**Praise for the novels of
Christopher Darden & Dick Lochte**

The Last Defense

"What do you get when you combine a shrewd former prosecutor . . . with one of the smoothest, most urbane mystery writers ever to come down the mean freeways of Los Angeles? A blockbuster legal thriller like this—crammed to the gills with pith, moment, racial insights, courtroom chicanery, sexual shenanigans, bizarre police behavior, and countless other delights. . . . Can be read as a modern *Candide* or even a *Faust*—the usual suspects being greed and pride. Or you can just take it at face value, and hold on tight for a smashing ride."
—*Chicago Tribune*

"Nonstop action from courtroom to barroom to bedroom. . . . Amid the simmering stew of sex, drugs, alcohol, violence, and courtroom pyrotechnics is a stable of memorable characters. . . . Darden and Lochte make a formidable team. . . . A fast ride with a jolting, surprise finish."
—*Publishers Weekly*

"Exciting and engrossing. . . . This crime-fiction dream team's most satisfying work yet . . . worthy of legal thriller masters such as Steve Martini and John Lescroart. . . . Crackles with lawyer lore and inside jokes, all smartly tucked into its complex story. . . . Moves with propulsive force toward its satisfying finale."
—*OC Metro*

"Will appeal to fans of John Grisham . . . fast-paced, hooking the reader from the early courtroom drama to the strong climax."
—*Midwest Book Review*

continued . . .

The Last Defense

Christopher Darden
& Dick Lochte

AN ONYX BOOK

ONYX
Published by New American Library, a division of
Penguin Group (USA) Inc., 375 Hudson Street,
New York, New York 10014, U.S.A.
Penguin Books Ltd, 80 Strand,
London WC2R 0RL, England
Penguin Books Australia Ltd, 250 Camberwell Road,
Camberwell, Victoria 3124, Australia
Penguin Books Canada Ltd, 10 Alcorn Avenue,
Toronto, Ontario, Canada M4V 3B2
Penguin Books (N.Z.) Ltd, Cnr Rosedale and Airborne Roads,
Albany, Auckland 1310, New Zealand

Penguin Books Ltd, Registered Offices:
80 Strand, London WC2R 0RL, England

Published by Onyx, an imprint of New American Library,
a division of Penguin Group (USA) Inc. Previously published
in a New American Library hardcover edition.

First Onyx Printing, January 2004
10 9 8 7 6 5 4 3 2 1

 REGISTERED TRADEMARK—MARCA REGISTRADA

Printed in the United States of America

PUBLISHER'S NOTE
This is a work of fiction. Names, characters, places, and incidents either are the
product of the author's imagination or are used fictitiously, and any resem-
blance to actual persons, living or dead, business establishments, events, or
locales is entirely coincidental.

For my in-laws, James and Gloria Carter
C. D.

For the members of The Suicide Club
D. L.

1

When the electricity finally kicked in again, restoring light and order to Courtroom Five, defense attorney Mercer Early automatically checked his watch. 4:18 P.M. The room had been dark and airless for nearly a half hour. Despite the best efforts of a thirty-year-old emergency generator tucked somewhere in the bowels of the aging courthouse, one of Los Angeles's frequent rolling blackouts had caused an unforeseen recess, not to mention a small degree of havoc, in the trial of *People* v. *Darion Mayfield.*

" 'Bout fuckin' time," Mercer's client drawled. The young black man had been slouched on a chair beside him when the power went out. He looked like he hadn't moved an inch. He yawned.

"We keeping you up, Darion?" Mercer asked.

"Barely," Darion said. He was a blasé young man who, at twenty-six, had been thrown out of a half-dozen schools, public and private, before entering the business sector. There he had served an apprenticeship running dope for an Original Gangster named Bumpy Lewis, who reportedly barbecued himself one star-crossed night while freebasing some of his highly valued product. Darion assumed control of the operation and, thanks mainly to his efforts, in the suburb of Inglewood, ecstasy, chronic and good, old-fashioned crack cocaine were as easy to purchase as aspirin from the corner Rite Aid.

Unlike just about everybody else in the courtroom, including his anxious, hand-wringing parents, he seemed unfazed by the blackout. It was just one more annoying inconvenience for him. "Fuckin' 'lectric power dudes should be the ones on trial," he grumbled. "They makin' more loot off the poor people than us dope dealers."

Mercer kept his annoyance off his face as he whispered to his client, "Say your occupation a little louder, Darion. I don't think the jury heard you."

Darion shrugged like he didn't care much either way. He was a punkass, no doubt, but, because his father, the Reverend Doctor Harlan Mayfield, was such a pillar of the black community, at the moment he was Mercer's punkass.

"Mr. Early." Judge Temperance Land was looking down her long powdered nose at him from the bench. "Shall we take up from where we were, before being so rudely interrupted?"

"Happy to, Your Honor."

The young attorney stood, straightened the jacket of his somber Armani suit, and assayed the prosecution's star witness, seated in the box to the right of the judge. Six feet something in a rumpled off-the-rack suit, rawboned, shaggy blond hair and bloodshot eyes, vice detective Claude Burris seemed as unmoved by the blackout and the heat and the stale air as Darion. Two of a kind, Mercer thought. Lower life-forms.

"Detective Burris," Mercer addressed him, "you've had a while in the dark to mull over your direct testimony. Want to change or retract anything you've put in the record?"

Claude Burris was a seasoned Narcotics bureau detective. He rolled his eyes in a gesture of boredom before letting them drift back to Mercer. "No," he said.

"So, Detective, it's your testimony that my client stated to you, at the time of his arrest, and I quote, 'I'll make it easy on you. The shit is all mine'?"

"That's what he said. By 'the shit,' he meant drugs worth roughly—"

"Thank you, Detective," Mercer interrupted before Burris could get into the mouth-dropping street value of Darion's stash. "You happen to record my client's statement?"

"You mean with a tape recorder?"

"That's what I mean. With a tape recorder. You officers do own tape recorders, correct?"

"Yeah, we do own 'em," the detective said, stirring a little now. "But the defendant's statement was . . . spontaneous. He blurted it out as soon as I had him proned out and was puttin' the cuffs on him."

It was what Mercer wanted to hear. He had to fight to keep the smirk off his face. Juries weren't fond of smirks. "Ever hear the term 'testi*lie*,' Detective?" he asked.

Burris nearly jumped from his seat. "Who the hell you think you talking to?"

Prosecuting attorney David Gomez did leave his chair to object. Standing there in his deputy D.A. Monday uniform—blue blazer, gray slacks, and spit-shined Weejuns loafers—Gomez looked about as straightlaced as a prosecutor could get. It was an accurate reflection of the man who'd been Mercer's mentor during his short, post–law school stint in the D.A.'s office. "Do everything by the book," Gomez had continually advised him, "and you'll never take heat."

You'll never get tapped by a firm like Carter and Hansborough, either, Mercer reminded himself.

"What exactly is your objection, Mr. Gomez?" Judge Land asked.

"I should think it's obvious, Your Honor. Mr. Early is badgering the witness. Detective Burris is a fifteen-year veteran of the LAPD with an impeccable reputation."

"Your Honor," Mercer said, "if the D.A. would like to testify to the detective's character, he can call himself to the stand. But he'll have to let me ask my questions first."

Judge Land's overpowered face showed neither

amusement nor undue annoyance. Merely impatience. "Objection overruled," she said. "Please continue, Mr. Early."

"You an honest man, Detective Burris?"

"Objection. The officer's character is not at issue. The evidence code requires that the prosecution first raise the character of a witness before the defense may delve into that area."

Judge Land sighed and suggested the attorneys approach her bench. "Thank you so much, Mr. Gomez, for reminding me of the evidence code requirement," she said. "We judges love little prompts.

"Mr. Early? Comment?"

"Your Honor, Mr. Gomez placed the officer's character at issue just moments ago when he stood before the jury, shouting at the top of his voice about Detective Burris's 'impeccable' honesty."

Judge Land's watery blue eyes shifted to the deputy D.A. "Considering how well versed you are on the subject, Mr. Gomez, it is a little surprising that you opened the door for Mr. Early. But open it you did. Your objection is overruled.

"However, Mr. Early, the court is not the least bit interested in rumors and idle gossip. If you have something that goes directly to the facts of this case, I'll hear it. Now finish your cross before the building goes dark again."

Mercer needed no further prompting. "Detective, what exactly did you mean when you said my client's statement was spontaneous?"

Burris frowned as if trying to see beyond the question. "I meant his . . . admission was . . . unexpected."

"You didn't say or do anything to elicit the statement?"

"No."

"Then what prompted you to say, just after my client's arrest, 'I kicked the crap out of him'?"

Burris blinked. "I never said that."

"You sure?"

"Yes, I'm sure."

"As sure as you are that my client stated, without prodding or coercion on your part, that 'The shit is mine'?"

"Yes."

Mercer paused, pretending to be mentally phrasing his next question. Actually, he was making certain the members of the jury were all on the same page with him. "You are aware that the jail physician has signed a statement that when my client arrived at the lockup there was a large bruise to his tailbone?"

"Yes."

"Could you explain the bruise for us?"

"That happened because your client refused to comply with our legal request to open the door to his domicile," Burris said, lapsing into copspeak. "We had to force entry. Apparently, he had been at the door observing us through the peephole. When he saw we meant business, he must have turned to run off to flush his dope just about when we kicked the door in. Anyway, the door hit him right where the good Lord split him, as they say."

"On that night, Detective, did you personally have contact with any of his neighbors?"

"Yes."

"The neighbor across the hall?"

"Can I check my notes?"

"Sure."

Burris removed a worn notebook from his coat pocket, flipped a few pages. "That would be . . . Mrs. Dobson. Clarita Dobson." He flipped the notebook closed. "Nice lady. Elderly Ne . . . African American. Stood in her doorway during most of it. She thanked us for stopping the sale of drugs in her building."

"Did you notice anything in her hand when she was thanking you?"

"In her hand? No."

"A cordless telephone maybe?"

"I don't recall," Burris said.

"Mrs. Dobson has a sister, Gladys Simmons, who lives in Shreveport, Louisiana. You know that?"

"No." Burris's face was showing splotches of red.

"Your Honor, what's the relevancy of these questions?" Gomez asked.

"Do tell us, Mr. Early," Judge Land said, "or pack up and move on."

"One more question should clear the air, Your Honor."

"Proceed, then. But don't try my patience."

"Detective Burris, did you know that as you exited my client's apartment, Mrs. Dobson was speaking to her sister Gladys Simmons's answering machine way off in Shreveport?"

Burris's face showed confusion. He opened his mouth to say something, but censored himself.

"I'm sorry," Mercer said. "I didn't quite catch that."

"No," Burris said flatly, "I was not aware of any answering machine."

"Well, guess who left a message on it?" Mercer turned to the judge. "Your Honor, I have an audiotape I'd like to have marked into evidence."

"It will be so marked, Mr. Early."

"Detective, why don't I refresh your memory by playing Mrs. Simmons's answering machine tape for you?"

"Your Honor." Gomez was on his feet. "Why were we not provided a copy of this so-called tape?"

"It only came into my possession this morning, Your Honor," Mercer said. That was fairly close to the truth. The tape had arrived at the offices of Carter and Hansborough the previous afternoon, but what with the trial and dinner and drinks and whatever, he had not listened to it until two A.M., which was definitely morning. "I have a copy for Mr. Gomez."

"Your Honor, I request a brief recess to review this so-called evidence."

Judge Land looked past Mercer to the witness chair, where a scowling Burris seemed to be gnawing the inside of his right cheek.

"Oh, Mr. Gomez, let's not drag this out any longer than we have to."

She nodded to Mercer, who retrieved a small portable recorder from his briefcase. As he plunked the tiny cassette into the machine and held it where its speaker could best be heard by the jury, Burris seemed genuinely puzzled.

From the small speaker, clear as a bell, came the sound of a woman, apparently the next-door neighbor, Clarita Dobson, saying, ". . . anyway, Gladys honey, the police jus' busted in on the boy 'cross the hall an' I'm watching 'em an' . . . hold on, now, they comin' out now . . ."

There was a hollow silence, then scuffling noises. A voice whined, "You busted my ass, man." All the jury had heard Darion say was "Not guilty," but they seemed to be having no trouble identifying the voice.

The next voice, though muddied by echo and telephone cables, belonged to Burris or to someone who sounded just like him. "Your ass is mine, pussy. You're toast. You gave it up."

Another male voice, unidentified but obviously a second lawman, asked, "The punk confess, Burris?"

"Sure. Pussies like him always confess. You just have to kick the crap out of 'em."

"What the hell . . . ?" Burris said.

Mercer snapped off the machine. "Was that your voice we just heard, Detective?"

The detective seemed distracted, confused. "My voice? Yeah, but—"

"Then my client's so-called confession was not voluntary, as you told us under oath, but the result of your 'kicking the crap' out of him?"

Mercer had seen a variety of responses from witnesses tripped up by their own words. Detective Burris's reaction was a new one. At first he seemed to be trying to work out some puzzle. Then he closed his eyes, as if the answer had come to him bringing not relief but despair.

"Detective?" Mercer prompted.

Burris's face had gone chalky white. "I . . . ah . . . refuse to answer on the grounds that it might incriminate me."

"It's a little late to be worrying about incriminating yourself," Mercer said.

Judge Land wasted no time dismissing the case.

Mercer was collecting his papers when he saw Claude Burris storming his way. The big Narcotics cop placed his huge hands on the table and leaned over to whisper, "You're gonna pay for this. You, your scumbag client, and all his . . . friends."

"Say what?" Mercer responded.

"You heard me. You piece of shit in a pin-striped suit. I got your number."

Mercer experienced a brief moment of paranoia in which he wondered if somehow this shit-kicker of a cop had stumbled upon the thing he'd been running from for the past six years, the thing he'd hoped he had put behind him.

"Some way, somehow," Burris added, "I'm gonna set this thing straight and all of you are gonna pay. You and all your *friends*." Was the Narc cop suggesting some kind of conspiracy against him? Good. That made him just another angry asshole not worth the worry.

"Damn, Detective, looky what's here," Mercer said, picking up the cassette recorder from the desk. "I musta left this turned on. Soon I'm gonna have enough of your voice—bragging about beatings, making threats—to fill a whole CD."

Burris's jaw dropped. His hand went out for the recorder, but Mercer was faster. He dropped the machine into his briefcase.

They were joined by Gomez and two somber dudes Mercer recognized as D.A. investigators. "Detective Claude Burris," one of the investigators said, "I'm placing you under arrest."

"For what?"

"Perjury."

Burris opened his mouth, but Mercer interrupted him. "If I were you, Detective," he said, snapping his briefcase shut, "before saying another word, I'd hire myself some piece of shit lawyer in a pin-striped suit."

As he was led away, a silent Burris seemed to be taking some of that advice to heart.

"Hey, Burris, who's the pussy now?" Darion shouted.

Mercer's client was standing near the rear door with his mother and father. The woman looked aghast at her son, who now was flipping off Burris. Her middle-aged husband, the Reverend Doctor Harlan Mayfield, shot his son a furious look and said, "Behave yourself, boy, before I have to slap you down."

The younger Mayfield was as tall as his father, maybe an inch below Mercer's six foot two. It looked like he might be carrying some muscle under his silk sport coat. But standing next to the formidable Reverend and feeling the full power of his fiery glare, Darion seemed to shrink back to childhood. "Yessuh," he mumbled.

The Reverend gave him a few more seconds of his wrathful staredown, then seemed to shake himself free of his anger. His eyes caught Mercer's. "Mr. Early, thank you for your excellent work on my son's behalf. On behalf of my whole family." His wife nodded her agreement.

"Glad I could help," Mercer said. He wasn't big on blaming anybody but the criminal for his crimes, but he couldn't help wondering how much the Reverend's mercurial anger and heavy hand had influenced Darion's antisocial behavior.

He picked up his briefcase and was on his way out when the Reverend said, "I don't believe I've seen you at service."

Aw, hell, Mercer thought. He'd worked his ass off keeping a low-life punk out of jail to earn the Reverend's good will, thereby strengthening his tenuous relationship with the Rev's good buddy, C.W. Hansborough, the senior partner of his firm. He didn't want to blow the whole deal now. "I . . . I'm not a Baptist, sir."

"But you are a religious man?"

"Yes, sir," Mercer said. Not a lie exactly. His religion was the practice of law.

"I thought so, the way you fight for truth."

Truth? Evidently the Rev was in serious denial or maybe he just didn't get the big picture: the truth would have sent his dope-dealing son into the slams. What Mercer had been fighting for was something quite different—he'd been fighting for a win. Winners advance. Losers take a step back. Simple as that.

Still, if the Rev wanted to think he was fighting for truth, so be it. He smiled and stood aside for Mayfield to usher his wife through the courtroom door. He expected Darion to follow them but the boy lingered, giving him a wink. "You the bomb, brother."

Mercer replied with a brief nod, nothing that would encourage further conversation.

He followed the boy from the courtroom and, sensing Darion was about to detain him further, headed in the opposite direction.

"Hey, Mer-suh."

Mercer pretended not to hear.

Darion ran to catch up with him at the end of the hall. "Whoa down. You and me goin' on the town tonight, Mer-suh. Do some celebratin'."

"Thanks, Darion, but I got other plans." It wasn't a lie. He'd be filling a chair at a fund-raiser for George Heathrow, the mayor of L.A., who had his eye on the governor's mansion in Sacramento. Later that night, he'd be prepping for a trial in the morning. But even if his evening had been one hundred percent free, he sure as hell wouldn't have spent it with the dope-dealing Darion Mayfield. Outside of the courtroom, he wanted nothing to do with drug dealers or hypes. Been there. Done that. Nearly lost it all.

"Bring your lady along," Darion said.

"Some other time."

"Shi-i-i . . . Mer-suh. We be drinkin' Per-re-a Jew-way in the flower bottle, snortin' dealer-choice blow."

"You might want to stay clear of blow for a while," Mercer said.

"Why?"

"You're a smart guy, Darion. Figure it out."

"I got it figured, bro. I can do the fuck I please." He grinned, flashed the young lawyer an assortment of hand signals and loped away. "All else fails," he shouted back, "I got you."

2

Mercer barely noticed the nineteen-minute trip from the courthouse to the firm. He was driving under the influence of something even more intoxicating than alcohol—the emotional rush of the win, or, as he thought of it, the kill. The callous immorality of his client, the look of malevolence on the vice cop's face, the disappointment he saw in the eyes of his old *patrón*, David Gomez, these things seemed irrelevant.

Downtown L.A. was in going-home gridlock stage, but Mercer's euphoria floated him through the traffic—past the county law library, then the civil courthouse, both invisible to him. His leased Mercedes stayed on autopilot all the way to One Wilshire Boulevard and the law firm of Carter and Hansborough.

The firm had been founded almost seventy years ago by two young members of the 1932 graduating class of the Howard University School of Law, Cordelu Wellington Hansborough II and Robert Hires Carter. The two young men had met while working cleanup detail at a Washington, D.C., speakeasy near the university. They became friends, roommates, and, on the strength of a handshake, business partners. They made the decision to practice law in what they thought would be the more open social climate of the new wild West, Los Angeles, California.

As close as the two men were, they did not share the same philosophies of life and business, something that might have been predicted by their reasons for attending Howard.

Even in those unenlightened days, it had been possible for a few blacks to struggle their way through Harvard or another of the more liberal law schools. Hansborough had the grades to prove he was the intellectual equal of the young men who grew up on the whiter side of the tracks in Holly Grove, Arkansas, and went on to study at the most prestigious universities. But Hansborough's daddy, and his granddaddy, too, convinced the boy that if colored people were ever going to achieve equality, they would have to do it by relying on their own kind. Howard University had been there for colored students since Reconstruction.

"Why go out of your way to be with white folks?" his granddaddy would say. "White folks are way too full of themselves. And they can't be trusted, neither. You think they yo' friends, but one of 'em gets caught throwin' a rock through a store window, the first thing they're gonna do is point their prickly pale fingers at you and say 'The nigger did it.' "

Howard was the ticket, his daddy told him. "We're investin' in our own kind."

Robert Carter's reason for attending Howard was more basic: he didn't want to have to deal with bigots. It took too much time away from studies . . . and partying. He was a likable, outgoing, social man whose oratorical skills made him a natural courtroom performer. But he was far from the workaholic that Cord Hansborough rapidly became. And he did not share his partner's strong conviction that the firm bearing their names serve the black community only. Particularly since in those days many blacks were convinced that the only good lawyers were Jewish. But Cord had graduated first in their class. He was smarter than Robert and he cared more, so he usually got his way.

For over four decades, Carter and Hansborough

maintained a narrow profit margin defending black
men and women charged with criminal offenses. But
times and basic philosophies eventually changed. The
founding partners moved on to that big courtroom in
the sky. The firm prospered and grew into one of the
most financially successful in the western United States,
thanks primarily to the micromanagement of the
founders' oldest sons, Robert "Bobby" Carter II and
Cordelu Wellington Hansborough III, or C.W., as he
preferred to be addressed.

The firm presently included a number of the brightest
and most promising young black lawyers in town,
among them Mercer Early. Over the years C&H had
signed its baby barristers to two-year apprentice contracts, providing them with enough resources, advice,
and practical experience to kickstart their careers. At
contract's end, the firm would provide loans to the more
promising young legislators who were interested in
opening their solo practices and feed them lower-profile
cases in return for 25 percent of the attorney fees. Depending on the month, C&H sometimes made more
money from its protégés than in-house.

Mercer liked the way C&H was run, really liked the
prestige and the sweet honey of success that spread
over even its freshest associates. And he liked its style,
as typified by the private elevator at One Wilshire that
went directly from the lobby to the penthouse offices
on the forty-first floor.

As he floated upward, surrounded by polished brass
and mirror images of himself, he realized he liked
nearly everything about the firm of Carter and Hansborough . . . except Hansborough.

That was a very large problem, all things considered.
But he was too high on his courtroom victory to let it
bother him that evening. Thinking about it made him
grin. Darion Mayfield had been sitting on a mound of
narcotics in his apartment. So what if Burris had put his
foot to the punk's ass. The idiot had still made the
damned confession. But none of that mattered once

Burris's credibility was damaged. The phone cassette had been a gift from heaven. But even without it, Mercer was confident he could have tricked up the cop some other way. "Excellent job, counselor," he said to his reflection in the elevator's mirrorlike finish, just before the doors opened onto the cool pastel colors of the firm's reception area.

"Good evening, Mr. Early." The greeting was repeated as Mercer walked past an array of six very attractive fair- to white-skinned black women still at work at 5:53, according to the surreal molded metal clock on the wall. Assistants with the appearance of concubines. Or possibly the other way around.

Past the dreamy pastel reception area, the décor of the hall area and the private offices, to Mercer's mind, took a sharp nosedive into nostalgia. The walls were covered with a cherry wood that old man Hansborough had had imported from his native Arkansas just after World War II. As Mercer had learned during his indoctrination, when the expanding firm moved from its humble Crenshaw Boulevard address to the downtown penthouse in the mid-seventies, Hansborough senior had insisted that the wood paneling be taken down and reinstalled. A brass plaque at eye level carried a familiar saying of the founding partner. "Don't forget where you came from."

How could you, Mercer thought, if you never left anything behind? They'd moved into new upscale digs and taken on new associates. They were a first-tier law firm and the old man had to bring that ancient funky-ass paneling along with him. The young lawyer shook his head in wonder.

Still, the offices were immaculate, the cherry wood polished to a sheen. And the view from the forty-first floor was breathtaking. From his office Mercer could see clear across town. To the west and Beverly Hills and Hollywood, the promise of money and fame. To the south and Inglewood and South Central, a very different kind of money and a different kind of fame. From the 'hood to the 'wood, he thought.

Sixteen months into a two-year contract, Mercer had managed to secure a two-window office on the opposite side of the building away from C.W. In the three-window office next to his was the only attorney, other than the partners, who was not on a two-year contract: C.W.'s daughter, Vanessa, a cool, conservative young woman unlike any he had ever known.

He began lusting her the moment he laid eyes on her. That had been his first day at the firm. Just off the elevator he'd been stopped in his tracks by the sight of her, bent over a desk, pointing out something to a secretary. Mercer lost track of where he was and why he was there.

Struck by this vision, he was unaware of his new boss, Cordelu Wellington Hansborough III, standing behind him, almost breathing down his neck. "Let me know when you've finished gawking at my daughter, Mr. Early," he said, "and we can get down to business."

The sting of the rebuke was salved by the fact that it caused Vanessa to look up at him. Mercer swallowed a large gulp of air. Damn, she was fine. Borderline gorgeous. No, full-out gorgeous. He stared at her. And, unless he was fantasizing to the extreme, she seemed to be staring back.

"You know each other?" her father asked, breaking the spell.

"Haven't had the pleasure," Mercer said.

"Good," Hansborough said, leading him away.

But something had clicked between him and Vanessa, and C.W.'s peevish attempt to cut it short had provided the perfect introduction.

Now heading for his office, Mercer noticed that Vanessa's was empty. "Where is everybody?" he asked Melissa French, his heavyset, plain-spoken, deadly efficient assistant.

"She's in the conference room," Melissa replied. "Something's going on."

"What?"

Melissa shrugged her hefty shoulders. "Nobody ever

bothers to put me in the know. But the old man was shouting for you a little while ago. You better get your butt in there."

Mercer grabbed a legal pad and pen and headed for the conference room next to C.W.'s office. As he approached the door, he could detect no noise or discussion coming from within. He knocked once. Still nothing.

He opened the door.

"Surprise!" The room was packed with attorneys, clerks, and staff. They surrounded the conference table, much of which was taken up by a large sheet cake. Red icing spelled out: "Mercer Early, King 'Gator." In L.A. courthouse slang, the term " 'gator" suggested both litigator and sharp-toothed predator. A bakery artist had decorated the top of the cake with a chocolate alligator in a charcoal-colored business suit.

The congratulations began.

"Way to stick it to those lying cop bastards," Eddie Baraca said sarcastically, giving Mercer a wink and a grin. Diminutive and pencil-thin in an immaculate, tailored pinstripe, Eddie was a rarity; an associate who'd scored so heavily in the courtroom that, according to office gossip, he was being groomed for partnership. For a man only a year or so older, he seemed to Mercer to be remarkably self-assured and sophisticated, someone who knew how the game was played.

Next came Joe Wexstead, an associate who had the misfortune of not being able to disguise his emotions. His round, brown face with slightly protruding eyes was a mixture of naked ambition and jealousy as he pumped Mercer's hand.

One by one the associates offered their sometimes genuine, sometimes artificial congratulations, until Wally Wallace, whose only reason for being in the firm was his kinship to the powerful Judge Claiborne Wallace, stepped before Mercer. Sweating profusely, his expensive but ill-fitting jacket twisted to one side, he said with obvious sincerity, "You d-d-did a good thing, Mercer. That f-f-fucker Burris has a rep for planting evidence."

Mercer did not feel it necessary to mention that the evidence found in Darion Mayfield's apartment had definitely *not* been planted by Claude Burris. Instead, he nodded his agreement.

Searching the crowd, he found Vanessa standing at the rear of the room. She'd been waiting for him to notice her and rewarded his attention with an approving nod. He knew that she had planned this little soirée, probably against her father's wishes. The old man didn't like him—a daddy thing, he assumed, that he would get around somehow. He wanted Vanessa and he wanted a partnership in the firm. He deserved them. He just had to prove it to C.W. The Mayfield victory was only the start of things to come.

The party was of short duration. Fifteen minutes after Mercer walked through the door, nearly everybody had headed back to his or her office. The young lawyers had quotas to meet: 280 billable hours per month. Fifteen minutes of frivolity translated into lost dollars, even at that time of evening.

Finally, Mercer and Vanessa were alone in the room. She began collecting the used plates. "This was really sweet, baby," he said.

"It was the least I could do for my 'gator man," she said. "You did good, G."

"How'd you put it together so fast?"

"Truth? The bakery had a plain cake. Took five minutes to do the icing art. I, ah, ordered the party stuff a couple days ago."

"Suppose I'd lost the case?"

"I figured you'd win one, sooner or later."

Mercer grinned and watched as she gracefully gathered more plates and stacked them on a side table. He'd never considered himself a voyeur before, but he loved to watch her. He had to watch her. She did the driving when they were together; he couldn't keep his eyes on the road with her beside him.

It came as a shock to realize he was sprung on the girl. Love hadn't been in his vocabulary. The last time he'd even used the word was in the ninth grade, when he'd thought he was in love with Becky Worner, the class queen. By the end of the eleventh grade he realized that it had been all about hormones, not love. Whatever it was that Vanessa the boss's daughter was doing to him, it went way beyond hormones.

So much so that two nights before, he'd asked her to marry him. He'd caught her by surprise. "I need time to think about it," she'd replied. Expecting a prompt and enthusiastic *yes*, Mercer had been devastated, but she'd told him not to give up on her. She loved him. They spent the night together, and in the morning she was especially loving. She promised to give him an answer soon and, until then, to keep his proposal a secret, especially from her father.

He moved behind her just as she was about to close the box on the cake. He pressed against her and she pressed back, turning her head far enough to receive the kiss she knew was coming. He closed his eyes and felt his lips touch hers and . . .

"Any cake left?"

Vanessa's father glared at them from the doorway. Mercer took a backward step away from her, almost tripping over a chair in the process.

"If you're finished pawing my daughter, Mr. Early," he said, "we have to discuss today's court proceedings."

"Thought you wanted some cake, daddy," Vanessa said. "Let me fix you a piece."

"Don't bother. I've lost my appetite. Mr. Early, I'm waiting."

Mercer gave Vanessa a helpless look and followed his boss from the room.

3

"Close the door," C.W. ordered, slipping into his huge, black leather desk chair. He spun around until he was facing a corner section of the windows that enveloped the room, offering his back to the young lawyer. "Sit down," he said.

There were three leather armchairs, one facing the front of C.W.'s antique desk, the others facing the sides. Mercer was moving toward the center chair when the older man said, "Not that one."

From his position, it seemed impossible that he could have known which chair Mercer had selected. It was a favorite parlor trick of C.W.'s, designed to keep a visitor off balance, make him wonder if the old man had supersensitive hearing or even eyes in the back of his head.

Mercer was too practical to consider such Addams Family bullshit. One day, while C.W. was at lunch, he snuck into the office and sat down behind the desk. Facing the side window, he discovered that the whole room was reflected in it. So much for the old man's magic.

C.W. turned as Mercer was seating himself. "This chair okay?"

C.W. ignored the question. "Let me tell you something, young man. There were over one hundred and fifty candidates for your position, most of them clearly more qualified than you. I've never understood why Bobby Carter was so determined to have you join us, but I did not object. I see now that was a mistake."

Mercer was confused. Sure, C.W. was pissed off about him and Vanessa. But wasn't this supposed to be about his courtroom victory? "Sir, I thought we were here to talk about the Mayfield trial."

"That's what we are talking about. What did you think?"

Mercer shifted uncomfortably on the chair. "I . . . thought I won that case."

"There is more to practicing law than winning."

Mercer felt suddenly warm, as if somebody had shoved a heat lamp close to his face. He stiffened. "I don't agree," he said. "In criminal law, winning is everything. Losing means your client is off to San Quentin. I don't believe in losing."

C.W. studied him for a moment. "Let me put it another way, so that even you can understand it. Law is a business. We are as much a business as Microsoft or General Electric. Sometimes, we win in the courtroom but lose in the boardroom because winning is bad for business."

Mercer was almost on the edge of his chair. "I don't get it."

"Obviously." C.W. placed his hands on the desk and slowly interlaced his fingers, controlling his impatience. "Carter-Hansborough has several Fortune 500 clients. I guess some of those good ol' boys feel it's in their best interest to throw a few bones to minority firms. As nice as these scraps are, they do not add up to all the capital we need or deserve. We are constantly searching for new sources of revenue."

"Okay, but—"

"Please. Let me finish. Recently, I approached Mayor Heathrow regarding one of the larger city contracts. I'm talking millions, Mr. Early. Enough to justify our donation of twenty-five thousand dollars for a table at tonight's rubber-chicken fund-raiser for His Honor."

"So?"

"So . . . your little courtroom fiasco has seriously undercut our chances of landing that contract."

"How?"

"Most of the city's litigation involves the LAPD. And the LAPD is the city contract I've been speaking of. Now do you understand?"

Mercer understood. He just couldn't believe it. "You're telling me I shouldn't have introduced the tape? That I should have allowed our client to be convicted on the basis of false testimony?" He shot to his feet, his body vibrating.

"Lower your voice and sit down." For a moment the two men glared at one another. Then, when Mercer obeyed, C.W. continued. "Out of respect to the Reverend Mayfield, I certainly did not want the boy to be convicted, as repugnant as I find the weasel personally. What you should have done was to let the D.D.A. know about the tape and suggest they quietly dismiss the case. If they'd foolishly demurred, you could have moved to suppress the weasel's confession.

"But Mercer Early doesn't believe in simplicity and subtlety. Mercer Early has to enact an episode of *The Practice.*"

"I was only—"

"I know what you were only doing. You were putting yourself above this firm."

Mercer's head was spinning with the conflicting emotions of ambition and anger. Anger won and he was up and out of his chair again. "You're making me sound like some kind of grandstanding fool. That's not me. It's not myself I put over the firm. It's my client. I don't care if he's Darion Mayfield or a true earth-walking saint. If it's between them and your deal with the city, then screw the deal."

"Sit down, Mr. Early. I don't like having to look up."

Mercer not only remained standing, he began to pace. "I don't get you, C.W. You call yourself a lawyer? A black lawyer? And you sit there, judging me, telling me that I should put money before my clients? That I should soft-deal a bad cop?" He stopped directly in front of the old man. "No fuckin' way. That pig had it coming to him and he got maybe half of what he deserves."

"You finished?"

The question stopped Mercer like a slap. "I guess I am," he said, feeling the anger drain away, replaced by the realization that he was about to be given his walking papers.

"Sit. Down."

Mercer sat down.

"Maybe the 'pig' did deserve to be taken down," C.W. said flatly. "But that's not your job. This firm employs thirty-one black men and women. Their economic livelihood depends on the decisions you and I make as lawyers. It is important for you to realize that the decision you made in the Mayfield case was a bad one." He reached for a folder on his desk, opened it. "In the future, you will copy me on all your outgoing correspondence and provide me with daily briefings prior to any court appearance. That includes your pro bono work tomorrow. What's your client's name?"

"Enrique Sanchez. He prefers the name Ricky."

"Well, I sincerely hope you will not be engaging in any theatrics on Ricky's behalf."

"No, sir. That it?" Mercer asked, wondering why he wasn't being fired.

C.W. looked up from the folder. "Reverend Mayfield called to sing your praises. We do like to keep our clients happy, especially clients as high profile as the Reverend Doctor."

It was his way of explaining why Mercer was still an associate of the firm.

He was headed out when C.W. said, "I could put my foot down about Vanessa going out with you, Mr. Early, but I prefer for my daughter to realize her mistakes on her own. Let me make it clear, however, that this marriage nonsense will not be tolerated."

The old man dug his nails in deep with that one. How had he known that Mercer had proposed unless Vanessa had disregarded her promise of secrecy?

Mercer paused at the door, trying to muster some reply that would regain at least a sliver of self-respect. But there was nothing to say. In any case, the old man had swung his chair around, once again showing Mercer his back.

Joe Wexstead, the most nakedly ambitious of all the associates, had been standing in the hall near C.W.'s office door.

"Everything all right, Mercer?" he asked, full of obviously bogus concern.

"Excellent," Mercer said, brushing past, mumbling to himself, "you eavesdroppin', sweat-drippin', chocolate doughboy son of a bitch."

He had to get away. Someplace where he could sort things out without a suckup like Wexstead lurking around to read his thoughts.

He grabbed his briefcase, mumbled something to Melissa about needing fresh air.

"Hey," she said. "The Sanchez trial, tomorrow morning at nine. Courtroom Eleven. Judge Dixon presiding. Don't forget."

As if he could forget Ricky Sanchez. Contrary to one of the first things he'd been taught as a lawyer, he'd allowed himself to become emotionally involved in Ricky's case.

The Sanchez brothers, Maximillian and Enrique, had been arrested months before, charged with aggravated mayhem, an offense carrying a possible life sentence. The victim, a forty-five-year-old assistant drugstore manager named Ellis Halpern, was suffering permanent brain damage. Mercer was convinced that Ricky, a simple-minded boy, barely eighteen, had been pushed into the crime by his much older sociopathic brother.

The prosecution's case looked to be a lock, but Mercer was going to give it his best shot. He'd been successful in convincing Max's attorney that it benefited both brothers to be tried separately, with Ricky, the more sympathetic, leading the way. In truth, he hoped Max got the full count. But he could not see how putting the naïve and confused Ricky in jail for the rest of his life would serve justice.

He retraced his steps, grabbed the folder from Melissa's plump, manicured fingers and jammed it into his briefcase. He'd been through his notes a dozen times, but he wanted to make sure there wasn't something he'd overlooked. Assuming he could get his mind off Vanessa long enough.

"And don't forget to pick up your tux," Melissa said as he headed out once again. But the words didn't register. His mind was too jumbled with other matters, like forcing himself not to glance into Vanessa's office when he passed by. This wasn't the time or the place for the conversation they had to have. She'd betrayed him. But just an hour ago, she'd kissed him like a woman in love. Shit if he could make sense out of any of it.

With the car's stereo blasting all thought from his skull, he drove aimlessly through the city. Eventually, he drifted into the familiar territory of South Central and wound up parked on the street in front of La Louisianne.

The restaurant, called LaLa's by its patrons, was famous for down-home food, jazz bands, and fast women, none of which had prompted Mercer's visit. He was just looking for a friendly bar where he could try to loosen up with a few tastes and get Vanessa out of his head, at least for the night. Then he'd drive home, take a final look at the Sanchez notes, and get a good night's rest.

After two tumblers of Red Bull and vodka he was mumbling to himself about Vanessa's betrayal. Around him the restaurant had started coming alive with the dinner crowd. He considered ordering something, but he wasn't there to eat.

He signaled the lady bartender for another Red Bull and vodka and considered his options.

From the jump, C.W. had been playing mind-fuck games with him while acting like a big brother to the Ivy League associates. That'd been okay, because each time C.W. dissed him, Bobby Carter had been there with the props, making him feel like he was important enough to the firm that the idea of a junior partnership was not the impossible dream. And, he'd been so confident of his courtroom ability he'd believed that he could turn C.W. around.

But now, facing an almost certain loss in court in the morning and with his professional life all twisted up with his personal life, he wasn't sure what the hell to do. Maybe this was the time to break with Carter and Hansborough. Bobby would give him a good recommendation. He'd take it and see what else was out there.

Hell. Who was he kidding? He knew exactly what was out there. He'd found that out at age fourteen, when his father had his stroke and passed away and the school district that employed his mother lost some of its funding. Through no fault of her own, she'd been transformed overnight from a bright, outgoing wife and mother and teacher to a fearful wreck of a woman. Her self-esteem had been so shattered she spent the rest of her life spiraling downward through a series of menial jobs that near the end barely provided a poverty existence. She'd let life beat her. No goddamn way would he allow that to happen to him.

Two well-dressed, dapper old gents sat down at the bar beside him, filling the cooled air with the scent of bay rum. The bar lady placed a freshly doctored Red Bull in front of Mercer and took the old dudes' orders. One of them noticed him and said, "Good evening, young man," in a courtly manner.

He returned the courtesy, wondering how they'd made their coin. Not the law. There were other ways of turning a buck. And Lord knows he had the ability to reinvent himself. He took a closer look at the man nearest him. Stoop-shouldered, overweight, smiling like the Buddha, talking bullshit with his pal about something he saw on TV last night. Retired, of course. But here he was sitting in the bar with another old grandpa, eye-popping the passing parade of past-prime sisters. What the hell had the two old dudes accomplished besides collecting their loot and staying alive to spend it? Did they ever save anybody from ten to twenty years behind bars? Did they experience anything like the elation you get from hearing those magic words "Not Guilty"?

He was a lawyer, goddammit. And he would remain a lawyer, no matter what. He took a bite of the Bull and started to feel just a little better . . .

Until he remembered Vanessa.

Why the hell did she go and tell Daddy he'd proposed? He finished the drink in one long pull. "I gotta do something," he muttered.

One of the old guys gave him an apprehensive look.

Uh-oh. Talking to himself. The booze had landed. Time to be moving on.

He paid his tab and, trying not to stagger, worked his way through the rapidly filling room and out into the night.

He drove to his apartment with some caution, avoiding the fast action of the freeways. He was almost there when he checked his messages and discovered that Vanessa was blowing up his pager. There were at least ten requests for him to call back.

He considered ignoring them. For about a second. He pulled over to the curb and grabbed his cell phone.

She picked up on the first ring. "Honey, where the heck are you?" she asked, whispering, annoyance in her voice.

"Where? In my car," he replied dumbly, the booze fuzzing things up.

"You're late. Bobby keeps looking at your empty chair and checking his watch."

Late? Empty chair? Then he remembered. The mayor's fund-raiser. Shit! Bobby Carter had been very explicit in his request—no, make that his demand—that Mercer attend the affair to meet some of the city's movers and shakers.

"Ah . . . tell Bobby I'm on my way." He broke the connection before he could say or do anything to fuck things up even more.

He sat in the car, clutching the steering wheel. He was still a little drunk, though sobering fast. It was late. It was a goddamned black-tie dinner. He was wearing a pin-striped suit and red tie. Even if he had the time to drive to the tux rental place, it'd be closed.

Well, what the hell? It was either go to the dinner as is or drive the car into the nearest telephone pole to give himself an out. He liked the car too much for that.

4

Detective Lionel Mingus had noticed the young man making a weaving exit through the crowd at LaLa's. He didn't think he'd ever laid eyes on him before, and if the dude was driving in that condition, he might never see him again.

Mingus was taking it easy on his night off, sitting alone by the picture window, sipping a Thug Passion, Red Alize and Courvoisier—alcohol with an alcohol chaser—and sampling the intoxicating aromas of Cajun food and booze mingled with expensive perfumes. Enjoying the sights.

One sight in particular. A handsome woman in a skintight skirt was damn near straddling the green velvet bar in search of an old cat daddy. Probably needed some help buying the groceries or maybe getting her nails done. There were enough old dudes in the house who were happy to pay for pedicures in exchange for a chance to pop a little blue pill. But the Viagra pill had a price. LaLa's had recently lost three of its regulars to heart attacks.

Mingus may have needed science's help in some areas, but, he thanked the good Lord, at forty-two, with only the hint of a gut on his big-boned six-foot-two frame, he was doing just fine in the dick department. That fact was becoming more and more obvious to him as he watched the lady working the old boys at the bar.

She wasn't a standout by any means and she might have been pushing fifty, which he'd previously considered a little too long in the tooth. But she looked hygienic, had a nasty laugh, and didn't have too many miles on her. Maybe she'd consider having a drink with a big, bald-headed black man with a mustache bristlier than a bottle brush and less than eighty bucks in his wallet. By the time he made up his mind to buy her that drink, his beeper started vibrating.

He unclipped it from his belt and squinted at the digital readout. The caller's number meant trouble of some kind. A robbery, at the very least, but more likely homicide. No sex tonight. Just violence. At the bar, the woman in the tight skirt laughed at something a cat daddy said and draped an arm on his shoulder.

Just as well he was being called back on duty, Mingus thought.

A restless nighttime crowd had already gathered by the time he arrived at 2000 Centinela Avenue, in the suburbs near Westchester. He was familiar with the area. In spite of the noise and fumes from nearby LAX, Los Angelinos, mainly of the Caucasian persuasion, had been paying upward of 400K for eighteen-hundred-square-foot, ranch-style houses built there in the 1950s. But the neighborhood, like so many others in the sprawling city, was undergoing an ethnic sea change. Newly affluent blacks from Baldwin Hills and Inglewood were moving in as fast as white home owners could put their properties up for sale and white builders could fill in the empty lots.

Mingus's nose told him the exact moment when his aging Crown Victoria entered the neighborhood. The exhaust from every kind of seven-forty-something jet hung in the air like a toxic fog. Years ago, when he'd been a patrolman at the old Pacific division station, the locals had insisted the exhaust was safe; the smell just took gettin' used to. Mingus never got used to it.

Two huge flamingo-colored apartment buildings had gone up on Centinela earlier that year and were leasing at exorbitant rates to anyone who could pass the credit check. A street-to-alley parking lot separated the twin buildings. The body was in a Dumpster at the far end of the lot. Many of the buildings' occupants were at their windows staring down at the show with what Mingus figured were probably not happy thoughts. Ten or fifteen Metro division cops were standing in a thin blue line, protecting the crime scene from the noisy, milling crowd in the street.

"No justice, no peace," one of the shufflers shouted as Mingus approached. As if on cue, others joined in. "No justice, no peace." The detective wondered what had prompted that little ditty. Probably nothing more than boredom on a slow evening.

He inched the big sedan through the crowd, trying to ignore their shouts and slapping and banging on the car, until he arrived at the blue line. There he lowered his window and stuck out his arm. One of the cops, buffed and tanned to a glowing red, flashed a light on his shield. He nodded his approval solemnly and shouted for his brothers to make way. The cop was an officious asshole. Six years back, Mingus would have told him so. Now he thanked him instead.

He could tell from the parked cars that the boys from Robbery-Homicide division were on the scene. Their Crown Vics and Buicks were brand-new. No dents or dings. They lived high, the dicks from RHD. Most of them dressed as well as the chief. Some dressed better. As everybody else in law enforcement was jealously aware, their cases carried special perks. Catch a celebrity stalking or, even better, a break-in at a film star's home, and by the end of the week you'd find yourself at some producer-director's compound signing a consultant contract. "Gritty Reality" was the name of the Hollywood game and the cop who consulted on a movie or TV show was as important as the guy who wrote it. More maybe, because he could give the director and stars private lessons in gunplay.

Mingus wedged his aging sedan in among the flashier vehicles and put it to rest. He reached into the glove compartment and grabbed a small canister of breath spray. He gave it one shot, then another to make sure. The original minty taste didn't taste too original. But if RHD was at the scene, so was the division brass. The last thing Mingus needed was for some asswipe captain to jam him about his alcohol intake prior to coming to work. He'd had enough of that before he left RHD for his current digs at Internal Affairs.

IAG didn't investigate murders. IAG investigated cops. Which made him wonder a bit why Captain Roy Jacquette, the top man at Robbery-Homicide, had sent for him.

As he stepped from his car, he saw that one unauthorized curiosity seeker had made it past the blue line. An ugly, slobbering pit bull the color and texture of a block of SPAM bounced along the lot following the smell of death. Or maybe just looking for trouble. Mingus gave the land shark a wide berth.

A light from a second-floor corner apartment in the north building cast an inappropriately warm glow over the group of dicks who were gathered around the death Dumpster, gaping into the crusted blue bin and frowning as if observing something both fascinating and nasty.

Detective Dennis Farley, an overweight redhead with a Captain Kangaroo mustache that matched his Captain Kangaroo gut, was the first to notice the approaching Mingus. "Lionel? Shit, man, what the hell *you* doin' here? Mistake this for a bar and grill?"

"It's your crime scene, fat boy," Mingus said. "You tell *me* why I'm here."

"Come on now, Lionel. You not still holdin' a grudge or anything? Wasn't me got your ass booted out of RHD. That was your pals, Johnnie, Jim, and Jack."

"Who?"

"Johnnie Walker, Jim Beam, and Jack Daniel's." The fat detective didn't try to control his mirth.

"What you got in the bucket, Farley?"

"Step right over, Mr. Mingus. See for yourself."

Mingus joined the others at the Dumpster. The garbage smell was waiting just inside the rim of the bin. The body was too new to add much to it, but that still didn't make it roses. Mingus's stomach suddenly lurched, and he had to hold his breath just to keep LaLa's southern fried chicken and red beans and rice dinner down where it belonged. A sour taste leaked into his mouth. He tightened his muscles, forcing the taste back where it came from, and wished to hell he'd passed on that last Thug Passion.

The body in the Dumpster seemed to be male, judging by the size-fourteen Nike on its left foot. Most of the torso was covered by your everyday garden-variety garbage—empty milk cartons, baby diapers, grapefruit rinds, chicken bones, and rotting vegetables—but judging by its mangled condition, Mingus figured that it must have fallen from somewhere near the top of the building. Sometimes a high fall resulted in separated body parts. Both of this corpse's legs were attached, but the knees and feet were pointing in at least four different directions.

Mingus was always surprised at the interesting positions murder victims wound up in. This dead man was lying on his stomach in the garbage, his chest pushed forward, with his pelvis extending outward to the side. His right knee was facing sideways. His right foot was twisted all the way around till it was pointed toward his rear calf. His left leg was clearly broken at the hip and the knee, since it was turned completely around with his left foot resting on his ass. The arms were both behind the body, attached but out of place. The right arm was clutching the air at a ninety-degree angle. The left arm extended across the back.

"Nasty shoulder break, huh?" Farley said gleefully.

There was a smear of blood on the outer rim and inside wall of the Dumpster. Probably the result of several large gashes made by triangles of glass embedded in what had once been the guy's spine. Smaller shards

were buried in his ass, arms, ankles, and shoulders—just
about everywhere. The corpse looked like some weird
kind of glass, cloth, and flesh sculpture.

There was one very unusual thing about the body, and
Mingus wondered why Farley hadn't mentioned it immediately.

"You take a close look at what you got here, Farley?"
he asked.

"Seen as much as I needed to, Lionel. Enough to
know that the corpse has answered once and for all time
the age-old question."

"What question's that?"

"Can niggers fly? 'Cause, son, the nigger sure as hell
flew out that window."

Farley's race baiting no longer got under Mingus's
skin, and he felt vaguely guilty about it. He took a step
back and looked up to where the fat detective was
pointing—a shattered lighted window at the top floor of
the five-story building.

"Musta got a little stoned and decided he had wings,"
the Homicide cop said. "Or maybe he just tumbled. Anyway, he gets my vote as Dumpster Diver of the Year."

Farley was good with the jokes, but, in Mingus's book,
he was worth less than dogshit as a detective. Dumb and
mean, with the bad habit of jumping to conclusions.

"How long has this scene been secure?" Mingus asked.

"Why? What's wrong?" Farley was immediately on
the defensive.

"You're missin' somethin' pretty important."

"RHD don't miss shit. If you're talking about what
happened to Mayfield's drug stash, my theory is he
didn't have any. The son of a bitch just got out of court
today. He probably was waiting till he cooled off a little
before going back in business."

"I sure hope you're not stupid enough to think a
dealer was going to close shop and let his customers
drift to another source. But it's not Darion's stash that
I'm saying you're missing. It's—"

"I don't care what it is. You just stay the fuck outta my

business, boy." He was in Mingus's face, his words having to work their way through clenched teeth. "I didn't send for you. The captain did. Go on upstairs and bother him and let us real detectives do our job."

Mingus stared at Farley. He could easily whip the fat man's ass and, Lord knows, the fat man had it coming. But what would that achieve? He stepped back slowly, turned, and headed toward the rear door to the building, feeling the detective's eyeballs on him. Suddenly he stopped and whirled, reaching toward his pocket.

Farley, tense and bug-eyed, reacted clumsily, stubbing his fingers on the weapon holstered beneath his sweat-soaked armpit. Mingus slowly withdrew a small cylinder from his pocket and tossed it to the detective. "You need this more'n me."

Farley juggled it before locking it in his pudgy fist. "Original mint taste?" he read from the tiny canister. "Breath spray, you fuck?"

"No need to thank me, Porky," Mingus said. "By the way. That corpse you checked so carefully?"

"What about it?"

"The thing that's missing is its head."

"What the hell you talkin' about? The head got lopped off when he hit the Dumpster. It's right over . . ." Farley gawked at a section of the lot that was now obviously bare and headless. "Mingus, you son of a bitch. This your idea of a joke, fucking with evidence?"

"Me? You been right next to me since I got here."

Farley had to face that fact. "Then what happened to the fucking head?"

"I don't know, but you might want to expand the crime scene and rope it off before one of those peace-screaming civilians stumbles over it."

"Dammit!" Farley shouted. He turned to the other detectives, demanding to know which one of them had moved the head. Nobody was copping to it.

Pleased with himself, Mingus left this amusing scene and went up to look for Captain Jacquette to find out why he had been called there.

5

The fund-raiser to help send Mayor George Heathrow to Sacramento was being held in the main ballroom of the Wilshire-Doheny Hotel. Mercer was not the last to arrive. That distinction went to an internationally famous Hollywood couple. Mercer watched them being ushered swiftly past the reception tables while he waited for a plump matron, decorated with what looked like the annual yield from an African diamond mine, to find his name on the guest list.

He was almost as surprised as she was when she found it. Raising one eyebrow (at his informal wardrobe, he supposed, though it might also have been because he was late and reeking of booze), she curtly provided him with the number and location of his table.

The ballroom resembled an underlit airplane hangar that somebody had dressed up with hundreds of roses and other flowers Mercer couldn't or didn't bother to identify. Couples rubbed butts and other body parts on a small, crowded dance floor, reacting to an orchestra that was playing what he called "ghost music," pre–Chuck Berry. The rest of the huge space was wall-to-wall tables where elegantly dressed men and women were seated. They proved their loyalty to the mayor by paying serious coin for the dubious pleasures of overcooked chicken, underaged wine, and half-baked speeches.

The Carter-Hansborough table was impressively close to the dais. It took Mercer a while to find it, because its only occupant was the firm's legacy associate, Wally Wallace. "M-M-Mercer, over here," he called out. He'd sweated through his tux shirtfront, making him look like a penguin who'd just been for a swim. "P-p-people been wondering if you'd m-m-make it."

"What people?" Mercer asked, looking at the empty table.

"They around," Wally said. "I think th-th-that's your seat," he said, indicating a place where the napkin and silverware were undisturbed and the dinner and salad untouched.

"Where's Vanessa?"

"Out on the dance floor with B-B-Barry Fox," Wally said.

"Barry who?"

"Fox. You know. The m-m-man you see if you want to see the m-m-mayor. They're out there ... I c-c-can't spot 'em now. They sure m-m-make a good-lookin' couple."

"Glad to hear it," Mercer said, scanning the dancers. He didn't see Vanessa, but he spotted Bobby Carter with Rose Heathrow, the mayor's wife. She was smiling at something he'd just said. She was in her forties maybe. Nearly as tall as Bobby's six feet, a red-haired, pale Irish American with a nice smile. A little too skinny for Mercer's taste, but she and Bobby, with his athletic bearing and chiseled features, formed a very handsome couple.

"S-s-she's the reason for the r-r-roses," Wally said, following his line of sight. "And for the m-m-mayor's theme song, 'Ev-Everything Comin' Up Roses.' "

"Who else is at our table?" Mercer asked, hoping to put a stop to Wally's Interesting Facts About the Mayor.

"C.W. He's across the d-d-dance floor t-t-talking with Chief Ahern." That would be Chief of Police Ahern. "Eddie and his w-w-wife are out there d-d-dancing."

Baraca. Well, it figured he'd be there, if he was going to be tapped for a partnership.

"There's a f-f-friend of C.W.'s named Arden who w-w-works for the city. K-k-kind of a blowhard. He's w-w-with D-D-Darnella from reception." He cocked his head and stared at Mercer. "You okay? You look a little, ah, f-f-funky."

"I've never been better, Wally," Mercer said. He shook out his napkin and draped it on his lap. He began to poke at the salad.

He'd eaten all the pieces of avocado he could find hidden among the wilted lettuce leaves when Bobby took a seat across from him. He stared at Mercer for a few moments, then said, "What happened?"

"I'm sorry. Things got . . . I'm just sorry."

"No matter. You're here now. Come with me. Some people I want you to meet."

"I'm . . . not dressed for this. I forgot to pick up my tux."

"Walk tall and they'll confuse your forgetfulness with rugged individualism."

Acting a little like a proud father, Bobby walked him around the room, pausing here and there to introduce him as "one of the firm's best and brightest."

When they arrived at the table on the dais, Mayor Heathrow said he'd heard good things about Mercer. The mayor was merely blowing politician smoke up his ass, but he smiled at the compliment all the same and shook the man's hand. If nothing else, Heathrow looked like a governor—tall, trim, gray of hair, with the strong jaw, sun-bronzed complexion, and steady blue eyes of a thoughtful outdoorsman.

Walking away from the dais, Mercer asked Bobby, "You figure he's the man?"

"I'm banking on it."

"What do you mean?"

"I mean that George's political future is important to me. To you, too."

Mercer stared at him. "Important to me? How?"

"That's something we'll have to talk about," Bobby said. "But not right now."

They returned to the Carter-Hansborough table to find it occupied by C.W., Eddie Baraca and his wife Helene, Wally, and a middle-aged black man who, considering he was pawing the well-endowed receptionist Darnella, was probably Arden the blowhard. Vanessa was there, too, wearing a black gown by some designer Mercer had never heard of, a necklace of fine pearls, and matching earrings. Simplicity and beauty. Wasted on him because he was too busy fuming at the way she seemed enraptured by her companion, a brother with the build and the dark good looks of a male model. He was wearing a midnight blue tux cut so perfectly it probably meant he spent a lot of time in front of a mirror.

"I think you're in my seat," Mercer said to him, interrupting the mood.

The male model looked up at him and showed him perfect, glistening white teeth. "This must be the tardy Mister Early," he said, standing and extending a large manicured hand. "Barry Fox."

Mercer braced himself for the power squeeze and was able to withstand it without crying out in pain. He managed to return the smile and lie, "Glad to meet you, Barry."

"As I was saying to the lady Vanessa, I'm having a few folks over for drinks at my place in Hancock Park when this winds down. Maybe a dip in the pool. Screen a movie. Just kick back. Love to have you two join the party."

"Thanks for the invite, Barry. Nothing I like better than just kickin' back."

"Do try to make it," Barry Fox said, missing the sarcasm in Mercer's reply or choosing to ignore it. "Van knows the address."

He turned to Vanessa. "See you later, beautiful. And thanks. You dance like a dream."

"What a sweetheart," she said, watching Fox head for the dais.

"I kinda thought he was more like . . . an asshole?" Mercer said. " 'Van knows the address.' Ah'm sure she do."

She turned to him, annoyed. "I've been to his home. With Daddy. What happened to you, anyway? You missed dinner."

"No. It's right here," he said, indicating the untouched, congealing meal.

She surveyed his clothes. "This your idea of black tie?"

He was furious with her but this was not the place to let it show. Slipping on his courtroom mask, he said quietly, "You disappoint me, girl."

"*I* disappoint *you*?"

"You told your daddy that I proposed."

She stared at him for a few seconds, then frowned in the direction of her father at the head of the table. "He swore he wouldn't get into it with you."

"What *he* swore isn't that important to me."

"I'm sorry, baby," she said, sounding as if she meant it. "It's just that—"

She was stopped midsentence by a popular, young, black television comic who was standing in a spotlight beside the band, using a wireless mike to welcome "the friends of Los Angeles's greatest mayor and soon to be California's greatest governor, George Heathrow."

Vanessa put her hand on Mercer's and whispered, "We'll talk later, at your place."

The impish, wiry comedian went on to do a sharply honed ten-minute routine heavily angled toward the current political scene. His standup was followed by a short set from a Grammy-winning female soul singer and a few more musical numbers by a very white boy group. Vanessa seemed fascinated by the entertainment, but Mercer suspected she was merely using it to avoid further conversation with him.

He settled back, simmering, and watched as the white boys, dressed in jumpsuits of some shimmering metallic gold material with fringed arms, whined their signature song, "Love, Love, Love the Way It Feels, Feels, Feels Inside You," accompanied by their trademark jerky synchronous gyrations. When he grew bored with them, he turned his attention to the mayor and discovered the good Reverend Mayfield bending His Honor's ear. He recalled Bobby telling him about the long-time friendship the two leaders shared, a friendship forged in the fires of the Watts riots, when both were still young men. Looking at them now, distinguished but definitely of a certain age, it was hard for Mercer to believe they'd ever been young. The Reverend seemed a bit agitated, as any man of God might, Mercer thought, finding himself in the presence of a bunch of blue-eyed choir boys in jumpsuits going on about how nice it feels to have sex with their girlfriends. The mayor looked like he was hearing the Reverend out. Then he nodded benignly. Mercer could almost hear him say, "It's just a song." Smiling with assurance, Mayor Heathrow reached out and adjusted Reverend Mayfield's black tie. It might have been one old friend fixing another's messed-up neckwear, but the gesture struck Mercer as patronizing—the big boss white man patting the darkie on the head.

Hell, he sure was in a mood, all right.

Two numbers later, the comedian returned to introduce a former U.S. vice president. It had been only a decade or so since the man had been in office, but he looked old enough to have served under Harry Truman and his voice threatened to give out once or twice during the fifteen minutes he spent extolling Heathrow's virtues before turning the floor over to him.

As the mayor's mellow voice filled the massive room, Mercer spotted Barry Fox positioned near the exit, probably there to discourage folks from sneaking out while the candidate was on stage. Nobody tried. Everybody in the room seemed to be hanging on the mayor's every word, except for the waiters and busboys busily shuffling the dirty dishes. And Mercer.

*   *   *

After the dinner, the young lawyer cooled his heels while Vanessa said good-bye to her father, who shot him a fiery glance. "You both have work to do, early in the morning," C.W. said.

"Yes, Daddy." Vanessa grabbed Mercer's hand and whispered, "Let's get out of here."

Waiting for their cars, she said, "I'll follow you home."

"Sure you wouldn't rather go to Barry's party?"

She gave him a smile as readable as the Mona Lisa's. "Here's my car," she said, heading for the just-delivered yellow Porsche Boxster.

Twenty minutes later she was in his apartment, looking so beautiful it took him a few seconds to remember that he was supposed to be angry with her.

"Why'd you tell him?" he asked.

"Because he's my father," she said. "A decision this big, it's something you talk to your daddy about. Especially since he's been your daddy *and* your momma since you were thirteen."

"What'd you say to him, exactly? That you were still thinking about it? That you were gonna shoot me down? Maybe that I wasn't worthy to be a member of that goddamned bourgie Negro family of yours?"

"No to all questions," she said, a tear rolling down her cheek. "I told him I was in love with you and I wanted to be your wife."

He stared at her.

"Assuming you still want me," she said.

His answer was to reach out and draw her to him. When they kissed, it seemed like it was longer and deeper than he had ever kissed any woman before.

Their romance had progressed slowly, at her request. The first couple times he asked her out, she refused, offering him no clear encouragement. But he stayed the course. It was a month or so before she said yes.

There had been no goodnight kiss after that date. Six weeks passed before they got together again. Either he was preparing for a trial or she was. Or the Lakers were playing ball or she was playing hard to get. When they finally did manage a dinner together, she'd forgotten much of what they'd talked about on their first date. Not a promising sign. But she seemed to like being with him.

She was not exactly wanting for company, she told him, a fact he'd figured out for himself. She had no time to waste on wannabe players or the dog-men who chased anything that moved.

"If I am going to date someone, he has to be a real man," she said. "No games. No bullshit." She'd observed Mercer long enough to believe he was neither dog nor player. But he did have issues.

Thinking about that now, as they walked hand in hand into the bedroom, he smiled. Yes, he had issues. More than she could possibly know. But that didn't matter. She was going to be his bride.

She unhooked her necklace and placed it and the earrings on a bedside table. Then she turned her back and let him unhook the clasp on her gown and slide the zipper down. The garment fell to the carpet and she stepped out of it. She turned, posing for him in the moonlight. She wore his favorite panties—the pink ones with lots of lace. Mercer knew that when they married, if he could afford nothing else, Vanessa would always have lots of lacy pink panties. He ran his index finger across the top of her waistband, and then drew it straight down the front. Vanessa quivered as he pulled the leg of her panties to the side, the better to touch her bare skin. She was already wet.

They'd agreed that they would take turns treating one another during their lovemaking. He made it her turn that night. She could lie back and let him do all the things she'd taught him, the way she'd taught him. She'd shown him where and how she liked to be touched, and made the learning process enjoyable for them both. Trial and error. Again and again.

Mercer dropped to one knee and gently rolled her panties down her thighs. They smelled of her, an aroma he loved. He leaned forward, parting her legs, and began to kiss her. Softly at first. Then with some insistence.

Her legs grew weak and she sat back on the bed. She came almost at once. He continued to kiss her until she pushed him away, muttering that she was "too sensitive."

He removed his clothes.

Standing beside the bed, admiring the length and the shape of her, he said something he knew he could not say often enough. "I love you." Then he covered his fiancée's body with his own.

He was just settling into a sweet postcoital sleep when the phone chirped. Without thinking, without even opening his eyes, he lifted the receiver.

A familiar, irritating voice said, "Mr. Early?"

He was immediately awake. Sitting up, coiled like a spring. Vanessa stirred next to him. He saw her about to speak and quickly raised a finger to his lips.

"Mr. Early? You there?"

"Yeah." Mercer cleared his throat. "I . . . what can I do for—"

"I wake you?"

"As a matter of fact."

Vanessa's lips formed the word "Daddy?" without saying it.

Mercer nodded and she rolled her eyes.

"Sorry about the hour," C.W. said. "Something on the late news I thought might be of interest."

"Sir, it's . . . what? . . . a little after midnight. Could this wait—?"

"Your client's dead," C.W. said.

Mercer's immediate thought was of the trial less than nine hours away. "Ricky Sanchez is dead?"

"Ricky Sanchez? No. It's Darion Mayfield. The Reverend's son."

Relief swept over Mercer. If one of his clients had to go, Darion wasn't a bad choice. "Overdose?" he asked.

"No. But drugs may be involved," C.W. said. "He fell out of the window at his apartment."

"He lives—lived—on the fifth floor."

"Yes. Evidently quite a mess. They say he was decapitated by the fall."

The image of Darion Mayfield's rolling head flitted through Mercer's mind. It was quickly replaced by a replay of Claude Burris's angry exit from the courtroom. "They sure he fell?" he asked.

"Did he strike you as suicidal?"

"No. If I had a guess, I'd say somebody shoved him."

"There's been no mention of foul play," C.W. said. "Of course, there was no mention of the boy's occupation, either. He was identified merely as 'the son of popular religious leader, the Reverend Doctor Harlan Mayfield.' As soon as the media makes the connection between the death and Darion Mayfield's trial, they may seek you out for information or a sound bite. Remember the firm's policy on personal publicity."

Beautiful. A client takes a fatal header and all C.W. can think about is the firm's public relations. "Yeah . . . well, thanks for the heads up. I'll try and stay clear of the press. See you in the A.M., sir."

Mercer expected his boss to ring off. Instead, C.W. asked, in a slightly strangled voice, "Is my daughter with you?"

"Here? You mean she's not at her place at this hour?" Mercer said.

Beside him, Vanessa had to restrain her giggle.

6

By eleven, the night had cooled down, not that it slowed the action at Buckie's. The Starbucks coffee shop owned by basketball legend Magic Johnson and located in the Ladera Heights shopping center had been affectionately renamed by the locals. It was the place to hang if you were young and single. The unmarried Mingus half-qualified.

He sat at a postage-stamp table, sipping a three-dollar coffee from a cardboard cup and observing the women strutting between Buckie's and the adjacent Friday's restaurant. The women were in their usual finery: scantily clad, ghetto-after-five, waist-high, tight-ass jeans with belly buttons exposed.

A honey dip bounced by wearing pants so tight they might have been spray-painted on. Mingus sighed. Nothing that round could be real. He wondered if anybody ever tried suing Levi Strauss for defrauding the public.

Not that that stopped him from looking. As his uncle, Fred Mingus the judge, used to say, "Ain't no harm in lookin'."

Redd arrived twenty minutes late. CPT, Mingus thought. Colored People Time. He and Redd went back to '96, during his first days in Internal Affairs. IAG, or

IAD as it was called back then, had received a tip that an officer at Wilshire division was trickin' with the females in the lockup. In exchange for a piece of ass and/or a blow job, he'd provide them with packs of cigarettes they could conceal in their most private parts and later resell in county jail. Because the facilities were filled with addictive personalities and smoking was prohibited at county, cigarettes sold for as much as twenty dollars apiece or four hundred dollars per pack. The only problem was that the jailers searched the girls and forced them to cough up, if not out, any contraband concealed on their persons. Redd made the most of her physical adaptability, easily transporting a pack of Kools and a lighter to go.

Mingus watched her slide out of a brand-new Cadillac Escalade, black on black and tightened up by 310 motoring accessories. Redd was pretty tightened up herself, in Manolo Blahniks, a yellow halter top, and black stretch pants that augmented yet another seemingly perfect ass. She paused to give the viewing audience a chance to let it all sink in before sashaying in the detective's direction.

There was something about Redd that made men like her. Maybe it was that walk, which few women could match. Maybe it was her accent which, when she wanted to, she could roll off her tongue in a way that West Coast men found too sexy to ignore. Or maybe it was that thing she liked to do so much. Either way, she had managed to snuggle up to some of the city's most powerful men, black, white, or anything in between; politicians, doctors, or lawyers. Over the years she had proved to be Mingus's most productive and reliable informant.

Strangely, she asked for nothing in return, except that she not be identified as the source of the information she provided. "I don't get it why your hand isn't out like everybody else's," Mingus had said to her one afternoon.

"Oh, I intend to get paid," she'd replied. "But a few hundred dollars don't mean shit to me. I mean, I *got* a few hundred bucks. But I'm keepin' track of your debt, honey. In fact, you owe me more'n you know."

"What do you mean?"

"Just that your tab is gettin' large, baby. I expect to be paid, eventually. Maybe, when I decide to settle down, I'll make you marry me."

She leaned over the tiny Buckie's table to kiss him. She reeked of Animale. His nostrils still hadn't quite recovered from the crime scene. With them inflamed and at full attention, he avoided her offered lips and barely brushed her right cheek with his mustache before gently nudging her away.

He noticed she'd done something new with her inch-and-a-half-long fingernails. The "2"s cut from real two-dollar bills had been laminated to their tips. He wasn't surprised by the concept, only by the denomination. He'd figured her for twenties. Maybe fifties. He said, "What kept you? I'm on my second coffee."

"I was with a friend." She smiled at him.

"Business is business."

"Not business. I got my own life, you know."

"Glad to hear it. Want some brew?"

"Naw. Didn't yo' mama ever tell you coffee makes you black?" Redd laughed.

Mingus didn't.

As a boy, he was often teased by other coloreds about the darkness of his skin. Blackie. Darkie. Midnight. Shoeshine. He'd heard them all. Jokes, too, of course. The fact that they came from members of his own race instead of some redneck crackers didn't do much to ease the pain. The first time he met his third grade teacher, Mrs. Hall (aka "Hot Miz Hall"), she'd remarked that he was "blacker than black. Baby, you so black you're blue-black. And you shiny, too." Back then, such things hurt. Back then, light skin was in; dark skin was out. Times had changed. But Mingus had a long memory.

"So what you got for me?" he asked. Redd had suggested the meet.

"I heard you been inquirin' about the dope dealer

who took a dive on Centinela." She smiled sweetly. "Somethin' special about that?"

Mingus was scanning the room, noting that Redd's fans had shifted their attention to a honey-skinned honey with fake tits wearing a long weave and tight red cargo pants. "What makes you think so?" he asked.

"Wel-l-l-l, the El Lay Pee Dee usually don't give a rat's ass what happens to a nigger drug dealer on the South Side. Y'all won't even visit after dark, 'less you' ridin' four deep with a helicopter escort. The fact you sittin' here with Redd makes it special, don't it, baby? Some cop mixed in it?"

There was, but Mingus wasn't there to give her information. The little chickenhead already knew too much about his street business. "Stick to the point," he said. "You holding anything about this dealer or not?"

"Would I be wastin' your time and mine? Ol' friend o' yours name Ken Loc Ansol been mouthin' off about bein' there when your dealer went down." She pronounced the man's second name "loak," like in "loco."

Mingus's recollection of Ken Loc was vivid enough, a skinny runt he'd popped some years back for carjacking an old lady at a Safeway parking lot. It had been Loc's third strike, but the old lady had been leery of testifying. Mingus and the D.A. had prevailed upon the public defender to convince Loc that a vacation at the state's expense would be wiser than risking a trial where grandma might suddenly find the nerve to finger him. Being a third strike, that carjacking would have carried a mandatory twenty-five-years–to–life sentence. Loc took the free vacation at San Quentin.

"I didn't know Ken Loc had touched down," Mingus said. "How long has he been out?"

"Couple months, I guess. I ran into him at the Liquor Barn."

"He happen to tell you where he's stayin'?"

"Like I would wanna know that?"

Mingus studied her for a few seconds. He couldn't think of any reason she'd be stringing him.

"His li'l bro' can prob'ly fill you in," she said. "You know Bay Bay, too, don't you?"

"I'm not sure," Mingus said. He had a dim recollection of putting the rap on somebody by that name, maybe busting his beak in the process.

"Come on now, nigger. You know Bay Bay. Used to be from the Sixties? Anyway, he must know where his big brother is hanging," she said. "He's workin' over at a prayer place, the Church of the Last Harvest, on 110th and Central."

"Boy got religion, huh?" Mingus said as if he didn't much believe it. "Okay. That it?"

"Your dealer man had a special hottie," she said. "No live-in, but she likes her megablast, which means she was at his place most nights."

"Name?"

"Can't help you there, Detective."

"Got anything? A description?"

"Hell, all them white girls look alike," Redd said, grinning.

"I was hoping you could do a little better than that," Mingus said. "You hear anything about what happened to Darion's stash?"

"First I'm learning it was missing. I'll check around."

"Guess I'll see if this Bay Bay can hook me up with his bro. Thanks for your help, Redd."

"My pleasure. Just don't mention my name to Bay, huh? Wouldn't want some folks to know I'm so tight with the po-lice." She smiled suddenly, as if in response to some private joke. "Bet Bay'll be surprised to see ya."

She got up and patted his cheek, letting those long, sharp two-dollar numbers scrape against his stubble. "Later, baby," she said and sauntered off across the room in a cloud of Animale.

Mingus sipped his coffee, observed her undulating ass as she departed and wondered if Farley had had any luck locating the dealer's head.

7

Shortly after her father's phone call, Vanessa left Mercer's bed to get dressed.

"You're not going?"

"Daddy will be calling my place every hour."

"So . . . ?"

"So, I don't want him worrying about me."

"Call him from here. Tell him you're home."

"I don't lie to him," she said. "Never have, never will."

"Then tell him you're here. With your husband-to-be."

She hesitated. "That wouldn't be a good idea. Not right now. He'll come around to the idea of our being together. But he isn't there yet."

"How long is it gonna take him?"

She bent over the bed and kissed him. "He'll come around," she said again.

An hour later he was still wide awake and staring at the ceiling in that midnight–to–three A.M. heart-of-darkness state when troubles appear like mental flashcards of despair. Sleep wasn't even in the negotiating stages.

Why was he worrying? He had found the perfect woman and she'd agreed to become his wife. He was with one of the major law firms in the country. Good stuff was happening. But there was Cordelu Wellington Goddamn Hansborough III, ready and waiting to fuck up everything.

He shook that idea from his head. No, he, Mercer, was the fuckup. He'd fucked up back in Alabama when, only by the merest chance, he'd escaped a very nasty fate.

Should he tell Vanessa about Alabama? No secrets? No way! She never lies to Daddy. Suppose she went running to him and ...

Aw, hell, did he trust her or didn't he?

He realized his hands were clenched. He relaxed, wiggled the tension from his fingers. Move on, he thought. Move on.

His thoughts drifted to Darion Mayfield, now headless, and the furious vice cop Claude Burris. Had Burris done the job on Darion? If so, wasn't he, Mercer, to blame for rattling the cop's cage? He'd been so proud of winning the drug dealer's freedom, but he sure as hell hadn't done the punk any favor. Jail may not be a picnic, but it definitely beat taking a long, head-chopping fall.

Move on.

He bounced from the bed and ran barefoot to his kitchenette where he downed a couple of aspirins. Then he searched the small apartment for his briefcase before remembering that the Enrique Sanchez folder was on the dresser in the bedroom where Vanessa had put it.

He took it to the bed, piled the pillows against the headboard, turned on the reading lamp and began to consult his notes.

The brothers, Max and Ricky Sanchez, had managed to get themselves arrested on two dozen or more occasions. Usually, Ricky, a juvenile until recently, took the rap for his older brother. It was Ricky who had appeared on the security tape breaking into an office building on Alvarado. It was Ricky who'd been in possession of the victim's wallet after a strong-arm job in Macarthur Park back in 1997. According to the victim, Ricky had been reluctant to take the wallet, but, after glancing a few times at his brother, had grabbed it, while Max watched approvingly but silently.

Max had learned in his developmental years as a criminal in the juvie system that mere presence at a crime scene was not enough to sustain guilt. This little legal tidbit, plus a brother who was just a few IQ points higher than the average dog and twice as obedient where Max was concerned, allowed the much older sibling to initiate any number of criminal offenses without fear of arrest.

But his luck had run out during the mugging of Ellis Halpern. Halpern, the assistant manager of Mid-city Drugs and the lock up man, had been so battered, the patch job had required more than two hundred staples in his head and face. On top of that, a brick to the head had left him even less mentally active than Ricky.

The police had arrived quickly enough to catch Ricky with his bloody hand in the store's till. Max was sitting on the front fender of their car. He told the officers that he'd tried to stop his brother from harming Halpern and looting the store, but he'd failed. What could he do? His brother was so powerful.

The cops wanted to know why he had blood on his clothes.

"I tried to protect the drugstore guy. I covered him with my own body, thinking that would stop Ricky. But he just pushed me away."

And the blood on his shoes?

"I guess maybe my foot rubbed against the poor dude when Ricky dragged me off him so he could whack him some more with that brick."

That night, in the interrogation room, the detectives had waved a surveillance tape under Max's nose. "We got you on tape in the act, Max," they'd told him. "You can't lay it on your dummy brother this time."

Back to the wall, Max had said, "My brother did the damage. All I'll cop to is aiding and abetting."

That was enough to put him in a cell next to Ricky's in the twin towers, charged as an accessory to aggravated mayhem. Only later did Max realize that he'd been scammed. The video camera had been set to pan a large section of the front of the building. The tape showed a male figure, allegedly Ricky, though the brothers were too alike in size and appearance, the light too poor and the picture too grainy to tell for certain, as he smashed a brick against Halpern's head. Another figure—Max, according to his statement—stood a few feet away gesturing at the man's head and presumably coordinating the beating.

Max's attorney, Edward Corey, was like Mercer, a former deputy D.A. and almost as disliked by the current crew. He'd agreed to Mercer's game plan to keep Max off the stand, thereby robbing the prosecution of the opportunity to confirm his previous conversations with the police—about his younger brother's guilt and his own participation in the crime.

Attempts at plea bargaining had failed. "Enrique isn't entirely responsible for his actions," Mercer had argued. "He suffers from a developmental defect. His IQ is in the low fifties." D.A. Dana Lowery wasn't buying. She had too much confidence in the strength of their case. And, after the bridges he'd burned with the Darion Mayfield trial, Mercer doubted she'd be inclined to agree to anything he might suggest.

He knew he had too high an emotional investment in Ricky Sanchez's fate. The law was too tough, the sentences too long. District attorneys cherry-picked their cases and the odds always favored the prosecution. "Here today, Folsom tomorrow," the old-timers often advised after a stiff drink at the saloon on Second Street. "Keep your distance or you'll drive yourself nuts."

But the past few months, whenever he'd visited the county jail, he found himself saving a few minutes to spend with Ricky. On one of those early drop-ins, the boy asked him when he could go home. He hadn't done anything real bad, he said.

"You gave a man a really bad beating."

"Oh. Right. I hit him with a brick and . . . maybe I stomped him?"

"Don't you know?"

"I have a hard time remembering. When can I go home, Mr. Early?"

By then he'd given up trying to get the boy to call him Mercer. Instead, he concentrated on the question, explaining that because of the severity of the crime, Ricky would be remaining in jail until the trial and possibly for a long time afterward.

"But can't I go home?"

Mercer explained the situation one more time and it registered. A little.

"I know what you're saying, but you got it all wrong. Max says they can't keep me, no matter what I do, 'cause I'm not old enough. I always go home."

"You turned eighteen, Ricky. No more juvie. You're playing with the big boys now. You don't get sent home."

Ricky's eyes started to tear up. "Well, papa Max says there's another reason they have to send me home. 'Cause I'm a re-tard."

"The doctors don't agree with Max," Mercer said. He'd managed to have Ricky examined by a handful of shrinks. The doctors had concluded that although the boy was borderline retarded, he was responsible for his actions.

"The doctors don't know what they're talking about, then. 'Cause papa Max is always right, Mr. Early."

"Why do you call him *papa* Max?"

"He's the closest I got to a papa," Ricky said. "He's old and he's smart, like a papa. He tells me what to do. He takes care of me."

"Yeah, he's taking care of you, all right," Mercer said.

On the next several visits, Ricky continued to ask when he would be going home and each time Mercer patiently explained the situation again. Eventually, the boy grasped and held the idea.

"How many years is life, Mr. Early?" he asked, surprising the young lawyer.

"That's real hard to figure. To give an exact number, I mean."

"I just hope it's not forever."

For a brief moment Mercer thought about grabbing the boy by the collar of his county jail blues and shouting, "Life is forever! They don't want you to go home. Ever. Life is forever."

He settled for cursing under his breath.

"That simpleminded boy doesn't have a mean bone in his body," he told Vanessa that night. "He just does what people tell him to. People like his goddamned 'papa' Max."

"You can't let yourself get emotionally involved with the clients," she said. "It'll beat you down. And you'll be less use to them in court if you lose sleep worrying about them."

That was the damn truth.

With a yawn, he closed the Enrique Sanchez folder. There was nothing more to be learned from his notes. All he could do was to try to play up the boy's childlike dependence on his brother. There were a few tiny cracks in the prosecution's case and he was as ready as he'd ever be to dig into them. He had to be alert. He needed sleep.

But as tired as he was, sleep wasn't on the docket.

His jumbled thoughts skittered from Ricky to Vanessa to her father to the image of a strung-out girl named Gisela in his arms.

"Stop!" he shouted, crying out against the memory.

But the painful images didn't stop. The price he paid for vanquishing the recollection of Gisela was the reprise of his most painful encounter with Ricky. The boy was in the prison's hospital ward. He'd been beaten and gang-raped by his fellow inmates. He'd smiled at Mercer and said, "They gotta let me go home now, right?"

Withdrawing from that soul-wrenching moment, he fell into a fitful sleep.

*   *   *

It was 8:20 when he awoke. Too late to shower. A dozen swipes of a Speed Stick and a cup of Listerine, a clean white shirt, and his suit from the day before, and he was on his way.

The Criminal Courts Building elevator was packed elbow to elbow with cops, criminals, and lawyers heading to the courtrooms above. A stench filled Mercer's nostrils. His first thought was that it might be coming from him. But this was more than one day's body odor. Turning his head, he discovered its source, a small, bearded man in handcuffs who seemed to be asleep on his feet.

He decided to hold his breath, hoping and then praying that the elevator hit the ninth floor without stopping first. But as it hummed upward, the lights flickered and it came to a screeching halt. Power failure.

The passengers struggled to maintain their balance. Someone began praying in Spanish. Almost immediately the backup generator kicked in. The lights flickered on and the car lurched upward.

Stepping gingerly off the elevator, Mercer gulped the relatively fresh air of the ninth floor. Composing himself, he refocused on the task ahead. The prospect of a good courtroom fight energized him, giving him butterflies in his stomach while at the same time providing the edge he needed to take on the state and win. "Better than beating a senior partner at handball," he'd recently told a class of high school pre-law club members.

But today was different. The fight before him was anything but "good." For the first time that he could recall, he was afraid. Afraid of losing. Afraid for Ricky.

Entering the courtroom he was met by a few of the guys he had clerked with at the D.A.'s who were heading out. He smiled and nodded, but the young prosecutors gave him the pariah treatment, looking through him and passing without a word.

A deputy D.A. was seated at the counsel table with an investigator from the D.A.'s office. Mercer knew them both. The prosecutor was a young woman named Anna Anapoli who'd once sought his help in nailing a black gangbanger. He wondered if any of the gratitude she'd expressed then still remained. The investigator, a black man named Rafe Collins, had previously worked in Internal Affairs, which meant he was neither liked nor trusted by his associates.

They seemed to purposely ignore Mercer's arrival, but he got a warm smile from Edward Corey, the lawyer for Ricky's brother, Max. Corey had put in just under ten years as a deputy D.A. before submitting a midnight resignation. According to office scuttlebutt he'd pissed off some cops in the major Narcotics unit after he failed to secure a conviction in a big trial. The cops claimed that Corey had thrown the case. There was also some talk about the evidence from the trial winding up a pound and a half light. Corey now lived in a million dollars' worth of house in Santa Monica that he claimed to have bought with his pension. Mercer didn't care about any of that, as long as the man was willing to let him call the shots on the defense of the Sanchez brothers.

Seated on a back bench was the boys' mother, Sylvia Sanchez, a short woman in a dark silk dress that accentuated her full figure. She waved to him, holding up the street clothes she had purchased for Ricky to wear before the jury. Mercer mentioned the clothes to the bailiff, who gestured the mother forward, accepting the garments and inspecting them carefully.

Mercer took one last chance to save the boy. The evidence against him was solid. All Anna Anapoli had to do was play the video of the victim eating brick and show Ricky's bloodstained clothes and the trial would be over. A life sentence was mandatory. He approached the D.A., extending his hand.

She offered hers reluctantly.

"Why don't we dispose of this for something less than ten?" he asked.

"Not much chance of that," she said in a flat voice.

The investigator, Rafe Collins, snickered. Anna Anapoli consulted her watch. "Where's the judge? The sooner we get started, the sooner we can go home."

"Home." The word hung in the air.

Mercer stared at the woman. He knew his presence unnerved her, so he decided to stand there as long as he could. The three of them were surprised by the sudden arrival of a detective assigned to the case.

Scowling at Mercer, he turned his back to the attorney and began whispering in Anna's ear.

"How in the hell did that happen?" she shouted. "Dammit, find it."

The detective scurried away, glancing at Mercer as he headed for the door.

Ed Corey approached the table as Rafe Collins asked Anna, "What's up?"

She seemed to be searching for the right words. Wrinkling her nose, she said, "The fucking videotape is missing from the evidence locker."

Mercer couldn't believe his good fortune, but he'd been around long enough to know that evidence was rarely lost for long. The cassette would be found misfiled or on some detective's desk and Ricky would still be looking at life. But the moment was his and he seized it. "What do you say, Anna? Let's plead out this thing."

She cocked her head. "What's your offer?"

Corey was suddenly very interested.

Balls to the wall, Mercer said, "My guy will plead to simple mayhem for a bullet." He'd admit to the felony and serve a year in county jail.

Anger added splotches of red to Anna's sallow Italian face. "With good time–work time credits, that's time served," she said, jumping to her feet. "It's a bullshit offer."

Mercer did not reply. He waited for her to calm down and return to her chair. Then he moved closer and almost whispered, "What kind of case do you have without the tape?"

"Your client was covered with blood."

"He showed up after the . . . mugging. Tried to help the guy."

Anna wrote a note to herself, then shoved it and her files into a briefcase. "Inform the clerk about the missing evidence," she instructed her investigator. To Mercer, she said, "I'll run your offer by the folks upstairs."

Corey said, "I'm offering the same deal for my client."

"Your client has confessed," Anna told him. "He is, in a word, fucked."

Before heading out of the courtroom, she said, "I hope to Christ you didn't have anything to do with making that tape go away, Mercer. You used to be one of the good guys, but these days you seem to have gone over to the dark side."

She flashed both attorneys a brief, insincere smile and strode from the courtroom.

8

Detective Dennis Farley sauntered into Robbery-Homicide, brushing lunch crumbs from his gut, to find Mingus at an empty desk studying the murder book on Darion Mayfield. "What gives, Lionel?" he asked. "I thought we were running separate investigations."

"Just keepin' current," Mingus said, continuing to turn the pages of the chronology log, a document noting the date and time for everything the detectives did in the course of their investigation. "Nothin' in here I shouldn't see, right?"

"Course not," Farley replied.

"Looks like you didn't get much help from the vic's neighbors."

"Nobody saw nuthin'," Farley said. "Them that bothered to answer the door."

"So much for community policing," Mingus said. "Most folks don't trust us enough to come forth when they're the victims, much less get messed up in the death of some drug dealer."

"Well," Farley said, after sucking excess lunch from his teeth, "you know your people, Lionel."

I know your people, too, you redneck bastard, Mingus thought. He pointed to an item that had been logged at 10:48 the night before: "Vic's head located. A neighborhood pit bull removed it from scene. Markings on face consistent with dog bites and animal consumption."

"Looks like you found that thing you were missin'," he said.

Farley glared at him. Then he managed a nasty smile. "I imagine you know how rough it can get if you lose things, right, Lionel?"

Lionel knew, sure enough.

The fat man's reference had been to the night Mingus lost . . . well, lost everything.

It hadn't started out much different than a hundred other nights, with the detective in a low dive throwing down doubles as fast as the barmaid could set 'em up. Too drunk to drive, he'd passed out in a storeroom at the rear of the joint, on a dirty cot that was there for hookers to use on busy nights.

When he awoke several hours later, his badge and weapon were missing. The thief hadn't bothered to take his money, even though he'd cashed his paycheck that afternoon.

He should have reported the theft immediately. But rather than face an Internal Affairs investigation and a layoff, he'd tried to get the badge and gun back on his own. It was a foolish decision. Three weeks later, a man identifying himself as a police officer knocked at the door of a young woman on Lockland Place. He flashed Mingus's badge and was allowed entry. He bound and gagged the woman and abused her every kind of which way before making his escape. He left Mingus's badge behind as a parting gesture.

The fallout had been heavy, with the city settling a lawsuit that was rumored to be in excess of two million dollars. Mingus was demoted in rank and fired from his position as lead detective at Robbery-Homicide. After that, he stopped living and settled for merely existing. His career over, there wasn't much left in his life worth anything. No wife. No family. No friends to speak of.

His gun was still missing, a shoe that would drop

sooner or later. Some asshole would use it to do a drive-by, killing a kid or maybe a cop.

Mingus had been living with the shame and guilt of that night for so long that Farley's zinger drew little blood. There wasn't much blood left.

"I'll be through here in a minute," he said, denying the detective the satisfaction of an emotional reaction. He removed a pen from his shirt pocket and began scribbling some reminders in his notebook.

He was conscious of Farley standing there, watching him for a beat, then shuffling off in search of the coffee pot. From his peripheral view, he saw the fat cop carry a steaming cup of the stale and bitter brew to a chair two desks away.

When Mingus finally closed the powder blue folder, Farley was right there at his elbow. "What exactly you lookin' for?"

"Just fillin' in my dance card," Mingus said, lifting his jacket from the back of the chair. "Anything not in the book yet?"

"Naw," Farley said. "But we still got the whole afternoon ahead of us."

"Nothing in here about the late Mr. Mayfield's girl-friend."

"What girlfriend?" Farley asked, frowning.

"I heard there was one, a white girl who spent a lot of time at his place."

"Well, you got a better source than me, Lionel. 'Cause I never heard of no girlfriend. I was beginning to think the boy was fruitpie. Got a name for me?"

"No," Mingus said. "You Homicide guys oughta do some of the work. Another thing I didn't see any men-tion of in the book is Detective Claude Burris."

"Burris? You talkin' about that bullshit over the drug bust? Mayfield was a dealer. Burris took him down."

"Heard there was some kinda ruckus in court yester-day. Bad feelings all 'round."

"It happens," Farley said.

Mingus stared at him.

"Fact is, Lionel, I was plannin' on talkin' with Burris, maybe later today," Farley said.

"He says anything interesting, I hope you'll let me know."

"You got any solid reason to think Claude's involved in the murder?"

"Detective Burris is just another suspect. Unless he's got himself an alibi. Then he isn't even that. Ask him about the alibi."

"Don't tell me how to do my job, Lionel."

"Somebody has to."

Farley almost lost it. "You got the questions," he said, eating his anger. "Why don't you talk to Burris?"

"It's your case," Mingus said.

"You got that right." Farley stuck out a red-rosy chin. He'd shaved it too close and Mingus could count the razor cuts.

"I got other things to do, anyway," he told Farley.

"Like what?"

"What I always do. Check the traps, see what's caught."

"You love this, don't you, Lionel? Love the idea that some real cop might have stepped in shit."

Mingus chuckled. "Look who's talking about real cops."

9

"You mean it, Mr. Early?" Ricky Sanchez said. "You're not fooling with me, are you?"

Mercer could hardly keep from smiling. "It's up to the D.A., Ricky, but we've got a shot. Now if you get out—"

"When I get out."

"Okay, when you get out, I want you to promise me you won't let Max lead you around by the nose ever again."

Ricky hesitated, then said, "I promise."

"Promise what?"

"Promise to never let Max lead me by the nose again."

After a while, the celebratory mood in the cell began to wane. Mercer checked his watch. Anna had been gone nearly an hour, more than enough time to get the plea bargain approved.

Returning to the courtroom, he was surprised to find Judge Carl Dixon on the bench, crewcut toupee in place, square jaw thrust forward. Seated before him were Anna Anapoli at the prosecution table and, at the defense table, Ed Corey . . . and Ricky's brother, Max.

"You understand, Mr. Sanchez," Judge Dixon was saying, "that in exchange for your plea of guilty to simple mayhem you will receive a year in the county jail, or time served, and you will be required to testify for the prosecution."

"I understand, Your Honor," Max said.

After the court accepted the plea, Mercer stormed over to Anna. "What the fuck just happened here? You sandbagged me."

Anna looked up at him without expression. "Courtesy of Mr. Gomez." She nodded toward the rear of the courtroom. Gomez was seated near the door, his legs crossed, smiling at Mercer. He adjusted his glasses at the bridge of his nose with his middle finger, then pointed the finger directly at Mercer.

Before the young lawyer could respond, Judge Dixon inquired, "I assume you're ready to proceed to trial, Mr. Early?"

Mercer turned to the judge, speechless.

The judge took this for assent. He instructed his clerk to "send for thirty-six jurors."

"But you said I was going home," Ricky shouted between hysterical sobs. "Life is forever. Life is forever."

"It's not over yet," Mercer said. "We can still win."

"Liar. Liar. Liar. Why did you lie to me, Mr. Early?"

Mercer hadn't lied, but he'd made a mistake. He'd let this childlike young man believe he was going home, and now he had to take it all back. A prudent attorney would have waited for the deal to be cut. A prudent attorney wouldn't have let his emotions overrule his common sense.

"You're lying about Max, too. Why would he do anything to hurt me?" The boy fell to his knees, weeping.

Mercer looked away. He was moved by the irony of the situation. If Ricky hadn't been such an innocent, he'd know why his selfish, scheming brother was serving him up. But the knowledge wouldn't help him. Mercer didn't try to answer the question.

He sat down on a chair near the cell. A pair of handcuffs dangled from its arm, one cuff locked to the chair, the other hanging and open like a trap. Unconsciously, he began toying with the locked cuff. Years ago, he'd made an interesting discovery about certain types of handcuffs. He took a pen from his pocket, unscrewed the top and removed the ink cartridge. He poked it into the cuff's keyhole.

Mindlessly working the cartridge point, he focused on the impossibility of his position. The judge was awaiting the arrival of a jury panel. The trial would start in a heartbeat. Max's testimony would be more devastating than the still missing video, which would probably be found any minute. His client was on the floor of the cell, weeping and useless.

He felt the lock give beneath the cartridge point and the cuff snapped open. "I've still got it," he muttered. Well, hell, nothing was impossible. It was time to start thinking like a litigator again. King 'Gator? Well, he'd give it a shot.

Standing before the cell, he shouted at the boy, "Get up, dammit."

Ricky stopped sobbing, whimpered, and began wiping his eyes. "I can't stay here, Mr. Early. I just as soon die."

Mercer slammed his hand against the door. "I don't want to hear that shit again, dammit. Ain't nobody gonna die. Now, get your ass up off the floor. Stop crying like a baby. We're gonna have to win. Okay? The tape is still missing and the best evidence they got is your brick-beating, sleazy fuckin' brother. He's the only thing standing between you and the street, and a just God ain't gonna let him continue to stand there."

The boy looked at his lawyer and slowly began to rise up. "Can you get me out of here, Mr. Early?"

"Hell, yes," Mercer said, stepping over the line again, except this time he was aware of it.

Reentering the courtroom, he asked the bailiff to give the boy the clothes his mother had brought for him. Scanning the back of the room, he saw that the faces had changed. Gomez was gone. Max was there, a free man, lank hair neatly combed, chin whiskers shaved, skull-and-bones tats covered by a cheap new dark suit. He was sitting next to Mrs. Sanchez. They were holding hands. More than a dozen prosecutors, most of them "baby cakes"—fresh from law school—were seated in a group. Gomez had probably made it compulsory that they witness the ass-whipping Mr. Mercer Early had coming to him.

Well, he'd try to make it as educational as possible.

As he took his seat at counsel's table, Anna called his name. Pointing to his hand, she said, "First blood, and we haven't even started."

Mercer looked down to find a line of blood running from a cut along the side of his hand, probably from when he'd banged the jail cell door. He removed his white handkerchief and wrapped it around the wound.

"Start me off with a little jury sympathy, huh, Anna?" He winked at her.

He saw her confidence falter in the face of his high spirits. "Just remember," he said, "I gave you a chance to do the right thing. Now you and Gomez are gonna have to pay for your sins."

She frowned, momentarily uncertain, then used a hand to wave away his words. She obviously had no idea what he was talking about. Unfortunately, neither did he.

Jury selection took the rest of the day. Ricky sat beside Mercer, growing more and more withdrawn. Shortly after lunch, the boy nodded off, lurching forward, eyes closed.

The judge called out to him, just to make sure he was paying attention.

By three o'clock, Mercer had to nudge Ricky repeatedly to keep him awake.

In most cases, D.A.s and defense lawyers choose different kinds of jurors. The D.A.s prefer white males from the suburbs, jurors who live in fear of crime and minority criminals and who would leap to convict a big Mexican charged with beating a man half to death with a brick.

Defense lawyers normally look for minority jurors who view the police with suspicion. This time, however, Mercer agreed wholeheartedly with Anna's selection. In the end, the jury consisted of ten whites and two Hispanics. Eight men and four women. The only black jurors were limited to the alternate pool.

The judge advised them to keep an open mind and not to discuss the matter with anyone. "The defendant is ordered back at nine-thirty tomorrow morning," he stated, banging the gavel. Then he left the bench, square jaw thrust out.

As the bailiff took Ricky toward the lockup door, the boy asked, "Mr. Early, can we talk before they take me back?"

Mercer was willing but the bailiff disagreed. "The bus to County is waiting for him. He's the last custody in the building."

Ricky stopped in his tracks, forcing the bailiff to tug his arms hard, dragging him in the direction of the holding cell. "Mr. Early, promise me you'll get 'em to let me go home. Promise me."

"I promise," Mercer shouted as the door closed on the boy.

10

Mingus spent the day trying to get a line on the vic's girlfriend and Ken Loc Ansol, tapping every source on the street available to him and developing a few new snitches along the way. All said the same things. They'd heard Darion Mayfield had some lady on the hook, but they didn't know who she was. A street hustler snitch called SassyBoy claimed to have seen the woman with Darion and described her as "built for the bedroom, if you like white fluff." He had no idea what her name was or where she might be found. No one admitted knowing anything about Darion's missing drugs.

As for Ken Loc, everyone agreed that he was "keepin' it on the down low," making himself scarce. It wasn't until he was on his own time that the detective realized he had gone about the search for Loc all wrong. What was it that Redd had said? Loc's big brother, Bay Bay, had been born again and was fellowshippin' at the Church of the Last Harvest.

On a slow Tuesday night, with nothing else pressing, Mingus drove to the address at 110th and Central in Watts on the odd chance of finding someone to point him in Bay Bay's direction. Judging by the fully lit church front and the filled parking lot, the trip hadn't been wasted.

The building's exterior was fairly commonplace. White clapboard, columns in front, all freshly painted. An illuminated marquee box planted on the square of lawn in front read: TONIGHT: BE NOT DECEIVED: LIVE FOR NOW. This was followed by the name, DR. MARCUS FOX-CROFT, HIGH PRIEST.

The interior of the church was a little less ordinary.

The walls of the alcove were covered in a rich red paint. According to a sign attached to the doors leading to the church proper, ONLY THE CLEANSED MAY ENTER. The second requirement was less open to interpretation: DONATIONS: $5, MINIMUM. BE GENEROUS.

When Mingus reached for the door handle, someone said, "Stop."

A figure in a red velvet hooded robe approached from a hall to the detective's right. All Mingus could see of the figure's face was a stubbled chin. "You didn't make your offering, brother."

The voice struck a distant chord with Mingus, but he couldn't quite identify it. As the figure neared, the light over the doorway lifted the shadow on a narrow male face. The detective put the man at a weary fifty-something. His three upper front teeth were missing, causing the lisp that had struck Mingus as familiar.

He brought out his wallet, but instead of pulling a fiver, he flashed his badge. "Police," he said.

"Usher," the man shot back. "I know you, Mingus. I know you a pig. We don't discriminate against anybody here, including pigs. But either you drop a dead Lincoln in the till or you get yo' ass out."

Mingus considered grabbing the snag-toothed man by the neck and introducing him face first into the near-est wall. But he *was* in a church, of some kind. He handed over a fiver. "Be sure it makes it to the till," he said, "or I'll have to ask for a refund."

The usher bowed and stepped away from the door.

Church was in session, but the Last Harvesters were evidently taking the city's energy crisis to heart. The place was almost as darkly lit as a movie house, though there was enough light for Mingus to see that the pews and fixtures picked up the red color of the walls.

The room's only bright spot was the altar where, in a raised bloodred pulpit, a minister—no doubt the promised Dr. Marcus Foxcroft—in a money-green robe with golden arm chevrons, rapped out a sermon. Hanging directly behind him was a sculpture of a crucifixion. Probably the Crucifixion, though Mingus had his doubts. The expression on the statue's face was not very Christlike. There was no hint of acceptance or sorrow or even peace. The crucified man seemed in the throes of terror and pain so horrific his face was twisted into a grotesque mask, while his body pressed back against the cross as if in fear. Nailed to the palms of each hand were hundred-dollar bills. On his feet he wore winged golden Nikes. On his head was a crown of thorns, but the crown was gold, inlaid with precious stones that glittered in the dim light.

As Mingus moved to a seat in the middle of the room, he caught stray phrases of Dr. Foxcroft's sermon. "One need only look to the Old Testament," the doctor's deep amplified voice rang through the church, "to know that the strong routinely invaded and enslaved the weak. The way of the world, my children."

"Oh, yes," the congregation answered.

"And whatever the conquerors claimed for themselves was righteous, because the taking of it meant that it belonged to them. God had put it on this not always sweet earth for them. God looked down in scorn at the weaklings and, in effect, said, 'You don't deserve happiness.' "

Mingus had no idea what point the guy in the green robe was trying to make. To him most religious oratory was bullshit, anyway, though this seemed to go even beyond bullshit. He tried to ignore it as he scanned the crowd of worshippers. It was a predominantly male group, with just a smattering of women. The men wore turbanlike headgear. The women covered their heads with sheer white cloths.

It was no place for a bald-headed stranger. The detective kept his hat on as he took a seat on the aisle.

Dr. Foxcroft descended from the pulpit and dropped to his knees on the altar. He began moaning and chanting words in some unfamiliar tongue. The worshippers left their seats to gather around him, dropping to the marble floor, contributing their chorus of loud groans while pressing their bodies against one another and touching each other's faces and arms and shoulders.

Like a sixties group grope, Mingus thought, but there was nothing remotely sexy about it.

Then, suddenly, a hand rose above the mound of bodies. It was holding something that caught the reflection of the altar light.

A knife.

Momentarily unsure of what to do, Mingus reached for his pistol.

He was too late. The knife was plunged downward into the mass of bodies. A woman screamed, nearly loud enough to wake the statue on the cross. Even after she stopped, the echo continued to bounce off the red walls. Mingus drew his gun as he ran toward the altar. The group had collapsed in a heap. Blood was everywhere, glistening on their faces and staining their clothing.

Mingus used his free hand to pull them apart one by one, like the leaves from an artichoke. At the heart, he found Dr. Foxcroft. In one hand he held the now-bloody knife. In the other was something dripping in gore—a thoroughly mutilated chicken.

"What the hell do you think you're doing?" Dr. Foxcroft shouted at him, rising to his feet. "Bringing that weapon of destruction to our service!"

Mingus was still pointing the gun at the man's head. He dropped his arm, but he didn't put the gun away. Not with the good doctor still holding *his* weapon of destruction.

"Be gone, you . . . you heathen." The minister waved the bloody chicken at Mingus, who felt a drop of something wet hit his cheek. "Be gone!"

Chastised, Mingus backed away. He holstered his weapon and turned. He forced himself to saunter out through the main door, trying to hide the shame he felt.

Standing in the foyer, embarrassed and confused, but also relieved that he hadn't shot anybody, he heard the scrape of a shoe against tile. Turning and ducking at the same time, he was able to avoid the gap-toothed usher's roundhouse right.

Mingus grabbed the usher by the neck and fed him drywall. The man's lip split and left blood to blend in with the red wall.

The detective maintained his hold. "Where can I find Bay Bay Ansol?"

The usher didn't answer. Mingus slammed his head into the wall a second time.

"Holy shi . . . wait a minute!" the man complained. "He . . . Bay Bay left, couple hours ago."

"Where to?"

When the man didn't answer quickly enough, Mingus started moving him toward the wall again.

"Okay," the usher shouted. "He say he was going to the Mustang. Had a little skeezer wif him."

Mingus relaxed his arm and the usher slipped away to sit on the tile floor. "Thanks for your cooperation," the detective said as he headed out.

But the man on the floor wanted the final word. "This the las' time you slam me, Mingus, you goddamned Oreo motherfuck."

Mingus paused in his tracks. The missing teeth. Slammin' him *again*? The same voice yelling the same Oreo insult he remembered from long ago.

He turned to the usher, who was still sitting on the floor. He had pulled off his hood and was wiping his bloody lip on his sleeve. Looking at him closely, Mingus wasn't completely convinced the man was Bay Bay. The weasel he remembered had been in his twenties, at least fifty pounds heavier, with a weird half-Afro. This was a skin-and-bones, bald-headed black man who looked old enough to be Bill Cosby's grandpa. But there was something . . .

"You're Bay Bay, right?"

"So you got me. Now what?"

"Why'd you take that swing at me?"

"I figured you'd be comin' for me one of these days."

"What are you talking about?"

"Fuck you, Mingus. I came at you 'cuz I thought I could take you. Even now." Bay Bay spit a clump on the tile floor.

Mingus didn't understand anything the man was saying. "Only reason I was lookin' for you was to find out where your brother is hanging," he said. He searched his pockets for a handkerchief or a tissue and came up empty. "It's Ken Loc I want."

Bay Bay stared at him, surprised. "No shit?"

"No shit."

Surprise turned to arrogance. "You expect me to rat out my own brother?"

Mingus reached beneath Bay Bay's armpits and helped him to his feet. The guy didn't weigh more than a big dog. "Whatever diet you on, Bay, you better quit now before you disappear."

"Diet, huh? You always was a funny man, Mingus." Bay Bay wiped his mouth across his sleeve, then ran his tongue over the few teeth he had left to make sure there weren't any new gaps. "You remember how it was in the eighties, huh? Too much good dope. Too much bad pussy. I got the HIVs. That's what I'm on: the HIV diet. I don't recommend it."

Mingus felt a stab of sorrow for Bay Bay. It was quickly replaced by the realization that he'd come in contact with the man's blood. "Uh, you mind if I . . . ?"

"Washroom's over there." Bay Bay gestured in the vicinity of a hall to the right. "I better come with you 'cuz Dr. Foxcroft don't like pig any more than I do. Wouldn't want you wanderin' aroun' by yo' bad se'f."

Washing up, Mingus kept his eye on Bay Bay, who was sitting on the closed toilet lid, staring back at him. "What's with this place?" the detective asked. "Some kind of voodoo religion?"

"You mean the chicken?"

"Yeah. And all the red."

Bay Bay hesitated before answering. "You know our name, right?"

"Church of the Last Harvest."

"That says it all, Mingus. All of us are on the HIV. It's our last chance at life, riches and salvation. We got nothing to lose."

Bay Bay rose to his feet. He handed the detective a clean paper towel from the dispenser. Mingus studied it briefly, looking for blood. When he was satisfied the towel was okay, he wiped his hands and face with it. "I dig the riches part. Grab what you can. What I don't understand is the salvation."

Bay Bay laughed. "With all the dirt I did in my life, Mingus, you think I'm going to heaven? Shiiiit. There's another place for people like me. Like all of us here. That's who we prayin' to. The head man at that stand. Get on his good side."

That helped explain the weird crucifixion statue. It was just a different spin on the event, Jesus as a frightened human, suffering defeat by his enemy.

"Didn't know Lucifer had a good side."

"Hope yo' wrong, Mingus," Bay Bay said. "What is it you think my li'l bro' did?"

"I'm not looking to jam him," Mingus replied. "He isn't a suspect. Maybe a witness. I need to ask him a few questions."

"What'd he witness?"

"Man he knew got tossed from a high window. I'm hopin' he can tell me something about the vic, maybe clue me in to the guy's foes."

Bay Bay frowned. After a brief silence, he said, "I spoke wif him around noon. Said he was seein' some skeeze later, maybe take her to the Mustang."

"That's the same jive you gave me before, when I asked about Bay Bay."

Bay Bay looked sheepish. "You got me unawares. I didn't have time to make nothin' up."

"If I miss him at the club, where's his crib these days?"

"I don't know."

"He's your brother."

"Yeah, well, he's not up with the HIV shit. He calls ever' now and then, check if I'm still breathin'. But he don't invite me over to dinner. No physical contact, nothin' like that." He said the words in a matter-of-fact tone, as though he didn't expect any more of his brother.

"You gotta have some idea where he's livin'."

"I'm too close to hell at this point to be doin' much lyin', Mingus. If he ain't at the Mustang tonight, he'll be there tomorrow. Or one of his other hangouts, like the Kittyhawk." He seemed to be studying Mingus intently. "That's the best I got."

Mingus threw his paper towel into the trash and headed for the door. Walking out, he stopped and turned. "You take it easy, Bay. I'm sorry I . . . well, I'm just sorry."

As the door began to close behind him, he heard Bay Bay say, "My dark God will redeem me."

Mingus drove directly to the Mustang Motel on Western and Martin Luther King. The hotel charged twenty bucks for the first three hours, an additional twenty for the second three hours or any portion thereof. Mingus arrived three hours and ten minutes after Loc had checked in. The ex-jailbird had already wet his beak and flown the coop.

11

A blast of sunlight peeping through the miniblinds struck Mercer smack in the face. Scowling, he pulled the sheet over his head. "What time is it?" he asked Vanessa. "I'm afraid to look."

When she didn't answer, he lowered the sheet, rubbed his eyes and tried to focus on the numbers on the digital alarm clock. 4:03. They were blinking on and off.

It sure as hell was not a four o'clock sun lasering through his window. There must've been a blackout during the night.

He groped for his watch on the table beside the bed, held it up in front of his still unfocused eyes. Damn. Almost eight o'clock. "Vanessa, wake up, baby. It's time."

He reached for his wife-to-be, only to grab a fist full of air.

She was gone.

He suddenly remembered that she had not slept with him. He'd spent the night alone, going over every minute aspect of the Sanchez case, wondering if there wasn't something he was missing, a key left unturned. That was when he recalled one of his conversations with Ricky. It was just a little odd thing the boy had said and he'd explained it, sort of. But there was something about it . . .

Shortly after two A.M., he'd awakened his assistant, Melissa, with a request that she do a little digging as soon as she got to work in the morning. He wanted as complete a list as possible of all of the Sanchez brothers' previous court appearances.

"What are we looking for?" she asked.

"A miracle," he said.

"Doctor," Anna Anapoli said to the young black man on the stand, "why don't you tell us what you observed when the victim, Mr. Halpern, was first wheeled into your ER?"

"Well, Mr. Halpern's face was battered and his head had been busted open. There was a tremendous loss of blood. The paramedics had tried to stanch its flow, but I noticed that the gurney was soaked and that blood had actually dripped onto the floor." Dr. Wayman Hoxie, a dark-skinned brother, was still in his twenties and fresh out of medical school. He had testified that he had done his residency at Martin Luther King Hospital, a facility in Watts internationally known for its triage. "Even doctors from the Marine Corps and U.S. Army trained their physicians at MLK," Dr. Hoxie had been eager to put into the court record.

"What was his medical condition?" Anna asked, pacing in front of the jury box.

"He was critical, ma'am. In critical condition."

Anna walked over to the counsel table and grabbed a file. At the same time, she motioned to a law clerk, a tiny, very young white girl who quickly exited the courtroom. Within seconds, the clerk returned struggling with a large four-foot-square placard wrapped in butcher paper.

Mercer knew Anna was a drama queen. Today, it looked like she was going for another Academy Award. She'd play to the jurors' emotions, bringing them to the point where they'd be deaf and blind to whatever the defense might offer. The placard was classic Anna. It would be a photograph of the victim at his bloodiest.

The photo would also have another purpose. To bait and anger defense counsel. To unravel him. To get him jumping up and down like a monkey in a zoo. But Mercer was determined not to bite.

"When they put up the picture," he said quietly to Ricky, "I want you to face it, then look down at the floor and give me some of those tears."

"I . . . I don't think I can cry like that."

"Do you love your mom?"

"Sure."

"Imagine it's her in the picture. Look at her. Then look down at the floor. If you feel like crying, cry. But I want you to look like you're sorry."

The judge ordered the little clerk to let him see the photo before placing it on the easel. The clerk unwrapped it, keeping it turned away from the rest of the courtroom and the jury, provoking everyone's curiosity.

Judge Dixon took a sharp breath and asked, "Do I hear an objection to a display of this . . . photograph, Mr. Early?"

Mercer replied in a calm voice, "We have no objection to the truth, Your Honor."

The color blowup of blood gushing from Mr. Halpern's gaping scalp caused many of the jurors to cover their mouths and eyes in horror, but the young lawyer did not stir in his seat. He watched as his client stared at the photo. The boy's eyes welled and he looked away. Mercer wondered if he'd have reacted that way even without his prompting.

"Doctor, is this what you saw when Mr. Halpern came in?" Anna asked.

Mercer looked at the blowup again. There was something odd about the gaping wound. At its edge was a crescent indentation, like a half-moon.

"Yes," Dr. Hoxie replied to the D.D.A.'s question in a raspy voice, choked with emotion. "It's one of the photos I took myself."

With the jurors still gaping in horror at the photo, Anna said, "Your witness, Mr. Early."

Mercer rose to begin his cross, but before he could say a word, Anna asked, "Would counsel like the photo of Mr. Halpern removed?"

"It's a terrible thing, very upsetting," Mercer said, studying the blowup. From the closer perspective, the half-moon was even weirder-looking. "But you apparently feel it serves a purpose, Ms. Anapoli. So let it stand."

He turned to the witness. "Dr. Hoxie, did I hear you say that you had just completed your residency?"

"Yes," Dr. Hoxie said, shifting in his seat.

"But you feel qualified enough to tell us that this man's wounds, left unattended, may have been fatal?"

"I do. But you wouldn't have needed a medical degree. Only a fool would not realize that this man was beaten within an inch of his life."

"A fool or a man with the mind of a child," Mercer said.

"Objection, Your Honor."

"Withdrawn," Mercer said. "I'm almost finished, Doctor. Were you able to tell what object or weapon was used to inflict these injuries?"

The doctor pondered the question. "My understanding is Mr. Halpern was struck repeatedly with a brick."

"Your understanding? You didn't make your own conclusions based on your observations?"

The doctor glanced toward the prosecution table, but the D.D.A. merely shrugged.

"I, ah, was told that a brick had been used. The wounds seemed consistent with that."

"Doctor, you say you took this picture?" Mercer pointed at the blowup.

Dr. Hoxie nodded. "I took numerous photos of Mr. Halpern's injuries. I brought them with me, together with the MRI results." He reached beside the chair for a thick file. From it he removed a stack of photos.

Mercer was going to ask the doctor if he had any opinion on what could have caused the half-moon, but decided to hold off on that until he had a better fix on whether the answer would help or hinder his case. Instead, he took Dr. Hoxie's photos and handed them to the clerk. "Your Honor, we'd like these marked 'Defense exhibit A,' collectively."

The judge scribbled a note. "They will be so marked."

"Thank you and thank you, Doctor."

Mercer returned to the defense table. A bit perplexed by the sudden loss of his photos, the doctor left the stand. He paused at the people's table to shake Anna's hand and wish her good luck.

Another piece of drama.

It seemed that Anna was still anxious to get home as quickly as possible. The next witness she called was her star: Maximillian Sanchez.

Clearly Max and his new best friend, the D.D.A., had spent most of the previous night preparing for his performance. It was also clear that they'd run out of time. Departing from her usual pacing before the jury, Anna stood at the lectern using a stack of notes.

"Maximillian, why are you coming forth now to give evidence against your brother?"

Max's thin, feral face made an effort to appear sorrowful. "It's an awful thing, having to say bad words about your baby brother. But Enrique did a terrible crime on that poor man. And I can't stand aside and say he didn't."

Having established Max's reluctance to speak ill of his brother, Anna began taking him through the various antisocial acts he'd witnessed his sibling commit. At one point she said, "Enrique seems a little slow. Is it possible he didn't understand what he was doing?"

"The boy is a bunch of cards short of a deck, that's for sure," Max said, "but he does know right from wrong. His mama sure taught him that."

Anna returned to her questions about Ricky's previous criminal activity. Finally, Judge Dixon ordered her to move on. Nodding, Anna clasped her hands and asked the big question. "Tell us what happened that night, Max."

Max looked down at the floor, and then at the jurors, and back at the floor. Speaking slowly, he said, "I'm sure not proud to be sitting here, talking about these things, these bad things my brother done. But that night, well, Enrique he takes a brick and near beats the man to death."

"Could you be more specific?" Anna asked.

Could he? He gave the jury a blow-by-blow account. The sound of brick against flesh and bone: "A sound I'll never forget." The blood: "Like a red sea." His brother: "Totally out of control, a real killer."

Max's eyes filled with tears. He blew his nose with a clean white handkerchief that had probably been given him by the district attorney's office for that purpose. "I try to stop him, may God be my witness if I didn't. But my brother is a powerful man. He won't give up the brick. Just keeps pounding it on that poor dude's head. I think he just gets so full of anger it's got to come out somehow. Lucky the police come when they did. Another minute and the dude is dead all the way."

Ricky had been sobbing during most of Max's testimony. During the last few statements he'd begun rocking back and forth in his chair, eyes shut, humming.

"Please restrain your client, Mr. Early," the judge ordered.

Mercer put his arm around the boy. Ricky opened his eyes and stopped humming. "Is Max over?"

"No. But you've got to be quiet," Mercer whispered.

The boy looked around the now-silent courtroom. Everyone seemed to be staring at him. He shut his eyes again, tucked his chin into his chest and pushed back against his chair as if he were trying to sink into it.

With a sign of exasperation, Judge Dixon asked Anna to continue.

"Max, you bear some responsibility in this, don't you?"

Her witness nodded yes, and used the handkerchief again. "I was there, Lord help me," he said, dabbing at his eyes. "I just can't stop him. I throw myself on the poor man, hoping to save him, but I just ain't no match for my brother when he gets like that. The cops come and they say I'm an accomplice, because I got the poor man's blood on me when I was only trying to help him. The cops say I got to plead guilty to helping in the assault. But I'll tell you now what my real guilt is—it's in not realizing how dangerous my brother was back before he done this terrible thing."

Satisfied, Anna turned the witness over to Mercer.

But Judge Dixon had another idea. "Ladies and gentlemen of the jury, it's eleven forty-five. My guess is that Mr. Early wants more than fifteen minutes for his cross-examination. Why don't we break until one-thirty? And please remember the admonition."

The judge made his exit and the jury, like the visiting spectators, began to file out of the room.

"Why you lie like that, Max?" Enrique asked as his brother paused at the prosecution table. "Why you lie? They trying to take my life forever!"

Max faced the boy. Grinning, he said, "Because, dummy, it's either you or me."

"That's enough," Anna said.

The bailiff intervened, leading Ricky back to the lockup.

Max sidled over to Mercer, who was gathering his papers. "Here's a little tip, counselor. Looks to me like you done pissed off everybody in this building. You might think about treatin' me kindly on the stand if you wanna get back in the D.A.'s good graces."

Astounded at the man's gall, Mercer watched him strut toward Mrs. Sanchez, who was waiting dutifully for him at the door.

He noticed that Anna was watching Max, too, her mouth hanging open in disbelief. Apparently she'd overheard the "tip."

"Remind me again, Anna," Mercer said. "Which one of us has gone over to the dark side?"

There was no time for lunch.

He was on the cell phone the minute he stepped from

the courtroom. Melissa told him she'd found fifteen
court appearances of the Sanchez brothers.

"Just give me the most serious cases."

There were two robberies and one sexual battery. The
robberies had been heard at the juvenile court at Mc-
Claren Hall. Too far to get to in an hour and a half. The
assault case had been heard right there in the Criminal
Courts Building because the D.A. had attempted, to no
avail, to try Ricky as an adult.

Mercer was at the clerk's office at five minutes to
noon. He hurriedly filled out the file request form.

The attending clerk, an attractive Latina with braces,
took one look at the form and told him to fill out a new
one. "Do it slower, so I can read it. Okay?"

"Wanted to catch you before lunch," he said.

"Well, you caught me," she said. "Now fill out the
form in English this time."

It was almost an hour before the file was in his hands.
Searching it, he found what he wanted. The prosecutors
in the sex case had tested both Ricky and Max for
DNA. The vic had subsequently refused to testify and
the case had been dismissed. But the DNA results were
there, and easy enough for Mercer to interpret.

He had the detectives who'd scammed Max into his
original confession standing by. His plan had been to
use them to stress Max's participation in the crime and
at the same time to challenge his credibility. He wasn't
sure he'd be needing them, but he had to talk to his
client first.

The bailiff was unlocking the doors when he arrived
at the courtroom.

"Can I see Enrique Sanchez now?" he asked.

"Sure. I got him cuffed to a chair so he could eat his
lunch. I'll go get him for you."

Judge Dixon began the afternoon by calling one of
the public defender's cases. When asked his occupation,
the armed-robbery defendant responded, "Well, Your
Honor, I like to think of myself as a venture capitalist."

There was a burst of laughter from the courtroom spectators. Mercer looked at his watch.

The defendant seemed pleased at the crowd's response to his joke. The judge said, "You know, son, I sentenced a venture capitalist about . . . it must have been about 1977. And you know something? He isn't out of prison yet."

The smile slid from the defendant's face. "I meant no disrespect, Your Honor."

"We'll see how much you respect me in twenty-eight days, at your sentencing hearing. In the meantime you're remanded to the custody of the sheriff. It'll give you a chance to catch up on all the economic news."

Mercer was so tightly wound he jumped when the bailiff tapped his shoulder. "Apparently, your client ain't nearly as dumb as everybody thinks," the bailiff whispered in his ear. "He ain't back there. He ain't in the building. Looks like he took a walk."

Before Mercer could reply, the bailiff was on his way to the judge, who, after reviewing a law book on his desk, ordered the attorneys into his chambers, along with the court reporter.

"The court has been advised that defendant Enrique Sanchez has escaped from the custody of the sheriff while in the middle of trial." He gestured to the leatherbound *Judge's Bench Book* that lay open on his desk. "There's precedent allowing us to proceed to trial in his absence."

"But that's sure to prejudice the jury, Your Honor," Mercer said.

"I will advise them that the escape should not be considered as proof of guilt." The judge gestured toward Anna. "Of course, all of this is assuming that Ms. Anapoli wants the trial to continue."

"I do, Your Honor."

Mercer rose to his feet. "Your Honor—"

The judge cut him off. "You've got till tomorrow to find your client, Mr. Early. If neither you nor the LAPD are successful, trial will start at ten o'clock without him."

12

Bay Bay had told Mingus that his brother Ken Loc frequented the Kittyhawk, a no-frills club on Florence and Market in Inglewood. There'd been a time when the detective had hung out at the bar himself, even though it had reminded him of the juke joint his mama used to send him to in search of his old man. "Get to him before he drinks up his whole paycheck," she'd say. Mingus tried, but he was usually too late. Not only could Daddy drink a lot, he drank fast. Leaving the garage where he worked on a five o'clock payday, he was dead broke by seven-thirty. Mingus eventually realized he'd have to shadow the old man after work. That way, when his daddy began to stray, he had a chance of nudging him home.

The Kittyhawk had convinced Mingus to put stock in the scientific theory about alcoholism being hereditary. The thing was: you could scarcely help but become a drunk there. Or so he kept telling himself. The drinks cost half of what they cost anywhere else in town, and when Eula was behind the bar in her tight leathers they were usually double shots disguised as singles.

Mingus waited until dark to give the K-hawk a try. He was parking his unmarked Crown Victoria when he noticed one of the local street rats slip into the bar's front door. The detective avoided that door and double-timed it to a side exit facing Market. In less than a minute, Ken Loc slid through that door dressed in an expensive warm-up outfit, his head twisted around, looking behind him like he was running from something. He bumped right into that something.

"You lookin' for me, Loc?" Mingus asked.

Startled, Ken Loc managed to answer a question with a question. "Why I be lookin' for you?"

Mingus could smell whisky on his breath. And fear off his body. "We're pals, aren't we?" he said.

"Wouldn't call it that, exactly."

"Let's go back inside and have a drink," Mingus said. "It'll improve your image, sharing a shot with a cop."

Loc began to back away. Mingus grabbed him by the collar of his FUBU sweatshirt. "Relax, brother."

Loc either couldn't or wouldn't obey. He tried to twist out of Mingus's grasp. The detective yanked his cuffs from his waistband and snapped one end on Loc's right wrist. Loc began squawking like a parrot getting his tail feathers plucked. When the other cuff clicked shut, securing both his hands behind his back, he quieted down and got a forlorn look on his face. "I don't deserve no cuffs, Mingus," he whined. "I paid the time."

"This is jus' for show, Loc," he said. "It don't do either of us any good for your low-life fellow inebriates to peg you for a snitch."

"Whatchu want from me, Mingus?"

"I want to know about Darion Mayfield. I want to know everything you can tell me, but mainly, I wanna know who killed him."

"We gotta stay here by the door?"

Mingus walked the ex-con to his car and placed him on the back seat.

A small group of men drifted from the Kittyhawk, not enough hair on any of their heads to make an eyebrow, mouths slack from too much whisky and not enough silence. One spied Mingus with Ken Loc.

"Evah notice how there's al'ays some Uncle Tom

bustin' his black ass to do the white man's dirty work?" a young, powerfully built, multitattooed man asked loudly.

An older barfly said, "Truth, brother. An' I don' recall any white folks in the K-hawk helpin' Mistah Mingus when he was fallin' off his bar stool."

"Sellout motherfucker," a third habitué of the Kitty-hawk added.

Mingus was saved from some lame response by an Inglewood PD unit. As it drove by in low gear, its uniformed occupants casting hard eyes, the boozers developed a sudden yen to reclaim their bar stools.

"So you used to do yo' drinkin' at the K-hawk?" Loc asked from the back seat as Mingus got behind the wheel.

The cop didn't answer. He stared at the gin mill. It wasn't much to look at. Essentially an old warehouse. "Eula still behind the bar in that leather belt and thong outfit?"

"Eula moved on to better things," Loc said. "Kareena there now. Got green hair, good jugs, and a bad attitude."

Mingus wasn't paying attention. His mind was moving through the bar's interior, back to the room at the rear, dark and full of junk furniture, to the sour-smelling cot the whores used, where he'd passed out, losing his badge and gun.

"Fuck the Kittyhawk," he said, surprising Ken Loc with his anger. "Fuck 'em all."

He drove the Crown Vic past the Inglewood swap meet, south on Prairie in the direction of the racetrack. There wasn't much traffic. "What you got for me on Darion Mayfield?"

The ex-con took his time replying. "His daddy's a big dawg minister, or somethin'. That what you want?"

"Don't give me your bullshit," Mingus yelled at him. "Tell me what you know."

"Don't know nuthin'."

Mingus was annoyed. He checked the rearview and,

without warning, stomped on the Crown Vic's brakes. Loc slammed face-first into the front seat, then flopped backward in an angry semistupor, blood draining from his nose onto his expensive FUBU shirt. "You busted by beak, you crazy muthafugga."

"Talk to me," Mingus ordered. "Your mouth still works, kinda."

"You know I cand talk about this shit."

"Why not?" Mingus asked, putting the car back in motion, dividing his attention from the road to the mirror image of the man behind him who was struggling to wipe his nose while handcuffed.

"You doe the deal. I don't say duthid' 'til Fat Mad Farley tell me to."

Mingus slowed and pulled into a Sizzler parking lot. "You talked to Farley?"

The ex-con wiped his bloody face against his shoulder, smearing red along his left cheek. "You doad doe shid-all about what's happedid, do you, Mi'gus?" He switched to his right shoulder, smearing blood on the other cheek and Mingus's seat belt.

"I'm here to learn," Mingus said. He found a wad of fast-food napkins he'd stashed in his glove compartment for just this sort of emergency, got out of the car, and took the seat beside Ken Loc. He was overly cautious to avoid the blood as he undid the cuffs.

"It's mah brother god the HIV, dod me," Ken Loc said. "All I god is a fugkin' brokid dose, thagks to you, you prick."

The detective continued to use caution while handing Loc the napkins for his bloody nose. "I don't think your nose is broke," he said. "It wasn't my intention to break your nose. You breathin' okay?"

Loc nodded, a little surprised by Mingus's concern. He repaid it by saying, "I was zare whed Darion wedt out the wid'dow. I tole Farley an' he tole me to keep it to myself till he say it okay to talk."

Mingus shifted on the seat, watching the man dab at his nose. "Farley says it's okay."

"Sure he does." Loc eyed him suspiciously. "You gudda jab me up, aret'cha?"

"You know I don't play that way," Mingus said. "If anybody jams you, it won't be me."

Loc nodded. "Used to be."

"Play straight with me, I play straight with you."

Loc stared at him. He said, "Well, fugk." Then he opened up.

Since getting out of the joint, he'd been looking for work. Trying to stay straight. He knew cars and he'd done some repair jobs and some chauffeuring. He wound up driving for Darion Mayfield every now and then. Nothing criminal, he was quick to clarify. On that fateful night, Darion called him crowing that he'd just been handed a Get Out of Jail card. He invited Loc to join him for a little celebration.

"There were other people at his place that night?" Mingus asked.

Loc didn't think so. He doubted Darion would have called him, if anybody else had been available. Anyway, he knew going to Darion's place was a parole breaker, but he figured he was due for a little fun. He'd just entered the lot beside the dealer's building when Darion went through the window.

"The parking lot crowded?" Mingus asked.

"Some cars. High-ed. The buildig aid't cheap."

"Okay. Tell me what you saw."

The ex-con's voice cracked. "Dariod come flyig through a widow up top. He hits the garbage bucket and his fugkid head come off. Fugkid *head* come off. Shit!" Loc slumped against the seat, eyes closed. Probably seeing a replay. "Dariod could be ad asshole, but he treated me good."

Ken Loc paused.

Mingus stared at him expectantly. He was surprised to find that the man was crying. The detective saw enough depravity on the job to take it in stride, but a hype expressing sorrow for somebody other than himself was as rare as a snowflake in summer. He took out a pack of smokes and withdrew one, handing it to Loc. Lighting it up, he asked what happened after Darion's death.

"This big white dude cumb ruddid' out the door and jumps into a Beemba. That weird ugly albost purple color."

Detective Claude Burris drove a BMW. Mingus couldn't remember if his file mentioned a color. "Describe the white dude," he said.

"Cave boy. Six foot supthid. Maybe forty-five. Blod hair. Cheap wambup outfid, like it a K-mart special. Looked too square to be a custober, but, hell, th' brotherhood of blow accepts all kides."

"You didn't recognize him?"

"Naw. Anyway, he peels off. So do I."

"You follow him?"

"Do I look crazy?"

"You told all this to Farley?" Mingus said. "Described the guy and his car?"

Loc nodded.

To close out any possibility of there being a legitimate reason the information hadn't made it into the murder book, Mingus asked, "When did you and Fats have your talk?"

"That sabe dight. 'Roud mid-dight. See, afta I saw that, I could-dit stay cooped. I dropped by the K-hawk add baybe tole one or two people I was there whed Dariod came dowd. Dext thing I dough, the Fat Bad's id by face, threatedid me if I doad do what he say."

"Fats tell you why he wanted you to zip up?"

Ken Loc took a long drag on the cigarette, then closed his eyes as he exhaled. "I doad ask; he doad tell." He held up a tissue and stared at his blood samples, then found a clean section and pressed it against his nose.

"You got any ideas on the subject?"

Loc took another drag and looked the black cop over. "You tell me. You brothers in the law. I doad dough why cops do addythig."

Mingus assumed that Farley was cleaning up after

Burris, who probably was a member of the same Aryan Brotherhood chapter. He didn't mention this theory to Loc. Instead, he asked, "Did Darion have a special woman?"

"Special? Shi' . . . ady bitch he could dig out was special. Less he was too wasted."

"There was supposed to be a white girl who liked her crack. Kept him company."

Ken Loc blinked and shifted his eyes to the street. "Yeah. I dough who you mead. Wild bitch. Crazy. Gets off slicid herse'f up whed she fucks. She got Dariod usid' a razor blade on his arms, too."

"What's her name?"

"Alice subthid . . . Adapts."

"Alice Adapts?"

"Thas it. I think she writes movies or subthid."

"You think?"

"I do' dough, Mi'gus. It ain't like I went gamid' od her. Oddy times I seed her, she's too high to talk or got somethid in her mouth."

"Any idea where I can find her?"

"What I bid sayid? No."

"You mention Alice to Farley?"

"I dough thick so. Ask him. I got duthid more for you, Mi'gus. Tha's the goddam' truth."

Mingus studied Loc for a few seconds, then nodded. He got back behind the wheel and pulled out into the street, made an illegal U-turn and headed back to the Kittyhawk.

He stopped the car near the juke joint.

"If the Fat Man should ask," he said, "tell him I tried to question you and you stonewalled me. Say I busted your beak, but you still held your mud. Didn't tell me anything, except to go fuck myself."

"Jus' to keep it real," Loc said, "go fuck yourself, Mi'-gus." He headed for the bar.

Neither man noticed the shiny sedan parked down the street.

13

Mercer pulled an all-nighter at his office.

He'd kept his cell phone on, hoping that he might hear from Ricky. But as the darkness melted into dawn there was no call. Not from Ricky. Not from the police.

Not from Vanessa.

As he sat in his chair, drifting between consciousness and something akin to sleep, he tried to keep his focus on the trial. His intention was to plot out every step in his cross-examination of Max, but his concentration wavered. One minute he flashed on Max's smirking face. Another caught Vanessa smiling at something he'd just said. Still another found Ricky, handcuffed to a chair, using a pen to pick the lock just like he'd seen Mercer do the day before.

Too many thoughts pulling him in too many directions.

At eight, he rushed home to shower and shave.

When he arrived at the courtroom, he found it filled with lawyers and clerks. The bailiff whispered to him that his client was still a no-show. "Between us, they don't have a clue," he whispered.

Judge Dixon was on the bench, involved in a pretrial matter. When he was done, he called the case. "*People* v.

Sanchez." He thrust out his jaw and scanned the room. "Both counsel are present. The defendant is not. Mr. Early, are you prepared to proceed without your client?"

Mercer straightened himself. "I am, Your Honor."

When the jurors were seated, the judge advised them that the defendant would not be present and they should not, at this point, draw any inferences from his absence.

When Max once again was seated at the witness stand, Judge Dixon reminded him that he was still under oath, then ordered Mercer to proceed with his cross-examination.

The adrenaline pumping in the young attorney's veins was doing a fine job of compensating for his lack of sleep. He felt remarkably alert as he stood before the witness. "Maximillian *is* quite a mouthful," he said. "Can I call you Max?"

"Sure."

"You testified yesterday about Ricky's prior criminal history. Do you recall that testimony?"

"Sure. It was just yesterday."

"How is it that you're so knowledgeable about Ricky's antisocial behavior?"

Max seemed puzzled by the question. "What do you mean? I've lived with Enrique his whole life. Except for when he's been in jail."

"Even when people live together, there are times when they go their own ways. But you and Ricky have been pretty tight. Right?"

"I guess. But I don't like the name Ricky. His name's Enrique, like the famous mariachi, Enrique Escobar."

"I'm not familiar with him, but he's a favorite of yours, huh?"

"Yeah, a real hero of mine. A beautiful musician."

"You figure that's why Enrique's parents gave him that name?"

Max stared at Mercer and said nothing. His expression was hard to read.

"Anyway," Mercer continued, "when you were telling us about the crimes Enrique has committed, that was firsthand knowledge, right?"

"Yes."

"In each instance you were present and got arrested along with him, at least until you explained that it was Enrique who was the active participant in the crimes. Is that correct?"

"Objection. He's badgering the witness."

"I didn't introduce the prior crimes, Your Honor," Mercer said.

"Overruled."

"Want me to repeat the question, Max?" Mercer asked.

"No. I was there, see, because I made a commitment to stop my brother from hurting people, including himself. This required that I spend a lot of time with Enrique, watching and taking care of him."

"That's very noble, Max. But just between us, didn't you tell Enrique to do these crimes?"

"No, sir."

"Isn't it true, Max, that Enrique will do anything you tell him to?"

"That's nuts. Why would he? I'm just his brother."

"Are you?"

"Am I what?"

"Just his brother?"

The question caught Max off guard. He turned to the judge. "Your Honor, I . . . I object."

It was Judge Dixon's turn to be surprised. "It doesn't work that way, Mr. Sanchez."

"Well then, Your Honor, I gotta speak to Miss Anapoli."

The judge frowned. "Ms. Anapoli is not your attorney, sir." He turned to the D.D.A. "Do you know what's going on here?"

Anna seemed to be chewing the inside of her mouth. She stopped long enough to answer, "I'm . . . not sure, Your Honor." But she was obviously hedging.

"Why don't you and Mr. Early join me for a sidebar chat?"

Mercer went to the defense table first, to pick up some papers.

When he and the prosecutor were standing before the bench, Judge Dixon said, in a lowered voice, "Mr. Early, what the devil is taking place in my courtroom?"

Mercer placed the DNA results before the judge. "Your Honor, I was going to request these be put into evidence, but since Ms. Anapoli apparently is aware of the relationship between Mr. Maximillian Sanchez and Mr. Enrique Sanchez, it may not be necessary. Her being an officer of the court and a seeker of just—"

"Enough of that. Ms. Anapoli, what is the relationship between the two men? Are they, or are they not, brothers?"

"They are brothers, Your Honor," she said.

"And they're also father and son," Mercer added.

The judge's heavy jaw dropped in surprise. "The hell you say."

"It's completely irrelevant to the charge, Your Honor," Anna said.

"You knew about this?" Judge Dixon asked her.

"We, ah, discovered it, yes."

"I'm guessing you didn't gift Mr. Early with your discovery, that he had to seek it out by himself."

"It's not relevant, Your Honor."

"Judge, the witness lied under oath," Mercer said. "I'd call that very relevant."

"Where's the lie?" Anna asked. "Max is Enrique's brother."

"And his father," Mercer said. "At the least, it's a lie of omission."

"Okay, okay," the judge said. "Give me a moment to take all this in."

The lawyers waited while he stared at his desktop, frowning. Finally, he turned to Mercer. "Tell me why you think this . . . unique relationship has relevancy."

"The father-son bond is different than the bond of

brothers, Your Honor. A boy, especially one as depend-
ent and childlike as Enrique, is more likely to trust his
father, to obey his father's commands, to do whatever
he can to help his father, even to the extent of taking
punishment for something his father did. Yesterday's
testimony wasn't just a brother turning against a
brother, it was a father turning against a worshipful son.
And lying while he was doing it. No wonder Ricky ran
away."

"Oh, please," Anna said. "Ricky ran away because he
nearly killed a man and he didn't want to pay for it. Max
Sanchez wasn't lying about that."

"But he was lying about his relationship to Ricky,"
Mercer said. "Which means he's untrustworthy. The jury
should be made aware of that."

"Enough," Judge Dixon said. "At the very least, I
agree with your last point, Mr. Early. Proceed with your
line of questioning."

As soon as the subject of fatherhood left Mercer's
lips, Max said, "I'm not answering that question, Your
Honor. I'm gonna take the fifth."

"You feel your answer would incriminate you?" Mercer asked.

"No. I mean, this just ain't right."

"What isn't right is having sex with your own
mother," Mercer said. "And then not acknowledging the
result of that misdeed."

The jurors looked like they'd been slapped awake.

Max glared at Anna Anapoli. "Ain't you gonna object
or anything? I tole you if you let this come out, the deal
is off."

"Mr. Sanchez, one more outburst and you will be
cited for contempt," Judge Dixon said. "You understand
what that means?"

"Yeah," Max said, still staring furiously at the deputy
D.A.

"As long as the 'deal' is off," Mercer said, "why not
tell us what the 'deal' was? What did the D.A. promise
you in return for your testimony against your . . . *son*?"

Max began to get out of the witness chair.

"Stay seated, Mr. Sanchez," the judge ordered. "And answer the question."

Max shifted on the hardwood chair. "The deal was: I get out and Enrique does the time. It's not like I'm lyin' or anything. He did beat that guy."

"You told the police you participated in the robbery, but not the beating. Right?"

"I didn't participate in nothing."

"The officers are here today. They have their notes and a signed confession."

Max turned again to Anna and mouthed the words, "Dumb bitch."

"I'm sorry, I don't think the jury caught that," Mercer said.

Max stared at him. "What's your question?"

"Did you tell the police you participated in the robbery?"

"Yeah. That's what I tole 'em. But I don't brick the guy. Is that it?"

"Not quite. When you were 'protecting' Mr. Halpern, did you happen to, maybe, step on his face?"

"No. Of course not. Enrique—"

"Enrique's as big as you, but he's got small feet." Mercer looked out over the courtroom to Sylvia Sanchez, sitting at the rear, dabbing at her eyes with a handkerchief. Not so proud of her elder son at the moment. "Probably inherited those tiny feet from his mama. Your mama. Anyway, you remember Dr. Hoxie, the doctor who was at the ER the night they brought in Ellis Halpern? He took a lot of photos of the victim's head. Ms. Anapoli was good enough to bring one of 'em to the courtroom for the jury. You happen to see it?"

"Kinda hard to miss."

"Yeah. Well, you remember seeing an indentation of something like a half-moon up near the victim's main wound?"

"I don't remember that at all."

"Something that might be the heel of a shoe?"

"Objection, Your Honor. Mr. Sanchez has said he doesn't remember seeing whatever it is Mr. Early is going on about."

"What size shoe do you wear, Max?"

"Objection. Relevance?"

Judge Dixon looked at Mercer questioningly.

It would have been nice if Mercer could have pulled one of Max's Adidas sneakers from one pocket and a photo of the half-moon from the other to compare them. But in fact he had no physical evidence except for the unexamined photo. He'd gone fishing with a speculation and only hooked himself. He shrugged.

"Objection sustained," the judge ruled. "Anything else, Mr. Early?"

"Just one thing more, Your Honor. Max, you're sort of a student of the law, right?"

"I watch Court TV." He offered a smile to the few spectators who'd giggled at the comment.

"Then you know what double jeopardy is?"

"A quiz show? No. I know what it is. You get found innocent, that's the ball game. You can't get brought up again for the same crime."

"Good. So you've been pardoned on the mayhem charge, which means they can't touch you on that crime, even if you confess. But if you commit perjury here today, it's open season."

"Objection," Anna said.

"On what grounds, Ms. Anapoli?" When she did not reply, the judge instructed Mercer to continue.

"So, Max, who was it busted up Ellis Halpern?"

Max turned to the judge. "It's straight about the pardon?"

"I'm sorry to say it is."

"Okay, then. Yeah. Enrique's only crime is he's too stupid. He's been takin' the heat for me. See, I'm short on cash that night and I figure the drugstore has got the green and maybe even some drugs I can move. So I give the Jew a couple hits with the brick and send Enrique into the store to look for loot. The dummy takes too

long and the Jew starts to come around, so I whack him
again, mainly for his own protection. Then he starts to
squawk, calls me a dirty Spic and I sorta lose it. Maybe
I use my feet on him. Enrique pulls me off the Jew,
which is how he gets the blood on him. Thing is, it really
ain't my fault. If the Jew man hadn't started hollerin'
out that racist stuff, I'd of never kicked him. I'm not a vi-
olent person."

Mercer saw that Anna had her head in her hands.

"You tell anybody the truth before this, Max?"

"What do you mean?"

"Your . . . mother. Did you tell her you beat Ellis
Halpern?"

"No way. I don't tell her dick."

"What about your lawyer?"

"That a-hole Corey? Think I'd trust him with that
kind of info?"

Max's face lit up. He turned to Anna. "I may have
mentioned it to my other lawyer, the lady D.A. over
there."

Anna suddenly sat bolt upright, stunned.

She'd withheld crucial information from him, but
Mercer couldn't believe Anna would send a boy she
knew to be innocent to a lifetime behind bars just to
spite his lawyer. "Max," he said, "perjury is perjury. You
don't want to mess up now."

Max stared at Anna for several long seconds, then
grinned. "Naa, she didn't know sh . . . didn't know nothing. She probably still thinks Enrique beat up the Jew."

Judging by the relief on Anna's face, the insult hadn't
registered. She'd stopped listening after Max let her off
the hook. She stood up, a bit unsteadily. "Your Honor,"
she said, "the people move to dismiss the case against
Enrique Sanchez."

"Motion granted," came the reply. "The reporter will
prepare a transcript. Bailiff, I want to see District Attorney Lowery—and not one of her minions—in this courtroom by noon. And if she declines, tell her to expect a
contempt citation by the time she's finished lunch.

"As for your client, Mr. Early, the warrant for his arrest is recalled. I hope you can find him and give him the good news before anything else bad befalls him."

Mercer was putting away his notes when Anna approached the table. "I'm sorry this got so out of hand," she said. "I really thought the boy was guilty."

"Uh-huh. You looked at that poor childlike young man and then you looked at his slimy, incestuous, mother-fucking, lying daddy and you made the honest decision that daddy deserved the pass."

"You can't tell anything by looks," she said. "Anyway, it wasn't my decision to make."

"Yeah, well, whoever made it, you did your best to carry it out."

"It's what we do. I really don't want there to be hard feelings between us, Mercer. This building makes for a very small world. We'll be butting heads in this room again before too long."

"I'd be surprised," he said, snapping his briefcase shut. "After Judge Dixon gets finished putting the D.A. on notice about what just went on here and after Too-Good David Gomez lays the blame on you, I figure I won't be seeing much of you 'round these parts. You'll be too busy spending the rest of your career pleading and bleeding in Compton. You have a good life, hear?"

14

Mingus knew of one witness who could place Claude Burris at the scene of Darion Mayfield's murder. In the hope of finding another, he had started out the day searching for information about the dealer's white customer and frequent sex partner whom Ken Loc had identified as a screenwriter named Alice Adapts.

The name "Adapts" had drawn a blank in the various L.A. area phone listings, at the DMV and even on the Internet Movie Database, a not very promising sign. The eager-to-help young man who answered the phone at the Writers Guild of America failed to find the name in the organization's directory. The strike-outs forced the detective to dial the number of a woman named Ida Bevan with whom he'd had a short, tempestuous affair that had ended badly. Ida worked for one of the largest talent agencies in the city. He left a voice mail message asking her to return the call, but he wasn't sure she would.

Then, keeping busy, he dropped by Robbery-Homicide.

He spent a couple minutes jawing with a few of the brothers, dissing the chief, trying to fit in, then casually asked a dick named Elgar if he could take a look at the Darion Mayfield murder book.

"Could if it was here," Elgar said. "Fats and Gervey

took it with 'em to the punk's autopsy." Al Gervey was Farley's partner.

Even though departmental policy required it, Mingus wasn't surprised that IAG hadn't been alerted to the autopsy. Farley was up to something and he evidently had such a disrespect for Mingus he wasn't bothering to be subtle about it. He'd even kept crucial evidence out of the murder book.

As Mingus saw it, there was only one conclusion to be drawn. An LAPD cop had tossed a drug dealer, a man who could send him to prison for perjury, out of a fifth-story window to his death. And the detectives on the case, his redneck brothers in blue, were making sure he got away with it.

Captain Jacquette had not been wrong in bringing him in to investigate the investigators.

He ignored speed limits driving to the coroner's office on Mission Road. He parked his Crown Vic alongside a much newer, shinier model in the spaces reserved for the LAPD and double-timed it into the four-story building. At the front desk, he waited impatiently while the receptionist took her sweet time locating the room where the Mayfield autopsy was being performed by the deputy coroner.

He rode the elevator down three floors beneath street level and stepped into a hallway lined with gurneys transporting every imaginable size and shape of corpse. Mingus barely flinched. It wasn't the dead bodies you had to fear, his uncle used to say. It was the living and breathing bastards with dead souls.

Speaking of which, Fats and his partner, Al Gervey, both gave him the fish eye when he walked into the room. After that they ignored him completely, returning to their study of Darion Mayfield's headless corpse.

Assistant Coroner Modi Saleem stood on the other side of the examination table, sea green eyes shining merrily in a brown face. "To briefly fill you in, Detective, the dead man did not take care of himself. Evidence of recently ingested alcohol and cocaine were found, along with partially digested doughnuts, sausage, peanuts. Also evidence of self-mutilation—razor cuts, mainly of recent vintage, along his left arm. To move to the crux of the matter, the poor fellow had pretty much broken every bone in his body. What we're left with is a sack of bones. The cause of death is obvious. Young man lost his head over something."

Fats and Gervey laughed. Mingus wasn't feeling amused.

"Why don't we step over here?" Dr. Saleem led the trio to a metal table where he removed a sheet, revealing what appeared at first glance to be a large hunk of meat covered with blood, hair and mangled tissue. Mingus realized with a lurch of his stomach that he was staring at Darion's head and neck, positioned as if it were a bust on display at the Getty. A long piece of bent neck bone extended from beneath the clump, making it look as if the thing had grown a tail.

The pit bull hadn't done much to improve the head. A piece of flesh had been ripped from the cheekbone, with a section of meat torn out and a three-inch flap of skin dangling by a sliver near Darion's left sideburn.

"Oh, my," Saleem said. "What in the world happened here, officers?"

Farley told him about the dog staking a claim on the head. "Before any of us got there," he lied. He looked at Mingus, almost daring him to contradict. But the Internal Affairs detective said nothing. His report would do all the talking.

"The animal appears to have dined well. Nibbled off the lips and the ears, yum yum," Dr. Saleem said. Using a shiny flat instrument, he probed the slightly parted gums. "The doggie made off with the tip of the tongue, too."

"Why just the tip?" Mingus asked.

"It's a guess," Saleem said, "but I imagine the dog's mouth was too big to fit into the dead man's."

He was poking about near the missing left ear when an assistant arrived with a stack of X rays. Saleem held them to the light, moaning and groaning with each one. Finally, he examined the last one and added a "hmmmm."

Grabbing what looked like a pair of chrome-plated pliers, he managed with some effort to pry Darion's jaw open. Next, he grabbed a narrow metal rod and began probing the inside of the mouth. "Come out, come out, wherever you are."

The three detectives watched in fascination as Dr. Saleem lifted the head from its perch and turned it face-down, shaking it. A huge clot of blood splashed onto the table, causing the detectives to jump back to avoid any contact with body fluid. Next came a row of teeth, apparently from the lower right jaw. Finally, a small piece of *something* fell onto the table.

"What the hell's that?" Farley asked.

The item was coated in blood. Saleem used forceps to pick it up and carry it to a sink against the wall.

After he washed away the blood, he said, "It's a small piece of plastic."

He placed the nearly flat, round object on the table under the overhead light, next to the head.

"It looks like a saucer from Barbie's dream house," Al Gervey said.

"Jesus, Al, you playin' Ken again?" Farley said.

"It's my daughter's, goddammit," Gervey said defensively.

"If you say so," Farley said, returning to the mystery object. "The mutt dragged the head through some-body's garbage pile. Broke plastic got in his yap. Nothing for us. Move it on, Doc."

Saleem withdrew a minirecorder from his coat pocket and began describing Mayfield's head injuries in a voice that seemed to Mingus a little too playful for the cir-cumstances. It was information Mingus either knew or didn't care about. He stared at the little piece of plastic and wondered if maybe Gervey hadn't been right about it being from a kid's tea set.

The doctor suddenly grabbed the head with his free

hand and angled it to give its various planes the full benefit of the light. ". . . consistent with the body falling from a considerable height and meeting with a raised surface—make that a *dull* raised surface. The subsequent trauma caused skin and bone to stretch and separate."

Dr. Saleem turned to his audience and said, "If the Dumpster's edge hadn't been so blunt, the separation would have been nice and clean."

"Yeah, well, there ain't much call for Dumpsters with sharp edges, Doc," Farley said.

Lost in his inventory, Dr. Saleem ignored the comment. "Left eye missing," he said. "Right eye sunken. Bones around both are fractured . . ."

Mingus looked at the empty left eye socket and winced.

"Extensive bruising of the entirety of the face, at least to that part that remains." Dr. Saleem shifted the head again. This time they heard shattered bone sloshing through blood and tissue. That unpleasant sound was followed by a rumble coming from Farley's stomach. The fat man belched and stepped back from the table.

"You okay, Den?" Gervey asked.

"Hell yes, I'm okay. Don't I look okay?"

"Actually, you look a little green."

"Yeah, well, fuck you, Al. Keep goin', Doc. None of us is gettin' paid by the hour."

Ordinarily, Mingus would have been amused by the fat man's blustering discomfort. But he wasn't feeling so solid in the stomach department himself. He experienced a sense of relief when the doctor's inventory was interrupted by the arrival of his assistant with a stack of photographs.

As the doctor studied each one, he handed it to the detectives. "Nothing outstanding about these," he stated.

Most of the pictures featured tight shots of the head. Farley and Gervey barely glanced at them. Mingus took a little more time. He'd had trouble confronting the head in an up-close-and-personal manner. But the photos were different. Images on paper, not flesh and blood. Easier to examine in de—

"What's this, Doc?" he asked, holding out a print, pointing his finger at a mark on the skin still hanging from Darion's cheek.

Dr. Saleem reached for a magnifying glass and then for the head. "Hmmmm. There is something . . ." He severed the dangling skin flap with a scalpel, then smoothed it out on the slab like a napkin on a picnic table. "Roberto, get the photographer down here for one more shot."

The assistant scampered away.

"Take a look," the doctor said, handing Mingus the magnifier. "Tell me what you think."

"It looks like a . . . swastika, maybe? Or an X," Mingus said. "Two long and skinny indents, intersecting in the middle. The ends are sort of, well, shit, they're eaten, but the lines are definitely there."

"Lemme see that," Farley said, grabbing for the magnifying glass.

Mingus gave it up and stepped back, watching the fat dick with a bemused smile.

"Yeah, I see what you're talkin' about," Farley said. He wasn't impressed. "The dog was dragging the damn thing all over the place."

"We can blame the doggie for some of the damage," Dr. Saleem said, "but not the indentations. They were made just before death or just after, during that narrow window of opportunity when blood remained in the tissue and while there was still some degree of circulation in the head."

Farley gave the doctor a bored look. "If you say so, Doc."

"Can I see?" Gervey asked.

"Be my guest, Al," his partner said, handing him the glass.

Dr. Saleem peeled off his rubber gloves. "Well, gentlemen, it's lunchtime and I'm famished. There's an excellent steakhouse just a few blocks away. Anybody for a nice, big, and bloody side of beef? I'm buying."

Until that moment Mingus hadn't realized that the doc was such a sadistic son of a bitch.

"I don't get it," Al Gervey said as the three detectives shared an elevator to the street level. "It's the middle of the day. We gotta eat something. Why not let the doc pick up the tab?"

"I may never eat meat again," Farley told him. "But if I do, it sure as hell ain't gonna resemble anything like what we just been in the presence of."

Mingus couldn't have cared less about what Farley would or wouldn't eat. He wanted to slam the detective against the side of the elevator and find out why there was nothing in the murder book about Ken Loc placing Claude Burris at the scene of the crime. But he'd given Loc his word that he wouldn't jam him up with the fat man. So he took another approach. "Farley, you ever have that conversation with your pal Burris?"

"Burris is your pal?" an obviously confused Gervey asked his partner.

"Don't mind Lionel," Farley told him. "He's just being ironical." To Mingus, he said, "Yeah, I talked to him."

"And?"

"He said he didn't do it."

The elevator door opened, and the men stepped out and headed for the parking area, dodging foot traffic and full gurneys. "That all he said?" Mingus asked.

"No. He said you were an ugly, useless bag of shit," Farley said. "But I took up for you, Lionel. I said I didn't think you were so ugly."

Mingus interrupted Farley's laughter by asking, "You remember to put the conversation in the murder book?"

Farley took a few seconds to reply. "He didn't say a thing worth writing down."

There was no more talk until they arrived at their cars, parked side by side.

As Farley started to get into his, Mingus asked, "Burris happen to say where he was the night of the murder?"

"You wanna know where he was, Lionel," the fat cop said, sliding behind the wheel and grunting while reaching for the door handle, "talk to the man yourself. Be my guest."

Mingus figured that wasn't such a bad idea. But there was something he had to do first.

He drove along behind the Homicide detectives as they left the lot and stayed with them on Mission Road until Farley's car turned off, heading for Parker Center.

He had another destination in mind. The dead man's apartment on Centinela.

Farley's casual disregard for departmental process made no sense. He wasn't exactly being tapped for Mensa, but he was smart enough to know he couldn't keep Loc in his pocket forever. Was he so arrogant that he thought he could get by with such behavior with Mingus looking over his shoulder? In spite of the insults and the bad feelings between them, Mingus didn't think that Farley considered him a total idiot. Fats knew that his boss, Captain Jacquette, had put Mingus into the mix. He must have at least suspected he might be under investigation. What the hell was he thinking?

And what was he hoping to achieve?

This was a murder that was already solved. Burris had opportunity and motive. And he'd been eyeballed leaving the scene of the crime. It was open and shut. Only Farley seemed to think he could hide the whole thing in his back pocket.

There was definitely some weird shit going down.

Mingus's worry was that he'd dropped the ball somewhere. Maybe right at the jump. He should have paid more attention to what Farley and his crew were doing at the crime scene the night of the murder. His meeting with Jacquette that night had been brief. The captain had simply passed on a rumor—that the dead man, Darion Mayfield, had had ties to the LAPD. What kind of ties, Captain Jacquette either didn't know or did not wish to convey. When Mingus had asked why he'd been given the assignment, the captain had blown smoke up his ass about his being the only IAG detective he could trust with such a delicate investigation.

Why delicate? Jacquette didn't answer that one either.

After the meeting, he should have stuck around, kept an eye on Fats and his boys and given the Mayfield apartment a thorough examination. Then maybe he'd know what put that swastika-looking mark on the dead man's face. Instead, he'd opted to meet with Redd at Buckie's.

When he turned into the complex's parking lot, he surprised a gathering of young black men who were hanging out at a white Jaguar sedan parked near the rear exit. He pulled into an empty space just off the building's entrance. He stepped from his car to find all eyes on him. Then, as if responding to a sound too high-pitched for his ears, they headed away in various directions, some walking quickly, some actually running, scattering like roaches.

Mingus squinted at the parked car they'd been draped around. It seemed to be empty. He was a little too far away for the license plates to be anything but a blur of yellow figures on a blue background.

It didn't look like the vehicle was going anywhere. He'd check the plates on his way out.

The apartment lobby had two elevator banks and a single stairway leading up. Mingus took the stairs. He'd learned a long time ago that good cops never leave a building the same way they come in. He figured he'd use his legs while he had the energy. And if anybody happened to be waiting for him on the fifth floor, they'd be watching the elevator, not the stairs.

Huffing and puffing past the third floor, he wondered if the climb had been all that good an idea. An older man in a gym suit passed him going down. The black men gave the traditional nod, exchanging "Wha'sup, brother?" greetings. Continuing on down, the older dude called back without breaking his stride, "You oughta get yo'self an EKG, brother, before you start running up stairs."

Mingus wanted to yell back that his EKGs looked fine, but he was too weary and out of breath. He staggered through the door marked with a large 5 and stopped, leaning against a wall to regain his wind. Sweat was dripping from his nose and chin. His chest felt like somebody was loading stone slabs on it.

Looking up, he saw that the door to one of the apartments down the hall was partially open. He'd have guessed whose apartment it was even without the splintered jamb and the torn yellow LAPD tape fluttering in the warm breeze.

He was heading for it when he heard an elevator door open . . . then close.

Panting, he fast-stepped to the bank of elevators, but the area was vacant. No one had gotten off. Whoever had gone down was way beyond his powers of observation.

Returning to the late Darion Mayfield's apartment, he drew his 9mm—a useless gesture, probably—and quietly pushed the door open wide enough to enter. Taking a swift tour, he saw that someone had done a number on the place. The bedding was turned over; the mattress was on the floor. The bedroom drawers were pulled out with some clothing dangling over the sides.

Fucking scavengers. A dealer dies, name and address in the paper, why not see if he left any samples around?

He holstered his gun as he reentered the main room. The only living things present besides himself were a couple of dozen flies that had found their way through the broken window. Mingus wondered if they'd made the trip all the way from the head-chopping Dumpster directly below at street level.

He made note of the dead man's state-of-the-art electronic wall, the CD and DVD players, the Playstation 2, the receiver and a half-dozen other matching black boxes, each with its own glass display window and unique set of buttons and dials, the monster TV, the speakers the size of refrigerators.

He frowned. How often did looters turn up their noses at that kind of pricey crap? The answer to that question was never. His curiosity about the passenger in that descending elevator suddenly increased.

He ran to the broken window and looked down through it to the parking lot and the Dumpster that had done the number on Darion Mayfield's head. Screeching tires drew his attention to the white Jag sedan as it left a layer of tread exiting the lot, turning right into traffic, and rolling quickly out of view.

Mingus wondered if the driver might not have been the mysterious Alice Adapts, strung out and looking for Darion's stash. If so, she'd be surfacing somewhere else soon enough.

Flies buzzed him as he moved back from the window. There were so many of the flying insects he wondered if there might not be a little piece of Darion lying around somewhere. He gave the room a perfunctory sweep and found nothing unusual.

Like the living room, the bedroom featured high-end Italian furnishings. For a dirtbag dealer, Darion had had style. If you happened to be fond of lacquer. Black lacquer dresser, black lacquer picture frames, bedposts.

Scattered around the bedroom were a variety of magazines designed to keep their readers up to date on the latest cars, digital shit, threads, and naked supermodels. On the dresser was a picture of Darion with Reverend Mayfield and an elderly woman who was probably his mama. The investigating officers or somebody had taken everything else.

In the living room, Mingus spied a splotch of white dust on the thick mauve carpet near the electronic junk wall. He leaned down and pressed a finger against the dust. He licked the finger and tasted cocaine. That's when he saw someone standing at the door—an elderly black lady, nicely dressed, carrying a purse and a brown paper bag. "You're not supposed to be in here," she said sternly.

"It's okay, ma'am," he said, getting out the leather case and showing her his badge. "I'm a policeman."

She looked from him to the badge and back to him again. She didn't seem convinced. "That why you eating off that dead boy's carpet?"

"I was checking . . . I'm investigating . . ."

"That why you busted the door and tore the tapes the police put up?"

"It was like this when I got here," he said. The old lady could teach the guys in Interrogation a few things.

"Well, it was still doing its job when I left for the grocery. Less than an hour ago." She continued giving him the eye. "Then I come back and find it all tore and you here, eating off the carpet. Nobody else."

"I'm Detective Lionel Mingus," he said, trying to relax the woman. "Who might you be?"

"Never mind who I am," she said, turning on her heel and going to the apartment across the hall.

He watched her place the bag on the carpet, open her purse, and get out a key. Before using it, she turned suddenly and shot him another piercing glance. Full-out embarrassed, he wished her a nice day and returned to his business.

If the neighbor lady was correct, the break-in had occurred less than an hour before. Not a lot of time to search a place. Still, Farley and his crew had had their way. Anything worth finding was probably long gone. But he had some time on his hands before LaLa's opened for cocktails.

He went back to the place where the coke had been scattered on the carpet. He hunkered down for a closer look, but there really wasn't much more to see. He wondered what had happened to Darion's drug supply. And his cash. Users usually didn't pay by credit card. He made a mental note to look into that.

As he straightened up, his knees got back at him for the climb, sending a bolt of pure pain down his legs. A fly did a rollover about six inches from his nose and made a dive for his mouth. Staggering, swatting, and spitting simultaneously, the detective lost his balance. His left knee suddenly unlocked and he fell to the floor with a thud, his shoulder and hip taking most of the trauma.

"Shit," he said, lying there, waiting for the intense pain. When it didn't come, he relaxed, thankful for Darion Mayfield's thick carpet. He put out a hand to hoist himself up and he felt the sharp edge of a piece of glass dig into his palm. Wincing, he pulled out the offending sliver.

It left just a little scratch with hardly any blood. He was about to toss the shard aside when he noticed it wasn't glass at all. It was plastic. And it resembled the piece of plastic Dr. Saleem had removed from Darion's jaw.

Mingus got out a pocket pack of Kleenex and used his teeth to pull one loose. He dropped it on the carpet and placed the piece of plastic on it.

A warm breeze floated through the broken window and tickled his perspiring face. He picked up the tissue to get a better look at its nestled content. He could make out raised letters that were far too tiny to be read by the naked eye, or at least his naked eye. Maybe a brand or manufacturer's name or copyright information.

Wrapping the shard in the tissue and placing it carefully into the breast pocket of his coat, he experienced a sense of elation he hadn't felt in a long time. He was certain he was on to something. If the two pieces of plastic matched, and he felt they would, it ruled out Farley's theory that the chip in the victim's mouth had been something the dog dragged in. It meant both sections were from an object that had collided big time with Darion Mayfield's face in the apartment just before he went for his air walk.

If there were two pieces, there were probably more. He'd find them. On his hands and knees, he crawled across the carpet, looking for glass that wasn't glass at all. The sound of his beeper made him jump.

He checked the caller's number and, smiling in spite of himself, sat down on the carpet and slipped his cellular from his shirt pocket.

Ida Bevan, talent agent and former Mingus flame, answered on the first ring. Her voice was wary but eager until he identified himself. Then it was just wary. "What can I do for you, Lionel?"

"I need an address for a screenwriter named Alice Adapts," he said.

"You and your women," Ida said flatly.

"This is business, Ida."

"What's she done?"

"She may be a witness to something I'm working on."

"No. I mean what's she *done*. What are her credits? Movies she's written?"

"I don't know."

Silence.

Mingus was about to break it, when Ida said, "She's not on our list. You have any clue of the kind of writing she does? Comedy? Suspense?"

"No," he said. "Well, maybe about the drug scene. Something kinda gritty." He was over his head. "Maybe not. I really don't know."

"I'll have to get back to you."

She hung up before he could thank her.

Well, at least she'd offered to help him, which was more than he expected. Must've been his lucky day.

He put the phone back into his shirt pocket and shifted on the carpet. Something cold and hard pressed against the back of his neck. "No sudden moves," a male voice instructed. "Hug the rug; keep your arm out."

It sounded like the guy was struggling to stay calm. Mingus did as he was told. He felt the cold object leave his head but sensed it had not gone far away.

"Okay. Now roll over real slow so I can tell which one of you motherfuckers I'm blowing away."

Considering that statement, Mingus decided not to roll over. That earned him a kick in the side. "I said roll."

With a grunt, keeping his arms stretched in front of him, Mingus rolled over. The first thing he saw was the nasty end of a gun, the barrel looking as big and round and ugly as an open pit. The second thing he saw was that the man behind the gun was Claude Burris.

"Easy now, Detective," Mingus cooed. "I'm—"

"I know who you are. You're one of the boys. And I know exactly what I've gotta do about it."

The rogue vice cop took a step forward, pushing his weapon closer to Mingus's face.

So maybe this wasn't his lucky day after all.

15

Mingus had been close to death before. In his baby cop days, he'd been stupid enough to turn his back on a battered wife while cuffing her abusive husband. That had earned him a butcher knife in his shoulder. Then there'd been a crack house shootout where a bullet found a soft spot just below the edge of his vest and the blood loss almost did him in. He'd faced guns, blades, broken bottles, been attacked by chains, saps, baseball bats, and, of course, a variety of nasty shit-eating guard dogs.

But he'd never before experienced the helplessness of lying flat on his back while a hot-eyed killer stood over him sticking an unwavering gun in his chops.

"This will be good," Claude Burris said to himself. "This will be goddamned good."

Mingus saw the man's bone-white finger start to move on the trigger. "Hold on there, Burris," he said, hoping his voice wasn't showing his fear. It never helped to show your fear. "You don't want to do this. You got no truck with me."

"That's beautiful," Burris said. "You're not up here trying to nail my ass to a murder. You just stepped in to get out of the sun. You Homicide pricks think the rest of us are dumb as clay. Well, fuck you."

"Whoa, whoa, whoa. Who said Homicide? I'm not Homicide."

Burris blinked. "You trying to tell me you're not on the job?"

Mingus was desperately trying to puzzle it out. Okay, the man had some major grievance with Homicide. But would he be feeling any more kindly toward IAG? Doubtful.

"I've *seen* you with Farley, you lying prick," Burris shouted.

"I know Farley. I used to be in Homicide."

Burris tensed.

"But I got kicked out. Years back. I'm Lionel Mingus."

Burris seemed to recognize the name. "The asshole who lost his badge and gun?"

"I'm the asshole."

Burris took a step backward. But he still wasn't happy. "What are you doing here, asshole?" he asked. "Working a bag job for that fat fuck?"

Mingus's head was spinning. Logic told him that Farley had gone out on a limb trying to help Burris. But Burris clearly had a homicidal hard-on for the fat man. "Nothing like that," he said. "Fact is, I'm here investigating Farley."

Burris blinked again. "Run that one down for me."

"I'm investigating a complaint against Farley and some others in the Homicide division. I'm IAG. I can show—"

"Keep your hands where they are." Burris was looking antsy. Unpredictable. Still, Mingus figured it was a step up from before, when he'd been ready to cap him. "IAG. Shit. Why ain't life simple? How do I know you—?"

"Drop the gun, sir." The command carried little conviction. It came from a very young patrolman of some Asian derivation: Vietnamese, Thai, Japanese. Mingus could never quite figure out the physical differences. He stood just inside the door, in an Academy-approved stance, aiming his weapon at Burris's back. Mingus noted that the boy had originally pointed the gun gang-style, arm extended, hand and weapon parallel to the floor. Then he'd caught himself and shifted to the conventional gunhand-on-palm position.

The boy's partner was a black man, older, slower, but hopefully more experienced. He moved warily to the side until Burris could catch a peripheral view of him and his weapon. "Lower the gun and drop it," he said calmly but with force.

Burris, considering his options, looked like he was starting to implode.

Mingus was working on a more basic level. There were too many goddamned guns in the room and one was still pointed at him. He didn't know what Burris might do, or what the uniforms might push him into doing. He waited until Burris's eyes shifted to the older cop again and reached out to grab the man's gun.

Burris stumbled back, yanking free from Mingus's grip.

His gun went off and Mingus felt a tickle across his scalp.

Burris stumbled into the young cop, who managed to keep from firing his weapon as they both thudded to the carpet.

With his ears ringing and feeling slightly light-headed, Mingus watched the black cop step on Burris's wrist and jerk the gun from his fingers.

The younger cop pushed Burris off him roughly and got to his feet. He looked at his weapon, confused.

"The safety," his partner said, keeping an eye on Burris.

"I'm on the job. Detective Claude Burris. Vice. Get your fucking foot off my wrist and your gun out of my face."

"He's Detective Claude Burris," the black cop said to his partner in a mocking tone. "Ain't that sweet?" He kept his foot and gun where they were.

"What's your story?" he asked Mingus.

Mingus wasn't feeling so good. He had a headache and his back was starting to sing a little, too, thanks to the position he was in on the floor. He told them who he was. The younger officer checked his ID.

"Looks good," he said.

"Okay. That makes it simpler. Go call in, Lee. Tell 'em we picked up Burris."

The elderly neighbor lady came to the door just as the young cop made his exit. "No," she said, distressed. "It's the other man I called you about. He's the one broke in. The man you're pointing your gun at, I've never seen . . . No, wait a minute. It's the detective who arrested Darion all those months ago. I remember now."

"I thank you for your help, ma'am," the policeman told her, "but I'd appreciate it if you went back into your apartment now."

"But you don't understand. The white man is a police detective. It's the other—"

"Ma'am, I have to insist you return to your apartment. This white man may be a police detective, but he's also wanted for murder."

The neighbor lady's eyes opened wide. She started to back away. "Well . . . I bet it was his shifty-looking associate there got him into trouble."

Mingus took his time getting up and straightening his clothes. Shifty-looking, huh? He knew what it was. The thing about his skin being so black. Even brown old ladies distrusted the black.

"There's no warrant out on me," Burris was saying to the cop.

"Guess somebody screwed up in Dispatch, then. We got the all-points about a half hour ago."

Burris turned to look at Mingus. "You know about this?"

"Nope. But I can guess. A wit came forward who placed you here when Darion Mayfield flew out of that window."

"That's bullshit," Burris said. "There's no witness, because I wasn't anywhere near this place that night."

"You're telling the wrong guy. Like I said, I'm not in RHD. It's a simple matter to clear up, I imagine, long as you've got an alibi."

"I . . ." Burris began, then shut up.

"You got an alibi?" Mingus asked.

"I didn't kill the man."

"You may have to do better than that."

"I don't kill people."

The patrolman chuckled, holding his gun steady. "You're saying that to a man you just shot. Another fraction of an inch and that cut on Detective Mingus's head woulda been a fatal wound."

Cut? Mingus touched the top of his head and his hand came away with blood on the fingertips. Damn, no wonder his head hurt.

"You oughta get that checked," the cop said. "Meantime, maybe that lady who called us in has got a Band-Aid you can use."

Mingus preferred to let his head bleed.

16

It had been a few nights since Mercer and Vanessa had been together, and they tried to make up for lost time. With not a lot of success.

She pushed him away, accusing him of being "somewhere else."

He assured her that he was definitely there, lying beside her. "It's just that I haven't had much sleep the last few days."

"And you're worried about that boy who's still missing," she said.

"Right," he said, trying to stay awake, to concentrate on the words. "Ricky's still out there. I thought he'd head for home by now. He's just a big kid. So many things could have happened to him. He could have—"

He felt the bed rock slightly.

She was crossing the room to where she'd placed her clothes on a chair. The fact that she'd placed them so neatly was an indication of the night's low level of passion. "I'm out of here," she said.

"I'm sorry, honey, I—"

"You've got to let it go. You proved the boy was innocent. That fulfilled your obligation. You shouldn't have brought it into our bedroom."

He liked the idea of "our bedroom," but there wasn't

anything else she was saying that sounded good to him. "I don't think of it as an obligation," he said. "I feel for the kid. I don't want him hurt any more than he has been."

"Wake up and smell the reality, Mercer," she said, completely dressed now. "This kid you feel for is an only-partially-functioning eighteen-year-old with the strength of a full grown man. He's out there somewhere, and maybe he is having a bad time or maybe he's giving somebody a bad time. When he eventually returns home, if he does, he'll be living with a mother who fucks her kids and a daddy who's also his brother and who uses him to rob people. Those are his so-called caretakers. It's a really ugly situation. And the boy's future is darker than his daddy's soul. But it's not your problem. You're a lawyer, not a social worker. I know you're smart enough to figure out the difference."

He opened his mouth to reply, but he checked himself. He was sleep-deprived and exhausted, physically and mentally. He was worried about the boy. He didn't want to make it worse by calling his fiancée a selfish, spoiled princess who needed to get her ass kicked. "I gotta get some sleep," he said.

She moved beside him, bent, and kissed him on the cheek. "I'm sorry," she said. "I guess I sounded like a bitch. We're both a little stressed right now. We need rest. In the morning, I'll be your nice sweet girlfriend again. You'll see."

"That's nice," he said. "Morning."

He was snoring before she closed the door.

He awoke early enough to fix himself a breakfast of eggs, toast, and coffee.

While he ate, he watched a show he'd taped the night before. Bobby Carter on *Geraldo Live!* jousting with a D.A. from Philadelphia about the civil rights of people who exist below the poverty level.

He and Vanessa had been looking at it together when he started to drift off, and she'd suggested they take advantage of the technology and record the show while they both were still awake enough to make love. As it turned out, they might as well have continued watching.

It was an entertaining segment, mainly because the D.A., a self-styled man of the people whose politics were somewhere to the right of Attila the Hun, was also a slow thinker. Bobby ran rings around him until the unfortunate dinosaur got so dizzy he toppled over.

Mercer clicked off the VCR, and the TV screen was filled by a live local news show. Which was how the young lawyer discovered that Los Angeles Police Detective Claude Burris had been arrested in connection with the murder of Darion Mayfield, whom the media was now describing as "a suspected Inglewood drug lord."

By the time he arrived at the firm, Mercer had absolved himself from any guilt over Darion's murder. All he did was a damn fine job of lawyering. He got his client set free. If anyone should feel guilt, it was whoever put Burris back on the street until his perjury hearing.

The reception area was abuzz with office chatter. Mercer doubted Burris's arrest was the reason. The receptionists had zero interest in any serious news unless it impacted in some way on them or the firm.

He moved past them, unnoticed in the din, and headed down the hall to his office. Vanessa's door was closed. He didn't know why, but that filled him with relief.

His assistant, Melissa, paused in her telephone conversation. "You're here early," she said with a hint of wonder. "I'll get your coffee in a second."

"Don't bother," he said. "I had two cups at home."

"Well, guess who finally figured out how to work his Mr. Coffee," she said.

"Back off. I know my way around a kitchen. I even fixed myself breakfast."

A few minutes later, she was in his office, filling him in on his phone messages. "Mr. Coulter called at a quarter to nine. And a Miz Doremus or Doramus phoned about ten minutes ago. She somebody you know?"

"Name's familiar. Doremus." He frowned, working on it, but the association didn't come.

"Old galfriend?" Melissa asked, smirking. "One of the many?"

"Them I remember. She say what she wanted?"

"No. And she didn't leave a number. Sounds real pushy and high-tone. Said she'd call back. Shall I get Mr. Coulter for you?"

Jerome Coulter was a wealthy elderly gentleman whose twenty-year-old granddaughter happened to be a klepto, among other things.

"Eugenia in jail, or out?" Mercer asked.

"Out, but he says she's been at it again. Fox Mall this time. Leather purse. He returned it and all she got was a warning."

"What's he want with me?" Mercer asked.

"He'd like you to scare her again. Said it kept her straight for nearly two months, last time."

It had kept him straight, too. The girl had thrown herself on his lap, grabbed his dick and stuck her tongue in his ear. It was her idea of innocent flirtation. He might have succumbed to it a) if Eugenia Coulter hadn't been a client, b) if he hadn't been involved with somebody else, c) if they hadn't been in his office, with the somebody else less than forty feet away, and d) if the girl wasn't such a freak. He'd stood up and dumped her on the floor. It must've hurt, but she just grinned and said it couldn't get too rough for her. Eugenia Coulter was nothing but bad news hiding out in a very tidy little package.

"Want me to schedule an appointment?" Melissa asked.

"Yeah. Do that. But tell the old man that because of my court schedule my associate Joe Wexstead will be laying down the law to her."

Melissa raised her expressive eyebrows.

"Joe needs the billable hours," he said, hiding his

amusement at the thought of the suckup keyhole peeper with his hands full of Eugenia. Literally.

"By the way," he said, "what's got the receptionists all lit up?"

"Barry Fox is in the office, meeting with Bobby," she said.

"So?"

"He's got the power. He's handsome. He's single. We can all dream."

"You, too?"

"You know I ain't into girls, Mercer."

A bit too casually, he asked, "Van in her office?"

"I guess. Her door was shut when I got in at eight-thirty."

"Nobody called about Ricky Sanchez?"

"Nope. Sorry."

She returned to her desk and he phoned the Sanchez home. Max answered, warned him to leave his family alone, and hung up. Mercer's next call was to one of the few friends he had left in the LAPD, a detective named Virgil Sykes who promised to snoop around to see if any information on Enrique Sanchez had come in.

The young lawyer busied himself for a few hours until, restless, he wandered from his office. He was heading for a cup of coffee when Vanessa's door opened and she walked out with Barry Fox. She seemed a little sheepish, like he'd caught her at something. Or maybe he was just projecting.

The mayor's man seemed happy to see him. "Well, Mercer. How's it going, brother?"

"Jus' fine."

"I got to say, I do like that name. Mercer. Family name?"

Mercer had no way of knowing. He said, "That's right. My uncle wrote 'Moon River.' "

Barry Fox cocked his head at the sarcastic reference to the white composer Johnny Mercer. In a less playful tone, he asked, "Where you from, brother?"

"Midwest."

"Oh? Where'd you study law?"

What the hell was this? Twenty questions? "Howard."

"Harvard man myself. But Howard's a hell of a good school."

"I've got to be back at one-thirty, Barry," Vanessa said. "If we're going to do lunch, we'd better get started."

"Right. Well, good seeing you again, Mercer. You play poker?"

"A little."

"Uh-oh. That's the hustler reply. We got a weekly game at my place in Hancock. Dime-quarter, just three bumps, so nobody gets hurt. Bobby sits in time to time. We gotta get you out."

"Just let me know," Mercer said, his eyes on Vanessa, taking some small solace from her discomfort.

When she finally pulled Barry Fox away, Mercer stormed back into his office, mumbling, "Harvard man."

He was still fuming a few minutes later when Bobby Carter appeared at his door to invite him to lunch.

They dined at the Los Angeles Cattle Company, a restaurant well known for its ultrapricey steaks and its secluded areas where conversation was unlikely to be overheard. When they were seated and their orders taken, Mercer said, "Sure beats the company cafeteria." His reference was to The Jury Room, a small restaurant-bar on the ground floor of the Carter-Hansborough building.

"I thought we both could use a treat," Bobby said.

"Heard you been jawing with Barry Fox," Mercer said.

Bobby smiled and waited for the waiter to deposit their iced teas and depart. "The Fox was doing the jawing. I was just listening."

"He's having lunch with Vanessa," Mercer said.

"That bother you?"

"Not much. He studied law at Haw-vard. He ever mention that to you? Bet he did."

Bobby smiled. "He may have mentioned it."

"Maybe at one of his poker games at his little place in Hancock Park."

"A word of advice," Bobby said. "Barry Fox is nobody you want to engage in a pissing match."

"Don't worry. I don't plan on engaging him in any kind of match. I don't suppose that's why we're having lunch, to talk about old Barry?"

Bobby studied him briefly before replying. "I'm going to give it to you straight from the shoulder, son. And I do not use the word 'son' lightly."

Oh, shit, Mercer thought. This was not going to be a free lunch.

"C.W. wants your ass out of the firm."

"Yeah. I picked up on that."

"What're you going to do about it?"

"I'm open to suggestions."

"Good," Bobby said, adjusting his napkin on his lap. "Stop fucking his daughter."

"That's not on the table."

"Put it on. For the good of your career."

Mercer felt the blood rushing to his face. "You wouldn't be asking me to free Vanessa up for your friend Barry?"

Bobby shook his head sadly. "You calling me a pimp, Mercer?"

"No. I was just . . . hell, no."

"I'm not thinking about anybody but you when I say you've got to make the break with Vannie clean and quick."

"That's not gonna happen."

Bobby sighed. "Wrong answer, son. I can keep you in your office until next March, per your contract. But you'll be doing shit work. And when the contract's up, you can bet C.W. will see to it that no other firm will hire you."

"Then I'll do something else. Vanessa and I are getting married."

Bobby leaned forward. "If I thought there was any chance of that happening, I'd tell you to go for it."

"What do you mean?"

"I've known Vannie all her life. Her mother passed away when she was barely in her teens. C.W.'s been everything to her. Daddy, mama, best friend. She's not going to go against him."

"She's going against him now," Mercer said, a little too defensively.

"She's having a romance with a smart young attorney who's got a bright future. How's she going to feel about the ex-lawyer who's scuffling to make ends meet?"

A worm of doubt began to grow in Mercer's mind, and he despised himself for making room for it. He decided he despised Bobby Carter, too.

He stood, dropping his napkin on the table. "I'll catch a cab back."

"Sit down, boy."

"I've lost my appetite, Bobby. And I'm fed up with this conversation. My resignation will be on your desk when you get back."

"Sit your ass down, now," Bobby ordered.

Mercer had never seen the man angry before. Even when that Philly D.A. was telling Geraldo that the poor got the kind of justice they paid for, Bobby had stayed chilly. At the moment, his eyes were blazing.

Mercer sat.

"You're behaving like some lovesick dog-man," Bobby said. "Keep it up and you'll make me start siding with C.W."

"You're telling me I have no options, Bobby. That no matter which way I turn, I wind up without the woman I love. I don't buy it."

"The reason you're so pissed off is that you do buy it. You know that girl won't stick with a loser."

Mercer realized his fingernails were digging into his palm. He relaxed his fist and tried to calm down. "I'm not gonna trade her for the job."

"Okay. When one is faced with only two choices and both of them are lousy, what does one do?"

"Vote Democrat?" Mercer said.

Bobby couldn't help smiling. "Besides that."

"You tell me."

"You find a third choice," Bobby said.

Mercer was about to reply, but Bobby raised a warning hand. Their waiter appeared with their steaks. When he'd left them alone again, the younger man said, "Do I have a third choice?"

"Maybe. As I mentioned the other night at the mayor's shindig, I've got something in mind. But it's still too early to discuss. What you have to do now is stay in place at the firm, which means keeping C.W. relatively content."

"I won't stop seeing Vanessa."

"Okay. Don't. Just stop dry-humping her while her daddy's in the room. Do what you have to do, but stay out of his face."

"What if he pushes? What if he fronts me about Vanessa?"

"You're a lawyer," Bobby said. "What do you do when you're hit with a question you can't answer?"

The two men stared at one another. "Vanessa says she won't lie to him," Mercer said.

"Then that should be a sign where her loyalty rests, push comes to shove," Bobby said, sliding the serrated edge of his knife through the splendidly prepared sirloin.

Mercer suddenly realized just how cleverly his mentor had manipulated him. He was not going to resign. Nor was he going to do anything stupid, like marrying a woman who'd side with her daddy over her husband. "Bobby, I guess I—"

"Enough talk," Bobby interrupted. "Eat your steak before it loses all its sizzle."

17

It took Mingus nearly three hours to have his cut scalp plastered and his statement taken. Another hour went into dropping the piece of plastic off with a police lab technician named Pascal who owed him a favor or two.

Then he began looking for Loc in all the wrong places.

Farley and Gervey had been too busy chatting with Burris in Interrogation to inform him of the basis for the warrant, but he was assuming it had been Ken Loc's eyewitness account of events surrounding the murder. Now he felt the need to talk to Loc again, not just to clarify that point but to try to make some sense of the whole Mayfield murder investigation.

Why had Fats tried so hard to convince him that Burris was not a suspect? Why had it taken so long for Burris to be officially charged with the crime? And, most disquieting of all, why did Burris sound so damned convincing when he denied killing Darion Mayfield?

Ken Loc seemed to be in the middle of it all. And he was among the missing.

None of Mingus's snitches was of any help. He finally consulted the boys at the Kittyhawk. The ones who would talk to him claimed they hadn't seen Loc since the evening they'd taken their ride together. "Hell," one of the men said, "all we know, your bein' here is some kind of fakeout. Loc pissed you off and you done a Burris on him."

"I left the man strutting high," Mingus said, "and heading here."

Nobody remembered seeing him return.

Mingus sincerely hoped that Loc had not disappeared permanently. If he had been the key to the warrant, Farley was probably keeping him in custody somewhere. Mingus had checked the usual places. Loc wasn't at the Glass House under his own or any temporary name. Nor was he at the 77th division jail or the county lockup.

He decided to skip the hide-and-seek bullshit and phone Farley, ask him about his witness straight out. But by then the sun had set and the fat man had gone off duty. Nobody answered his home phone. Annoyed, Mingus snapped his cellular shut and slipped it into his pocket.

The K-hawk waitress, a big girl in a tiny leather outfit, sidled over to his section of the bar and said, "You look like you could use a nice cocktail to chase away the blues."

It was a tempting idea, but Mingus decided to take it to a place where he wasn't as well known. Or disliked.

The next morning, with a bandage on his scalp covering the gunshot wound and nursing a hangover and heartburn, Mingus marched up to Dennis Farley's desk at Robbery-Homicide and asked, "Where've you got Ken Loc?"

Farley looked at the tape on Mingus's head and said, "You doin' those hair plants, Lionel?" He said it loudly, playing to the other six detectives in the room. All male, and not a black face among them. Mingus guessed that was the way the fat man was working things—assigning the undesirables to overnight duty or sending them out to handle the morning shit work, and saving the nine-to-five for the Aryan brotherhood.

Mingus ignored Farley's little joke. "I want to talk to Ken Loc."

"Me, too," Farley said. "That boy's our primary witness. And we want to talk to you about your little run-in with Burris yesterday. Gotta give you credit, Lionel, you were on the money about that bent cop prick."

"You sitting on Loc somewhere?"

"Sittin' on him? Hell, I don't even like being in the same room with him."

Mingus's eyes dropped to the detective's murder book lying open on the desk.

"Take a gander," Fats offered. "Cooperation is my middle name."

Mingus lifted the book and scanned its pages. Not surprisingly, notes of an interview with Loc were now in the chrono log.

"What the hell's going on, Farley?" Mingus asked.

"What do you mean?"

"I don't get this game you're playing."

"Tell me something new, Lionel. You haven't had a clue about anything since you traded in your baby bottle on a fifth of gin."

"Let me be specific. What took you so long to add the Loc interview to the murder book?"

"You clocking me, Lionel? I put it in when I put it in."

Mingus placed the murder book back on the desk. "I'm filling up a file on you, Fats. Loggin' in every one of those little tricks you've been playing over the years."

"You're scaring the shit out of me, Lionel. I get all trembly when I think of the great Mingus on my ass. A guy so smart he lets some hump powder his booze and steal his badge and gun."

Mingus stared at Farley, suddenly oblivious to everything else in the room. "What makes you think my booze was powdered that night?" he asked too quietly.

The smirk left Farley's face for a beat. Then it was back in full force. "Just giving you the benefit of the doubt, Lionel. Hate to think you fucked yourself up all on your own." He tilted his chair back, his hands cupped around his fat head.

Mingus was furious with himself. All those years he'd

known the fat man hated him and resented his position in the department. But it had never once occurred to him that Farley might have set him up, might have sent some lowlife to slip something in his drink and steal his weapon and badge. Hell, it had never even occurred to him that his drink might have been messed with. But he understood now with complete certainty exactly what had happened and who had been responsible.

He swept his foot beneath the back leg of Farley's chair, sending him crashing to the floor like a sack of rocks. Before the rest of the cops could react, Mingus was on top of the fat man, relentlessly pounding his pale, freckled face.

A big cop named Hibbler grabbed him by the collar and dragged him up, but Mingus drove an elbow into the man's gut and went back to his original plan, burying a knee in Fats's chest. Fists began flying at Mingus from all directions. Exhausted, he grabbed as many of the cops as he could, dragging a bunch of them onto the floor and on top of Fats, who lay grunting and bleeding.

A white hand reached for Mingus's holster, ripping away his handgun. Too slow to stop him, Mingus reached toward the waistband of the cop nearest him.

"Gun!" somebody shouted.

The cops rolled every which way, running for cover while at the same time pulling their own pieces.

Slide. Click. Click. Click. Slide. The sounds of weapons cocking filled Mingus's ears. Standing alone and surrounded, he drew down on the one detective who hadn't scattered. He was a big white boy, in his twenties, who looked like he hadn't been eating right, all puffy and pale. And terrified. He dropped to his knees with his eyes shut, as if in prayer.

Mingus counted five cops pointing their weapons at him.

"Drop it," an older cop named Lewis demanded.

"Fuck you, Lewis. You drop it." Mingus wanted the cops to know he meant business. He pressed his piece against the head of the kneeling detective who, he realized, had pissed his pants.

"Tell you boys what," Mingus said. "I'm walking. You be cool, I'll be cool. We can settle this later."

The RHD cops didn't seem interested in making any deals. "I say we kill the nigger," Hibbler growled, clutching his damaged stomach.

"That makes my mouth water." Farley had somehow recovered enough to be standing right behind Mingus. "It'd give me great pleasure to shove this .45 up his black ass and fire off a few caps. But Lionel's a good old nigger. My guess is he'll probably drink himself to death one of these days and save us the trouble. So let's us put our toys away. For now."

The other cops began slowly to holster their guns, keeping their hostile eyes on the black detective.

Mingus didn't give a damn about them. Farley was at the center of his focus. The fat man was tucking his gun back into its leather sheath. His nose was bleeding and a mouse was forming under his right eye. That was good for openers, Mingus thought, but it didn't begin to pay the bill on what he'd done.

Farley tapped Mingus's hostage on the shoulder. "Get up off your knees, Charlie. And go change your diaper."

His face burning from embarrassment, the young man rose and ran from the room.

"Who's got my gun?" Mingus asked, holding out the weapon in his hand.

A ferret-faced cop moved from behind a desk. Before handing Mingus's gun over, he looked to Farley for approval.

Farley considered the situation and finally nodded. "Jesus, Lionel," he said with disgust. "I oughta make you clean up that piss."

"Gives the place a little class," Mingus said, exchanging the gun in his hand for his own. "It's not gonna end here, Fats. Not with me knowing what you did."

"You don't know shit, Lionel. I didn't have nothing to

do with your troubles. Now, get outta here, let me tend to my throbbin' head."

"That throbbin' head is just the start of it," Mingus said, holstering his gun. He took his time making his exit. At the door, he bumped into Captain Roy Jacquette. The head of Robbery-Homicide looked at his torn jacket, his shirttail hanging over his belt, his pulled and twisted tie. "What the hell happened to you, Mingus? You on the sauce again?"

Trying to ignore the laughter in the room, Mingus assured the captain that he hadn't had a drink all day.

Then he made his getaway down the hall.

18

When Mercer arrived back at One Wilshire, he drifted through the reception area, then cruised down the carpeted hall to his office. Vanessa's door was open, but she wasn't there. Probably still at lunch. With Barry.

Melissa was dining in at her desk, putting the finishing touches to an industrial-size carton of cottage cheese that she firmly believed was a diet meal.

Detective Virgil Sykes had not called with news of Ricky Sanchez.

"No phone calls at all," Melissa said, gesturing with a tiny plastic spoon, "but that Miz Doremus who called earlier . . . ? The one whose name you said sounded familiar . . . ?"

It still did. He nodded.

"Guess you didn't recognize her when you walked right by her," Melissa said.

"What're you talking about?"

"She's here. Out in reception. Been waiting for you for about fifteen minutes."

Mercer vaguely recalled seeing a well-dressed woman, but he'd been too focused on his personal situation to pay her much mind. The fact that she'd assumed she could just arrive and barge in on his business day won her no favors from him. He had more pressing matters to occupy his afternoon. "Any idea what she wants?"

"No, but—"

"She just drops in? No appointment? Tell her I'm tied up."

"Well, actually—"

"And don't bother apologizing for my not seeing her," he said. "It's her bad. Explain to her how it works. We meet clients by appointment only."

He still wasn't paying attention to his surroundings or he'd have noticed that Melissa was looking past him. She said, "Ah, Mr. Early . . ." Trying to give him some clue.

"We don't just sit around here waiting for clients to walk in off—"

"I didn't mean any offense, Mr. Early."

Mercer caught a whiff of expensive but pungent perfume. He turned to see the elegantly dressed sister he'd barely noticed in reception and wondered how he could have been so blind. She looked to be in her late twenties, but she might have been older. The unlined face, bright deep green eyes, well-coiffed dark red hair and firm, well-proportioned, couturier-draped figure suggested that the woman spent a lot of time and money smacking down the aging process.

The emblem on the bag she was holding in one gloved hand said Gucci and, unlike a lot of the swap-meet G-bags some sisters were known to carry, this one looked real. She extended the other gloved hand and said, "I'm Mildred Doremus, Mr. Early."

He hesitated just a beat before taking her hand. "Nice meeting you, Miz Doremus. But as my assistant should have informed you, you'll have to make an appointment before—"

"I'm sorry," she interrupted him. "Your assistant did tell me about the appointment thang, but I don't have a lot of time for formalities. My . . . *affianced* is in serious straits and needs your help."

He suddenly realized that his first impression of her as

a well-married woman of some means might have been a little off. The "thang," mixed with the pretentious "affianced" and "straits" suggested some playacting might be going on. No well-heeled matron, then. But well-heeled nonetheless. Probably the mistress of some high-rolling cat daddy. And the cat daddy was in trouble.

"What sort of straits is your fiancé in?" he asked.

Her expressive green eyes stared at him, sizing him up. "He's in jail." Then, anticipating his next question, she added, "They say he murdered somebody."

Melissa made a little gulping noise.

"You think we could continue this discussion in your office, Mr. Early? I talk better when I'm off my feet."

"Of course," Mercer said. His attitude toward drop-in business had done a 180, now that it might provide him with his first murder trial.

Melissa followed them into his office, carrying her pen and steno pad.

"If you don't mind, I'd like this to be private," Mildred Doremus said, taking the client's chair to the left of his desk. "At least until we can come to an understanding."

The comment caught Mercer off guard. He had no problem with Melissa leaving. But was it smart to let a client start calling the shots right from the jump?

Melissa took the decision out of his hands. "Before I go, Miz Doremus, is there anything I can bring you? A bottled water or soft drink?"

"No, darling, I'm fine."

Melissa made a swift exit, pausing to shoot Mercer an eye-roll before closing the door behind her.

He turned his attention to Mildred Doremus, whose green eyes held an arrogance that seemed out of kilter with a woman seeking help. He was leaning forward, a bit too anxiously, he thought. He forced his body to relax, lean back, and provide the image of attentive but objective professionalism. "Ready when you are," he said.

"Well, like I told you, my good friend was arrested for killing a man."

"I thought you said he was your 'fiancé'?"

"In the eyes of God," Mildred Doremus said. "In the eyes of man, I have a husband, though he's not exactly in the picture. Nor will he be for the next seven years, unless . . . But that's part of the problem."

"I'm sorry," Mercer said. "I'm not quite following you. It sounds like your husband is . . . what? In jail, too?"

"Servin' a dime at TI." Ten years at the facility at Terminal Island. "And I sincerely hope they keep his knife-wielding abusive ass behind bars for the full term and then some."

"Okay. I'm clear on that. Now, about your friend . . ."

"He didn't kill anybody."

"Let's put that aside for the moment."

"Let's not. That's why I'm here, to make that point. He was with me, in my bed, when they say the punkass went out the window."

Mercer frowned. There couldn't be that many punkasses who'd gone out of windows lately. But it didn't figure that a black woman . . . "What's your friend's name?" he asked.

"Claude Burris." She smiled. She looked younger when she smiled.

"You and Burris doing the nasty? Is this a joke?"

"No joke. Claude is my man."

"You got a fucked-up case of jungle fever, sister," Mercer said.

"You don't know anything about it, *brother*."

"Maybe a little bit." He caught a whiff of her heavy perfume and decided he didn't like it any more than he liked her. "I know your *man* is a fucking ugly racist son of a bitch who kicked a confession out of my client, Darion Mayfield. I know your *man* was making ten kinds of threats after I took him apart in court. I know the minute Darion was set free, somebody tossed him out of a fifth-story apartment. Sounds like your *man* to me."

"Like I say, you don't know nothing. To begin, Claude's no racist."

"It's not just my opinion. It's his rep."

"That's why he's keeping time with me?"

"If rednecks didn't keep time with good-looking black women, both you and I would be a few shades darker."

She glared at him, annoyed. "If all white men were rednecks, you and I might be dead," she said. "Prejudice works both sides of the street. Tell me about his rep, as you call it."

"Nineteen claims of excessive brutality," Mercer said. "All coming from black men."

"Black cons," she corrected. "And did Internal Affairs check each one out?"

"Yeah. All that proves is there wasn't anybody around with a camcorder when he—"

"Don't give me your lawyer jive. I'm not some doo-dah sitting in a jury box. You researched Claude. You know damn well he'd been a cop for nearly thirteen years before anybody laid that racist bullshit on him. Your research tell you the first convict to file a claim against him?"

It suddenly hit him why her name sounded so familiar. "Joe Doremus," he said.

"Joe 'Sweets' Doremus," she said. "Man I married when I was a schoolgirl and dumber than dirt. He was handsome, threw money around like it was confetti. But as I quickly learned, what he really was was a lowlife son of a bitch pimp. Truth be known, Claude did beat the shit out of him. Didn't have anything to do with racism. See, Sweets cut up one of his whores."

"You telling me white knight Claude beat up your husband just because he didn't like the way he treated his stable?"

Her green eyes sparked. "I was the whore got cut up."

She paused, waiting for him to show a little sympathy. But the image of her and Burris that had lodged in his head did little to soften his heart. When he said nothing, she continued. "Mr. Sweets turned me out to the first high roller who showed some interest. He always saved me for the 'special' customers; I give him that. No riffraff. And, because he was not a smart man, I managed to put away a considerable amount of cash. Enough to get dekeloided by somebody who knew his stuff."

She raised her hair off the back of her neck, letting him see a line that might have been drawn by a very fine point. "There are a few more under the dress. See, Mr. Sweets only cut me in places not immediately noticeable. Didn't want me so scarred up I'd lose my top value, but enough for me to remember not to try and leave him again."

"He cut you because you wanted out?"

"Actually, it was because I was leaving him to be with Claude."

"Let me get this straight," Mercer said. "You were married to a pimp and you fell in love with a vice cop? Kinda went out of your way to mess yourself up."

"I should think, Mr. Early, you'd be a little more understanding about the funny little tricks life plays on you."

Mercer felt the hairs on his neck start to tingle. Could she know the trick life played on him back in Alabama? "What do you mean?"

"Just rambling," she said, waving a hand as if to dismiss the statement. "In any case, about Claude and myself, it wasn't that unusual that we met. He was trying to arrest Sweets, and he was a smart enough cop to figure it out that I might be willing to help him if it would help me get control of my life."

"And you crazy kids fell in love, huh?"

"We did," she said, ignoring his sarcasm. "Right away Sweets suspected something. I mean, I wasn't on call for his 'clients' twenty-four-seven like the other girls. I had my off time. Still, Sweets sensed something was up. He figured I might be knocking back with another man, but he didn't have a clue that I was helping the other man put him away. I guess if he'd known that, he wouldn't have just scarred me with that knife, he'd'a slit my throat.

"As it was, he left me lying in my own blood. Went off drinking. I managed to call Claude, who came and got me to the hospital. Then he went after Sweets. I'm gonna tell you something now. I assume our conversation is privileged?"

"It is. But don't take that as a sign I'm gonna be defending Burris."

"I wouldn't want anything I say here to get him in more trouble."

"I can't guarantee that. You tell me you saw him commit a crime, like, say, throwing the Mayfield boy out that window—"

"The crime I'm talking about, I wasn't a witness to."

"Then it's hearsay and inadmissible."

"Okay. Here's what he did to Sweets. He waited for the big man to leave the bar he was at. Then he followed him, dragged him into an alley, and pounded the shit out of him. He was gonna claim Sweets resisted arrest. But Sweets wasn't carrying his knife and Claude wanted hard evidence, to make sure Sweets was put away proper. So he left him fast asleep in the alley. He got hold of another blade and visited me in the hospital.

"We opened up one of my cuts, put my blood on the new blade. Then he and the cop he was partnered with at the time went and arrested Sweets. When Sweets saw them takin' the knife outta his pants pocket, he started yelling setup."

"And he was right," Mercer said. "His lawyer musta been asleep at the wheel."

"What could they say?" she asked. "That Sweets knew the knife had been planted because it wasn't the one he'd used on me?"

"Maybe not. But they went the racism route when they had a much more effective motive for false arrest. The damn cop was involved with you."

"They didn't know about that. My husband still doesn't know Claude's my lover. That's the problem."

Mercer took a minute to let the bits of information shift into some sort of order. "I get it," he said. "You're

Burris's alibi for Darion Mayfield's death. But if you testify for him, it'll come out that you and he have been hitting the sheets since way back. When your husband hears that . . ."

"He's got what he needs to have his conviction overturned. He gets out, a free man. And the first thing he does is come see me with a brand-new knife."

"And Claude won't be around to protect you, because, even though your testimony will set him free in the murder trial, he'll be going back inside for what he did to Sweets."

"Exactly. That's why he wants you to defend him. 'Cause you so good, I won't have to take the stand. I'll have my bank prepare a one-hundred-thousand-dollar cashier's check to serve as a retainer for your services."

The hundred grand had its appeal. So much for C.W. and his claim that the fees from criminal clients didn't amount to petty cash. But it was a no go. "I can't defend Claude Burris."

"Why not? You quit practicing law?"

"I don't know you. You come in off the street, tell me this story. By your own account, you've got a good reason to be lying about where Burris was the night of the murder. I'm inclined to believe the cops are right: he killed my former client. It would be a conflict of interest for me to defend the son of a bitch. Hell, I might even be called as a witness for the prosecution."

Mildred Doremus seemed to consider everything he said. "Claude's an innocent man. The main reason he's in jail now is because of you and the damage you did to his reputation in court."

"Your innocent man kicked a confession out of my client and lied about it on the stand. All I did was bring that to the court's attention."

"It was a setup," she said. "If that's news to you, then you were set up, too. But your client had to be in on it. He knew damn well Claude didn't kick him. And don't tell me about that tape just appearin' like by magic. I can get one made with *you* sayin' you kicked Darion

Mayfield in the ass *and* threw him out a window and have it on your desk by morning. Claude never lied on the stand."

Mercer shook his head. He was tired of listening to her bullshit, tired of looking at her in her fine clothes, waving her Gucci bag, doused in expensive perfume, pretending to be something other than what she was—the hooker-wife of a pimp and the mistress of a bent cop. "Yeah, Burris never lied," he said. "It's all a setup. I'm sorry, Miz Doremus, but I've got clients who aren't delusional who need my help." He stood up and started around his desk to usher her out. "What I ought to do is go have a long talk with your husband about how his legal rights were violated. But I'll settle for just showing you the door."

She made no move to get up. Instead, she opened her purse and withdrew a card. She scribbled something on its back and handed it to him. "I was hoping I could appeal to your sense of justice, Mr. Early. Now I'll have to appeal to somethin' else."

She'd written two names on the back of the card. The first, "Gisela Redmond," belonged to a ghost. The second was the name that was on his birth certificate, "John Parker."

"How did . . . ?" He couldn't quite finish the sentence.

"See, that's the thing about Claude," she said. "You hit him, he hits back. You attack his character and . . . well, a while back, a pal of his tipped him you were digging through all that racism bullshit Sweets and his jailbird gangsta pals were spreading about him. That's when Claude started looking into *your* backyard. He was expecting something stupid, like maybe you got some girl in trouble." She smiled. "Well, I guess that's what you did."

"I didn't do anything to Gisela," Mercer said softly, leaning against his desk. "I sure as hell didn't hook her on crank."

"Well, she ODed at your place. And the Huntsville Police are still carryin' John Parker in their fugitive file."

"I was studying at the school library when it happened," Mercer said. "She knew where I kept the door key. She let herself in, shot up, and died. I got back in time to see them taking her out in a bag."

"And you ran."

"Yeah. It may have been the 1990s, but it was still Alabama."

"And she was dead in your apartment. A white girl."

There was a little more to it than that, but there wasn't any use getting into it. "How'd Burris find out?" he asked.

"He paid off a guy in the lab to lift your prints from the defense table after one of your trials. Kept running them through files until he got a match. He didn't get the chance to find out how you turned John Parker, fugitive, into Mercer Early, hot young lawyer. How did you swing that?"

The thought crossed his mind that she might be wearing a wire, though he couldn't imagine where under that tight dress. Maybe the G-bag. Not that it mattered. The fingerprint match was all anybody needed to hold over his head.

"Cat got your tongue, huh?" she said. "Well, Mr. Early, or whatever the fuck you want to call yourself, I don't know if your problems back in 'Bama are bad enough to put yo' ass in jail, but they sure as hell will get you kicked out of the legal profession. So, you *are* gonna take this case. You *are* gonna take this money. And you *are* gonna make sure Clyde walks. 'Cause if you don't, at the very least you're gonna find yo'self working graveyard at 7-Eleven."

She stood. "I won't take up any more of your time. Fact is, time is running out. The union stuck Claude with a shyster who didn't impress him too damn much at the arraignment. Putz didn't even try for bail."

"No bail for a capital case," Mercer said.

"Well, he could have done somethin'. He let the D.A. walk all over him. Agreed to a speedy trial. No end of bullshit. Claude told the guy to fuck off and sent me to get you. Consider yourself got."

Mercer sighed. "Seems that way."

She indicated the card in his hand. "My phone number's on the other side. Ring me when you ready to pick up your check. You got damn little time to prepare your case."

Prepare his case? A murder case? Shit, he was in trouble.

She removed the glove from her right hand and extended it toward him. He stared at it and the odd images on her fingernails. "You can shake it or kiss it," she said, "long as it seals our deal."

He shook it, wondering why anybody would want to decorate their nails with the numbers from two-dollar bills.

"Since we old friends now," she said, "it's okay I call you Mercer?" When he nodded dumbly, she added, "Well, good. I'll call you Mercer and you call me Redd."

19

Mercer stood at his window watching little toy cars play stop and go along the Wilshire corridor without really seeing them. He wasn't even in the present. Mildred Doremus's very effective blackmail threat had sent him back to that night in Huntsville when everything changed.

He could see the scene as crisply as if it'd been captured on a DVD. The ambulance blocking some of the street, the empty prowl car with its squawking radio, the gathering crowd, the emergency team in working green scrubs carrying the body bag down the front steps of his apartment house.

He pulled to the curb, asked a sister what was going on.

"Say some girl ODed," was the offhanded reply. "Got herself all tagged and bagged."

There were only four apartments in the old brownstone, all serving as home for students at the university. If the building had been a high-rise, he still would have known with certainty that the dead girl had been found in his apartment and that her name was Gisela. Crazy Gisela.

Her father had been the president of an advertising agency somewhere in the state. In Mobile, he thought, but wasn't sure. The main point was that neither her daddy nor her social butterfly mama paid a whole lot of attention to what Gisela and her even crazier brother, Hank, were up to. Hank was part of a gang of stupid, bored, and usually stoned frat boys who spent their hungover Saturday mornings puffing weed, then skateboarding down Riker Bluff and zooming across Highway 72 against the traffic. Gisela preferred to court death with pills and blow.

She'd been a sad girl and Mercer took full blame for contributing to that sadness. They met in an English Lit class. She came on to him and he, not the most sophisticated of college juniors, had eagerly embraced the rounded white body that was being offered up so freely. He had not seen past the hungry flesh to the damage that years of rejection and pain and indifference had caused. He had not understood how close she stood to the brink of despair.

Once again he replayed the sequences of his failure to her. He'd done it so often, they'd taken on the disorienting aspect of a recurring dream.

He was in his apartment in the brownstone on the night their romance ended. The lights were dim. He and Gisela had just spent the last hour or so making love. He heard the familiar and oddly comforting hiss of the steam heater beneath the one window. He was drifting off when he felt the thin mattress stir. Through half-lidded eyes he saw Gisela remove something from her suede bag—a small vial.

She tapped a portion of its contents onto her palm. Her use of cocaine was her affair, but he'd asked her— no, he'd told her—not to bring it to his place, because then it became his affair, too.

"Hey."

Her body jerked in surprise. The vial fell to the carpet. "Damn," she said and dropped down until her face was inches from where the vial rested on its side. She pressed her nose close to the spill. Then her tongue.

"Damn, Gisela, that carpet's been down there since the fifties. You might as well lick a garbage can."

She paid him no mind. She wasn't going to let one snow white granule go to waste.

The sight of her on hands and knees, frantically inhaling off the grimy carpet, was more than enough to chase away any lingering sexual desire he might have for her. Maybe forever. And without that, what was the point?

She returned to bed, brushing her nose, then licking her fingertips. "Okay now," she said. "You lie there and let me do all the work."

Only after she'd straddled his body did she bother to look at his face. "Aw, hell. You're pissed. It's okay, baby. It's just a little blow."

"I told you I don't want it here. I don't use it. I don't like it. I sure as hell don't want to get jammed up because of it."

"O-kay," she said in the little singsong voice she used to mock her genuine insincerity. "It will ne-ver hap-pen a-gain."

You got *that* right, he told himself.

She leaned forward, placed a small warm hand on his naked chest.

Nothing.

She ground her lower body against his.

Still nothing.

"Oh, Johnny, don't . . . please. I swear I'll never bring drugs here again."

"Okay," he said. He turned on his side, forcing her to slide off him.

She snuggled against his back, whispered in his ear, "I love you, Johnny."

He felt a chill. They'd made love. But they'd never talked love. He was black. She was not. This was never meant to be a lovers-forever kind of thing. He thought she understood that.

"Get some sleep," he said, closing his eyes.

He realized she was crying.

He turned toward her.

"Tell me you love me," she said. She was so close that even in the dim light, he could see flakes of cocaine trapped inside her nostrils.

"I'm wiped out, Gisela. We'll talk about this in the morning, when I'm awake and you're straight."

"Tell me you love me or I'll die," she said.

He didn't recognize it as a promise she meant to keep. "We'll talk about it in the morning," he said again, closing his eyes.

But they didn't talk about it.

He dodged her on campus the next day and avoided her calls. When she finally connected, he told her that he was feeling pressured by his studies and needed some time alone.

There was a momentary silence, then a dial tone in his ear.

A few days later, her brother, Hank, stopped him on campus. Delivering a message. Gisela was in rehab. She'd nearly overdosed on a speedball. She wanted to see him.

He went to the hospital, but she was resting. He watched her through the observation window, sleeping peacefully, the bed covers tucked around her. Relaxed, her face resembled an innocent child's.

Relieved that he'd been able to fulfill whatever obligation he felt without actually seeing her, he started to go. An orderly stopped him, a big brutish white man. For a brief second, Mercer feared the man was about to make a scene, blaming him, because of his race, for Gisela's addiction. Instead, the man thanked him for coming and asked him to return later. "She could use a friend," he said. "So far, you and her brother have been her only visitors."

He couldn't bring himself to go back. He didn't want to be her only friend.

The moment she was released from rehab, she phoned.

He told her he didn't need her kind of trouble in his life.

"If you break up with me I'll die," she said.

And so she did.

Mercer had given up playing the what-if game a long time ago. All that was left was a soul-deep feeling of sorrow and regret that he would never lose, and the fear of being found out that Mildred "Redd" Doremus had just released again like an evil genie from a bottle. The idea of being dragged back to Alabama did not appeal to him. He would be charged with something: reckless endangerment or murder or something in between. But he would be charged. And probably convicted. There was a cell waiting for him inside Huntsville Prison.

He had three choices as he saw it. First, he could try to call the Doremus woman's bluff. She and Burris knew his secret. But he knew theirs. If they went public with his fugitive status, he would return the favor, setting her abusive pimp of a husband free and adding another crime to the cop's scorecard. The problem with that scenario was that the woman had freely provided him with the story of Sweets Doremus and his illegal arrest, which meant that she and Burris understood that in a show of cards, Mercer had the most to lose. No bluff.

Choice two: he could run. He'd done it six years ago. Drove to a nearby state, spent most of his cash on fake IDs, wangled a janitorial job at the University of Arkansas at Pine Bluff and began searching the obituary pages of back issues of the local newspaper, the *Pine Bluff Commercial*. It took him less than a month to find the perfect dead man. Mercer Edgar Early had been a black man, born the same year as he. He had been a student at the university when he'd died in an automobile accident two years before.

It had been a simple matter for him to turn off his waxer one night in the registrar's office of the administration building and log on to a computer. It took him less than an hour to resurrect the late Mercer Early. He was not a cheat. In creating Mercer Early's new scholastic record, he was scrupulous in using the precise grades he'd earned at Alabama. They were high enough for most schools to accept a transfer. The following September, armed with Mercer Early's birth certificate, driver's license, and even a credit card, he'd joined the Howard student body.

He'd left very little behind in Alabama. The graves of his mother and father. An aunt and uncle and some cousins he barely knew. A few friends. The meager contents of his apartment. The meager contents of a life.

The situation was a bit different now. He was at the beginning of a promising career. He was in love. He had a life. Too much to give up.

That left him with choice three.

Bobby Carter's assistant, Claudine, a big, very black woman with an athlete's build, looked up from her desk and said, "He's busy with . . . Hey!"

By the time she was up and starting to head him off, Mercer had Bobby's door open and was gliding past it. His mentor was seated at his desk. But he wasn't alone. C.W. was standing beside the desk, pointing to papers that were laid out across its surface.

Both men stared at him, frozen in surprise.

"I, ah . . . I'm sorry. I didn't mean to interrupt . . . I'll come back."

"What's wrong?" Bobby asked. "If it's about our discussion at lunch . . ."

"No. This is . . . something else." Mercer tried to collect himself. His plan had been to tell Bobby about the Burris case, playing up to the partner's often expressed belief in the necessity of providing a defense for everyone, even those accused of the most reprehensible crimes. Then the two of them could confront C.W.

"I'll come back."

"You have something to say, spit it out." C.W. made it an order, not a request.

Well, it *would* get things moving faster. And C.W. had hopped all over his ass for blackjacking Burris on the stand. Maybe he'd see this as a way of mending fences with the LAPD. Or maybe not.   •

"It's a little complicated."

C.W. pulled a chair around and sat on it, staring at him. "Dumb it down for us."

He told them about Mildred Doremus's visit and her request. He neglected to mention a few things. He figured it would not help matters if they knew that Burris had planted a knife on Sweets Doremus or that the tape he, Mercer, had used to set Darion Mayfield free had been a fake. He sure as hell wasn't going to say anything about the sword that Burris and the Doremus woman were holding over his head. But he was clear on every other point.   •

When he finished, both men were silent for what seemed like an interminable time. Then C.W. shook his head and said, "No. The money's tempting, but it's bad business."

Bobby said, "What do you want to do, Mercer?"

"I want to take the case."

"There's no—" C.W. began, but Bobby waved him into silence.   •

"Go on, Mercer. Tell us why you want to defend him."

"Starting out, the cop's innocent. He was with Mildred Doremus."

"Assuming she's telling the truth," Bobby said. "Wasn't like she was under any oath sitting in your office."

"No, but—"

"If she's in love with the man, she's got a strong motive to lie for him."

"Yes, but—"

"And even if she's telling the truth, which is a highly speculative notion, it'll do nobody any good because she's not going to be appearing in court."

"I can win—"

"You do know why he wants you?" Bobby asked. "He thinks being defended by a black man will wipe off some of that racist taint. And if the same black man who was poor Darion's lawyer is willing to defend him, that by itself may be enough to give at least one juror reasonable doubt of his guilt."

Mercer understood all that. But he also had enough pride in his work to think that the cop had been impressed by the way he'd defended Darion Mayfield. "Do you think there's a conflict of interest?" he asked.

"Not legally, I suppose."

"That's the only real issue, isn't it?" Mercer said. "We're supposed to be defense lawyers, right? We don't judge our clients. We don't measure their guilt. We don't refuse to represent a client just because he may be unpopular."

He was a little surprised to see Bobby shifting in his chair in obvious discomfort.

"Those words came right out of your mouth, Bobby."

"It's nice to know that you've been listening. But you must have been asleep when I told you never to take a case that goes against your conscience. A bachelor lawyer may not have a problem defending an accused child molester, but for a lawyer who's got children, that's a different situation. It's not fair to him and it's not fair to the client."

"It's not fair to the firm," C.W. said. "The public relations fallout would be disastrous."

"For once we're saying the same thing, C.W.," Bobby said. "Or almost the same thing. Defending a racist cop charged with murdering a young black man . . ."

"A black man who was one of the firm's clients," C.W. said.

". . . that defense would be harmful to our *collective* conscience."

Mercer gave his mentor a look of profound disappointment. "This case is consistent with everything you taught me. You used Timothy McVeigh as an example, a damned baby killer and mass murderer. He had a right to a lawyer. I remember hearing you on CNN saying that any lawyer who refused to defend McVeigh was a hypocrite. Who the hell's the hypocrite now?"

Bobby seemed surprised by Mercer's attack, but not shamed or silenced. "Son, here's your lesson for today. First, like any man, McVeigh had a right to counsel. But not to counsel of his choice. Understand? And second, that's my daddy's name and my name on the front door. I will not have it sullied by our association with this maggot of a cop. Claude Burris is the latest in a long line of thugs who have used a badge to terrorize our community for years. I cannot in good conscience deny him the right to counsel. But happily I will deny him this firm's counsel. God, what would Kweisi Mfume say the next time I see him?"

"That hundred thousand," C.W. said to Bobby, "maybe Mercer should refer Mrs. Doremus to one of our former associates."

"Absolutely not. If the firm is even remotely involved in this trial, it will be to assist the district attorney in whatever way we can." He turned to Mercer. "And that's my final word."

Mercer said no more. What else was there to say?

Melissa interrupted his rush to his office. "Detective Virgil Sykes wants you to call. Is he . . . involved with anybody? Man has a very sexy voice."

"I don't know what his status is," Mercer said, barely giving it a thought. "You want to get him for me?"

"Yes, indeed."

His office reeked of Mildred Doremus's perfume. He searched his desk drawers for a match to burn off some of the odor. He was still looking when Melissa buzzed him that the LAPD detective was on the line.

"Enrique Sanchez is with his family," Virgil said. "He'd been hanging with some homeless badasses in the park. They worked him over a little. Busted his nose. Cracked a rib. Stole his shoes. Somehow he found his way to a people's clinic and they patched him up and notified his mama. She's taking care of him now."

"Thanks for checking it out," Mercer said glumly.

He immediately called the Sanchez home. Max picked up.

"Let me talk to Enrique," Mercer said.

"I know who this is," Max said. "Stay away from him. You give him bad ideas."

Mercer could think of no threat that would get him past Max. "Maybe it's you I want to talk to anyhow," he said. "If you ever try to bring harm to him again, I will fall on you like a sword of steel. That's a promise."

"Yeah, yeah," Max said. "Bye bye, and go fuck yourself, shyster."

The line went dead.

Replacing the receiver, Mercer tried to convince himself that Ricky was better off with a roof over his head, no matter how screwed up things were at his home.

Damn, what a day!

He got out Mildred Doremus's card. He might as well bring her up to date. Hell, maybe the partners' refusal would get him off the hook. How could he provide Burris with an adequate defense without the firm to back him up?

The scent of the woman's perfume floated up from her card. A little of it might have been okay, but she must've bathed in it.

It had become part of his office.

He grabbed his coat, deciding to call Mildred Doremus from his apartment, where the air was fresh and he could clear away the cobwebs with a vodka and Red Bull.

"Melissa," he said, "I don't care how you do it, but get that sweet stink out of my office."

"It's Animale."

"Smells like animal shit. Call maintenance. Maybe they got industrial-sized Odor Eaters or something."

Mercer headed out. Vanessa's office was still empty. He wondered if she'd ever made it back from lunch.

20

After the roughhouse at Robbery-Homicide, Mingus brushed himself off, patched up a little, and headed for the lab, where his friend Pascal informed him that the shard had been plastic, all right, "a part of some kind of dish, maybe. It has the letters 'ist' stamped into the surface. Manufacturer's name probably. But which one? That'll take some work to find out."

"Anything else?"

"Well, it looks like a residue of something on it. I can't tell more without cutting into it a little and you said you didn't want that."

"How much do you need?" Mingus asked.

"A real thin layer should do."

The detective told him to go ahead. Pascal promised him the results within forty-eight hours.

Mingus returned to his office. He stayed there until the sun went down, creating a report on everything he knew pertaining to Detective Dennis Farley's involvement in the investigation into the death of Darion Mayfield.

Then his thirst got the better of him and he went off the clock.

The Santa Anas were blowing through the city, tossing and twirling every piece of trash that wasn't nailed down as he drove south on Arlington. He noticed that everybody in the hood seemed be spending the night out of doors. No surprise, since their apartments were too hot for comfort and the wind, warm as it was, provided some relief.

Mingus's apartment would be cool enough, but he wasn't quite ready for it all the same.

At La Louisianne, a couple of women in their late forties were standing just past the entrance, jawing and sucking cigarettes that were outlawed inside. "How you doin', big man?" one of them said to Mingus as he approached.

"Fine, thanks."

"You hurt yourself?" another woman asked, gesturing toward his head with her cigarette. He touched his scalp, the pain reminding him of the gunshot wound. He'd removed the big adhesive patch and substituted one clear Band-Aid, but it evidently was still an eye-catcher.

"Nothin' serious," he said.

"I thought you mighta cut yourself shavin'?" she said.

She and her friends seemed to think that was hilarious. Mingus, whose sense of humor was poor when it came to his appearance, moved past them with his face burning. Jesus, what was happening to him that he had a bunch of grandmas dissin' him or hittin' on him, or whatever they were doin'?

He slapped hands with Big Timo, the security guard, gave a pound to a couple of regulars who had all but taken up permanent residence barside, then surveyed the scene. The place was jumping. A small jazz quartet was finishing a set, its leader giving props to the members of the group and letting the crowd know that the star of the show, Mr. Greg Rose, would be taking the stage in ten minutes.

Mingus dug Rose, who sang many of the seventies R&B hits he'd grown up with. He thought the performer's renditions of Harold Melvin and the Blue Notes' songs were better than Melvin's own. Rose sounded a lot like Teddy Pendergrass. Looked like him, too. Enough to have picked up the nickname, "Teddy *Pretend*ergrass."

Mingus couldn't imagine why the record labels weren't falling all over the man.

The detective had barely taken his seat when the sister fixing the drinks laid a small white napkin on the bar in front of him and set down his usual Thug Passion.

"Thank you, my beloved," he said, lifting the drink, sniffing it like a fine wine before taking a taste. He had one brief moment of pure pleasure. Then he began to wonder why he hadn't heard back from Ida Bevan. He hadn't expected her to drop everything to look up Alice Adapt's address for him, but how long could it take?

On the other hand, what did it matter now what the woman might or might not have seen the night of Darion's death? His killer, Claude Burris, was behind bars. That aspect of his investigation was finished. It hadn't done the job of nailing Farley to the wall, but it had given Mingus a hard look at how confident the fat man had become. Playing games with a witness. Screwing around with the murder book. Farley obviously felt he was living in clover.

Mingus took a bigger pull at the Thug Passion. There was definitely something fucked up with the Mayfield murder, but he didn't see any immediate way of finding out what it was. Farley wouldn't talk to him. Burris wouldn't talk to him. And Loc and Alice Adapts were still among the missing.

The drink was just starting to do its magic when he noticed the tall, fair lady seated across the bar. Miz High-Yella was giving him the eye. He had seen her before, a big, well-rounded woman, had even sent a drink or two her way. She had a couple of years on him but looked like she took pretty good care of herself.

She slid off the bar. As she passed Mingus, she said, "I'll be right back. Don't you go away."

She continued on in the direction of the restrooms.

Every male on that side of the bar turned to watch her swing her round, shapely ass into the john.

Mingus was happy to put his mind on something other than the job. It had been a while since he'd been with a woman. Particularly one so spectacularly proportioned. The night was filled with promise.

Fantasizing a little about things to come, he swung around on the stool and found himself face to face with Redd.

"Let me get this straight," she started in on him. "You'd fuck that fat old horse but you won't let me hit it?"

She ran her hand behind her neck, at the same time pushing her breasts tight enough against her T-shirt they almost popped out of her scarlet felt Ellen Tracy jacket. Then she tested her navy stretch pants by crossing one shapely leg over the other, nuzzling his calf with a red suede mule. "I must be losing my touch," she said.

For one brief moment Mingus thought she might be serious. Then she laughed lustily and said, "I don't know, Detective. Maybe I been fooling myself about your bedroom action if that old granny is the best you can do. She the one who beat you up?"

His hand automatically went to the wound on his scalp. "No, that was line of duty."

"What about that lump on your jaw?"

"That was just fun," he said, remembering how it felt bouncing Farley's head off the floor of Robbery-Homicide. "I didn't know you hung out here, Redd. This crowd seems a little . . . slow for a happenin' honey like yourself."

"I don't *hang out* here," she said, looking around. "Maybe I should. Some of these cat daddies look like they be carrying some cash on 'em." She gave him a wink and waved over the sister behind the bar, ordering a split of Moët.

"So what brings you here?" Mingus asked.

"You. This is your home away from home," she said. "I was wondering how your investigation is going."

"It's not so pressing now that they caught the Mayfield boy's killer," he said, watching her drop a hundred-dollar bill on the bar to pay for the champagne.

"You're a smart man, Mr. Mingus. That what you think?" She sipped her champagne, her eyes studying him over the rim of the glass. "That they caught the real killer?"

"You know something about it?"

"I know they arrested the wrong man."

Mingus frowned. "How's that? I heard they got him cold."

"He wasn't there," Redd said.

The big high-yella woman with the sexy figure passed by on her way back to her barstool. She turned to give Mingus a disappointed look. He shrugged.

"Guess I'm keeping you from something, huh?" Redd said. "Something more important than justice."

"What the hell you talking about?" He was suddenly annoyed. He didn't know if it was because she was messing up his plans for a romantic evening or because she was playing into his doubts about the Mayfield murder. "Since when do whores give a damn about justice?"

She stiffened and surprised him with the hurt look on her face. "I didn't mean . . ." he said. "I . . . aw, shit." He took another gulp of Thug Passion. The strong sweet taste of the liquor coupled with the strong sweet odor of Redd's perfume made him wish he'd ordered something a bit simpler, like an O'Doul's.

She cocked her head to one side and smiled. "You're right, Detective. I am a whore. Not a cheap one. And not a lyin' one. I'm speaking the truth when I say Claude Burris didn't kill that boy."

"What makes you so sure?" he asked.

"Let's us take a walk," she said.

"Why?"

" 'Cause what I got to tell you isn't for the street. You can bring yo' drink."

She slipped off the barstool and began to gather the change from her hundred. She took a twenty and waved it at the sister behind the bar. "This is for my uncle's cherry Coke," she said, pointing to Mingus's drink, which he was in the midst of shooting. "Keep the change."

On his way out, Mingus noticed with regret that the big sexy woman had settled for second best—a cat daddy with dyed jet-black hair and a gold front tooth.

Redd led him to a black Land Rover.

"What happened to your Caddy?"

"Think I got just one set of wheels? An expensive whore like me? Hell, I got a vehicle for every mood. Sometimes I feel like speed. Sometimes like luxury. Tonight, I felt like roughin' it."

Settled behind the wheel, she offered him a cigarette. When he refused, she lighted one for herself and broke her window to let some of the smoke escape.

"What you got to tell me, Redd?"

She studied him for a beat. Then said, "Claude Burris was with me when the boy was killed."

He wasn't sure he'd heard her right. "With you?"

"At my place. He and I been keeping company for a time."

"You and the cop? The white cop?"

"Love don't have no color," she said.

Man, he had to lay off that Courvoisier and Alize. Stuff was fucking up his sense of reality. He touched his wounded head. "You asked about this. Your fucking white cop shot me."

"When?" She seemed genuinely surprised.

Mingus told her about Burris drawing down on him just before his arrest.

"He didn't mean to shoot you. He's not like that."

"I got a creased skull says different."

"I tell you, I know Claude Burris. You don't love somebody and not know what kind of man he is."

"Love?" Mingus shook his head in disbelief.

"You don't think us *whores* ever fall in love?"

"You got a husband out at TI, right? And you hittin' the sheets with a white cop?"

"That's the way it is. And I'm not lying when I say he was with me that night the dope dealer got shoved."

"The whole time?"

"Least until I left to go meet you at Buckie's. Well after the deed been done."

Mingus stared at her, looking for some sign that she was lying.

"Didn't you ever wonder how I was able to get such good information on the streets? Hookin' in with a vice cop didn't hurt."

Mingus was having a hard time buying it. He felt he was being set up. He tried to move her into her pitch, whatever it was. "If Burris didn't kill the boy," he said, "who did?"

"Claude isn't sure. He thinks it might have been a Homicide cop. Irishman named Farley."

Mingus stared at her. "Burris got anything looks like proof?"

"The only proof I know of is me. I'm proof he didn't kill the boy."

"Then you wasting your time with me," he said. "Stand up at the D.A.'s."

"That's not gonna happen. Like you said, my husband is at TI, and this is how it is . . ." She explained the situation with Burris and Sweets Doremus.

"Burris and you were bumpin' before he arrested Sweets? Damn, Redd, you know better than to be telling me all this. I investigate cops for that kind of shit."

"I believe I can trust you, Lionel."

Long as he'd known the woman she had never used his first name before. He was trying to figure out how to deal with this new, vulnerable Redd, when she said, "You asked me a hunnert times what I wanted in exchange for my information. I been sayin' I'd collect on your debt later. The time has come."

He relaxed a little. They were back in familiar territory now. Wheeling and dealing. "So? You want me to go plant some fake evidence on Fats Farley so he can take Burris's place inside?"

"No, Lionel," she said. "I'd never ask you to do anything illegal. I just need you to do one thing: be a good
cop."

"Don't try and tell me how to do my job, woman."

"That's not what I'm saying. My man is innocent.
Somebody set him up and you gotta put things right."

"Why should I bust my ass for a cop who tried to part
my head?"

"Cuz he ain't no murderer. Cuz you owe me. Cuz I
have always looked out for you."

"Looked out for me how?"

Redd hesitated, then reached over him to open the
glove compartment. She removed a heavy object and
placed it in Mingus's hand. He knew from the cus-
tomized Houge pistol grip exactly what it was: the handgun stolen from him while he lay passed out at the
Kittyhawk.

"Where the hell . . . ?"

"I heard about what happened way back then. You
got your gun and badge taken away and then the white
girl got herself raped on the west side. I put the word
out I was in the market for the gun. It cost me dear, but
I bought it and put it away where nothing else could
happen to it. Or to you."

As good as the gun felt in Mingus's hand, his mind
started to fill with the memory of all those nights in all
the years he lay awake worrying about where the
weapon might be.

She must've read the thought on his face. "No way I
could give it to you back then."

"Why the hell not?"

"That was part of the deal I made. So I did the best I
could. I kept it in a safe place where it wouldn't do you
any harm."

"You get this from that fat cop?"

"They all look fat to me."

"Farley?"

"Never met the man."

"Maybe your goddamn boyfriend gave it to you?"

"Claude wouldn't do that kind of shit. I didn't get it from no cop."

"Who, then?"

"I can't tell you."

"The bastard didn't just steal from me. He beat and raped a woman."

"I know. But I can't name him. Not now. Maybe soon, but not now."

"What the hell does that mean?"

"It means I don't go back on my word, not even for you."

"Fuck that. I want this guy and I want him now. I can make you tell me."

"I don't think so," she said. "Dammit, Lionel, ain't it enough I got your gun for you?"

Mingus settled back against the leather seat and hefted the weapon in his hand. "I don't know about you, girl," he said. "I just don't know." He slipped the pistol into his waistband.

"Holdin' back stuff isn't the same as lying," she said. "Don't make the mistake of thinking I lie. And I surely ain't lying when I say Claude didn't kill that boy."

"Even if I believed you, the D.A. won't. They got an eyewitness who puts your man in the apartment at the time of the murder."

Redd gave him a crooked grin. "That crackhead, Loc? Some witness. Man'll say anything to keep the boys in blue off his ass."

"Why'd you send me to him in the first place?" Mingus asked.

"I wanted you to hear the bullshit he was spreading about Claude firsthand, while you could."

"You knew they were going to bottle him up?"

"Claude figured they'd want their little liar boy off the market till the trial."

"Why would cops use Loc to put another cop on the spot?"

"I guess for some reason—like maybe this Farley killed the boy—they needed somebody to blame," Redd said. "Claude made a damn good suspect."

Mingus had to admit it sounded plausible. That fat bastard Farley could have been yanking his chain, pretending to give Burris a free ride knowing that would lead Mingus into focusing on the vice cop. He could have prepped Loc to lie about seeing Burris. But what was Fats's motive for wanting Darion dead?

"What makes Burris think Farley is involved?" Mingus asked.

"I don't know. All I know is they used to be partners in the long ago."

"They must've had some serious breakup. Claude tell you about it?"

She shook her head. "He would've if I'd asked. It wasn't anything to me. Is it important?"

"Hell if I know," Mingus said. Through the car's windshield, he saw that the smokers were drifting back into LaLa's. Greg Rose was probably taking the stage.

"Claude's not just gonna roll over," Redd said. "We working on a plan, but it's got sidetracked a little."

Mingus's stomach growled. "They generally run out of fried catfish suppers pretty quick," he said. "You want to tell me about your plan, you better make it fast."

She explained that she had tried to secure the services of Mercer Early, the young attorney who had set the perjury trap for Burris. "Claude says the kid's good enough and sly enough to get him off. And the kid is willing, but the big dogs at his firm won't let him."

"What firm?"

"Carter and Hansborough. Top of the line."

Mingus was familiar with the firm. Thanks to his late uncle, the judge, he knew quite a bit about many of the law firms in the city. "They only represent brothers and sisters," he said. "They probably won't be changing that policy for a honky cop charged with killing one of their clients.

"Which reminds me, if your *man* is as innocent as you

say and he didn't have any ax to grind with Darion May-field, why'd he kick the boy and then lie about it in court?"

"He never kicked the boy."

That was all Mingus had to hear, a denial of proven fact. He reached for the door handle. "They got a tape sayin' he did."

"It's fake."

"Yeah. Sure it is. I'm missing my dinner, Redd."

She clutched his arm. "The lawyer who was set to de-fend Claude on the perjury case got a copy of the tape. I took it to one of my homies, a rapper named G-Spot, who's got a studio in his garage. He showed me how it wasn't even a good fake."

The bullet ridge along Mingus's scalp started to tingle.

"When you slow the speed down, you can hear a voice in the background saying, 'this tape is doctored; this tape is bullshit' over and over."

Mingus was getting tired of her story. He could see the last breaded catfish dinner being set before some-body else, probably the old dude with the gold tooth who'd already profited enough from Redd's interrup-tion. "If the tape was bullshit, and easily recognized as such, what was the goddamn point?" he asked.

"At first Claude thought it was a warning Farley was sending him. The perjury case would be tossed out, but it'd give him an idea of the trouble he'd be in if he didn't keep his nose out of Darion's business. Then the May-field boy was killed and Claude figured the doctored tape served another purpose. It made folks look to him for the murder."

"I'm a simple man, Redd. Somebody starts talking about conspiracies or three- or four-step crimes, my in-clination is to go get myself a drink."

"Go ahead and get your drink and your food. And your hot big ol' grandma. Don't worry about repayin' me for the years of keepin' you informed or for getting your gun back. But don't call me again, Lionel. We got nothing more to say to one another."

"What the hell you want me to do, woman?"

"Somebody got to give Loc a shot of truth juice."

"I can't find the son of a bitch."

"The other thing, the big thing we need is that boy lawyer, Mercer Early, to defend Claude."

Mingus's patience was decreasing in direct proportion to the increase in his hunger. "You're losing me, Redd. Early was Mayfield's lawyer. You don't think he was part of the fake tape deal?"

"The young man's too straight up and Carter-Hansborough's too high and mighty to let him play like that."

"You'd be surprised what Carter-Hansborough might do."

"You got something on the firm? That's what I was hopin', Lionel."

Because of his late uncle, the judge, he did have a card to play. But he wasn't sure he wanted to. "It's not the way I do business."

"My man's innocent," she said. "They gonna drop the pill on him."

Dammit, he did owe the woman. And it would give him a chance to pump Burris for whatever he knew about Farley. "Lemme see what I can do," he told her. "But I need a sitdown with yo' boyfriend first."

"I'll take care of that tonight," she said.

He wondered whom she'd have to pressure to get through to a prisoner at night, but he didn't bother asking because he knew she wouldn't say.

"You do that."

"Okay. Uh . . . if you happen to meet Mercer Early at the lawyers'," she said, "it might be better if you don't mention you and me are acquainted."

He frowned at her. What was this now?

"No big thing," she said, answering a question he hadn't actually spoken. "It's just me and him got . . . issues. It'd confuse things."

"I don't plan on seeing your Mister Early," he said. "If I pay the firm a visit, it'll be the big boys I'll be talking to. Now go give Burris the word and let me grab what-ever's left of the night."

Before he could get the door open, Redd leaned over and planted a kiss on his cheek. "Thank you, Lionel."

He stood on the sidewalk in front of La Louisianne watching her drive away, his face burning from the kiss. He felt the gun pressing against his stomach under his coat. He patted it. It gave him a sense of comfort he hadn't had in six years.

21

Mercer sat at the counter that separated his kitchenette from his living room, staring at a silent but active television screen. Elsewhere in the room, the view through sliding glass doors proved conclusively that it was night, but the sports network was insisting that it was a bright sunny day at Malibu with girls in bikinis engaged in a furious game of volleyball. Ordinarily, a sporting event of that magnitude would have captured at least a small fragment of his interest, but he might as well have been watching paint dry. From time to time he remembered to sip from a vodka and Red Bull he'd made so long ago the ice had melted.

His last conversation with Mildred Doremus—or Redd, as she had insisted he call her—had not gone well. She didn't care if the partners had ordered him not to take the case. "Claude wants you to represent him," she'd said flatly. "And that's what you're gonna do. You got him into this with your fake tape and you're gonna get him out. Unless you'd prefer to be Alabamy bound."

"I can't take on a trial like that without the firm backing me up. I need researchers, jury experts, investigators . . ."

"You're gonna have a hunnert grand. Buy yourself some help. Thanks to that asshole lawyer the union stuck Claude with, the trial's almost on us."

That'd been her last word.

He considered fixing a fresh drink, but he really didn't want one. There were times when booze was a nice leveler, smoothing out the rough edges, but at the moment, smoothing was not what he needed.

He needed a main plan and a backup plan.

Actually, he was prepared for the latter. In his bedroom closet, stuck in the pocket of a dirty wool poncho, was a plastic pouch containing a birth certificate, a driver's license, and a Visa card. The credit card and the license were illustrated by his photos. All three items of identification carried a name that was nothing like his own.

He was resigned to the fact that the situation he'd left behind in Alabama would remain unchanged forever. He was wanted in connection with a death by drug overdose. He could think of nothing that would alter that fact or remove the consequences. He would always be a wanted man, and for that reason he'd decided to have another change of identity in the hopper.

He'd almost convinced himself that he was safe, all those years and several thousand miles away from trouble. But Redd and her vice cop had proven just how vulnerable he was. So, what to do?

As much as he hated Burris for dredging up his past and using it as a weapon to hold over him, he realized that he was actually eager to defend the son of a bitch.

He believed that Burris was innocent. He also believed that he was at least partially responsible for the cop's predicament. It was the goddamned tape recording. He should have checked it out. Hell, C.W. had been right: he went for the grandstand play instead of meeting with Gomez and showing him the tape. The deputy D.A. would definitely have tested it and that would have been that. Darion Mayfield may have wound up in prison, but he'd be alive. Burris would be hitting the sheets with the Doremus woman, and the only thing Mercer would be worrying about was . . .

Vanessa.

He looked at his watch and wondered if it was too late to call her. He thought that hearing her voice might help to push him in the right direction, whatever that was.

He picked up the phone and dialed her home.

No answer.

He looked at his watch again.

Frowning, he tried her cellular phone. She answered on the second ring. In the background he could hear hearty male laughter and the clink of glasses. "Hello?"

"Me, honey," he said.

"It's after eleven," she said. "I figured."

Someone called her name, a man's voice he didn't recognize.

"I just wanted to—" Mercer said.

"I'm sorry," she interrupted him. "I really can't talk now. See you in the morning at the office."

And the phone went dead.

Shit.

So much for help from his beloved.

He tried to shift his mind back to Burris and the trial. But now he had to deal with jealousy which was overriding even the desire for self-preservation.

He was unable to sit still. He began to pace. When that didn't work, he decided he had to get out, take a drive. The drive ended on the shady residential street where Vanessa lived.

He knew he was behaving at best like a teenage puke, at worst like some demented stalker. He left his car and walked to the barred door leading to her underground garage. He spied her yellow Porsche Boxter parked in its spot on the aisle.

Good. She was back home.

He walked into the street and looked up to the third floor. Her windows were dark.

He returned to his car and dialed her apartment.

No answer.

He dialed her cellular.

She was off-line.

Annoyed, jealousy really kicking in, he settled in behind the wheel. There he waited, alternately experiencing anger, frustration, and self-disgust, until way past midnight, when a silver Bentley sedan rolled up in front of her apartment. A Bentley, for Christ's sake.

He watched Barry Fox get out, circle the car and open the door for Vanessa. Together, they walked into her building. A couple minutes later, the lights went on in her apartment.

Sick at heart, Mercer drove home.

22

Once Redd had gone, Mingus changed his mind about going back inside LaLa's, even though he could hear Greg Rose working his magic on "Turn Out the Lights," a Teddy Pendergrass classic. He was going to have a busy morning, and a hangover wouldn't help.

He picked up a bag of burgers on the way home.

He was working on burger one when the apartment phone rang.

Ida Bevan's voice was slurred by drink and accompanied by electronic static. "Hope I din' innerup' anything," she said.

"Just my dinner, Ida."

"You're a prick, ya know?"

Mingus sighed. "Rough night, huh?"

"Like you care." The combination of her attitude and the static was starting to annoy him.

"You got something for me? Or did you just phone to bust my balls?"

"Nobody named Alice Adapts has ever written a movie anybody's ever heard of."

"Well, thanks anyway for—"

"There is a writer named Alice *Adams*, now. Wrote that piece of shit, *The Price of Sisterhood*."

Adams. Considering the way Ken Loc's busted nose had been messing with his speech, that might work.

"Like some white bitch knows the first thang about sisterhood."

Mingus was actually familiar with the movie: life in South Central as seen through the eyes of three teenage girls. Thinking about it made him feel bad. Not because of the movie itself, which he'd hated, but because he couldn't bring to mind which of his old flames had dragged him to it. He didn't think it was Ida. He was a man who remembered old movies but not old loves. No wonder he was still living alone at his age.

"You there, Li'nel?"

"Yeah. Sorry. Sounds like this Alice Adams might be the one."

"You sure picked yo'se'f a fine new playmate." He imagined Ida sitting at the counter of the barely used kitchenette in her expensive apartment, swigging from a bottle of Remy. "Miz Alice Adams got a pretty low rep, even by yo' standards. Rumor is she's stoned half the time."

"You got an address, Ida?"

"A crackhead who still gets A-movie assignments. Tell me how your playmate manages that, Li'nel."

"You know a hell of a lot more about her than I do," he said. "But when I see her, I'll ask."

Ida Bevan slurred a phone number and an address in the Hollywood Hills. "Jus' ask her if she needs new representation."

"Thanks, Ida. I appreciate this."

"Sure you do. Only, Li'nel, don't call me for any more fuckin' favors," she said, hanging up.

Fair enough, he thought.

He picked up the phone again and was dismayed to discover that the static was still there. He wiggled the receiver cord and that seemed to clear it up a little. He punched in the numbers Ida provided. One ring. Two. Three. Then a throaty voice saying, "I'm here, honey. Where the hell are you?"

"Alice Adams?"

Momentary silence, then, "Who is this?"

"My name is Lionel Mingus. I'm—"

"Who?"

"Lionel Mingus. I'm a detective with—"

"Leave me alone, for God's sake. I don't know anything. I've already told you people that."

"I'm sorry, Miz Adams. What people we talking about? Somebody with the LAPD?"

"I don't need this aggravation. I'm very busy. Don't call again."

For the second time in less than five minutes, a woman had hung up on him. He stared at the remnants of his fast-food dinner, rapidly turning as chilly as his brief conversation with Alice Adams. He got down only two more bites before the phone rang again. He stared at it warily until curiosity got the better of him.

"It's all set, Detective," Redd informed him without protocol. "Claude'll be expectin' you tomorrow morning at nine."

"Good," he said, scowling at the static. "You hear that?"

"Bad connection," she said. "I gotta go, Detective. Give gran'ma a big wet kiss for me."

"No gran'ma here," he said.

"You poor lonely man. Want Redd to come over to put you to sleep?"

"Appreciate the offer, but I got a little work to do yet."

"Awww," she said. "You know what they say about all work. Later, Detective."

At least she didn't go away mad.

He finished the burgers and fries, washing them down with a soda instead of the beer he'd opened. He could still feel the effect of the earlier Thug Passions and he wanted to be as sober as possible when he forced himself on the already spooked Alice Adams.

An evening concert was in progress at the Hollywood Bowl which meant, though every spare inch of curbing in the vicinity was occupied by parked cars, the streets were relatively empty.

Heading up Outpost Drive, Mingus lowered his windows to listen to the music. Something thunderous. Classical, maybe, but judging by the few times he'd wound up at the Bowl, more likely a movie score.

He was turning onto Impala Road, paying a little too much attention to the music, when a dark sedan came barreling down the narrow, car-lined street heading straight for him with the force of a bullet train.

With a curse, he shot the Crown Vic into a driveway, moving too fast to straighten out. His left rear wheel caught the curb, twisting the car and throwing him against the steering wheel. He jammed his foot on the brake pedal and managed to stop a few inches shy of the front of a million-dollar residence. Behind him, the sedan—what the hell was it, a big Mercedes maybe?—zoomed down the road with the blare of its horn and, Mingus thought, the sound of laughter.

Shaken, his face coated with tension sweat, he pried his fingers from the steering wheel. He took a few deep breaths and began the process of backing away toward the now-safe street, trying not to damage the strip of front lawn any more than he already had.

Stone sober and on full alert, he continued up Impala Road, following the street as it turned into Impala Terrace, a cul-de-sac. Number seventeen was a ranch-style home overlooking the Bowl. It sat in darkness, outlined by the glow from the lights below. Mingus supposed Alice Adams had to be pretty successful at her screenwriting, being able to afford a house in that location and a heavy-duty coke habit to boot.

He pulled into her drive and parked behind a green Ford Explorer so new it was still using a dealer card for a license plate. Less than an hour ago, when he'd talked to the woman, she'd sounded a little too high strung to be heading for bed. More likely, the dark house meant she'd gone out.

But the Explorer was there.

A second car, maybe. Or the "honey" she'd been expecting to call her had picked her up. He should have left his place sooner. But, as long as he'd made the trip . . .

He got out his cellular and dialed her number.

He heard the phone ringing inside the house. Heard it too clearly, easily cutting through the Bowl's crescendos.

He got out of his car. As he approached the house, he saw that the heavy front door was standing open. Through it, he heard Alice Adams's voice, but it was on an answering machine responding to his call. From what he could see, the interior of the place was lit by the glow coming from the Bowl below, filtered through a glass wall at the rear. "Yo, anybody home?" Mingus called out.

He didn't expect an answer.

Maybe Alice Adams left in such a hurry she forgot to close the door. Or maybe . . . something else.

He backtracked to his car and popped the trunk where he kept his bag of tricks. He removed latex gloves, a penlight, and a little Berretta he'd picked up on his travels. He rolled on the gloves, clipped the pen light to his top pocket, and stuck the gun in his belt. Then, just to play it safe, he also worked a pair of rubber galoshes over his shoes.

"Anybody home?" he called out again, before entering the house. "LAPD."

His overshoes squeaked as he crossed the parquet entryway and stepped down to a slightly recessed living room. The furniture, what he could make of it without clicking on the penlight, was standard California casual. A couch with plump suede pillows and matching easy chairs. A coffee table containing magazines, newspaper sections, a glass, and a wine bottle. And something else.

He clicked on the penlight and aimed it at the table. The wine bottle, an inch or two from empty, had a label identifying it as a merlot from the vineyards of a famous movie director. The dregs in the glass were fresh. Some of it had spilled on the table. The object that had moved him to use the light rested beside the bottle, a large black enamel tile containing three lines of white powder and the remnants of another few lines. On the carpet next to the table was a large plastic baggie containing what looked like maybe a half pound of dope.

Mingus was impressed by the quantity, but also disturbed by the presence of the three unused lines. He didn't know many crackheads who'd walk away from the table leaving such a nice, neat, tempting display.

The circle of light picked up something else on the beige carpet. A line of wine drops leading away from the table. Or, since the bottle and glass were still on the table, maybe leading toward it. Or maybe the drops weren't wine.

He studied the splotches on the table. A little thick for merlot.

Man, he wanted a drink.

He followed the drops across the carpet to a sliding glass door leading to a patio and lighted pool. There were more of them on the flagstone surface of the patio.

The door slid open easily, letting in night air that was almost chilly so high in the hills. The music from the Hollywood Bowl below seemed familiar. He realized he knew the words. "Flintstones, we're the Flintstones." The orchestra was treating the cartoon theme song as if it were a symphony. The dumbbell song lyrics kept popping into Mingus's head as he followed the splatters to a chaise longue near the pool.

The waterproof cover of the chaise was smeared with blood.

Abba-dabba-fucking-do.

The body was on the tiles just beyond. It seemed to have slid from the chaise. It was feminine, compact, motionless, except for the fluttering of blond hair tendrils in the cool night breeze. He assumed it was the lady of the house, dressed in tight faded jeans and an antique white blouse with its sleeves rolled to just above the elbow. Some of the blood from a deep cut across her left wrist had been absorbed by the shirt, but most of it had drained over the patio tiles to the pool's gutter, where it turned the lighted water a cloudy pink.

Mingus pressed his index finger against the woman's neck. No pulse. In the corpse's right hand was a bloody razor blade, probably the same one she'd used to do her lines. It had served double duty. Her arms were striped with scar tissue. As Ken Loc had told him, she'd been a cutter. But Loc had been wrong. Cutting wasn't about sex. It was about pain. Mingus had had it explained to him a while back by a shrink who'd said pain and mental anguish built up in cutters to the point where they felt they had to slice themselves to reduce the pressure.

He guessed that's what Alice Adams had been doing, only she was so stoned she cut a little too deep and ended her pain forever.

He wondered how long it had taken her to bleed out. Ten minutes? Five?

The blood hadn't done much congealing on that cool night. She hadn't been a corpse very long. If he hadn't finished his dinner . . . No. No sense going there.

He retraced his steps to the front of the house and out. There wasn't anything he could do to help Alice Adams and he sure as hell wouldn't be helping himself if he stuck around to explain why he was there and why he'd entered the house illegally.

On his way down the hill, he phoned in the death anonymously to the Wilshire station, thereby avoiding the 911 Caller ID system. He was halfway home when he started thinking like a cop again. Had the bag of blow been part of Darion Mayfield's missing stash? he wondered. An even more pertinent question: if Alice Adams had accidentally killed herself, as he'd originally assumed, why had her front door been open when he arrived?

23

"**I**'m going to defend Claude Burris," Mercer said. He'd just burst into Bobby Carter's office and had stopped far enough to the right of his mentor's desk to avoid having to stare into the bright morning sun.

"No, you're not," Bobby replied, almost cheerfully, and took a sip from his mug.

"You don't understand."

"Sit down, son. You look like you just staggered out of one of the lower depths of hell. Need some coffee?"

Mercer felt himself falling under the man's magic and shook free of it. "No coffee, Bobby. Look, I got to get this straight."

"Hear me out first." Bobby placed his cup on his desk beside a neat manilla folder.

Mercer noticed that Bobby's mug was decorated by a caricature of him in top hat and tails. Under that was the nickname "Mr. Smooth." He was that, sure enough.

Bobby picked up the folder. "I've just been going over your personnel file," he said. "I think it's time we closed it out."

Mercer blinked. He was being fired! He'd come in to give Bobby an ultimatum, either he be allowed to defend Claude Burris or he'd quit. It looked like Bobby and C.W. had already made up their mind on that score.

"If that's the way you want to play it," he said.

"You think that little fight we had about the racist cop changed my feelings toward you?" Bobby said. "It'd take a hell of a lot more than that."

Mercer wanted to believe him, but the "racist cop" comment made him wary.

"Lawyers fight and disagree all the time," Bobby continued. "It's in our nature. It's what we are trained to do, what we get paid to do."

"Where exactly are we headed with this, Bobby? You firing me, or what?"

For a moment, Bobby Carter looked like a lot of the witnesses he had cross-examined, a man trying to decide whether he should tell nothing but the truth, a small part of it, or lie like a rug. "I think you know C.W. wants the firm to get out of the criminal law business," Bobby said. "His plan is to concentrate on civil litigation, catering to several big clients."

"I'm aware of that," Mercer said. "He calls the cases I handle 'petty cash,' though that's certainly not true of the Burris case. I'm also aware that you don't agree with C.W. Lemme see if I can quote you. 'We cannot turn our backs on the people who got us here. As long as there exists a disproportionate . . .'"

". . . a disproportionate number of black men filling our prisons and awaiting their fate along death row," Bobby said, completing his own statement, "the firm of Carter and Hansborough will remain in the practice of criminal law."

"That's why I've been bringing talented and dedicated young men like yourself into the firm these many years. But those days are coming to a close, I fear. C.W.'s going to have his way."

"Why?"

"I'm taking a leave of absence," Bobby said. "If things work out like I hope, I may be gone quite a while."

"What things work out?"

"George Heathrow has asked me to join his team in a rather major position."

"Lieutenant governor?"

"If he'd offered me that, I might have turned him down. No, George is giving me the chance to do some serious ass kicking in the way justice is handed out in the state. He wants me to be his chief law officer."

"Attorney general?"

"You better believe it."

Mercer found himself grinning along with his mentor. But the feeling of elation lasted only until he realized the full impact of the news on his situation. "I'm happy for you, Bobby," he said. "But I guess I can see now why you're telling me my days here are over. Even if C.W. didn't hate my ass, soon he'll have no more use for criminal lawyers."

"I think I've got that covered," Bobby said. "You leave with me."

"What?"

"Join us on the campaign trail, Mercer," Bobby said, "and, the Lord willing, in Sacramento. I want you to be my right hand."

Mercer was stunned.

"Think about it, son. Once we get to the capital, you can take your pick. Start out poking around the division of criminal law, figuring out how to improve the way justice is served. Then move on to civil law or any of the other divisions. Looking on down the road, when it comes time for me to run for governor, you can take a step up yourself."

It was an amazing offer. But it solved none of his current problems. Quite the contrary.

"What do you think?" Bobby asked, a wide smile on his friendly open face.

"It's a beautiful plan," Mercer said.

"Sounds like there's a 'but' coming," Bobby said.

"I've got to defend Claude Burris."

Bobby's face seemed to turn older and harder. "You'd throw away your career for this fucking racist cop?"

"What makes you think he's a racist?"

"You proved it in court," Bobby said.

"That's one of the reasons I have to defend him. I didn't prove jack shit in that trial. My so-called evidence—the tape recording that nailed him—was a fake."

Bobby was momentarily speechless. "You knowingly used manufactured evidence?"

"I didn't know it wasn't real. Somebody used me to destroy the man's reputation and set him up as a prime murder suspect."

Bobby mulled that over, then said, "The only reputation you sullied with that evidence is the firm's. Burris's reputation was in dispute before you even got out of law school."

"He didn't kill Darion Mayfield."

"You don't know that. The woman you talked to, what makes you think she's playing straight with you? I'll tell you what your problem is, son: you've got a messiah complex. You think only you can save this son of a bitch?"

"I don't see any other messiahs stepping forward."

"Don't do this foolish thing, son. I'm giving you a chance at a brilliant future, a chance to make some changes in the lives of all our brothers and sisters. Don't give that up for some cracker cop."

Mercer was tempted to tell his mentor about his fugitive status, that his secret tied him to Burris's defense just as it denied him the hope of a political career. But he couldn't see any benefit from such a disclosure. Instead, he said simply, "I have no choice."

"I don't usually make mistakes about people," Bobby said, looking Mercer hard in the eye. What he saw seemed to defeat him. He slumped back against the chair. "If you are committed to this idiocy, you better clear out now," he said, turning to face the window. "I don't want you anywhere near this firm."

Mercer took his time leaving, hoping that Bobby would stop him, tell him they would at least part on a friendly note.

That didn't happen.

Out on the floor, he wandered toward his office in a daze.

On the way, he passed the voluptuous receptionist, Darnella, leading a big, very black man with a Band-Aid on his dome in the direction of the partners' offices. The man, who was clutching a scarred leather briefcase, stared at him as if he might know him. Mercer didn't think he'd ever seen him before.

His attention was diverted by a couple waiting for the elevator—the weasel Joe Wexstead and Jerome Coulter's klepto granddaughter. The girl's reaction, when she saw Mercer, was to stick her tongue out at him and casually place her hand on Wexstead's crotch. The weasel nearly jumped a foot. Ah, young love.

As Mercer passed Vanessa's office, she waved him in. "Well?" she asked, happy as a lark.

"Well what?"

She hesitated, surprised that he didn't seem to share her cheeriness. "Didn't you and Bobby just have a talk about your future?" she asked.

"You know about that?"

Her smile returned. "I had dinner at Daddy's last night. Bobby was there."

"And Barry Fox," Mercer said.

She was momentarily flustered. "Yes. Barry was there," she said. "They were discussing the wonderful news about Bobby. And he mentioned his plans for you. It's a great opportunity."

"You wouldn't mind moving to Sacramento?"

"Oh. Well, actually . . . I . . . was thinking . . . it's not that far away. I mean, it's less than an hour by plane. We'd have weekends . . ."

He sighed and was reminded of a primary rule of the legal profession: never ask a question unless you are sure of the answer. "You won't come with me?"

"I guess I could," she said, "but . . . some couples even manage to work on different coasts."

"It doesn't matter," he said. "I'm not going anywhere. Except out of here."

"What are you saying?"

"I turned Bobby down."

"Why, in God's name . . . ?"

"I'm going to be too busy defending Claude Burris."

She couldn't have been more shocked if he'd slapped her. "I thought . . . Daddy said the firm—"

"The firm won't be defending him," Mercer said. "Just me."

"But—"

"I got a hundred things to do," he said. "Why don't we talk about this over dinner?"

"Tonight? Umm, I . . ."

"Or not," he said.

"No," she said. "Dinner tonight. My place?"

"Let's make it mine," he said. He didn't feel comfortable at her apartment. It always seemed like she was following him around, slipping coasters under his glass or tidying up in his wake. "Eight okay?"

"Eight will be fine," she said, blessing him with a smile that just a few days ago might have melted his heart.

24

Mingus thought the young man he'd passed in the hall looked like he'd just had the rug pulled out from under him. That figured. He recognized Mercer Early from a photo in the *L.A. Times* that had accompanied an article on Darion Mayfield's acquittal. Thanks to an uncommon memory for faces, the detective thought he'd seen Early in LaLa's a few times, too.

"This way, sir," the extraordinarily fine young sister said, hoping to move Mingus along. Her exaggerated professional tone underlined the point that once she had delivered him to the office of Cordelu W. Hansborough III, she never expected nor wanted to see him again.

She turned him over to Hansborough the three's secretary, or assistant, or whatever the hell the current name was for a black hightone who spent her day sitting in front of a closed door waiting for her buzzer to sound. She let him cool his heels for five minutes or so, then walked to the closed door, knocked once, and stuck her head in. "Mr. Mingus to see you," she announced.

"Good. Good," the man in the corner office said. "Show him in."

The woman gave Mingus the barest hint of a smile

and gestured toward the open door. The room he entered was large and bright, so full of windows it reminded him of a time he'd chased a perp along the top floor of an unfinished building.

Hansborough was circling his desk, a tall man in shirtsleeves, offering a hand.

"It's Detective Mingus, right? That's what you said on the phone."

"That's right, sir. Detective Lionel Mingus."

"Well, have a seat, Lionel, if I may call you that."

"Sure," Mingus said.

"C.W. is what people call me," the lawyer said, leaning back against his desk. "You were a little vague on the phone, Lionel. Said it was something about your uncle. Judge Fred was a fine jurist and a good friend of my daddy's. Mine, too, of course. We were all very sad when he passed away. Is this about your aunt?"

"Not exactly," Mingus said. "Isn't Mr. Carter gonna join us?"

"He'll be just a minute. How about a cup of coffee while we wait?"

Mingus said that would be fine.

He was starting to have his regrets about being there. His meeting with Claude Burris at twin towers, the county's new high-security jail, first thing that morning had left him with conflicting feelings about the man. He had serious doubts that Burris had killed Darion Mayfield, but that didn't make the vice cop a saint or even somebody he wanted to go to the mat for. In fact, Mingus thought the guy was a cracker and probably crooked as a corkscrew.

Even though his girlfriend, Redd, had set up the meeting, Burris, slouched in his chair in the sparsely furnished interview room, had seemed guarded and suspicious. "Your head don't look so bad," he told Mingus, breaking the ice. "It was your own damn fault the gun went off."

"Let's forget about me and concentrate on Darion Mayfield."

"I was at my place with Redd when he got what was coming to him."

"A witness puts you at the building."

"I wasn't there. Not at any time that day or night. Anybody says different is a fucking liar. Look, I'm coming up for retirement. Would I blow that and all my years on the job, just to squash that little turd?"

It had sounded right, but Mingus had been on the job long enough to realize that nobody knows what they'll do, given the right set of circumstances.

"You ever hear of a woman named Alice Adams?"

"We get the news in here, you know. She offed herself last night. She connected to Darion?"

"I heard she might have been one of his customers."

"Then she's better off now."

Nice man, Mingus thought. He asked, "What's up with your hard-on for Dennis Farley?"

Burris's eyes glazed over. "I got nothing to say about that."

"I'm here because our mutual friend asked me to help you," Mingus said. "Even if that wasn't the case, you been on the job long enough to know that nothing you tell an Internal Affairs officer can be used against you in court, long as it's not you I'm investigating. So if you and Farley got some history you're worried about, you can unlax. It's *his* sins I'm interested in."

"I partnered with the son of a bitch and I know that fucking with him never made anybody healthier. But I'm not afraid of him. I don't have anything on him to give up. Just suspicions."

"That's a start."

"There's been a hell of a lot of drugs funneled through Inglewood for a long time. Back six or seven years ago, when Farley and me were partnered up, we were on Bumpy Lewis's ass more often than his Levi's. But we never seemed to be able to catch him holding or selling. Then he gets careless, in more ways than one. First, he takes up with a little gal who's got a big habit and a mouth to match. She tells our mutual red-headed friend that Bumpy places all the cash he gets from his street hustlers in a little tin box. Every other night, he takes the box out of his safe and goes off with it, all by his lonesome. Doesn't trust his stooges. He comes back with the box empty."

"Making a night deposit," Mingus said, "but probably not at Wells Fargo."

"I got it all set up to follow him on one of his night deposits," Burris said. "But before that can happen, Bumpy does a little freebase and barbecues himself and the girlfriend. At least, that's how it got written up." He paused, then added. "By my old pard, Farley, who, next time I look, is top man at RHD."

Mingus felt a chill and wondered if Burris's paranoia was starting to infect him. "You sayin' Bumpy's death wasn't an accident and Farley was messed up in it?"

"Bumpy was a moron who used his own product, but he knew enough about drugs not to set himself on fire. And the woman burning, too, is pretty damn convenient."

"If Darion Mayfield was the next in line, maybe it was him held the match."

"Darion didn't have the balls. I studied these guys, Mingus. I know 'em. Bumpy was fronting for somebody else, and so was Darion. When they got too stupid, they were goners."

"Who's doing the dealing now?"

"I don't know. Maybe this Ken Loc weasel." That prospect seemed to excite Burris. "Yeah. That'd explain why he's lying about seeing me. He's the goddamned key, Mingus. Get to him."

The detective did not share Burris's enthusiasm. He doubted anybody would be dumb enough to trust Ken Loc with even an ounce of low grade, much less a whole street shop. Still, Loc was at the top of his to-see list. "Soon as I find out where the RHD boys are keeping him."

"I hear they're looking for him, too," Burris said.

That was interesting news, if true. "I'll check on it,"

Mingus said. "Meanwhile, you got anything at all linking Farley to the drug operation?"

"You mean like proof? Hell no, or I wouldn't be sitting on this side of the bars."

"Well, here's the thing," Mingus said. "You're telling me it's Farley who's tied in with the drug operation. A suspicious person might wonder if it wouldn't make more sense for it to be a vice cop. Maybe one who got so big for his britches his bosses put him in a murder frame to show him the error of his ways."

Burris's face reddened. "I figured this meeting was a mistake," he said. "Maybe Redd thinks you can walk on water, but I say you're just another just IAG puke with an ax to grind. Probably get a large charge out of bustin' white cops. Well, fuck you and the slave boat that brought you."

Burris leaped from his chair, knocking it over with a loud clatter. He pounded on the door. "I'm through in here," he shouted to the guard.

The slave boat that brought him. Dammit. Sitting in C.W. Hansborough's office, Mingus felt his face burn at the memory of Burris's last words. What the hell was he doing there, anyway, about to go up against two very powerful men just to help that cracker son of a bitch?

Thinking rationally, he knew he wasn't doing it for Burris. He was there to show Redd he could walk on water. Why that was important he couldn't say. But it was.

Robert Carter joined them, a trim, expensively dressed brother who exuded the sort of quiet dignity that Mingus admired even though he didn't want to. When C.W. had performed the introductions, Carter asked, "What's this meeting all about, Detective?"

"A fellow I know needs a good criminal lawyer," Mingus said.

Carter said, "We have the best. What's your friend's problem?"

"He's not my . . ." Mingus had to censor himself.

"They say he committed murder. Look, I'm talking about Claude Burris. He wants one of your associates, Mercer Early, to handle his case."

C.W. blinked, but Carter didn't. He was immediately in Mingus's face. "Let me get this straight, brother. You come in here trading on your late uncle's name, expecting that to be enough to get us to represent a dirty cop who killed a client of ours?"

"Man says he didn't do it."

"That's not the point," Carter said. "Who gives a damn if he did it or not? We're talking about the man. This firm would never represent such a client." He stared at C.W. "Not as long as I'm still an active partner here."

"If we could just talk about the firm for a minute," Mingus said, opening the briefcase, "there's something I'd like to show—"

Mingus paused to stare at a handsome big black woman who'd just arrived at the doorway.

"Sorry to interrupt, gentlemen," she said, "but, Bobby, you've got a call from Mr. Fox. Says it's important."

Bristling, Carter said, "I'm through here, anyway," and stalked from the room, taking a whole load of tension with him.

C.W. sighed. "Well, Detective, I'm afraid that about covers it. I'm sorry."

Mingus shifted in the leather chair, hand still inside the briefcase. "If you bear with me, I'm not quite finished."

"Something you want to show me?"

"I'd like to wait till Mr. Carter gets back," Mingus said, bringing his hand out empty, "so I only have to go through it once."

The lawyer frowned. "My partner is pretty adamant. I doubt there's anything you can tell us that'll change his mind."

Mingus glanced at the open briefcase. His uncle had given it to him a while back for safekeeping. He'd been curious about its contents, but his uncle had trusted him not to peek inside and he had not betrayed that trust. Until the old man's death. Then he'd discovered a ledger indicating that several firms, from the high to the low, had been slipping His Honor Fred Mingus a little somethin' somethin' under the table in exchange for special favors. When the original Carter and Hansborough had hung out their shingle, times had been tough for a black-owned, black-only law firm. They'd cut a deal for his uncle to favor them when appointing defense attorneys. This had resulted in millions of dollars over the years, a percentage of which was returned in cash to his Uncle Fred. Mingus hadn't really warmed to the idea of blackmailing the law partners with the sins of their fathers. But he was feeling a little better about it, now that he'd met the two men. "I'd still like to give it a shot," he said.

C.W. glanced at his watch. "Why don't I ask his girl how long he'll be?"

He reached for the phone, but before he could pick it up, Bobby Carter entered the room, his face void of all expression.

"Bobby," C.W. said, "Detective Mingus would like just a few more minutes of—"

"Actually, Detective," a very subdued Carter said, "I may have been a bit unreasonable about this whole matter. Claude Burris certainly has the right to the best counsel available." He turned to his partner, who was staring at him in obvious confusion. "This should act as a sign of our firm's eagerness to assist the members of the LAPD in whatever way we can. And it might just help the mayor make up his mind about that city contract."

C.W. nodded as if he now understood his partner's about-face. Mingus still couldn't quite pin it down. It had to have been the phone call from Mr. Fox. There was a slick named Fox who worked for the mayor. He had just promised Carter a city contract in return for the firm defending Burris. The big question was: why the hell did the mayor want to save the vice cop's ass?

"You can assure your ... colleague," Carter said to the detective, "this firm will provide him with the best possible defense."

Mingus figured with the mayor on his side, why not push it? "By that, you mean Mercer Early?" he said, clicking his briefcase shut.

"Early is a little fresh," C.W. said. "He takes too many chances. We have a much stronger attorney named Baraca—"

"Claude Burris wants Early. With the firm backing him, I bet he'll do just fine."

Carter looked as if he were in pain. "Did Mercer send you here?" he asked.

"Never met the man," Mingus said. "This is all Detective Burris's idea."

"I'd like to believe that," Carter said.

"Got no reason to lie."

Carter stared at him for a beat, nodded, and excused himself, leaving C.W. to walk Mingus out.

Both men moved briskly down the hall without conversation, but just after the detective stepped into the elevator, C.W. held the door from closing and said, "Mr. Early mentioned something about a hundred-thousand-dollar deposit."

"You'll have to talk to him about that," Mingus said. "I don't know anything about that side of it."

"That briefcase," C.W. said, "was there something in it you wanted to show us?"

"Nope," Mingus said as he pressed the down button. "I just carry this thing to make me feel important."

25

Life had to go on, Mercer thought as he emptied the contents of his desk into a cardboard box, even if he didn't know where it was going. Whatever happened, at least he'd have a parachute of sorts, the 100K Redd had promised for defending Burris. As for Vanessa, he felt he'd already lost her. He'd make sure at dinner, but there were too many signs.

Hell, he'd known all along she wasn't the kind of girl for him. In his mind, he was hardcore. Raised by a weary woman who had worked too much of her short life to keep a few inches above the poverty level. Vanessa was soft. She'd grown up with a silver spoon in her mouth and had never wanted for anything. She'd never give all that up. Not for him anyway. Maybe for a Harvard man.

He was so involved in packing up and playing out the future in his mind that when Bobby called his name he nearly jumped out of his skin. He turned to see that both partners were standing only a few feet away.

"You guys'd make good Indians," he said. "Come to say good-bye?"

"You don't know why we're here?" Bobby asked.

"Checking to see I'm not stealing any pens?" He held out the cardboard box for their inspection.

Bobby ignored it and the comment. "You know an LAPD detective named Lionel Mingus?"

"Sounds familiar, but maybe I'm thinking of the old jazz guy. You gentlemen seem to have something on your mind. What's up?"

"We've . . . reconsidered the situation involving Detective Burris," Bobby said as if the words were sticking to the roof of his mouth. "We've decided that your defending him would *not* conflict with the policy of the firm. So you can unload that box and get to work."

Mercer was clearly dumbfounded. "What changed your mind?"

For the first time the young lawyer could recall, Bobby seemed at a loss for words.

C.W. took up the slack. "Bottom line, this is a law firm. Defending people is what we do. We've handled unpopular cases in the past, black men and women who have been accused of crimes against brothers and sisters. It would be inconsistent for us to deny Detective Burris's request simply because of the color of his skin."

Mercer was listening to C.W., but he was watching Bobby, trying to read the odd expression on his face. Was it resignation or disgust? "You up with this, Bobby?"

Bobby gave him a fleeting smile. "I'm up with it. Of course, the decision is yours. Maybe you'd prefer to dissociate yourself from the firm and defend the detective on your own."

"No, no," Mercer said enthusiastically. "I want very much to continue being a part of this firm."

"Good," C.W. said. "That's what we want, too."

Mercer wondered if he were in a dream. C.W. was going beyond mere civility. He was even smiling and offering his hand. The young lawyer realized he was still holding the cardboard box. He placed it on his desktop and accepted C.W.'s enthusiastic handshake. He turned to offer his hand to Bobby, but his mentor merely nodded and took a distancing step backward. The two men seemed to have switched bodies like in one of those dumb science fiction movies.

"We'll be taking a tremendous amount of heat on this," Bobby said glumly. "From our clients and from the black community."

"Your pal Reverend Mayfield certainly won't be welcoming you with open arms this Sunday, Bobby," C.W. said. "But I think that when Mercer brings in a 'not guilty' verdict, the ill will will fade away. The firm will come out of it bigger and stronger. Miracle workers always prosper. Their sins are quickly forgiven and forgotten."

"I'll get the verdict," Mercer said.

"Start picking your crew, then," C.W. said. "Things are about to get very crazy, very quickly."

Watching the two partners leave, Mercer was struck by the idea that the craziness had already begun.

26

"Yeah?" Redd's voice on the line was thick with sleep.

Mingus glanced at his watch. Nearly eleven. "Sorry to wake you," he lied.

"Tha's okay," she said. "I had to get up anyway. To answer the fucking phone."

"This couldn't wait. I need you to float some bullshit for me," he said. "Get the talk out."

"Name it."

"Your friend Burris tells me Loc's slipped away from the RHD boys. Spread the word that he's been out and about, hitting the clubs, getting high. Out of control."

"Your wish be my command," she said.

Mingus put the phone back on its cradle and it rang almost immediately.

"You kill her?" Ida Bevan's depressed voice was unmistakable.

"Kill who, Ida?"

"Alice Adams. I give you her address and she's dead within the hour."

"Paper said she took her own life."

"You have that effect on women, Lionel."

"I sure hope not. In any case, she was gone before I even had a chance to talk with her."

"Wish I had her luck," Ida said and broke the connection.

Jesus, he thought, as he replaced the phone.

He stared at the papers littering his desk. Pink message sheets, interoffice communications, notices. He ignored them to take a quick survey of the bullpen. A couple of his fellow IAG dicks were standing before the bulletin board shooting the shit. He considered, then dismissed each one of them, settling on a man with the height and build of a basketball player who sat in the corner of the room with his huge feet up on his desk, reading the morning paper. Stan "the Man" Foster. Mingus didn't particularly like Foster, who was cold and arrogant and light-skinned. But he was a pro and he owed Mingus a favor and liking had no bearing on the situation.

When Foster reluctantly agreed to assist him, Mingus, armed with the big detective's cellular number, left the office for the nearest 7-Eleven. There he purchased a jug of Coca-Cola, a bunch of candy bars, mainly of the chocolate variety, and a box of Twinkies. Since his plan might require him to remain glued to his car for very long periods of time, he also got the clerk to throw in an empty half-gallon water bottle to take care of the after-effects of the Coke.

He drove back to Parker Center and took a tour of the underground parking before nesting the car in a slot that best served his purpose. He removed a Walkman from the glove compartment. Listening to Irma Thomas singing, appropriately enough, "Time Is on My Side," he skinned the wrapper off a Twinkie, settled back, and waited for Farley to reclaim the shiny Crown Vic that was parked near the entrance.

It was nearing noon when the fat detective and his pasty partner, Al Gervey, strolled past. They were shuffling along, laughing at something Farley said.

This wasn't good. If they'd got the word that their loose cannon, Loc, had been doing some heavy rolling in the night, they'd be moving with a bit more purpose. So Mingus was in for a little more shadow work than he'd hoped. He really didn't like tailing people, mainly because he'd never quite mastered the art.

The new Crown Vic's first stop was a big-man shop on Sixth and Broadway. Farley stayed behind the wheel of the idling car while Gervey rushed into the building. Mingus, caught without a place to linger, had had to drive past Farley and hope that he had not been seen. He circled the block and took his sweet time creeping up on the RHD cop. He was four or five car lengths back when Gervey left the shop with a plastic-covered garment on a hanger.

The next stop was at Gary's Guns on San Pedro just before Little Tokyo. Both dicks entered that shop and stayed there for the better part of a half hour. They might have been working, but, judging by their high spirits and the boxes in their hands and the glum look on the store owner's face as he watched them from his entrance, it was more likely that they were shaking the guy down for ammo. Worth checking out when he had the time.

Stop three was a steak house in Little Tokyo.

The Homicide dicks had been in the restaurant for about twenty minutes when Mingus heard a tapping on his car's passenger window. He'd been staring at the front of the restaurant so intently that the noise startled him, causing him to tear off the Walkman's earphones.

An Asian in a business suit stood on the curb beside the car, grinning at him. He gestured for Mingus to roll down the window. When the detective did that, the man raised his right hand. In it was something covered with a white napkin that he shoved through the open window.

Mingus automatically reached for his gun, but the Asian was too quick for him. His free hand whipped away the napkin with a flourish, displaying a very appetizing sandwich on a plate, surrounded by crispy brown potato curls and little clumps of shredded carrot. "Businessman steak sam-wich," the man said, continuing to grin. "Median-rare. Please take."

Frowning, Mingus accepted the sandwich, which, in fact, he desperately hungered for.

"Here, more," the Asian said, pulling a bottle of Kirin from his coat pocket and twisting off the cap. "From your friends."

"My friends," Mingus said flatly.

"Yes," the smiling Asian said, gesturing with the beer bottle at something in the street.

Mingus turned to see Farley and Gervey in the Crown Vic, waving at him before zooming off in the opposite direction. With a sigh, he turned back to the smiling Asian and took the beer. "Thanks."

"Next time, you come inside," the man said. "Your friends say you shy, but my establishment happy to serve black men."

"That's mighty white of you," Mingus told him.

The call from Stan "the Man" Foster came a little before three.

"You were on the money, my brother," Foster said. "Soon as your buddies ditched you at the Jap steak house, they hopped on over to Watts like little white bunny rabbits. Stopped at 110th and Central. Church of the Last Harvest. You know what kinda church that is?"

"Yeah," Mingus said. He also knew that if Farley and his partner went there, it meant they'd lost track of Loc and were hoping Bay Bay could set 'em in the right direction.'

"What business do a pair of lily-white Homicide dicks have at an AIDS church in Watts?"

That was a big problem dealing with Stan the Man, his curiosity. Mingus said, "I'll ask 'em when I see 'em."

"Word is there's some serious shit going down at RHD. Is that what this is all about, Mingus? If you working on that, plug me into it, too, long as I'm doing the assist."

"This is personal, like I told you," Mingus said. "A

personal favor, like the one I done for you." He had tipped Foster that a woman he was seeing on the sly had been planted on him by a cop he'd been investigating. The tip had come in time to save Stan the Man's job and marriage.

"Yeah, well, anyway, they were in the church for about five, then it was back in the car, traveling across town to Inglewood. An apartment house on Maverick. 2047."

"Maverick, huh?" Mingus said, as if he weren't all that interested. Actually, his head wound was tingling. It had to be Loc's hidey-hole. "They still there?"

"Left about fifteen minutes ago."

"Where are they now?"

Foster hesitated, then said, "I don't know. I, ah, lost 'em. I'm still parked in front of the apartment house."

"How'd that happen?" Mingus said, trying not to sound too pissed off.

"They go into the building. I figure it's whiz and Whopper time. I wasn't gone longer than ten minutes, tops. But they'd flown. I'm sorry, man, I really am."

"It's okay. You did fine."

"The apartment they went to was 203."

"How do you know that?"

"Before I took my pee break, I went into the place. Only got ten apartments. I heard 'em jawing inside 203. Second floor, just off the stairs. They were deep into something, which is why I figured they'd be there a while."

"You hear anything they said?" Mingus asked.

"Naw. The walls are paper, but there was music playing and they were in a back room."

Maybe Stan had heard something, maybe not. Mingus knew better than to completely trust him. Internal Affairs was a highly competitive department. "Thanks for your help, man," he said.

"I could go inside, brace the folks in 203. Find out what Farley and his buddy was up to."

"Waste of time," Mingus said, trying to keep his voice casual. "You say there are 'folks' at the apartment?"

"I'm not sure. You comin' here? I'll stick around, case you need backup."

"I don't think I'll bother," Mingus lied. "I'm gonna see if I can find where Farley went. Thanks for your help."

"We square then, brother?"

"We're square," Mingus said.

It took him eighteen minutes to arrive at the apartment house on Maverick. He was glad to see that Stan the Man wasn't still lurking around trying to get a fix on his business. He entered the building and went up the wooden stairs. He paused in front of 203. Music was playing. Hip hop. Snoop Dogg rapping about being shot.

He knocked.

Nothing, except Snoop going on about dying.

He knocked again.

He was getting that bad feeling in his stomach. Like maybe Loc was there, but he wasn't hearing the knocking. Or Snoop Dogg. Or anything else.

He tried the knob.

It turned and the door opened.

Mingus drew his gun. In spite of the situation, having his old weapon back in his hand again gave him a feeling of confidence as he stepped into the apartment.

The front room was a mess: newspapers scattered on the floor; grease-stained take-out boxes; empty beer cans, whisky bottles. An old armchair faced a silent TV. Against one wall, an ancient faded green couch was partially covered by a rough woolen blanket. There was an unpleasant odor in the apartment. Stale food mixed with rubbing alcohol.

The sounds of Snoop were coming from another room. As Mingus worked his way there, his foot connected with a bottle and sent it spinning on the bare floor.

"Somebody out there?" a weak voice called from the other room. "Kenny?"

The room was bright with the afternoon sun, but that was the best Mingus could say for it. Bay Bay was lying on a rumpled bed, a soiled pink blanket pulled up to his neck. His condition, which hadn't been so hot at the church, had apparently worsened. Beside the bed on a battered card table rested a white plastic radio, a real antique that reminded Mingus of a similar box his mother had owned, plus an assortment of pill bottles and a tall glass half full of a cloudy fluid that may have been tap water. There was also a small gray plastic cup filled with a thick, red substance. A chorus behind Snoop kept repeating the word "Murderrrrr."

Bay Bay's heavy-lidded eyes opened wide briefly, then went back to half-mast. "Mingus," he said with neither joy nor despair. "Come to use that gun on me, I hope?"

"Where's your brother?" Mingus said, slipping the weapon back into its holster.

"Everybody wants my brother. Nobody wants me."

Snoop was carrying on about a pact with the devil. Mingus clicked him off mid-rap. "Where's Ken, Bay Bay?"

"Fuck I care. I'm sick as shit, case you blind." He shivered and pulled the blanket tighter.

"He's cooping here, right? Sleeping on the couch in the other room?"

"Wrong. He tried it for a night, then said he'd had enough. He thinks I'm sending germs into the air that'll give him the sickness, too. The hell with him."

"He happen to tell you where he was relocatin'?"

Bay Bay's face contracted in pain. "Jesus, I can't go on like this."

"Something I can do?" Mingus asked, moving near the bed, looking at the array of medication.

Bay Bay shook his head. "None of it does nothin'." He poked his chin at the tiny plastic cup filled with something thick and red. "Not even Satan's blood."

"What is that red stuff, Bay? Not what I think it is, I hope."

"Sacramental wine," he said. "Dr. Foxcroft brung it when he give me the last rites."

"Maybe I should get him back here. Or your real doctor . . . ?"

"They can't help me," Bay Bay said. "But you can. Drop the pill on me, man. Buy me a ticket to hell. I'll be received there like the prodigal son."

Mingus stared at Bay Bay, perplexed by his mixing a Bible story reference in with his desire to hook up with Satan.

"Those other fucks, Farley and the gray ghost he hangs with, they wouldn't do nothing for me. But you're a black man. You'll shoot me, right, put me out of this pain?"

"I don't think so," Mingus said.

Bay Bay's eyes narrowed. "I'll tell you where my brother is, if you promise."

Mingus hesitated, then said, "I'm not gonna shoot you and get jammed up, Bay. But I might do it with a pillow, you sure it's what you want."

"Oh, man, I do want it. I'm ready to leave this life and meet my Dark Master."

"First, you got to tell me where Ken is."

"With a bitch named Eula Montgomery, in her place over to Florence Street."

"Eula? The one used to sling booze at the Kittyhawk?"

Bay Bay's death mask of a face broke into a brief smile. "You remember her, huh? Pouring you drink after drink. Yeah. She and me and my little bro, we grew up together. She and him was always tight." He took a deep breath, coughed, and said. "Okay, Mingus, I'm ready to meet my beloved Lucifer."

"I can't drop the pill, Bay," Mingus said. "I don't do murder."

"It's not murder, you fuck, it's mercy." Yelling, Bay Bay rose up for a second before weakness and gravity pushed him back against his gray, sweat-stained pillow. "You worse than the fat man. He's a miserable son of a bitch, but at least he . . ."

Mingus was headed to the door when the unfinished sentence made him turn. He expected to see the man taking his last gasp. Instead, Bay Bay was giving him a sly look. "I see you got your gun back," he said, almost a singsong. "That bitch Redd musta give it up to you. You her cat daddy now?"

"What do you know about my gun?"

Bay Bay winced in pain, then the smile returned. "She didn't tell you, huh? Watch out for the bitches. They don't tell you everything."

Mingus understood what Redd meant when she said it wouldn't be long before she could give him the name of the thief who stole his gun and badge. "Why'd you rob me, Bay?" he asked. "Just because I pushed you around once?"

"Hell, no. Wasn't nothing personal. But I can't say I didn't get my en-joys seeing you in the squeeze."

"And you beat and raped that woman?"

"She was sweet, man. Even in my condition, I'm bonin' up right now thinking about her."

"You sick son of a bitch," Mingus said, drawing his gun.

"Yeah, she was sweet," Bay Bay said. "Kinda like a extra treat for that little job. Not only did I get all that money to set you up, but I got to work out on that sweet bitch."

Mingus pointed the weapon at Bay, then realized from his grin it was what the sick man wanted. He lowered his arm.

Bay Bay looked crestfallen. But not for long. "Don't you wanna know who paid me?"

"I do know."

"Bullshit."

"Farley," Mingus said.

"Where'd you come up with that idea?" Bay Bay asked, grinning.

"Farley slipped up. Said something about me being fed knockout drops. Not even I knew that."

"Yeah, the fat man found out about it, sure enough. The prick-bastard tried holdin' it over my head, thinking to get me to be his rat. But he came by his knowledge a little too late. That's one good thing about bein' terminal: cops got nowhere to go on you."

"How'd Farley get tipped it was you drugged and robbed me if he wasn't the man behind it?"

"Probably my baby bro' who seems to be kinda tight with him." He managed a sly grin. "Course, it coulda been yo' girlfren' Redd tole him."

It wasn't what Mingus wanted to hear. He wanted Farley to be the architect of his fall and no one else. But thinking about it, he had to admit that back when Bay Bay stole his stuff, he'd barely known the fat man. Their animosity hadn't started until Farley was on the upswing within RHD. The architect of Mingus's downfall was probably somebody he'd put behind bars. Too many to choose from.

"Give me a name," he said.

"You want the answer, you know the price."

"You got a deal. Tell me."

"Bullshit. You reneged before. Put the gun to my chest and let me hook my thumb on the trigger."

Mingus pushed his gun against the man's bony chest and Bay Bay smiled. His hand caressed the barrel and slid toward the trigger.

As badly as Mingus wanted the name, there was no way he would kill a man in cold blood, even a worthless piece of trash like Bay Bay who wanted to die. He considered letting the sick man stick his thumb on the trigger. He was pretty sure he'd be able to keep Bay from moving it. But people on their last leg were able to find untapped strength when they wanted it. He couldn't take the chance.

"Not today," Mingus told Bay Bay, jerking the weapon from his desperate grasp.

"Do me," Bay Bay screamed.

"Do yourself."

"I . . . don't got a gun. Gimme yours."

"Yeah, sure. You want my badge, too. Been there, done that."

"Gimme something. A knife. Anything. I'll tell you what you wanna know."

"Not at that price, Bay. You stay healthy, huh?"

The sick man's curses followed him down the stairs and out of the building. Halfway to Eula's address, they were still ringing in his ears.

27

"I thought I could handle anything, Early, but this place is getting to me," Claude Burris was saying in the twin towers interview room. His eyes shifted to a thick glass window in the wall, beyond which a yawning uniformed guard observed their conversation, supposedly without being able to hear them. "Always watching. You can't take a shit without fifteen people watching you. Up here in high-power, they get you to spread your cheeks twice a day so they can stick a finger up your ass. Lookin' for drugs, I guess. I told the goddamned guard, 'You just searched my ass three hours ago. Now you're back with your finger out. You in love with me or what?' "

"Win him over with that kind of sweet talk?" Mercer asked. Even if his metal chair wasn't digging into his back, he was running short on patience. Prisons did that to him. He picked up the pen that was resting on the table in front of him.

"They got me sleeping on a slab of cement," Burris said, "using a worn-out blanket for a mattress. And the fuckin' food'd gag a maggot."

"You don't look like you're losing weight."

"Yeah, well, lucky me." Burris lowered his eyes and mumbled, "There's a deputy been smuggling in some deli for me. But that don't make it Fun City in here. The place is a hellhole."

"It's jail, Burris. It ain't supposed to be the downtown Hilton. You probably never thought about the conditions inside when you were out on the streets putting the long arm on my black brothers."

"Jesus. Are you my lawyer or did you just come here to gloat?"

"I don't much like you, Burris. I think you're an arrogant man who abused the power you got from wearing a badge. I think you've put black men in here who shouldn't be here. But I am your lawyer. That's why I'm getting my gloating out up front."

"I respect the badge and I do the job," Burris said. "I arrest people accused of crimes. Black, white, yellow, or maroon. I arrest 'em. It's judges and juries who put 'em away."

"Uh-huh. Well, on that subject, since Darion Mayfield was set to be a witness against you in the perjury case, that makes his murder a special-circumstances crime, punishable by the death penalty, if that's what the D.A. wants. And the D.A. does want it."

Burris stared at him, a big pale man in a blue jumpsuit, apparently unmoved by the decidedly bad news.

"No comment?" Mercer asked.

Burris didn't reply. Nor did he blink or move or show any sign of having heard the question.

Mercer felt frustrated and annoyed by the man's silence. "The way Ms. . . . the way Redd put it," he said, "my defending you was your big idea. So here I am. You gonna talk to me?"

Burris shifted in his chair. "I was just thinking, you might have some idea what it's like being locked up for something you didn't do."

"This isn't about me," Mercer said.

"Maybe I'm wrong," Burris said. "Maybe you did it. You kill that college girl, Early?"

Even ruled by temper, Mercer realized what Burris was doing. "You don't want to talk about your defense?" he said with remarkable self-control. "Okay. That's up to you. You the guy complaining about fingers up the ass."

Burris shifted his glance to the floor. His lips started to move, but no words came out. It was as if he was arguing with himself. Mercer felt the hairs on the back of his neck curling. *The man's nuts*, he thought. Or setting the groundwork for a diminished capacity defense.

The vice cop seemed to get a grip on himself. His chin dropped to his chest and he took a long, deep breath. "Okay. You got a point, counselor."

Burris licked his lips. As much time as Mercer had spent facing down the cop in the courtroom, he had never noticed how seriously lacking the man was in the lip department. He had George Bush lips.

The thought caused Mercer to chuckle out loud.

"Something funny?"

"I was just thinking that, with that pale face and the little liver spots, you aren't just a cracker, you're a saltine cracker."

To his surprise, Burris grinned and started laughing, too. "Yeah," he said, "I wouldn't last an hour in your hot jungle sun."

The comment sobered Mercer, but Burris was caught up in his own hilarity, laughing harder and harder. "That's me, a fucking saltine in the shade." When he began pounding on the table, the guard opened the door. "Everything all right in here?"

Burris was laughing too much to reply. The guard looked from him to Mercer who said, "I just told him the joke about the pig with the wooden leg."

The guard's expression said he thought they were both nuts, but he left them to their craziness.

When Burris finally quieted down, Mercer asked, "All laughed out?"

Burris nodded. "Yeah. Jesus, this place. I really lost it, there."

"You okay now?"

"Yeah. I'm under control. So here's the deal. The

basic fact is that I didn't kill the scumbag. Now ask me what else you want to know."

"Were you there?"

Burris scratched an itch beside his right eye. "That depends on how you define 'there.' "

Mercer sighed. " 'There' meaning 'positioned,' 'located,' 'situated.' 'There' meaning 'present at the precise moment in time when Darion Mayfield got tossed from the goddamned window.' "

"Given your definition I can say in all honesty I was not 'there.' "

Mercer stared at him. "You weren't at Mayfield's apartment that evening?"

The detective dropped his head into his hands. For the first time, Mercer saw in Burris something he had seen in others he had defended. They were sad desperate people, caught up in a system that could easily roll right over them, destroying anything and everything important in their lives. And there was always that moment when they arrived at the crunch—did they trust their lawyer enough to give the truth up to him, or not? That trust wasn't always necessary, but it always helped.

"I was there," Burris said. "But long gone by the time the dope dealer bought it."

"What were you doing there?"

"When I finally got out of the goddamn lockup, I checked in at Vice. Mayfield had left a message he wanted me to call him. That much curiosity I got. He said he wanted to make peace, that he might be willing to testify that I hadn't beat the confession out of him if I stopped raggin' on him. I told the fucker to go climb a rope and was about to hang up when he said a name. Sweets Doremus."

"He knew about you and Redd."

"Said he wanted to talk about it. So I went to his place."

"What time?"

"Seven, seven-thirty. He was by himself up there. Stoned and throwing it in my face that there wasn't anything I could do about it. He told me I'd have to find some other dealer to harass, unless I wanted to wind up taking Sweets's place in the jug."

"And you slugged him, right?" Mercer asked.

"Wouldn't you?"

"Aw, shit," Mercer said.

"I hit him. I didn't kill him."

"Well, here's the situation," Mercer said. "See, we want the D.A. to continue thinking your motive for murdering Darion was to get rid of the key witness against you in your perjury trial. We can fight that with the doctored tape which suggests you may not have committed perjury at all. If you weren't guilty, Darion was not a threat. Then, all that's keeping you from freedom is a witness who's a well-known flake.

"But if Darion knew about you and Redd and Sweets, that gives you a motive we can't fight. All we can do is hope the D.A. doesn't know about it." Mercer's mind was racing. He'd been figuring that, if worse came to worst, he could convince Redd to take the stand and provide Burris with an alibi and worry about future recriminations later. But now she could easily be part of the murder motive, which would make her testimony worthless, if the D.A. found out that Darion had been aware of their relationship.

"How did Darion learn about you and Redd?" he asked.

"I dunno."

"Let me put it another way. Who knew about it?"

"Just me and Redd," he said, scratching beside his right eye.

"Who do you think killed Darion, Burris?"

The man in blue shrugged. "No idea." His face seemed to be itching him again.

"You're lying."

"Fuck you."

"Okay, fuck me, but you're still lying and I know it."

"Sure you do. I'm an open book."

"Something like that," Mercer said, watching the cop scratch his face. "Who killed Darion?"

"That's something you're better off not knowing."

"You don't think it might help me just a little with your defense?" Mercer asked.

"Maybe. But I'm doing you a favor."

"I don't understand."

"There are some bad people out there, Early. We don't want to piss them off. Let's move on."

Burris's comment opened the door to "an assortment of scenarios," to use a term his mentor, Bobby Carter, often employed. "Some of these bad people cops?" Mercer asked.

"Let's move on," Burris repeated.

"What about this detective you tried to waste, Mingus?"

Burris grinned. "That was an accident."

"Not the way it's written up. They got you dead bang. Shooting a fellow cop. Even if we beat the murder count, you could do life for Mingus."

"Don't worry about it," Burris said. "Mingus isn't one of the bad guys. Least, I don't think so."

"Who are the bad guys?"

"Next question."

Reluctantly, Mercer shifted from the unknown to the known. Burris said he was not present when Darion was killed and there'd been no face-scratching tell. So, either the vice cop had been playing him when he scratched his face or the D.A.'s main witness was lying. Not a hard choice to make, especially since he'd seen the two-and-a-half-page rap sheet on Kenneth Ansol, aka Ken Loc.

"How well do you know the witness against you, Kenneth Ansol?" he asked Burris.

"Kenneth . . . Ken Loc? I hear he's an ex-con."

"You know any reason he'd lie to put you on the scene?"

"No."

Mercer shook his head. "Man, you don't make it easy. You ever arrest him, beat up on him, or give him any other reason to do you harm?"

"No. Never had any dealings with him I can recall."

"Okay. Let's talk about your work record."

"Sure," Burris said.

For the rest of the meeting, he responded with candor to questions about his work, associates who might be willing to testify on his behalf, why others would be unwilling. Whenever Mercer returned to the subject of who may have murdered Darion Mayfield, Burris closed down.

Packing up to go, the lawyer said, "I don't get you, Burris. Seems to me somebody out there put you in a frame. You're not exactly a turn-the-other-cheek type of guy, but you're holding back. What's the deal? Some kind of twisted honor code?"

"Call me a fool, but winning the case don't mean shit if we're dead the next day."

"We?"

"Welcome to the real world of cops and robbers."

"You serious?"

"Just watch out for yourself."

Slightly unnerved, Mercer rang the buzzer. A shift change had brought on a female deputy. As he headed for the door, a thought came to him. He turned and asked Burris, "What about your woman? Is she in danger, too?"

"Don't worry about her," Burris replied. "She can take care of herself."

28

"**Y**ou missed Kenny by at least a half hour, Detective," Eula Montgomery said to Mingus at the door to her little Florence Street cottage, "but c'mon in. I imagine you want to see for yourself he ain't here."

Eula had gone through some changes since the last time he'd seen her. Then, she'd been working just a few blocks down Florence at the Kittyhawk, showing herself off in some kind of leather thong outfit with a necklace of spikes. Now she had on slacks and a man's plaid shirt with the sleeves rolled up. She also was wearing gold-framed bifocals low on her nose and had let her hair grow out kind of wild and wiry with some spots of gray. She was still a fair-looking woman, but a little matronly, and Mingus felt wistful at the loss of her dominatrix glamour.

"Want some coffee?" she asked. "Don't keep nothing stronger in the house."

"No thanks," Mingus said.

"Well, you go look aroun' to your heart's content. I got work to do."

The house was clean and ordinary, except for the occasional religious relic. Holy pictures were taped to the side of the refrigerator in a spotless kitchen. A bible rested on a window ledge in a bathroom that smelled of roses and pine oil. A statue of Jesus, arms outstretched, stood on a dresser top, looking out on a neatly made four-poster in the bedroom. On the floor not far from the bed a large black canvas-and-leather bag was spilling its contents: a man's shirts and underwear. He wondered if Jesus really was blessing everything that went on in that room.

He found Eula in a tiny space, about the size of a walk-in closet, that she was using for an office. She was seated at a white desk tapping away at a computer keyboard. "Satisfied?" she asked.

"Where'd he go?"

She shrugged. "Wherever you cops take him."

"Cops took him?"

She swung around on her chair. "Two white cops," she said. "One of 'em they used to call Detective Fats."

"Ken go voluntarily?"

"I imagine so," she said as if it were of little interest. "Bay Bay phoned to let him know they was coming."

"He phone about me, too?"

She nodded and turned back to the computer. "Yeah. He don't think too highly of you."

"That's 'cause I wouldn't put him out of his misery."

"The Lord'll take care of that soon enough," she said.

Mingus was puzzled by the image on Eula's monitor. It looked like a light bulb almost lost in fog. "What's that you got up there?" he asked.

"My web page. I'm Madame Juanita, ever'body's psychic sister."

"How's that work?"

"I advise folks on their future. At my psychic site, I do it in kinda broad strokes. You know, is this a good month to take vacations in the south or the north? Or, if you're a Taurus, is this the time to hop the broomstick with the man you been seeing? Like that."

"This information just sorta comes to you out of the blue?" Mingus asked.

She smiled. "Guess I got the gift."

"Where's the payback?"

"Anybody can access the site for free. But I got a 900 number and a bunch of subscribers who get one-on-one e-mail advice. A little healthier than standin' on my feet all night pourin' booze for loud drunks. Pays better, too."

"Might be worth twenty bucks or so, if you could conjure up where Fats took Ken."

"I'd be taking your money for nothing, Detective," she said. "I don't know where he is. He went off with his razor and toothbrush and some clothes stuffed in a paper bag, so I imagine I won't be seeing him for a while."

"You and him talk about Darion Mayfield's murder?"

"No," she said, swinging around to face the monitor. "See, I do sorta believe in keepin' my aura clear of that kind of negativity. Kenny and me go way back. We tend to talk most about the old days. The innocent time, you know."

Mingus didn't know if she was bullshitting or not. It didn't matter much either way, so he changed the subject. "I once asked you about the night I lost my gun and badge at the K-Hawk."

"Yeah," she said, facing him. "Like I tole you then, you fell off the stool. Took three of the brothers to carry you to the back room."

"You see Bay Bay slip a knockout powder in my drink?"

She stared at him. "What you talking about?"

"He told me somebody paid him to jam me up that night."

"I hope you not implying I was part of that?"

"No ma'am."

"That little weasel didn't say I was part of it?"

"No. He took sole credit."

"I did stuff at the K-Hawk back in those days I ain't proud of. Mainly of a sexual nature. Some drugs. Never did no thieving. And I sure as hell wouldn't have let nobody fuck with the drinks I was serving." She shook her head, more in wonder than anger. "Bay Bay is a lowlife. Always was, even when we was kids. Doing bad and layin' it off on poor Kenny."

"Kenny isn't exactly a Boy Scout."

"He's done stuff, sure enough, but he's not bad through and through, like Bay. That's why the good Lord come down so hard on Bay with the AIDS. You know he serves in the devil's church." Mingus nodded. "Kenny's a Christian, worships the true God."

Oh, man, Mingus thought, if this wasn't a sign of the way his world was headed. His fantasy dominatrix-barmaid had turned into a born-again true believer. But she was pouring the holy water a little deep when it came to Ken Loc. "He may worship God, but he saves a little room for the white powder, too," he said.

"Kenny doesn't use no drugs. Where'd you get that notion?"

"He did some work for Darion Mayfield, the dope dealer who got himself murdered."

She shook her head. "No, he didn't."

"Ken told me that himself."

"You got it confused. Kenny works for the church. The real church."

Damn, Mingus thought. She's in love with him. Only a woman blinded by romance would believe a mutt like Ken Loc would go into a church for any other reason than to steal from the poor box. But why argue with a true believer? "You know him better than me," he said.

She smiled. "What about you, Mingus? You still looking for happiness in a bottle?"

"Naw. I don't know where it is, but I know it ain't there."

"You always were a gentleman, even when you were shit-faced." She smiled. "I caught you giving me the cat-eye time to time, but you never moved on me. I used to wonder why."

"I don't know," he said, suddenly embarrassed. "Figured you had your own thing going."

"I had a few things going. But I wouldn't have been averse to a little strange jammy. Course, that was then. Come a little closer."

He obeyed, warily but hopefully.

"Let's see what you got in store, romance-wise."

Before he could step back, she pressed a hand to his forehead and closed her eyes. "I see some good . . ." She paused, scowled, and drew back her hand as if his forehead had burned it.

"What?" he said.

"Nothing," she said. "It's all jive anyway."

"What'd you see?"

"A long and happy life," she said.

"Bullshit," he said. "You saw something."

She was about to protest when his pocket started to beep. He removed the noisy little object, read the message on its face, and asked, "There a phone I can use?"

She pointed to a complicated telephone setup beside the computer on the desk. "Use line three," she said. "The first two are for my 900 calls."

He fumbled with the phone and couldn't get a dial tone. She punched the one button he'd overlooked. Waiting for a connection, he caught her staring at him, a worried look on her face.

"District attorney's office," a voice on the phone said.

"Deputy D.A. Gomez, please."

Eula stood up. "I'm getting me some coffee. Sure I can't tempt you?"

He stared at her, then hurriedly shook his head and focused his attention on the phone, identifying himself to the woman who answered at D.D.A. Gomez's extension.

Almost immediately, Gomez was on the line. "How soon can you get here, Detective?"

"I guess I'm about a half hour away. This is in connection with what, exactly?"

"Claude Burris. What else would it be?" The D.D.A. sounded testy. "Don't delay. I'm waiting."

"On my way," Mingus said.

Eula was filling her cup in the kitchen. She rested it on the sink and walked him to the front door. "You take it easy, Detective," she said.

"When Ken gets back, you think you could get him to call me?"

"I'll try. Really."

"You see something bad in my future?" he asked.

"I don't have the power, Detective. What I do is like show business. You worried about your future, put your faith in the Lord."

"I may just try that one of these days."

"Don't wait too long," she called after him.

Mingus didn't much care for David Gomez, or as he was known in some of the more cynical areas of Parker Center, Too-Good Gomez, a nickname that suggested his rigid adherence to the rules of law probably was hiding some really sick and nasty shit underneath.

The small brown man in his starched white shirt and muted tie sat at in his orderly office with his small brown hands resting, fingers linked, on an open folder on his neat desktop. His lips pursed, he stared at Mingus as if he were an oil stain on the carpet.

Gomez unlinked his fingers to tap on the folder. "Been reading about you, Detective," he said. "Colorful material, but not very helpful to the cause."

"The cause?"

"The prosecution of Claude Burris," Gomez said, obviously annoyed. "Get with the program, man. You got a history of drunkenness. Are you drunk now?"

Mingus stared at the man without expression. "No. I'll walk a line for you, if you want."

Gomez made a throat-clearing noise and said, "I don't know what the hell to do with you. A man I'm prosecuting for murder tried to kill you. You're a cop. You should be a perfect witness. But this," he placed a small hand down on the folder, "this says you're the prince of Fuckup City. There are eighteen excessive-force complaints against you. Drunk-on-duty citations.

And then we got your masterwork—the incident where you pass out in a bar and lose your gun and badge."

Damn, Mingus thought. He wondered if this was just the beginning of the bad luck Eula had seen in his future.

"So here's my quandary: is your testimony worth the risk of putting a potential train wreck like you on the stand?"

Mingus knew that Gomez didn't expect him to answer the question. He was just talking to hear himself talk. The fact was, the detective hoped the little bastard would not call him. He wasn't wild about testifying against Burris, mainly because of Redd. But he wouldn't shrink from it, if called.

Gomez nodded his head a few times. "Yes," he said. "I think I will risk it. Here's my logic, Detective. One way or the other, I'll have to use you. If by some fluke, Burris should be acquitted of the murder of Darion Mayfield, I will then put him on trial for attempting to murder you. We've got him dead-bang on that."

"Not exactly dead-bang," Mingus said. "I can't rightly say he meant to pull the trigger. I was fighting him for the gun."

"He drew down on you."

"He drew his gun in what he thought was self-defense."

"You didn't identify yourself?"

"I did that," Mingus said, "but Detective Burris still felt I meant to do him harm."

"I don't understand," Gomez said.

"He seemed to think there were some cops out to get him and I was one of 'em."

Gomez frowned at that. "Let me get this straight. You identify yourself as a lawman. You tell him he's under arrest, and—"

"Excuse me. I wasn't trying to arrest him," Mingus said. "I didn't even know he was wanted."

"Then what the hell were you doing at the crime scene?"

"At the request of Captain Roy Jacquette, I was and still am investigating some men in his division."

"Didn't Jacquette kick you out of Robbery-Homicide?"

"He approved my transfer to Internal Affairs," Mingus said.

"Same thing. And yet he sicced you on his own men?"

"That's what we do in IAG."

"I'm still confused," Gomez said. "Burris is in vice, not RHD."

"Right. Like I said, Burris wasn't why I was at the crime scene."

Gomez paled. "Goddammit, don't tell me any of the detectives assigned to my case are under investigation."

Mingus stared at him and said nothing.

"Shit," Gomez said. "What've you got on 'em?"

"Right now I'm just looking."

"Is that the truth or is it something Jacquette told you to say? No. Don't answer that. I don't want to know the answer. Let me put it this way: if Burris's defense attorney asks you that question in court, what do you tell him?"

"I tell him I'm just looking," Mingus said. "I got nothing solid. Yet."

Gomez seemed relieved. "Okay. So let's you and I go over the questions I'll be asking you on the stand and—"

He was interrupted by the arrival of district attorney Dana Lowery, a lean, large-boned brunette with a shock of white hair in front that, along with her disposition, had earned her the nickname "Cruella." Her dark, nervous eyes barely flitted over Mingus before resting on Gomez, who seemed frozen at his desk.

"I've got the Reverend and the spin boys in my office, David," she said. "We need your input on Carter-Hansborough and this Early character."

"I was just—" Gomez began.

"Pronto," the D.A. said. Her always-in-motion eyes took in Mingus for a nanosecond, weighed his importance, discounted it, and she was gone.

Gomez stood nervously. "You stay right here, Detective. This won't take long." He headed for the door. Then, thinking better of it, he returned to his desk and closed Mingus's folder and took it with him.

What a dick! Mingus thought as he settled in for what would undoubtedly be a long wait.

29

Mercer steered his sedan through the going-home traffic, creeping from one congested freeway to another, until finally settling in for a bumper-to-bumper crawl along the Santa Monica. The slower the Benz's progress, the faster his mind raced, hopping from the upcoming trial to his dinner with Vanessa. The prosecution figured it could establish motive and opportunity, but to hang on to the latter, they'd be forced to rely on Ken Loc, a two-time loser with every reason to do and say whatever the D.A. wanted, true or not.

True or not? Was Vanessa playing straight with him or was she moving on to Barry Fox? Maybe she was having dinner with Mercer just to give him the bad news. He shook his head. No. He was not going to psyche himself into a wrong position tonight. He had to start thinking positively. Focus. He had a very important dinner to prepare.

He crept off the freeway at Fairfax and swung into the nearest supermarket where he collected a couple of pre-baked potatoes, a bag of chopped salad, two filet mignons, fresh flowers, including a bouquet of roses, and a bottle of Zinfandel.

He was no cook and meal planning was not his forte. As far as he knew, the oven in his apartment had never been used. He figured he'd rely on the skills he'd perfected in college. He'd 'cue the steaks on a hibachi grill he kept on the balcony. It was the same balcony where a maintenance man had recently earned twenty bucks getting rid of the mess a bunch of pigeons had made. Mercer thought he might scrub down the hibachi a little. But, on the other hand, why waste the time? The fire would burn off the birdshit and feathers.

At eight o'clock sharp, Vanessa was knocking at his door.

She'd come directly from the office without bothering to change or freshen up. That was fine with him. He'd prepared a bath for her, floating the bouquet's red rose petals on the water. An ice bucket and two glasses sat on the floor next to the tub. He'd never tried taking a bath with anybody in the apartment before and wasn't quite sure they could both fit in the tub, which was looking smaller by the minute. But he was anxious to give it a test run.

She greeted him with, "My man. You got it made, honey."

Did he ever, he thought, as she came into his arms. Then he realized she wasn't talking romance. "The media's gonna be out in full force," she cooed into his ear. "And they're gonna love you, just like I do."

"I'd rather the media not get that personal," he said, flashing on a pack of newshounds digging up old bones from his past.

She slipped from his arms and headed for the couch where she dropped her purse. "Heading up your own defense team. Calling all the shots. And you made 'em both back down. Not just Daddy, who really seems impressed by you, but you turned Bobby, too. Others have tried to do that and failed. You are the man. King 'Gator."

He gave her what he thought was a humble smile, while he wondered once again why Bobby had changed his mind. Was it something political that—

"Can a lady get a kiss around here?" Vanessa asked.

He took her in his arms and answered the question. But though she'd requested it, the result was a little short of the ultimate in passion. Especially when she pulled away to yawn.

"I'm sorry, honey," she said. "I'm a little out of it. I didn't get much sleep last night."

The line, delivered casually, was like a one-two punch. First, a blow to the solar plexus: I didn't sleep because Barry Fox and I had sex all night. And then, a right to the heart: Now I'm too tired (and too sex-weary) to sleep with you tonight.

Reeling, Mercer was still determined to make the best of her presence.

"I have a surprise for you," he said, taking her hand. "Close your eyes."

Giggling, she obeyed, letting him lead the way. When he reached the bathroom, he whispered, "Surprise."

At first she said nothing. Then she acted as if she was really surprised. But regretful. "It's a beautiful idea, baby," she said. "But that tub's a little tiny and I'm way too wasted for what you've got in mind."

Rather than lose the moment, Mercer reached for the bottle of wine and handed her a glass. As he began to pour, he saw her staring at the label on the bottle. Her face—a lawyer's face—was impossible to read.

He filled their glasses and made a toast. "To our love."

She barely wet her lips, then led him to the sofa in the living room.

He'd thought he had done a fair job of straightening up the room, but sitting there he was conscious of the streaks on the coffee table, the dust on the lamp shade, a section of the newspaper poking from under a stuffed chair.

Past the glass sliding doors leading to the balcony, heat was rising from the hibachi. "Looks like the coals are ready for the filets," he said. He started to stand, but she placed a hand on his arm.

"I'm not very hungry," she said. "Let's just sit and talk for a minute."

"Sure," he said, hiding his disappointment. "No" on the tub, "no" on the wine, "no" on the dinner. It looked like a strikeout to him.

"Daddy said you were meeting with your client earlier. What's he like?"

"Like anybody behind bars, except that he's a cop. And white. Which makes it a little unusual."

"Did he do it?"

The question surprised him, coming from an attorney.

"He says he didn't." Mercer knocked back his glass of wine, grabbed the bottle, and refilled.

"You believe him?"

"I don't know," he said, which was the truth. "Frankly, at this point I don't care."

She smiled as if she approved of the answer. "You're going to get him off, aren't you?"

"Oh, yeah." He took a gulp of wine.

"Then you'll be able to write your own ticket."

He shrugged, tried to fake a little humility, and took another gulp.

"I'm so proud of my man," she said and—surprise!—pulled him closer.

This time their kiss lasted longer, had enough passion for him to forget he was holding a glass of wine, which he spilled down her back.

Vanessa stiffened and pulled away. "Damn," she said, reaching over her shoulder to test how bad the spill was.

"I'm sorry, honey," he said.

She raced to the bathroom, where she adjusted the mirrors to give her a view of the red stain on the back of her blouse. "Damn," she said again.

He started to repeat his apology, but he didn't think that would help. Besides, she was unbuttoning the blouse.

"I don't suppose you've got any *white* wine?" she said, removing the blouse.

"I could go buy some," he offered, a little dulled by

the Zinfandel and the sight of her standing there in a satin half-bra.

"How about club soda?"

"Yeah. Maybe."

He found a bottle stuck way in the back of a cabinet in the kitchen. She poured the bubbling liquid over the stain, seemingly oblivious to him standing in the bathroom doorway. After a few minutes, he wandered back into the living room and, ignoring the glass, took a long swig from the wine bottle.

He eyed the two raw fillets resting on a plate in their blood. Well, *he* was hungry. He carried the steaks to the balcony and dropped them onto the glowing hibachi.

He was back near the coffee table and the wine bottle when Vanessa emerged from the bedroom wearing his Lakers T-shirt and a half-smile. "Hope you don't mind," she said, pointing to the shirt.

"Course not," he said.

"You went to a lot of trouble for tonight, didn't you?" He started to shake his head, "No," but she put up a hand to stop him. "I know you did and it must seem like I've been acting like a real bitch; but my day has been hell."

She sat down on the couch, away from the wine spill.

"What happened?" he asked, sitting next to her.

"Daddy happened. I was supposed to respond to a discovery motion, but I, well, I was a little late. Like a day. And Daddy had a fit. So I told him I'd fix it. But it took me forever to find my postman's home phone number. They won't tell you that sort of thing at the post office."

"You lost me," Mercer said. "Why did you want your postman?"

"To get him to backdate the postmark on my response."

"Your postman would do that? Hell, mine won't even stick my mail in the box. Just leaves it on the counter downstairs."

"Well, Louis—that's his name—is kinda stuck on me.

So he does me little favors. But even though I got it taken care of, Daddy continued shouting at me all afternoon."

"He's not known for cutting slack, that's for sure."

"Well, I did screw up," she said. "Fact is, I'm bored silly with the civil cases. I think I'm ready for criminal law."

"Your daddy may have something to say about that. He thinks the big money is in civil litigation."

"You got him to change his mind about the Burris case."

"It was probably the hundred-grand retainer changed his mind about that," Mercer said. "But your average criminal case is a whole lot of work for very little coin."

"I'm not talking about average criminal cases," she said.

"Those are the cases you have to cut your teeth on," he said.

"Unless you're lucky enough to wind up assisting in a very important murder trial."

He'd been listening to her without hearing what she was saying. He understood now that this was the main reason, possibly the only reason, she'd agreed to have dinner with him. "Without some practical experience," he said, "that's not likely to happen."

She looked crestfallen, but only for a moment. "You know I'm a hard worker. And I'm smart. And it would be exciting, you and me in it together."

"Yeah, it would," he said. He took her hand and held it. Her fingers were long, her hands were strong and yet incredibly soft. She was wearing, at his request, an apple-red nail polish. She wore it on her toes, too. Just for him. Why was he doubting her affection?

"Problem is," he said, "David Gomez will be prosecuting. I may have mentioned him before."

"Sure," she said. "He's the deputy D.A. you beat in the Darion Mayfield trial."

"It goes a little deeper than that," Mercer said. "The man used to be my supervisor when I was working for the D.A. He was bummed when I left to join the firm, and then I really kicked his ass in court. He's out to get me good, which means he doesn't just want to put Burris away, he wants to drop the pellet on him."

"But you won't let him," she said.

"No. But I need a second chair who's got some experience in murder trials. That's Eddie Baraca. He's a slick son of a bitch. The problem is gonna be holding him down. Of course . . ." The crestfallen look on her face stopped him. "Aw, honey. You're a damn good litigator, but that's not what I need. The man's on trial for murder."

Vanessa withdrew her hand. "How different is murder from wrongful death?"

He was silent for a beat, trying to think of how to put it without sounding patronizing or insulting. "I love you, honey. But this is going to be real ugly. Darion Mayfield had his head chopped off. The prosecution is going to be hanging autopsy pictures all over that courtroom. A severed head, with a lot of the flesh ripped off by a dog and—"

"You see me as some bourgie princess who can't handle a little blood, right? You don't think I'm tough enough?"

"That's not—"

"Lemme tell you something, Mr. Clarence Darrow: I can run a case just as good as you—anytime, any day."

"Yeah? How many cases have you tried in court?" he asked.

When she remained silent, he answered for her. "None. Zero. How many criminal cases have you handled? Same answer. Not even a petty theft. You think runnin' a couple of motions in some dry-ass civil case makes you ready to handle a murder trial? A trial where a man's life is at stake? What kind of a jackass lawyer would I be to put my client's life in the hands of an amateur?"

It took him a second to realize that his anger had shifted him into a very nondiplomatic mood. Vanessa was glaring at him. Her eyes seemed to be filling with tears, but he knew she wouldn't cry. He considered an apology, but it would serve no purpose other than to make him sound weak and ineffectual.

"Exactly how many murder cases have you tried?" Vanessa asked.

"None," he said. "That's why I need a backup like Eddie."

"Yeah, well, Eddie didn't do so fine for himself in that Lincoln trial."

"The prosecution had Elroy Lincoln dead-bang," Mercer said. "Eddie beat the death penalty."

"Great," she said. "You want to settle for life in prison for your white cop, you did the right thing. You got Eddie."

She was off the sofa and grabbing her purse before he could stop her.

"Hold on," he said, following her to the front door. "Baby, this whole night got turned around. I just wanted to spend some quality time with you. To show you how much I love you."

"I think you showed me that," she said. "With those supermarket flowers in your pathetic little boy's bath tub and your rotgut wine and your cruel and insulting remarks about my . . . professionalism."

"I guess Barry Fox woulda done better."

"Barry Fox *has* done better," she said, exiting and slamming the door on him.

He stared at it for a few seconds. When he turned, he discovered that flames were shooting up from the hibachi. He filled a glass with water and raced for the balcony, getting there before the fire did any serious damage to the building. The dousing resulted in a screen of smoke and ash around the charred steaks.

He was trying to rescue what was left of the meat when he heard the rat-tat of heels down below, then the slam of a car door and the rumble of a Porsche engine. The Boxter's top was down. Heartbreakingly beautiful in her fury, still wearing his Lakers shirt, Vanessa roared

by and away, not looking back. Just as well, he thought.
All she would have seen was a sorry fool with a forkful
of inedible steak in his hand, standing in the smoke and
ruins of his evening of romance.

30

Mingus's stomach was singing a symphony by the time Gomez decided to cut him free.

During the two hours the D.D.A. had kept him waiting, he'd wandered around the area looking for and not finding a candy-bar machine. Failing that, he roamed the floor, chatting up the secretaries and picking up enough bits and pieces from the meeting to realize that Gomez, the D.A., some white-haired dude in a minister outfit, and a couple of pasty suits were deep in discussion about how they could most effectively use the court of public opinion to aid the prosecution of Burris.

When Gomez finally emerged from the meeting, he put Mingus through another hour and a half of questions, many of them repeated, about the events leading to Burris's arrest and his ongoing investigation of Detective Farley.

"I get the feeling you're not really working with me, Detective," Gomez complained, after Mingus had balked for the eighth or ninth time at getting too deep into the Farley case.

"I'm doing everything I can per Captain Jacquette. Maybe you should take this up with him." The RHD captain had told Mingus to button up, but the real reason he was not giving the prosecutor his full cooperation was more basic: he simply didn't want to. His initial dislike for Gomez had grown by the minute to the point where it was all he could do to stop from reaching across the desk and bitch-slapping the smug smile from his chubby tan face.

He resisted the urge.

As he and Gomez waited for the elevator, the prosecutor said, "Remember, Detective, you never answer a question the defense asks you without thinking through the consequences of your reply. Take all the time you need. And try to answer with a yes or a no. Never ever offer more information than is requested."

"I'm not exactly a rookie," Mingus said.

"No," Gomez said, his smirk turned on full force. "Rookies have cleaner records."

Wearily, Mingus returned to his office. Considering that he'd been away nearly all day, there was very little waiting for him. Most of the Internal Affairs personnel had gone home. He picked up his phone and caught Pascal just as he was leaving the lab.

"The residue on your plastic was white wine," the tech told him, "so I guess we're talking some kind of drinking cup."

"Who drinks white wine out of a plastic cup?" Mingus asked.

"Anybody who doesn't have a wineglass at his disposal," Pascal said. "I've used a jelly glass from time to time."

Mingus had, too. "You mind sticking what's left of that shard in an envelope, Pascal? Leave it at the front desk for me?"

The lab technician said he would.

Mingus leaned back in his chair and closed his eyes. Just for a second, he told himself.

He was awakened with a start by the ringing of his phone.

It was Captain Jacquette, speaking over the roar of a crowd somewhere. "Where are you with the Farley investigation?"

While Mingus tried to clear his head to reply, he could hear through the phone the hollow sound of feet pounding the floor, yells, grunts, and a pattern of slapping sounds. "I'm trying to locate a man who I think can give me the whole story. Problem is, he's a witness in the Claude Burris trial and Farley has him tucked away somewheres."

"So you've got nothing for me?"

"No nails to put in the coffin, but—"

"Close the file," Jacquette said.

"Say what?"

"You've got nothing. The investigation is finished. As far as the world is concerned, it never even began. Understand?"

Mingus was stunned. "I don't think I do."

A universal groan came from the crowd where Jacquette was and he said, "Shit."

"You at a ball game, Cap?"

"Yeah. My daughter plays basketball. My son goes to cooking school. That's the fucking kind of world it is. Drop the case."

"This got anything to do with the Mayfield trial?" Mingus asked. "Like maybe the D.A. wants to make sure Farley stays all nice and shiny?"

"That's not your concern," Jacquette said. Then he dropped some of his surliness and added, "Sorry I wasted your time on this. I . . . ." Whatever he was about to say, he thought better of it. Instead, he said, "Stay the course, Lionel," and clicked off.

Stay the course? What the hell did that mean? Stay the course, Lionel. Was the captain telling him to do as he was ordered? Or was he suggesting that Mingus ignore the order and stay with the investigation?

Confused and beaten down by the events of the day, he decided he owed himself a small bit of relaxation.

Sitting at his favorite table at LaLa's, awaiting the arrival of his first taste of the evening, he allowed his eyes to scan the bar area, searching for the big, beautiful high-yella lady of his dreams. What he found instead was Burris's lawyer, Mercer Early, drunk and at the mercy of a willowy, walking mantrap he had nicknamed the Barracuda.

She was working the lawyer over in fine fashion, pressing against him, one hand inside his shirt, the other possibly fondling his butt, more likely involved in some far-from-benign activity.

The waitress placed the Thug Passion in front of Mingus. "You waitin' for anybody, Detective," she asked, "or do you want to order your dinner now?"

Mingus's plan had been to grab an early dinner, alone, then hang around to see what developed. But he abruptly changed his mind. "Catch me in five, huh?"

The Barracuda had lifted the young lawyer's wallet and was on the verge of dropping it into the purse at her feet when Mingus grabbed her wrist.

Startled, she glared at him, mouth open, ready to unleash a flow of invective. He stopped her with, "I'm a cop. You wanna go to jail?"

"I was jus' helpin' my fren' pay his bill."

"Wha's goin' on?" Mercer Early was looking at them both, slack-jawed and glassy-eyed.

"Lady's leaving," Mingus said. "You better get something to eat."

"What?" the young lawyer asked with a hint of anger.

"I ain't goin' nowhere," the Barracuda screeched.

Mingus sighed, turned to the door, where Big Timo the security guard had filtered out the noise in the room to pick up on the woman's aggressive tone. The detective nodded and Timo crossed the floor with surprising grace for a man who weighed in at 260 pounds, most of it muscle.

He grabbed the Barracuda's upper arm and lifted her off the stool. "I tole you last time it was the last time, Lucinda," Timo said.

"Gotta get my goddamned purse," she said, snagging it from the floor as he propelled her toward the door.

"Where's he takin' that girl?" the young lawyer asked.

"They don't like thieves in here," Mingus said, slapping the wallet on the bar top.

Mercer blinked and squinted at the object. "Tha's mine."

"Your *girl* seemed to think it was hers."

"My girl. My girl doesn't love me."

"What she loved was your cash," Mingus said, waving to the barmaid.

"No. Don't mean that girl. My girl. Vanessa." He tried to stand, but his legs wouldn't hold him.

"You better get some food in you, man. Pay the lady and I'll help you to my table."

Mercer seemed to have trouble getting the bills from his wallet so Mingus took it from him, tossed two twenties onto the bar and shoved the billfold into the lawyer's jacket pocket.

Then he dragged Mercer to his table, the cowardly lion dragging the scarecrow.

The lawyer sat across from him, staring down at the tabletop in silence. When the waitress arrived to ask for their order, he said, "No barbecue. Meat all burned."

Mingus ordered catfish dinners for them both and a cup of black coffee for Mercer.

"She's gone. Vanessa."

"That happens sometimes."

"I tried to make it perfect. Ever'thing got fucked up."

"Drink up," Mingus said, when the waitress had placed a steaming cup of black coffee in front of Mercer.

"My life's going great and . . . wham. She's gone and what else matters? Answer me that."

"Hard to say." Mingus watched the lawyer take a sip of coffee and wrinkle his nose at its bitter taste. He looked too young and, frankly, too naïve to be the kind of hotshot lawyer who'd busted Burris on the stand and cut Gomez off at the knees. Of course, he wasn't at his best. Moaning about some soured romance. Mingus couldn't remember the last time a woman meant that much to him. Maybe that was what was wrong with his life. Didn't some poet say it was better to have loved and been shit on than never to have loved? Still, judging by Mercer Early's present condition, it wasn't necessarily better.

"Who the hell are you?" Mercer asked, staring at Mingus for the first time.

"Just a guy thought you could use some help."

Mercer took another sip of coffee. "Jesus," he said. "I'm drunk. Do I know you?"

Mingus considered the question. He was tempted to answer it in full. But Redd had begged him not to confide too much in Mercer, should they meet. And he wasn't sure how much the lawyer could take, operating at less than full capacity. "My name's Lionel Mingus."

"Thanks, Lionel, for . . . Mingus?" The lawyer squinted at him. "You're the cop?"

"Yeah."

"Aw, shit. I can't . . ." Mercer tried to stand, but he was still too wobbly. He plopped back down. "This is no good. I can't be . . . You're on Gomez's list."

"Yeah, but right now you're in no condition to—"

"No. This is wrong. We could both—"

He was stopped by the waitress placing two aromatic catfish dinners in front of them.

When she'd gone, Mingus said, "Eat up. We don't have to talk about the trial. We don't have to talk at all."

With a groan of exasperation, Mercer picked up his knife and fork and began to devour every morsel of food on his plate.

During a mainly silent dinner, Mingus was struck by an idea how he could continue to investigate Farley without actually doing it. When they'd both finished eating, he put it into play. "There's a way we can help one another."

Mercer's eyes had lost their glassiness. They were now bloodshot and wary. "Not about the trial."

"I think you want to hear me out."

"You got me at a disadvantage. I'm not sure I could stand up and walk away."

"You seriously want me to shut up?"

"I wouldn't be that rude to a man who saved me from getting my wallet lifted."

"Gomez's key witness is an ex-con named Kenneth Ansol. Also known as Ken Loc."

"So?"

"So you might want to know the felon claims to have worked for the deceased."

"Okay. I'm with you so far," Mercer said.

"There's a question you might want to ask him when you get him on the stand," Mingus said.

Mercer stared at him. "We gotta watch ourselves here," he said. Then he grinned. "What question?"

"What's his relationship with the officer in charge of the investigation?"

"That'd be Dennis Farley?"

"Most definitely."

"What's his answer gonna be?" Mercer asked.

"I don't know for sure. Maybe that Farley threatened him with prison time unless he put the finger on Burris. Maybe it's an even stronger tie, like he might know of some connection between Farley and Darion Mayfield."

"You got anything approaching proof on any of that?"

"If I did, I wouldn't need you to ask the question."

"And you can't ask him yourself because . . . ?"

"Farley's keeping him out of sight."

"What's your interest in this? Since my client put that notch in your head, I don't suppose you two are pals."

"I don't give a shit about Burris, one way t'other."

"What were you doing at the crime scene when he got arrested?" Mercer asked.

Mingus was amused by the fact that the more sober his dinner partner got, the more lawyerlike he became. "Following my curiosity," he said.

"You're Internal Affairs, right? Were you investigating my client?"

Mingus yearned to tell Mercer that Farley was his target, to turn him loose on the fat man when Farley took the stand. But he'd been told by both Captain Jacquette and Gomez to keep his mouth shut on the subject. "Can't talk about it," he said.

Mercer stared at him. As glassy and red-rimmed as the man's eyes were, they were pretty fucking intense. "You'll have to tell me in court."

"Might not be an answer you and your client want to hear," Mingus said.

Mercer cocked his head and grinned. "You're after Farley."

"I'm after him, all right. But it's personal. The IAG isn't interested in him."

"What'd he do to you to make it personal?"

"That's another thing you don't need to know," Mingus said. "But I could put you wise to a few facts that might help."

"Lay 'em on me, Detective. You're sobering me up faster than the food and coffee."

So Mingus told him a few things. He recapped his meetings with the Ansol brothers and described the autopsy, including the discovery of the piece of plastic in Darion's throat. "I found a similar piece at the crime scene. A friend in the lab says it had wine residue on it."

Mercer seemed to absorb that information. He asked, "What's Farley's angle?"

"Talk to your client."

"I have. You think it's possible Farley framed him?"

"Maybe. They're about as friendly as two dogs with one soup bone. Burris won't say what set 'em at one another, but I figure it was something happened when they were partners."

"They were partners?" Mercer asked.

"Oh, yeah. Don't you and your client talk at all?"

"Not nearly enough, it would seem," Mercer said. "Could Farley have killed Darion?"

"Pushing him out a window? That's not exactly Fats's style. Even if Darion had done something to rile him up, Fats most likely would have drawn down on him and shot him."

"Well, it was a nice idea."

"Mercer, there's something . . . I'm not sure it's connected, but there's a woman named Alice Adams who died last night."

"Yeah. There was something in the paper this morning. She wrote movies."

"She was a big customer of Darion's and, according to Ken Loc, she hung at his place a lot. I know they're calling her death a suicide, but if she was with Darion the night he died . . ."

"That's one hell of a what-if. Unless you know something to make it more likely."

"Well, there were no drugs found at the crime scene."

"I know," Mercer said. "That's one avenue I want to explore, the possibility that somebody killed Darion for his stash."

"Who does your investigating?"

"Ex-cop named Lonny Hootkins."

Mingus recalled Hootkins, a salty old dog who'd unloaded his feelings about the chief of police to a *Los Angeles Times* reporter just before taking early retirement. "Maybe you should get Lonny to have a talk with the officers who found Alice Adams's body. See if maybe there was a large quantity of Darion's white powder on the scene."

"There was nothing in the paper about drugs," Mercer said.

"Wasn't any mention of her connection to Darion, either."

"So you think . . . what? That she witnessed the murder, grabbed some dope and lit out? Then the killer came after her? Made it look like suicide? Man, that's thinking way outside the box." The young lawyer suddenly got a strange look on his face, like his dinner was going to make a reappearance.

"You okay?" Mingus asked.

"Yeah. I just remembered something Burris said about there being 'bad people' we had to watch out for."

"I'm not suggesting any major conspiracy, just wondering if there might be a link between the two deaths. And, if I may say so, I don't think you ought to take everything your client tells you as gospel. He carries a lot of bullshit with him."

Mingus turned to signal the waitress that she could take away the dishes and saw that the big woman of his dreams was sitting at the bar. All alone.

"Dinner's on me, Detective," he heard Mercer saying. "I owe you that and more."

"Think you can make it home okay?" Mingus asked.

"What I got is mainly a hangover now," Mercer said. "I'm beat on my feet. I'm going to grab a few hours' sleep and get things rolling in the morning. Put Hootkins on the case."

"Then I'll say good night," Mingus said, rising. "You got any other questions or if you find out anything about Farley, give me a ring. You can call me at—"

"I have your number at my office," Mercer said.

Mingus nodded and started away. Then he stepped back. "I almost forgot. I was down at the D.A.'s today. They moving kinda fast on this, aren't they?"

"Burris had an attorney before me who let the D.A. con him into a speedy trial. I got weeks to work with instead of months."

"Yeah, well, the D.A. had quite a party going on down there. A bunch of slick-looking white dudes and this white-haired reverend who was loud-mouthin' some nasty stuff about you and your law firm. My guess is, the D.A. is out to trash you folks big time."

"Thanks," the young lawyer said. He looked suddenly stricken.

"You sure you're okay?"

"Just wondering how far back David Gomez might go looking to—no, don't worry, I'm okay. You go on."

Mingus turned to the bar again and saw with some dismay that the big woman was gone. How could that be? She'd been sitting there just a second ago . . . Her bar stool was still there. Unused.

As he moved closer, he saw that her drink—it looked like a martini—was still on its coaster, barely touched.

He sat on the empty stool and signaled the bartender for a cocktail.

"That seat's occupied," the bartender cautioned him. "Lady's in the powder room."

"Good," Mingus said, grinning. "That's what I want to hear."

He watched his dinner companion pay the tab and get to his feet, a little wobbly. He made it to the door without too much difficulty, turned, and waved to the detective.

Mingus waved back, hoping Mercer was sober enough to be driving.

The lawyer went completely out of his thoughts when the big lady with the serious curves returned, a Betty Boop pocketbook clasped in her hand. He stood and offered her the stool. "Just keeping it warm for you."

She raised one eyebrow. "Not too warm, I hope. My dress is kinda thin." She climbed up on the stool, placing her purse on the bar next to her glass. She wiggled around on the red leather and said, "Nice and warm, just how I like it. You waitin' for your redhead friend?"

"Nope," he said. "You waitin' for your friend with the dyed-black hair?"

"Dyed? You mean that lamp black with the gray roots ain't natural?" She smiled. "Coulda fooled me. But no, I'm not waiting for him."

"Isn't this something," he said. "Two people not waiting for anybody."

"We should drink to that," she said.

31

Mercer's head was throbbing so hard from the booze, all he wanted to do was get home, crawl into bed, pull the sheet up, and hide from the world. The world wouldn't let him. The apartment smelled of burned meat and stale wine, reminding him of the dinner from hell. His answering machine was blinking like a turn signal. Before he could decide what to do about either of those situations, the phones in the apartment broke into a one-note duet.

He froze while the answering machine kicked in, expecting to hear the voice of doom, speaking with an Alabama accent.

"This is Carl Tunis from the *Daily Journal*, Mr. Early. Please give me a call at . . ."

Ah, no police, just the media. Mercer breathed a sigh of relief and ignored the man's phone number. The *Daily Journal* was a leading legal newspaper. No doom tonight, thank you, I have a headache.

Just when he found the aspirin bottle hiding in the kitchen cabinet, the phones began to ring again. Damn, they were shrill. Well, that was a problem easily solved. He stumbled to the bedroom, unplugged the phone by the bed. By the time he returned to the main room, another reporter, this time a woman from a local TV station, was asking him to return her call. He pulled the plug just as she was finishing her spiel.

He was in no condition to answer questions about the trial, or to even speculate on why so many people were calling him at home at so late an hour. He was not a well man. Maybe the aspirin would help. Probably not.

He ignored the temptation to simply flop down on the bed and undressed instead, meticulously placing his suit on a hanger and his shoes on a rack before slipping between the sheets.

He closed his eyes with a half-contented sigh.

And couldn't sleep.

Every little sound caused him to stir. The most crucial trial of his short career was upon him and he had a hundred things to do in the morning. His head, hard as it was, seemed mushy inside, the combination of stress, liquor, and sleep deprivation taking its toll.

He could not quite figure out the detective, Mingus. The man had stepped up and saved him from himself. Then he'd actually fed him information to use at the trial. Why was he showing such a weird lack of animosity toward a man who came damn close to putting his head on a pike alongside Darion's? Burris said Mingus was one of the good guys. Considering the source, that may not have been a compliment. But maybe the IAG cop was different from the rest, somebody who put justice above everything else. Mercer wanted to believe that, but he'd seen too much of the other breed of lawman.

One of the main reasons he'd left the D.A.'s office was because he couldn't stomach the D.D.A.s who believed in their moral superiority. They were so goddamned judgmental about every defendant, regardless of the strength or weakness of the case, regardless of the severity of the crime. It seemed easy, sitting in the prosecutor's chair, to condemn a sad dude so beaten by failure he decided to get strung out on junk, or a woman so leveled by life that she sold herself to keep a roof over her kids' heads.

Some D.D.A.s drew distinctions, for example, as between the petty thief and the child molester. But as Gomez used to say, "Among criminals, it is a distinction without difference." They were all scumbags.

Still full of law school notions of morality and justice and harboring his own secret past, Mercer found it hard to accept this cynical broad overview. The final test of his tolerance occurred during a lunch with an old-timer who'd been at it since the days when then-D.A. Vincent Bugliosi put the hex on Charlie Manson. The old dude had been carrying on about his fondness for the death penalty and Mercer asked him how he'd feel if he learned he'd sent an innocent man to the white room. "My duty is to convict them," the codger replied. "Let God sort out the innocent ones."

The comment had drawn laughter from the rest of the clerks. And disgust from Mercer. He'd been waffling about pursuing a career as a D.A., mainly because of his concern over the background check that would precede his swearing in. But it was that day, that moment, that convinced him to submit his resignation.

He groaned and pushed deeper into the pillow. Too much dwelling on the past. Besides, the thought of the D.A.'s office and Gomez reminded him of the trial and the last thing he needed was a sudden shot of adrenaline.

Vanessa's face floated above him. Too damned beautiful.

The night dragged on. A car passed, its speakers blasting rap music as it trailed off into the distance.

A fly buzzed about the dark apartment, then began testing a window to see if it was real. Buzzing and bouncing. Mercer felt a kinship with the insect. Constantly bumping into solid things he could not see. Objects bigger than he, tougher than he. Like the fly, he had limited options. He could not break through or get around the things in life that trapped him. Like the fly, he would have to accept his fate, make the best of his situation, and expect that he would eventually die, looking at the world going by just outside that window.

The sun broke through the blinds at a little after seven A.M., waking him from a very light sleep. He checked the clock, turned off the alarm, and headed for the bathroom. There was a meeting at the office at ten A.M. He had all the time in the world. He would take a long shower, dress, have a dose of caffeine from his single-guy, four-cup coffee maker, and then drive to One Wilshire. He forgot he'd unplugged the phones.

It was eight-forty-five when he sat down at the small kitchen table, the one that must have been built for dwarfs, to sample the coffee. It was lukewarm and weak. He tossed it and decided to treat himself to a decent cup.

Aiming the leased car in the direction of the 'hood and Buckie's, he clicked on the radio for "The Beat" and its mix of hip hop and humor. What he got wasn't so funny.

"I just want to ask Mercer Early one question: how many pieces of silver did they give you, Judas?"

"Who the hell . . . ?" Mercer said, momentarily losing control as the car almost kissed a vehicle in the next lane. His question was answered when the speaker was identified as a Reverend Eldon Patterson, a "leader of the black community."

"I'd love to know how much money those white cops gave that colored firm to betray the assassinated son of my brother in Jesus, the beloved Reverend Doctor Harlan Mayfield, and our entire community."

The radio DJ was a hyper guy named T-Break. Mercer knew him, infrequently played bungle ball with him at the beach. That wasn't stopping T-Break from egging the Reverend on. "Tha's what you think of Carter and Hansborough? That they're just *colored*? Not enough color in them to be considered black?"

The Reverend cleared his throat. "I can only say this: those godless people are no longer welcome in my church. They certainly need Jesus, but they'll have to go off with their own kind to find Him."

T-Break opened the phone lines to callers. The listeners were unanimous in their view of the firm and particularly critical of Mercer. "Sellouts. Uncle Toms. House nigguhs," said one caller, before he was cut off.

"Y'all got to control yourselves on the AM," T-Break chided his audience. "This ain't NPR or HBO. No profanity allowed. Now, if you feel the need to cuss, write those lawyers a letter or say it to 'em direct. But don't do it on the radio, 'cause there are kids out there listenin'."

T-Break took more calls.

In one rare instance the firm got some support. "So, y'all sayin' that if a black man killed a white boy that white lawyers ain't supposed to defend him?"

"We ain't here to talk about O.J.," T-Break said, shooting the caller down fast. "That's old news."

Mercer's cell phone began to chirp. Bobby Carter. "You on your way? All hell's breaking loose here."

"Uh . . . yeah," Mercer said, swinging the Mercedes sedan in a 180 and heading for Wilshire. "I've been listening to some Reverend Patterson on 'The Beat.' Rough stuff."

"Didn't you catch his news conference last night?"

Mercer suddenly recalled the phone calls, the messages. "No," he said. "I turned in kinda early."

"Patterson has good legal help. He went right up to the libel line, but he never crossed it. Anyhow, we'll discuss it when you get here."

The word "traitors" had been spray painted on the front of One Wilshire. Several uniformed security guards were shooing picketers and reporters from the entry while two workmen tried unsuccessfully to wipe away the letters with some kind of paint remover. Mercer thought a sandblaster might be in order.

Two black guards stopped his car just after it descended the ramp to the underground parking area. One stepped to the window to ask his business.

He explained he was an associate member of the firm. The guard asked to see his driver's license. He didn't have to check it against the list on his clipboard. "Okay, Mr. Early. Please move on."

The second guard asked, "That's Early?"

Both men studied him with barely veiled hostility. And they were on the firm's payroll.

Mercer moved on.

The brass walls of the elevator had been keyed, ugly gouges spelling out ugly words.

When he stepped off the elevator it seemed as if every phone in the place was ringing. The yella girls at the front were turning redder and redder with each call. "Sir, I will not sit here and listen to your profanity," one of them snapped and slammed the phone down hard.

Passing his own office, he instructed an obviously harassed Melissa to tell the receptionists to switch his phones to voice mail. "You can start picking up after ten."

Mercer moved toward Bobby's office.

Both partners were present. As he was taking a seat, Vanessa walked in. She was yawning and her hair was uncharacteristically out of place. Had she gone directly to Barry Fox's after leaving his apartment? Mercer considered telling her how much he liked her new 'do, but there was enough tension in the air.

"So, young man," Bobby said, "here we are, getting everything I thought we would. Since you're the one who created this problem, why don't you give us the benefit of your wisdom on how to fix it?"

Mercer had spent the rest of his drive time arriving at the answer to that question. "The truth will set us free," he said.

Bobby frowned. "It's a little late for bromides. We've got a mob downstairs, and half our client list is moving on to a 'truly black' firm."

"Not quite half, Bobby," a strangely genial C.W. said.

"Thirty percent, tops. And that loss will be more than made up by the business we'll be getting from the city."

Bobby started to say something, thought better of it.

"When Mercer wins his case," C.W. continued, "the others will come back. Everybody respects success."

"Meanwhile, we've got a building that identifies us as traitors," Bobby said. "What do we do about *that*?"

"Think about what this firm is, Bobby," Mercer said. "It's a reflection of our community, a community that's always prized truth, fairness, justice."

"Where you going with this?"

"In our zeal to protect the rights of Darion Mayfield, we inadvertently placed a fake tape recording of Detective Burris's voice into evidence. We allowed some still-unknown party to use us to discredit him. When we discovered that the tapes had been doctored, we felt we had a moral duty to correct the injustice we'd helped create."

"You honestly think people will believe that's why we're defending Burris?" Bobby asked.

"Isn't that why?" Mercer said.

C.W. smiled. "I suppose you want to convey this information to the media, young man?"

"No way. It should be somebody with a reputation built on integrity. Bobby."

Bobby scowled. "I don't think so."

"You could get a lot of mileage out of it," C.W. said. "The white folks in this state would be more inclined to vote for a black attorney general if he has proven he believes in equal justice regardless of race."

"You are one cynical son of a bitch, C.W.," Bobby said. He turned to Mercer. "I'll do it. But it comes to this. If the D.A. proves to the world that Burris is a murdering, racist cop, we'll all take the fall with him. My political career will be over and this firm will go straight to chapter eleven."

Nothing like a little more pressure.

"He's not guilty, Bobby. I'm going to win this case."

"Where are you? Should we bring Eddie in here?" Bobby asked.

"He's getting depositions from the scattered friends Burris has in the department. One of them, happily enough, is his boss, Lieutenant Cubert."

"You putting Hootkins to work?"

"I got a nice long list of things for him to do. We may need to hire one or two of his retired buddies to help him out. Time's the big enemy here."

"Hire whomever you need to get the job done," C.W. said.

Mercer rose from his chair. "I'm going to have another talk with the client. Got some things to check out."

He took a few steps toward the door, then stopped to ask, "This Reverend Patterson, he got white hair?"

"Like white Brillo," C.W. said.

"Then the D.A.'s office is behind his publicity tour."

"You're wrong," Bobby said. "The conference last night was organized by Patterson's own Brother-to-Brother Coalition."

"The Coalition might have fronted it, but I have it on good authority that Patterson and a bunch of spin doctors had a long session yesterday evening with the D.A. and Too-Good Gomez. The plan they came up with was to cover us with as much mud as they can. But mud washes off."

Bobby frowned. C.W. looked bemused. Vanessa gave Mercer a smile of approval. It was a little short of the kind of smile that used to make his heart sing, but, for the moment, it would do.

Burris wasn't exactly thrilled to see him and tightened up even more when Mercer began asking him questions about Dennis Farley.

"Okay, we were partners. So fucking what?"

"So you guys don't seem to be friends anymore. What happened?"

"Why do you want to know?" Burris said.

"If I can bust Farley on the stand, you're on your way out of here. How do I get the guy?"

Burris glared at him for what seemed like an eternity. Then he lowered his voice to a harsh whisper. "You don't. It's too dangerous."

"Convince me of the danger."

"Okay, but it stays here," Burris said.

"If that's how you want it."

"Back when Fats and I were partnered up, we'd get a little gift every month from Bumpy Lewis, who was the dealer man in Inglewood. Not a fortune, but we didn't have to do much to earn it. Then Farley gets tapped by Robbery-Homicide. Why, I've got no idea. The guy was never much of a cop. No major arrests. Nothing like that. The only reason he wound up on the job was because of his dad who, as far as I could tell, wasn't much of a cop, either.

"Anyway, he gets a job in RHD, but he expects to keep getting his share of Bumpy's good nature. I tell him to go fuck himself. Within weeks, Bumpy is turned into a crispy critter and Darion is the new top dog. Then Fats informs me that I'm gonna get a much smaller bite of Darion's action. Talk about your brass balls, he says it's only because he likes me I don't get cut off entirely.

"Well, hell, I'm not gonna take that lying down. I pull Darion in. He's on the street faster than I can write up the bust. Then the shit begins. Little stuff at first. A dead rat in my mailbox. Flat tires. Mouth-breather phone calls. I get to the apartment after work one night to find that somebody broke in. Nothing stolen. They just wanted to take a dump on the living room carpet.

"I still don't get the message. I find Fats, slap him around, and tell him if the bullshit doesn't stop I'll pound him into dog meat. The next day, the very next day, the brakes go out on my car.

"So, I figure life's too short. I'll spend the rest of mine ignoring Darion Mayfield."

"What changed your mind?"

"Darion. I was in this Cuban joint with some friends, minding my own business. The scumbag had to come over and pretend like we were old buddies. He all but told 'em I was on his pad, the fuck. So, I'm so pissed I find a judge in the morning and the next night I bust him. And here I am, paying the price."

Mercer felt his hangover coming back strong. His client had just admitted to being a bent cop. Now he was spouting some bullshit conspiracy scenario. Neither situation was going to help much to get him acquitted.

"Burris, we've got to bring this down to jury level. I'm pretty sure I can pull the pants off Ken Loc Ansol, but I need to get Farley to bare his teeth on the stand, show 'em who he really is."

"I'm telling you, Early, don't fuck with the fat man or you'll get us both whacked."

Mercer nodded, but made no promises. He wasn't going to go soft on a potentially damaging prosecution witness because his client was acting paranoid about payback.

"You have a line on any of Darion's customers?" he asked.

"Why?"

"It's that shadow of a doubt thing," Mercer said. "In the jury room, somebody's going to start asking who killed Darion, if it wasn't you. I'd like to float the theory that a hype may have killed him for his drugs. None were found in his apartment."

"What makes you think there were any? The place got cleaned when I busted him."

"He invited me to party with him that night. He promised me 'dealer-choice blow.' "

"And you didn't go?" Burris laughed nastily. "Or maybe you did."

Mercer wasn't amused. "You got any names?"

Burris shook his head.

"Thanks for your cooperation," Mercer said, standing to go.

"I hear you're taking a little heat out there from your people." Mercer, sensitive to such things, could find no sarcasm in his client's tone.

"A little."

"Once your reputation gets tarnished, it's goddamn hard to shine it up again."

"It helps if you make the effort to apply some polish," Mercer said.

32

The sex had been good for Mingus. The big woman—her name was Bettye (she explained she added the "e" to make it "just a little different") Hiler—had been eager to please him. Some of the things she had wanted to do seemed more than a little freaky. But he did 'em anyway. And in the end, he was glad he did. What he wasn't happy about was what happened when he woke up.

First, he was surprised to find himself in Betty Boop land. The walls were covered with Betty Boop memorabilia. The bedspread and linen were also Betty Boop. When he finally got up to take a leak, the toilet was covered by a black and red velvet Betty Boop.

Then, emerging from the bathroom, he found Bettye exploring his wallet. "Jus' tryin' to find out a little about you," she said, handing him the worn piece of leather.

They hadn't talked much about themselves. Hadn't talked much about anything.

"You need a few bucks?" he said.

She nodded. "I got a husband doin' federal time until somewhere around 2010. It's been a little rough. But I didn't touch your money. I don't do that. And I'm not a ho."

"I didn't think that," he said, taking a few bills from his wallet and putting them on her dresser.

She fixed him a breakfast of meat and eggs.

While they ate, she told him she was originally from Culpepper, a small town in Virginia. Chowing down on the meat, Mingus wondered aloud what kind of sausage he was eating.

"That's not sausage. It's scrapple."

Mingus had never heard of it.

"It's scraps of pork and corn meal all mashed together."

Mingus suddenly had trouble swallowing the meat, if that's what it really was.

"You know what I'd like right now?" she said, moving one long leg until her toes found his under the table. "To go back to bed and fool around a little more."

Mingus wanted to, but it was already nine o'clock. "Gotta get to work."

She seemed disappointed as she followed him back to the bedroom. "Am I gonna see you again? I mean, I hope you don't think badly of me because I was lookin' in your wallet or because I took you to my home."

"No. Not at all."

"I mean, heck, I be needin' love just like you. Plus, we both been eyeing each other for the longest."

Mingus was already buckling his belt and placing his 9mm in its holster. His old gun, the one Redd brought to him, lay on the dresser. He didn't remember putting it there and that fact sent a chill up his spine. The night could have been a replay of that last blackout.

He took another bill from his wallet, a hundred, and placed it on the dresser, too.

"Good-bye money?" she asked.

"No. Just to help out."

At the door, Bettye said, "You wanna have dinner here tonight?"

He wasn't sure he did. She had a husband at the stone house. The same lousy situation Burris was in with Redd.

She must have sensed his reluctance. "I bet you could use some good home cookin', all that restaurant food you eat."

Why not? he thought. What else did he have to look forward to that night? "Dinner sounds fine," he said. "But, uh, no scrapple, huh?"

"You didn't like it?"

"I'm a real bigot when it comes to food. I believe in meat segregation."

"How's about fried chicken, potatoes, and gravy?"

"No problem there," he said. He took out his wallet, but she shook her head.

"No. You already give me all I need." She smiled. "And then some."

"I'll bring wine," he said.

"Beer's fine with me," she said, which, in Mingus's mind, almost made up for all the Betty Boop bullshit.

A depression hit him about halfway through the day, prompted by his failure to turn up anything of substance on the Farley investigation. If he'd worked faster and more productively, the captain would have let him complete the job. Instead, he was back at the daily grind.

He and a detective named Opaka, a sometimes partner, were sent to poke around an incident in Hollywood in which an off-duty cop shot a man who was robbing a liquor store. Opaka was a sullen little Hawaiian who had the odd habit of giving a lilt to his normal conversation, so that it sounded like he was singing rather than talking. Mingus figured that if they were to run into trouble, Opaka would probably draw a ukulele instead of a gun.

At the shooting scene, Mingus went through the paces without really giving it much thought. It looked righteous enough. The dead man had a gun near his hand—maybe a throw-down, but why be pessimistic? The dead man had served time for armed robbery. The Vietnamese store owner corroborated the cop's statement that lives had been in danger. Open and shut. Only, Opaka must have been watching too much *Law and Order*, or something, because he began throwing questions at the store owner. "Where was the robber pointing his gun when he was shot?" "Whose life was in danger?" "Did you have any history with the robber?" "Do you know Officer Bernard?"

The store owner, for whom Hawaiian-accented English was definitely not a first language, particularly when sung, seemed to be confused. Which Opaka, not knowing how fucking weird he sounded when he talked, found very suspicious. He told Mingus he thought something was hinky.

Mingus shrugged and headed for some Slim Jims he spotted on the counter.

They arrived back at IAG near quitting time. Mingus left Opaka to type up a report on the day and made a trip to the lab.

Pascal was a small, sallow man with what appeared to be the pincer of a large scorpion tattoo on his neck showing above the starched white collar of his smock. He ragged on Mingus for pushing him to get his precious piece of plastic ready and then picking it up a day late. He then suggested that maybe it was piece of a "shot glass sort of thing that people who are really into wine use when they test vintages and stuff."

Mingus said it was as good a guess as any, then took the shard to his apartment where he tried to catch a few winks before dinner. Even well rested, it would be hard to keep up with the energetic Bettye Hiler.

She greeted him at the door dressed in panties and a bra, both of them in matching red satin with peekaboo cutouts. "It was so warm in the kitchen," she said, taking the twin six-packs from his hands. "Hope you don't mind the casual dress."

He let her get a few paces in front of him before following her to the kitchen. "Don't mind it at all," he said. The apartment smelled of chicken frying. On the stove, pieces of the bird browned in hot oil. Cooked pieces dried on a bed of paper towels.

She put the beer in the refrigerator. As she moved to the stove she purposely backed into him, rubbed herself against him and said, "You a hungry man, Lionel?"

"Getting hungrier by the minute," he said, pulling her to him and turning her for the kiss.

Her tongue darted into his mouth. She had him horns up within seconds, then pulled free. "First we eat," she said. She turned her attention to potatoes in a pot that she began to attack with a masher.

Mingus tried to catch his breath.

"Think you could open a couple of your beers, Lionel?" she said.

"Sure," he said and withdrew two cans from the fridge. "Where do you keep your glasses?"

"In the cabinet just to your left, but don't bother with a glass for me," she said.

Yes, she was okay, he thought.

33

Mercer spent the weeks leading up to the trial like a skier on a giant slalom, totally focused on maintaining speed and staying on his feet while avoiding the next obstacle. He left the overseeing of the clerks and the investigators and the specialists to his cocounsel, Eddie Baraca, who regularly kept them working into golden time.

Though his routine was far from inflexible, it usually consisted of a prebreakfast scanning of the clerks' labors, a postbreakfast meeting with Eddie and the investigators, more meetings with the client or the partners or strategists, and a final, late session with Eddie during which they would discuss their progress or lack thereof and fill in the blanks in the following day's schedule. Since he was averaging less than five hours of sleep each night, he also tried to catch a quick nap whenever he could fit it in. Of course, any of these events would be shifted or skipped to allow for unforeseen emergencies, including the countering of personal attacks emanating from the D.A.'s office.

Bobby Carter's press conference was generally well received. It cast a slightly more friendly light over the firm and helped to keep in place the clients who had been teetering on the brink of departure. It also seemed

to have stemmed the television and radio activity of
Reverend Patterson and may have been the reason for
Reverend Mayfield's surprising public refusal to en-
dorse Patterson's crusade, adding a few more nails to
the blowhard's coffin.

The publicists employed by the firm anonymously
"leaked" a copy of the tape from Darion's trial to the
Los Angeles Times with typed instructions to play it at a
speed slow enough to hear the voice describing it as
"doctored bullshit." The resulting article made the front
page, and legal pundits, prompted by those same publicists, began to ask why the district attorney's office
hadn't tried to authenticate the tape before allowing its
use in court.

Mercer went out of his way to dodge the media but
eventually was cornered by a persistent reporter who
pressed him about the tape. How much had he known
about it when he placed it into evidence? He replied
truthfully that the tape had been found on a desk at the
firm the night before he was scheduled to cross-
examine Detective Claude Burris in the Darion Mayfield trial. He should have been more suspicious, should
have tried to authenticate its contents, but he'd been too
excited by what he thought to be proof that Detective
Burris was a liar.

The reporter tried to elicit a theory about who might
have made the tape and what motive they may have
had. "I wish I knew," Mercer said. "That person is probably responsible for Darion Mayfield's murder. All I
know for certain is that Detective Claude Burris is innocent of all charges brought against him. And I will do
everything in my power to prove his innocence."

Poking around in the death of Alice Adams, investigator Lonny Hootkins had found nothing to support
Detective Mingus's theory linking it to the Mayfield
murder. The unusually large quantity of illegal drugs
present in the home was considered merely the by-
product of the woman's wealth and addiction. The only
odd item of note was the absence of the deceased's lap-

top computer which, according to those in the know, had been like a part of her.

Hootkins and his associates were a little more successful in uncovering Darion Mayfield's other former clients. Those without alibis were cajoled or intimidated by threat of subpoena into sitting still for an interview. Some might have served as remotely possible suspects, but only one struck the defense team as prime, a skeletal ex-athlete named Armando Petty who looked and acted as scary as Freddy Krueger and who claimed to have been asleep in an earthquake-condemned building while the murder was being committed just three blocks away. His addiction had already cost him his career, his marriage, and his health, and Mercer wasn't exactly up with adding to his grief by parading him before a jury. But, as Eddie Baraca pointed out, "Our obligation is to Burris, not Petty. Besides, the dude can't get any lower and he's not making any moves to climb back up. And, hell, maybe he did the murder."

The Hootkins squad's other assignment was to go over every witness with a fine-tooth comb. Witnesses for the prosecution in a murder trial are under no obligation to submit to a defense deposition, but Baraca and his team conned some of them into believing otherwise. The interviewees said they'd heard Burris mouthing off about wanting to "get" Darion Mayfield or that they'd seen the vice cop's anger in full bloom. A couple of ex-cons claimed to have felt his unprovoked wrath. None of them had anything substantive to say about the specific crime.

Even if Detective Lionel Mingus hadn't been savvy enough to know he was not supposed to talk to the defense, David Gomez brought that legal point to his attention on a regular basis. It hadn't stopped Mingus from making a few phone calls to Mercer. The week prior to the start of the trial, they accidentally wound up sharing a crowded elevator in the Criminal Courts Building. The two men barely acknowledged one another until they were alone on the parking sublevel.

Then, grinning like schoolboys who'd put one over on the teacher, they slapped hands.

"You look like you been taking care of yourself, brother," Mercer said. "Working out?"

"Something like that," Mingus said. "What about yourself? You're slimmin' down to Chris Rock size."

"Got no time to eat," Mercer said.

"You covered for next week?"

"I think so. The info you've fed me—the business with the dog, the background on the Ansol brothers— it's priceless. Still, a couple things could be better. It'd be nice if my client stopped his silent hard-ass act and opened up to me a little. And I'd love to get about an hour with Ken Loc before dealing with him in court. Don't suppose you know where I can find him?"

Mingus shook his head. "They still got him cooped."

"That's got to mean they're afraid he—"

Mercer's comment was halted by the sound of the elevator doors opening and people getting off.

The detective turned and started walking away. "See you next week," he said over his shoulder.

Mercer watched him go. "Next week," he said, mainly to himself.

34

Since hooking up with Bettye Hiler, Mingus had undergone something of a sea change. He'd been spending just about every night with her. Eating well. Fucking well. Cutting way down on the booze. Saving a buck or two. He'd even lost a couple inches of gut. Instead of dragging his lonely ass to some club or bar, he'd been spending those hours in Bettye's comfortable little living room, sock feet up on the end table, telling her about his day or watching TV with her.

The woman's influence had been so positive that it brightened even the dreary daily grind of peeking into cops' dirty laundry. He still felt regret at having failed to find the evidence needed to get Farley's badge yanked but the desire to do the fat man in had waned. His interest in the Burris case might have diminished, too, if it hadn't been for Gomez's frequent calls seeking assurance he'd be ready and able to take the stand when needed.

Every so often he'd seen something—a cable blabbermouth putting some weird spin on the Burris case—or remembered something—the odd scratches on Darion Mayfield's face—that moved him to put through a call to Mercer Early. He genuinely liked the young man and thought the feeling was reciprocated, but that didn't stop him from worrying a little about what Mercer might do to him in court. He knew enough lawyers to understand that a good one, which he felt Mercer was, would break his mama's heart if it set his client free.

The evening before the commencement of trial, David Gomez called him at IAG to remind him to be on the ninth floor of the Criminal Courts Building twenty minutes before the fireworks started at ten o'clock in the morning.

"You putting me on first?" he asked.

"Don't worry about when I'm putting you on. Just be there."

"Sure," he said, "since you asked me so nice."

He arrived at Bettye's just after sundown to find her banging pans in the kitchen. "I can't find the goddamn meat thermometer, 'scuse my French."

He was about to make some obscene remark about a meat thermometer when he realized how stressed she was. "Don't worry about it," he said.

"But we had a 'lectricity blackout and the roast was only partways done. And now I don't know if it's too rare. Overcookin' dries the meat out. An' you sure as hell don't want to undercook pork roast."

"Nope. Got no taste for pork tartar. I'll go get you a thermometer. Tell me where."

"I can get it, Lionel. They have 'em at the Ninety-Nine Cents store down the street. You just sit down and relax, I'll fetch you a beer."

She was a fine woman, all right. He took off his jacket and sat down on her sofa, while she got him a cold beer.

She handed him the bottle and stood there, looking slightly ashamed. "The roast and all, I'm a little short. That's why I didn't buy the thermometer 'fore you got here."

"Oh, hell, I'm sorry, honey," he said, reaching into his pocket for his roll. "How much you need?"

"Ninety-nine cents, plus the tax, I guess."

"Yeah, right." He handed her a five.

Both of them noticed the plastic chip that fell out of his wallet.

She bent to pick it up. "Why you carrying this little piece of cup?"

"I'm not sure I know," he said. "I'm not even sure it's from a cup."

Bettye was a big girl and she had a big girl's laugh. "Well, that's 'cause you sleep in on Sunday."

"Say what?"

"It's broke from a cup like we use on the first Sunday. For the Lord's supper."

He was frowning at her.

"The blood of Christ. Hello! Communion? You evah step inside a church?"

Mingus stared at the sliver. Yeah. It could be part of that kind of cup. He had drunk wine from cups like that in church, back in what seemed like another life. And he'd seen one recently, but it wasn't being used for the blood of Christ, exactly.

"Shit," he said, getting to his feet. "I'm sorry, baby, but I got something I have to do."

"Now?" she asked.

"Somebody I gotta see who's very sick. I have to catch him before he passes on."

"My Lord!" she said.

"I just got some questions to ask him."

"There's all this food. You coming back?"

He moved to her, gave her a hug and a quick kiss. "Be back soon. You get a thermometer and cook that pig good. And then keep everything warm for me, huh? And I mean *everything*."

The door to Bay Bay's apartment was open a few inches.

Mingus did not like open doors in neighborhoods as bad as that one. He drew his gun and, hunkering down to avoid a bullet in the head or upper body, pushed the door open fully.

He looked in on a shadowy, silent apartment.

He entered, closing the door behind him. He did not put his gun away.

The only light in the apartment came from the bedroom where he'd left Bay Bay. He walked cautiously in that direction, eyes scanning left to right, right to left.

Bay Bay was half in, half out of the bed. It looked like he'd tried to get out but his feet had been tangled in the sheet. He was dead with his eyes open and a look of permanent surprise on his face.

His body was still warm. He hadn't been dead long.

There was an odd smell in the room. Sort of medicinal, but very pungent. Ammonia? Cleaning fluid? He looked at a couple of open bottles on Bay Bay's table and wondered if the smell was coming from them.

Without moving the body, Mingus couldn't even guess at the cause of death. The guy wanted to leave the earth behind. Maybe he just willed himself to stop breathing.

The detective caught a whiff of a familiar smell mixing with the medicinal odor. Spicy and strong. He took a few steps away from the bed and the corpse until his back was to the wall. He said, "Come on out, Redd."

When there was no response, he said, "Dammit, Redd, show yourself."

The bathroom door opened and Redd stepped out, wearing one of her skimpy little boutique originals. "Hi, Mingus," she said. "Fancy meetin' you here."

He gave her a slow once-over. He couldn't see where she could possibly be hiding a weapon, so he put his away. "You kill him, Redd?"

"I look like I kill him? The man be like that when I got here five minutes ago."

"What are you doing here?" Mingus asked.

"I was kinda hoping Bay Bay might tell me where his brother is."

"You got business with Loc?" Mingus asked.

"Trial starts in the A.M. I want to make one last try to talk some sense to him, tell him to stop lying about Claude. What do you suppose happened to Bay?"

"Looks like he coulda been scared to death," Mingus said.

"Sure is ugly."

"No uglier than he was when he was alive," Mingus said. "Guess he's happy now, shoveling coal to keep his true master nice and warm. Don't suppose you called the cops?"

"Thought never occurred to me," she said.

"You strolled in, saw Bay Bay lying there, and decided to stick around?"

"I was just startin' out when I heard you clompin' in," she said. "Figured you might be the boogeyman. But I think I'll be going now." She started for the door.

"Hang on . . . Back when you were buying my gun from that sorry piece of shit over there, he happen to tell you who got him to rob me?"

"No, honey. We never discussed any kind of stuff like that. He was just waving yo' gun around, braggin' on how it belonged to a cop. I ast him what cop and when he said your name, I commenced to hagglin'."

"I appreciate what you did," Mingus said.

"Okay with you I leave?"

"Yeah. Go on."

"We could have a drink or somethin', if you want?"

"Not tonight," he said. "I'll be kinda busy."

"Right. Filling out death forms. Shit like that."

"Yeah," he lied. He wasn't about to let that pork roast get all cold and greasy while he got hung up in red tape because of a sewer rat like Bay Bay. He was getting used to making anonymous death calls.

Redd blew him a kiss and left.

He waited until he heard her close the front door, then began a quick search of the apartment. There wasn't much there beside Bay Bay's medicine bottles, a packed suitcase, a few shirts and pants on hangers, and a pile of dirty clothes on the closet floor.

A take-out container from a place called Fong's Palace rested on the floor beside the bed. The little plastic cup he'd noticed during his last visit was down there, too. Like the container, it had probably been knocked from the table when Bay Bay slipped from his bed. Mingus used a pencil to lift the cup, carried it to a lamp where he compared it to the sliver. It looked identical. But where did that get him?

He returned the cup to precisely the same place on the carpet where he'd found it. What now?

On a whim, he used his handkerchief to lift the phone, then hit the redial button. After a few rings, a voice said, "Madame Juanita, your psychic sister."

"Hi, Eula," Mingus said. "Just givin' you a buzz to see if Ken ever turned up?"

"Still somewhere with those cops," she said. "He calls me, time to time. While back, I mentioned you was looking for him. He said your business with him was done."

"Not completely. Don't suppose your crystal ball could tell you where he is?"

"Not really. What's going on with you, Detective? You taking care of yourself?"

"The best care. You ever hear from Bay Bay?"

"Funny thing. I haven't heard from Bay in a while. Then he calls earlier today lookin' for Ken."

"Say what he wanted?"

"No. He sounded like he might be pickin' up. You want to talk to Bay? I've got his number—"

"No, thanks. If you hear from Ken, tell him we still got business and he should give me a call?"

"Will do."

Mingus placed the phone back on its cradle.

He crossed the room and paused at the door to give the room a final check. He stared at Bay Bay's corpse. "Pickin' up, huh?" he said. "Some psychic."

Later, after the roast pork dinner and nearly an hour of Bettye's imaginative lovemaking, he lay in bed, awake, wondering about Bay Bay's death. AIDS, murder, or suicide? Take your pick. Maybe all of the above.

He was still mulling that over the next morning when he arrived at the CCB.

As was the ritual on the ninth floor, he was forced to walk through metal detectors and X-ray machines. Cleared, he wandered down the hall in the direction of the courtroom, where bailiffs were putting visitors through a second weapons check. What he could see through the open doors indicated that it was nearly a full house. There were quite a few brothers and sisters in attendance, none of them smiling. Just as well they were unarmed. He strolled by and entered the attorney conference room where he selected one of a half-dozen empty chairs to roost on.

He'd barely had a chance to lean back and close his eyes when a familiar voice said, "Well, if it ain't battlin' Lionel Mingus." Dennis Farley waddled into the room, a paper cup in one hand, some weird looking doughnut in the other. He plopped on the seat next to Mingus, put the steaming paper cup on the floor, and brushed doughnut glaze from his stomach. "How's it goin', shoofly?" he asked.

"You losing weight, Farley?" Mingus asked, eyeing the man's outstanding gut.

"Maybe a pound or two," Farley said, missing the intended sarcasm. "Secret is walking. Walk for an hour and it's like the calories in your lunch don't count."

"Farley, you could walk five hours a day for the rest of your life and they're still gonna have to put you in a square coffin."

Farley shrugged off the insult as the door opened on Deputy D.A. Gomez and his cochair, a buxom and famously humorless young black woman named Gloria Olivette.

"You men ready?" Gomez asked.

"This man is," Farley said. "My cousin Lionel seems a little moody this A.M."

Gomez's head snapped toward Mingus. "You with the program, Detective?"

"Sure," Mingus said. "Don't pay any attention to Fats. He's suffering from sugar shock from the bag of doughnuts the defense just bought him."

Gomez saw that Farley was shoving the tail end of a cruller in his mouth and for a moment, Mingus had him going. Then reality kicked in. He gave the IAG detective a disapproving head shake and departed, followed by the unsmiling Ms. Olivette.

"Between you and me," Farley said, lowering his voice, "you figure Too-Good is playin' hide the salam' with Glo-Glo-Gloria?"

"Haven't given it too much thought," Mingus said.

"Whatdya think of *him*, Lionel?"

"No better, no worse," Mingus said.

"I don't like the prick. Too much attitude for a wetback."

Mingus felt uncomfortable sharing a dislike with the fat man. He hoped his wasn't based in any way on the deputy's ethnic background, but you could never be sure about things like that.

He watched Farley sip from his cup. "What the hell you drinking?" he asked.

"Coffee. Whatdya think?"

Mingus pointed at the assortment of Chinese letters printed on the cup. "I figured it might be ginseng or bee pollen. Shit that's supposed to help wake up a tired pecker."

"My pecker's fine, thank you, Lionel." Farley studied the Chinese figures on the cup. "Anyway, it's coffee. Black. No sugar. And hold the soy sauce."

Footsteps sounded down the hall and two men walked by the open door. One was Mercer Early, consulting his watch as he headed for the courtroom.

"That's the son of a bitch we gotta deal with," Farley said.

"He sure beat up Burris in the Mayfield trial," Mingus said.

"Yeah, well, that's Claude Burris, for you. No big trick to beat him up. Hell, you and me, we're gonna be doin' a fair job of that in this trial."

"Maybe," Mingus said, as if he weren't so sure. He was staring at Farley's coffee cup again. Along with the Chinese letters were the words "Fong's Palace."

Sure is a popular place, he thought.

35

At nine o'clock that morning, Mercer had been summoned to C.W.'s office. The senior partner greeted him with a smile. "Sit."

The new affection C.W. was expressing made him feel off, but he supposed it was better than having the man hate his ass like before. "What's up?" he asked.

"I won't keep you. Just wanted to let you know that I had a nice talk with Mayor Heathrow. He couldn't be happier we're defending Claude Burris. The happier he is, the happier it makes me."

"Happy is good," Mercer said.

"With Bobby all involved in politics, we're going to be a little short on partners around here. I'm not saying this would happen overnight, Mercer, but I want you to think about that in court today. We all have quite a lot riding on the outcome of this trial."

"I guess we do," Mercer said, fully aware that C.W. was being C.W., putting the pressure on without actually promising him a thing. Still, it didn't hurt to dream. "I won't let the firm down," he said.

Eddie Baraca drove using just his left hand, freeing the other for smoking, gesturing, and tapping the dash along with the loud rap music from the radio. He'd been full of advice on the drive downtown, most of it unbidden and unwanted. "You shouldn't have worn that canary yellow tie, Mercer," he'd said. "Gotta keep it subtle for the jury." And, "Remember to hold their eyes. If you can hold their eyes they'll believe everything you tell 'em." And, "There are five brothers and sisters on the jury, Mercer, and they're the ones you got to snake charm. The blue-eyed devils are gonna be siding with Burris and in our pocket from the git-go."

"You ever listen to yourself, Eddie?" Mercer said finally. "You got diarrhea of the mouth, man."

Eddie wasn't offended in the least by the comment. "Well, sure," he said, "I'm a lawyer."

There was considerable activity in front of the Criminal Courts Building. Pickets yelled angry and inflammatory slogans both for and against Claude Burris. The media milled, cameras searching for something besides other cameras. TV was being kept outside of the courtroom and the promise of a single pool camera was not going down smoothly for the members of the press. They smelled LAPD butt on the barbie and they wanted to make sure they got their piece.

It was not quite the circus of some high-profile trials of the past, but enough to make life a little more difficult for pedestrian and street traffic. With a minimum of wheel spinning, Eddie maneuvered the sedan past all the action and down a slight ramp to the car park floor beneath the courthouse. With blind luck he found an empty space immediately.

In just minutes, he and Mercer were on the ninth floor, home for high-risk, high-security cases. Here, the McMartin Preschool defendants, most of them now deceased, had earned more than sixty guilty verdicts. Orville Simpson and the Menendez boys had profited from the gullibility of jurors on that floor. More recently, defense attorney Barry Levin had lost and then earned a new trial in the case of four cops charged in the LAPD's Rampart division scandal.

Then Levin took his own life. Too bad, Mercer

thought. He could surely use a guy like Barry today. He would have to make do with Eddie.

Outside Department 110, they were searched for weapons by a cadre of bailiffs. When they entered the packed courtroom, the noise was loud and intense, like a plague of crickets caught in a chat room. That stopped temporarily while the spectators turned to gawk at them. Mercer was only mildly surprised to see Redd smiling at him from a corner of the room, looking very chic in a crisp linen outfit. The woman seemed to have easy access to everything.

Quite a few members of the black community were present, some of them glaring at a group of whiter-than-bread visitors wearing "Support Our Police" buttons. Reporters who had covered all the high-pro trials in L.A. were welcoming each other to yet another feast.

Almost a dozen bailiffs secured the courtroom. Two were at the door, two at the defense table, and one each in the jury box and at a small table near the lock-up door, where Burris would enter the courtroom. The rest were strategically placed near the clerk or in the small lobby located directly outside the courtroom door.

As Mercer headed for the defense table, Eddie nudged him and pointed to Gomez. "Your friend don't look so friendly."

The D.D.A. was, in fact, sending rays of pure hatred his way.

He nodded politely and Gomez turned to his co-counsel, Gloria Olivette, an unsmiling but formidable-looking black woman whom Mercer could not recall from his time at the D.A.'s.

Burris was escorted into the courtroom and delivered to the defense table by a trio of bailiffs. He had been treated to a fresh, close-to-the-bone jailhouse buzz cut, which went well with an off-the-rack dark suit showing some shine on the elbows. His cop suit, Mercer thought.

Burris held his head high as he scanned the crowd. He turned to Eddie, extending his hand. "Claude Burris," he said.

"I figured," Eddie said, shaking Burris's hand and introducing himself.

"I like this guy, Mercer," Burris said. "He looks slick."

"That's his big thing," Mercer said. He could feel the adrenaline pumping through his veins. He was ready and anxious.

"You see her?" Burris asked him. "My woman?"

"I saw her."

"Damn, it's been a long time."

"Right." Mercer didn't know what else to say. He consulted his watch. Still a couple minutes to go. He'd been careful to get to the courtroom a few minutes shy of ten A.M. As he'd learned during the Darion Mayfield trial, Judge Temperance Land was a freak for time.

Sure enough, at ten on the dot, the bailiff commanded, "All rise."

Judge Land entered the courtroom, taking her seat on the bench. "This is the matter of the *People* versus *Burris*," she announced. "Your appearances, counsel."

"Good morning, Your Honor. David Gomez and Gloria Olivette for the People. We are ready to present our opening statement."

"Good morning. Mercer Early and Edward Baraca for the defendant, Detective Claude Burris of the Los Angeles Police Department. We stand ready to proceed, Your Honor."

"Be seated, gentlemen, Ms. Olivette. I'm a bit disappointed that counsel are maintaining their positions in this matter. The defendant faces the possibility of death by lethal injection. He has everything to lose. The prosecution's case relies heavily on the testimony of a convicted felon. I think it is fair to say that the district attorney may once again find herself facing public criticism for failing to convict yet another high-profile defendant. Clearly, both sides stand to benefit from a plea bargain."

Rising slowly, Gomez addressed the court. "With all due respect, Your Honor, our office has no interest in any plea or penalty short of first-degree murder and death in this case. Mr. Burris has harmed more than just the victim and his family. He has caused injury to an entire community. He tarnished the badges and reputations of every peace officer in this city. He has violated the public trust and brought shame onto all of us who believe in the law and who are responsible for its enforcement. The public must be assured that we cannot—will not—tolerate lawlessness on the part of our law enforcement officers. Under the color of authority, he has taken a life. It is only just that he pay with his own."

"Your Honor." Mercer stood to speak.

"Brevity, Mr. Early. I do so treasure brevity." She shot Gomez a reproachful glance.

"Your Honor, if a plea bargain had been offered, we would have declined. My client has no interest in pleading to a crime he did not commit. Mr. Gomez speaks of Detective Burris's guilt as if he were the judge and jury. I would respectfully remind the prosecutor that the document filed in court is merely an accusation, nothing more. Our prisons are filled with innocent men who in the face of overzealous prosecutors pled guilty to crimes they did not commit. We will not stand idly by and let the same thing happen here. Mr. Burris's only plea is 'not guilty' because he is *not guilty*."

Peering over her metal-rimmed glasses, Judge Land seemed to take a moment to measure both lawyers. "Promise me one thing, gentlemen. Minimize your verbosity." She sighed as she realized there wasn't much chance of that. "Nettlesome," she mumbled, shaking her head. Then, as if to reassure herself that she had some control over her world, she announced, "The bailiff may call in the jury."

Gomez's opening statement was, as Mercer had anticipated, moderately compelling, focusing on racism and revenge as motive while tap dancing around the fact that his case was weak on identification.

Mercer's advisors had impressed upon him the statistically proven fact that juries tend to form strong opinions based on opening statements, but he had precious little to tell them up front to counteract the charges made against Burris. He could say his client was not a racist, but that was a claim impossible to substantiate no matter how many African American fellow officers were to come forth to speak on his behalf. And in fact, Baraca's crew could locate only four and one of those was waffling. On the charge of murder, it would have been lovely to mention an alibi, corroborated by a black woman, but he wasn't allowed that luxury. He decided that the only course left for him would be to present his client as the victim of a different sort of prejudice.

"In a democratic society," he began, "a man is presumed innocent unless proven guilty beyond a reasonable doubt. Unless you are a police officer. Unless you are Claude Burris, a guardian of the law who in the course of a long career has been guilty of only one thing—of trying to do his duty and bring drug dealers and other purveyors of vice to justice." The words almost stuck in his throat. In his mind he could hear Burris admitting to being on Bumpy Lewis's pad. *Lose that thought,* he commanded himself. *Forget that damned conversation. Forget what Burris confessed to. It's murder we're talking about here. He is innocent of murder.* "The prosecution will not show you any evidence that Detective Burris pushed Darion Mayfield through a window to his death. There is no such evidence. No physical evidence. No credible eyewitness.

"What this trial will demonstrate is that the only guilty people in this courtroom are my client's accusers. No, they're not guilty of murder, either. They're guilty of sloppy police work. Guilty of conducting a biased investigation. Guilty of hiding the truth. Guilty of charging an innocent man to further their own personal and political gain. In a democratic society, one is supposed to be presumed innocent. Not now, not in this room.

"Some members of the prosecution may actually believe that Detective Burris is guilty as charged. But it is a prejudiced belief because there is no tangible evidence to back it up. The fact is: Claude Burris is not guilty and with or without the People of the State of California, I am going to prove it."

In his zeal Mercer had pushed the envelope a little, said a few things he probably shouldn't have. Opening statements were not supposed to be argumentative. They should be an introduction to the evidence to be presented by the defense. That was what his professor in Trial Advocacy had told him. His professor hadn't told him what to do if he found himself without evidence or expert witnesses or even a cooperative client, but it's doubtful he would have suggested preaching to the jury and telling them he would prove his client's innocence, something not even the law required.

When he returned to the counsel table, Eddie Baraca whispered, "Proof? Who the hell you think you are, the black Perry Mason?"

Mercer was annoyed by Baraca's critique but even more by his own hubris. He didn't have much time to think about it. Gomez had called his first witness, Detective Dennis Farley.

The rotund dick gave a mind-dulling account of his brilliant career in vice and RHD, claiming to have investigated more than two hundred homicide crime scenes. At the end of his lengthy resume, Gomez asked, "Detective, what if anything did you observe upon your arrival at the scene of Darion Mayfield's brutal death?"

The question was D.A. standard issue, designed not only to let the detective sum up everything he saw but to allow him to sneak into the record information that otherwise might be found objectionable. Assuming that the defense attorney was taking a snooze.

Mercer gave Farley about thirty seconds to respond before lodging an objection. This prompted Judge Land to order Gomez to move on to his next question. Which the prosecutor did, time and again, before turning the witness over to the defense.

Mercer approached the plump witness with a friendly

smile. "Detective, you've been sitting here answering Mr. Gomez's questions for about an hour, right?"

Farley glanced at his watch. "One hour and thirteen minutes, to be exact," he said. The courtroom crowd chuckled.

"That's a nice watch," Mercer said. "Looks like a real Rolex."

"It is real," Farley said, then realizing he may have made a mistake, added, "I didn't buy it. I mean, it's too expensive . . . It was a gift."

"Nice to have wealthy friends," Mercer said. "In any case, you strike me as a man who's a stickler for detail. Am I correct?"

"Yes, sir. I believe God is in the details."

"Can make or break a case, right?"

"Absolutely. Details are a Homicide cop's best weapon. I've got more than twenty years' experience in paying attention to detail. That's why I was picked to become a member of the department's elite Homicide unit."

"I see," Mercer said, moving to counsel table and retrieving a manilla folder. "Detective, when you just testified on direct, did you happen to leave out any relevant details?"

"I answered the questions put to me."

"Mr. Gomez asked what you observed at the scene. Right?"

"He did. But you stopped me kind of short by objecting." More titters from the crowd.

"Then let's correct that," Mercer said. "You did inform the court that Darion Mayfield had fallen into a Dumpster beside his apartment building; and when you approached it, you saw the victim's body, right?"

"Yes."

"All of it?"

"It was partially obscured by trash."

"But at that time, you used your radio and advised the coroner's office to roll. True?"

"Yes."

"You informed the coroner's office, and I quote, 'Victim's body is contained within a large trash bin. Scene is secure.' Is that what you said?"

"Yes."

"That wasn't exactly true, was it?"

Farley frowned.

"The victim's body wasn't contained within the trash bin, was it?"

"No. Not entirely."

"Something was missing?"

"Yes."

"Would you tell us what?"

Farley coughed, covering his mouth at the same time. "The, uh, head." A half-dozen jurors leaned forward, trying to hear.

"I'm sorry. What was that?" Mercer asked.

"The head. The head wasn't in the Dumpster."

"The victim's head," Mercer said. "And that was the little detail you missed during your first, let me check your logs, your first *two* hours at the scene?"

"Yeah, well, you see—"

"How important was that oversight, Detective?"

Farley looked perplexed. He turned to the D.A., as if to ask, what do I do now? When Gomez offered no legal assist, he said, "I don't think I understand the question."

"Let me help you. Drawing on your vast experience as an observant lawman, which part of the human body contains most of what you in the homicide arena would call 'clues'?"

"That would be the head, but—"

"In this case, hadn't the victim's head been subjected to a fair degree of damage?"

"Yeah. The guy fell a long way."

"I'm glad you used the word 'fell,' because it is entirely possible he stumbled on his own and fell through that window. But to get back to that missing head . . ."

Mercer moved to the defense table where Eddie Baraca handed him a poster, approximately two feet by two feet. It was a black-and-white blowup of Darion

Mayfield's head. Cropped to eliminate the severed area, it was still gruesome enough to cause several of the jurors to gasp.

"This is a photo of Mr. Mayfield's head?"

"Looks like," Farley said, relaxing a little.

Mercer pointed to two crossed lines along the dead man's cheek. "Any idea what might have made the marks?"

"Not offhand."

"Well, with all your experience, would you recognize the object that made the marks if you saw it?"

"I suppose I would," Farley said. "If I saw it."

"These marks may have been the result of an attack by the killer, right?"

"Maybe."

"Detective Farley, did you recover from my client any item that might have caused those marks?"

"No."

"Was anything found in his apartment that might have caused those marks?"

"No. But the marks could have been made after the man died."

"Is that what the coroner says?"

"Well, actually, I think the report says the marks were made before."

Mercer nodded, as if this were an admission of something. The jury seemed fascinated. "Detective Farley," Mercer said, "to get back to the severed head, if it wasn't in the Dumpster when you arrived, just where the heck was it?"

"Can I check my notes?"

"If you need to."

Farley, sweating profusely, removed his notebook and, licking his thumb, used it to riffle through the pages. He paused at a page and studied it, holding the notebook at arm's length as if he were having trouble with his eyes. Satisfied, he closed the book and put it back in his pocket. He sat a little straighter in the witness chair. "It was found approximately two hours after our investigation began. A, uh, dog had taken it away."

"Let me get this straight, Detective. While you and your ever vigilant crew were containing the crime scene, a dog was eating the evidence? That's what you're telling us?"

"Well, he'd kinda dragged it away from where the body was ..."

"That was a pretty serious oversight, wasn't it, Detective? Failing to realize the head was missing in the first place and then letting Rover play with it for a couple hours?"

"Your Honor," Gomez said, "does Mr. Early have a point with all this severed head business?"

The judge turned to Mercer.

"Goes to the credibility of this witness, Your Honor," he said.

"Overruled, Mr. Gomez, assuming you were making an objection. Mr. Early, will you be spending a great deal more time with this witness?"

"Probably, Your Honor."

"Then you'll do it after lunch. We'll resume at one-thirty."

But they didn't.

At 1:14, another of the city's rolling blackouts temporarily shut off the building's electricity. Most of the participants made it back, but Detective Farley was stuck in a crowded elevator.

The trial did not resume until nearly two-thirty.

Farley looked a mess. His suit was rumpled and sweat-stained. His tie was twisted and pulled down from his shirt collar. His pallor was milky, with unnaturally red splotches on his cheeks, as if he'd been pinching them. "You okay, Detective?" Mercer asked, resuming his questions. "You look a little under the weather."

"I been stuck in a dark, airless fu—in an elevator with about a hundred and fifty Third Worlders, none of whom know the meaning of the word 'deodorant' and . . ." He paused, evidently realizing that he was surrounded by a rich ethnic mix. He cleared his throat and smiled and tried to look like a man who loved everybody.

"To return to our previous topic, Detective, I assume that the victim's head did finally make it to the coroner's office?"

"Yes."

"You were present?"

"Yes. My partner and I and a detective named Lionel Mingus."

"Who did the examination?"

"Dr. Modi Saleem."

"Did you witness Dr. Saleem's discovery of anything that, in your experience, might be considered vital evidence?"

"Vital? Not that I recall."

"You want to check your notes?" Mercer asked.

Uncomfortable and on edge, Farley tried to repay Mercer for his sarcasm by taking his sweet time examining his notes. Finally, he replied that, with the exception of some tattered skin and the crossed indentations on the victim's cheek, "nothing of significance was recovered."

"Detective, let me show you what has been marked 'Defense Exhibit B.' 'Exhibit A,' by the way, is your detailed report. Here."

He handed the fat detective an X ray of Darion Mayfield's severed head. "Hold it up to the light and tell us what you see in this area." He pointed to the corpse's mouth.

Gomez was on his feet. "Objection. Detective Farley is not an expert in the interpretation of X ray photography."

"I'm not asking for expert interpretation, Your Honor," Mercer said. "Merely what the detective sees."

"I'll allow it. Continue, Mr. Early."

"What do you see there in the mouth, Detective?"

Farley furrowed his brow, peering at the X ray. "It's, ah, a hunk of broke plastic."

"You see all that in the X ray?" Mercer asked.

"Just the outline. But I saw Dr. Saleem take this plastic shard from the victim's mouth."

Mercer turned to the jury box, looked at the faces staring back at him. He was heartened by their alertness and vital interest. He saw their eyes shift to Farley as he asked, "Did you book that item into evidence, Detective?"

The reply was an almost whispered "No."

"What was that, Detective?"

"I said no. I did not book that item."

"Why not?"

"I didn't feel it was . . . significant."

"A foreign object, a hunk of plastic, found in the throat of a murder victim? Not significant? That's what you're saying?" Mercer asked.

Farley seemed at a loss for words. "The, uh, head," he croaked finally, "was dragged pretty far by the pooch. I figured that's why the plastic got lodged."

"Considering the sudden importance of the dog in these proceedings," Mercer said, "it would appear that it had more to do with Darion Mayfield's death than my client. So, Detective, do you have any idea what happened to the piece of plastic?"

"I imagine Dr. Saleem might still have it."

"But you wouldn't be too concerned if the doctor tossed it, since you didn't consider it to be evidence?"

"I don't know what the doctor did with it."

"Isn't it possible, Detective, that the reason the piece of plastic is missing is because it may have provided us with something—a fingerprint, maybe—that would unequivocally prove my client's innocence?"

"Ob-jection, Your Honor," Gomez screamed.

"Withdraw the question," Mercer said. "Detective, one final thing. What you've told us here today is that you not only ignored a key piece of evidence, you have no idea where it might be at present. Is that correct?"

"Yeah," Farley said.

"I'm finished with you, Detective. Thank you for sharing your . . . expertise with us."

"I imagine you'll want to redirect, Mr. Gomez," the judge said.

The prosecutor bounced to his feet, but Judge Land waved him back down. "You'll have to save that enthusiasm until the morning, counselor. I'm ending this session a little early today. You will have your quality time with Detective Farley first thing when we convene.

"You know the admonition, folks," Judge Land said to the jury. "Do not discuss the trial with anyone until it is appropriate. We will resume at nine-thirty A.M. with Mr. Gomez's redirect questioning of Detective Farley."

The judge rose from the high back, black leather chair. Anticipating the bailiff's next commands, the crowd got to its feet. A group of four bailiffs led Burris from the courtroom while three others stood guard at the courtroom door.

On his way out, Farley moved close to Mercer and leaned in to say, "I hope you don't have any plans of ever becoming a judge in this town, 'cuz it ain't never gonna happen, smart guy. Me and the union will see to that."

Mercer smiled. "Detective, I'm gonna give you a heads up on another detail you apparently missed."

"Yeah?"

Mercer looked around, as if making sure no one else could hear the little nugget he was about to drop. He said, "Your mouthwash ain't doing its job."

Farley reared back, unamused. "You fuckin' blacks always got jokes, don'tcha? We'll see whose laughing after I lock your ofay buddy up for life, asshole."

Mercer looked around for potential witnesses to this odd vignette. Eddie was waiting for him by the door. The clerk was busy completing the court's docket. Only Gomez had heard them. He grinned, said, "You gotta love him, right?" and followed his key witness out of the room.

Eddie walked back to the defense table. "What was that all about?"

"Hell if I know," Mercer said.

"You got any idea what Gomez is up to?" Eddie asked. "He must've known how much they screwed up at the crime scene. Even a third-year law student would have made an effort to prepare the jury for the missing head. In the opening statement, in the direct, somewhere."

"I can't figure it either," Mercer said. "And just now, Farley threatened to put me on the police-union shit list."

"He got that kind of clout?"

"Maybe he was blowing smoke, but he seemed to think he did," Mercer said. "And if he does, what else is he capable of?"

"Hell," Eddie said, "long as you're gonna prove Burris didn't do it, Perry, maybe you better find out where Farley was the night Mayfield stepped out for some fresh air."

36

Barely fifteen minutes after Judge Land's adjournment for the day, Dennis Farley was walking along the rows of cars beneath Parker Center, singing an Irish melody on the way to his Crown Victoria. Mingus, who'd slipped down on the front seat of his sedan at the sound of the fat man's garbled rendition of "Clancy Lowered the Boom," edged up to peer over the dashboard just as Farley settled himself behind the wheel.

The Crown Vic jounced out of the parking facility onto Los Angeles Street, took a left, and slipped into traffic like a salmon joining a school swimming upstream. Mingus was about four fishes back. He wondered where Farley's pale partner was. Well, somebody in RHD had to be doing work.

Mingus was expecting Farley to lead him into the neighboring Chinatown. That was the home of Fong's Palace, source of the fat cop's morning coffee and the takeout carton that had been in Bay Bay's apartment. He figured Farley was keeping Ken Loc somewhere near the establishment.

But Farley wasn't going to Chinatown. He made an abrupt right turn onto Third. Mingus, caught short, had to wave his badge to convince a truck driver to let him switch lanes. By the time he made it to Third, the Crown Vic was almost fading into the distance.

But not quite.

As Farley crossed Rampart, Mingus had the car clearly in his sight. By the time the Crown Vic entered the exclusive Hancock Park area, Mingus was in complete control of the tail.

That stretch of Highland Avenue had once been the wealthiest section of the city. It still was the neighborhood of choice for old money. An odd place for either Farley or Gomez to be stashing a witness. So maybe Mingus was wasting his time. Well, it was his to waste. Until he was called to the stand, he was off the IAG duty roster.

Farley stopped his car in front of a somber two-story Tudor set way back from the street behind a high wrought-iron fence.

Mingus drove past, forcing himself to maintain his speed rather than engage the fat man's attention. After a couple of blocks he made a U-turn and returned to where a small pair of binoculars from the glove compartment provided a good view of the Crown Vic.

Farley was still in the car. Judging by the motion of his mouth, he was continuing to brag on Clancy's ability to lower the boom.

Mingus shifted his view to a man opening the Tudor's gate and heading for the Crown Vic. He got in, taking the passenger seat. He was a tall, handsome man built and dressed for an afternoon of tennis. The only thing that didn't quite fit with the outfit and the neighborhood was that he was black.

Mingus recognized him, sort of. Maybe a movie actor. No. A city official. High powered. The name would come to him. Eventually.

The man's visit, judging by facial expressions, was not very friendly. He was laying down the law to Fats and Fats was grinning under the abuse. Then the man was out of the car, passing through the gate and heading back inside the home.

Fats gave the dude's back a one-finger salute, then started up his vehicle.

If Mingus had been working with a backup, he'd have opted to stay there until he discovered the tennis player's name and relationship to Farley. But when the Crown Vic zoomed past him, Mingus hung a U-turn and followed.

Farley took Santa Monica Boulevard toward downtown. He was in a hurry now.

Mingus stayed with him, traveling a series of freeways, ending on the Golden State as it merged with I-5. When the Crown Vic exited I-5 at Mission Road, Mingus assumed they were headed for the coroner's office. He'd been planning on going there himself. He'd spoken with Dr. Saleem that morning about the corpse of Robert Bay Bay Ansol. No autopsy had been planned. There'd been no rush to work on a body carrying the AIDS virus. Saleem, in fact, had been quite annoyed with Mingus for suggesting that an autopsy might be called for.

"Why, Detective?" the man had almost whined. "The unfortunate Mr. Ansol was terminal."

"It's still murder if somebody helped him die," Mingus said.

"But no one has suggested this to our office." Dr. Saleem really wanted to get rid of the body ASAP.

"I'm suggesting it."

"You cause me grief, Detective. Is this request official?"

"Yes," Mingus lied without hesitation.

"You are a bad man, Detective."

"I always speak well of you, Doc," Mingus had said.

Now he was parked next to the four-story building on Mission Road, observing Farley's entrance. Was it possible he was there because of Bay Bay? Could Ken Loc be inside, making the official identification of his brother?

Mingus got out of the car.

The building was busy with orderlies pushing gurneys, some transporting corpses, covered and uncovered, some waiting for arrivals. Farley was nowhere to be seen.

Mingus pushed past the death march into a less frantic reception area. No Farley.

Where could he be? With Saleem, probably.

It was a short elevator ride down to the autopsy area. He had no perfumed handkerchief or Vicks to block the odor, but it wasn't strong just off the elevator. Only that unpleasant collards, funk, and Mr. Clean mix.

He stopped a woman in scrubs who told him Saleem was in Operating Room Five.

He was a few feet away from the pneumatic doors when he heard screams from inside the room. The doors flew open and two lab assistants staggered out. The female fell to her knees and fainted. The male, a sturdier specimen in his twenties, tore off his mask and yelled, "Gas . . ." and fell to the floor, too.

The hall was suddenly filled with people, mainly rushing to the stairwells and elevators.

Mingus was feeling a little light-headed. Through the open door, he saw Saleem beside his autopsy table, staggering and falling, his smock covered with what appeared to be intestinal fluids of varying, disgusting shades. Mingus caught a sudden whiff of something so ghastly and powerfully cloying he began to gag.

Saleem was on the deck. Dead? If not, he soon would be. No human could breathe the air in that room.

Mingus backed away from the open door, took a deep breath, and rushed in.

Immediately his eyes began to sting and water. There was a burning sensation at the back of his throat. On the operating table, the horrifying, diseased body of Bay Bay had been split open, a shimmering steam rising from the cavity. Blood and bile covered his lower body, spilling over onto the table and the floor.

Wiping away tears, holding his breath, Mingus grabbed the collar of Saleem's powder blue scrubs and dragged the big man toward the door.

It was only fifteen feet away, but he wasn't sure he'd make it. His body was closing down at an alarming speed. His strength was going. Saleem felt like he weighed five hundred pounds. Mingus's legs were turning to lead. He'd been concentrating on holding his breath, but he must have taken in some air, because he was struck by a nausea so profound that he gagged and backed away from the doctor to throw up on the floor. Damn if it didn't look like scrapple.

Sicker than he'd ever been in his life, he grabbed the doc again and struggled toward the corridor. He might have made it all the way to fresh air, but he stopped to slam the doors on the toxic stench. The whoosh of the doors swinging shut was the last thing he remembered before hitting the floor beside Saleem.

He was lying on a metal table when he awoke.

Some kind soul had stuck a foam rubber pillow under his head.

He was in a small operating room. An oxygen tank was beside the table. Dr. Saleem was sitting on a chair. An Asian nurse stood by watching them both.

Saleem had his own oxygen tank. Attached to it was a breathing apparatus that the doctor placed over his nose and mouth. He inhaled, then removed the apparatus.

"That doin' any good?" Mingus tried to say. Even to him it sounded like "Aadnnneeegooo." The nurse crossed the room, staring at him with open curiosity.

"So he lives," Saleem said. Mingus had been expecting some word of thanks. What he got was, "You did this, Detective."

"Me?" Mingus tried sitting up. Even with the nurse, a remarkably strong woman, helping, his body kept telling him it wanted to tip over to the left.

"Try a hit of this," the nurse said, placing his oxygen mask over his face.

The gas seemed to open up his throat to allow him to breathe. The nurse removed the apparatus and he said, "More."

"Bad man," the doctor said.

Heady from illness and oxygen, Mingus said, "What's with you, Doc? I saved your butt in there."

"What happened in there was of your doing," the doctor said. "Mr. Ansol's body nearly killed us all."

"AIDS caused that stink?" Mingus thought he knew a little bit about the disease. He'd never heard of toxic gas being part of its devastating package.

"Not the disease," Saleem said. "The gas came from the thing that killed him."

"Not AIDS?"

"No. I have only read about this thing. A mixture of corrosives—bleach, oven cleaner—causes a gas, which has proven as fatal for others as the concoction was for the victim."

"Damn, that's some bad-news cocktail," Mingus said.

"Most unpleasant. The corrosives erode the throat, preventing the victim from crying out. Then, gravity takes its course and the fluids eat through the stomach lining. Mr. Ansol couldn't have lived for longer than two or three minutes. Then his corpse was transformed into a toxic bomb which, thanks to you, I detonated."

"Guess we're lucky it wasn't fatal, huh?" Mingus said.

"How much luckier I would be," the doctor said, "if I'd never met you, Detective."

"You're not alone," Mingus said with a sigh.

37

"So it went okay?" Redd asked.

Mercer was in his office, feet on his desk, phone against his ear. "Yeah. 'Okay' is how I'd grade it."

"You sound like it coulda gone better."

"The prosecutor's acting like maybe he knows something I don't. Which isn't that big a stretch since my client hasn't exactly been an open book. Claude says he gave Darion a bloody nose earlier that night. Any chance Claude was bleeding, too? Maybe left some DNA around the apartment?"

"I don't recall seein' any blood when he got back that evenin'," Redd said.

"If Gomez has got anything, I imagine we'll find out soon enough," he said.

"You sound a little stressed, Mercer. Maybe you need some smoothin' out tonight, a little professional unwinding."

"I don't think so."

"Don't knock it till you try it."

"I'd just as soon—"

Melissa was in the doorway waving to catch his eye. She was carrying her purse and dressed for leaving. He glanced at his watch: 6:20.

"Sorry, Redd. Gotta go," he said into the phone and cradled it before Redd could reply.

"Heading home?" he asked Melissa.

"I try to do it every night, usually a little earlier. Did you know there's a meeting going on in Bobby's office? Eddie's there with the partners."

"Great," he said, swinging his legs around and getting to his feet. "Thanks for the heads up."

"It's what I live for," she said.

The floor was deserted except for one telephone receptionist reading a paperback novel.

As Mercer neared Bobby's untended office, he heard Eddie holding forth through the half-opened door. "Yeah, the cross went fine, but I gotta tell ya, I'm concerned about that opening statement. Mercer says he's gonna prove Burris didn't do it."

Mercer entered the room.

Bobby was seated at his big desk. Eddie was in the visitor's chair opposite him. C.W. was on the suede-covered couch. Next to him was Vanessa.

"This a private meeting?" Mercer asked.

"Hey, Mercer. I was just giving the partners a rundown on the trial."

"Sounds like I was the one being run down."

"I was just sharing my perspective," Eddie said.

"Your perspective? I'm first chair, Eddie. Any perspective you feel the need to share ought to be shared with me to my face. Right?"

Eddie stared at him for a beat, then said, "Yeah. My bad."

Mercer gestured to the mug on Bobby's desk and asked, "Any more of that coffee around?"

"I'll get it," Vanessa said.

"What about *your* perspective?" C.W. asked Mercer as he took the remaining chair.

"It went pretty well. Maybe too well. It's almost like Gomez isn't taking us seriously. Like he feels he's got a dead-bang case."

"That's what I was saying before . . . you got here, Mercer. Too-Good wasn't making any moves to shore up the weak spots in his case."

"Some D.A.s aren't exactly known for their pretrial prep," C.W. said.

"Gomez is a detail man," Mercer said. "And he's usually in your face. Unless he was on heavy medication today, something's up."

Vanessa's knee touched his thigh as she handed him a full coffee mug. He tried not to read too much into that.

"You don't have any idea what he's got in his bag of tricks?" C.W. asked, shattering the moment.

Mercer shook his head.

"He sure didn't seem very upset about the X rays or the missing piece of plastic," Eddie said. He explained the references to the others and added, "What was that all about, anyway, Mercer? Where you going with those autopsy questions?"

"Just trying to make Farley look like a jackass."

"If the X rays and the pieces of plastic hadn't been put into evidence by the D.A., how did you even know they existed?" Bobby asked.

"The assistant coroner who did the autopsy told me about them," Mercer said. That was not the whole truth. Lionel Mingus had given him a play-by-play of the autopsy, which is why he'd been able to ask Dr. Saleem the right questions and get him to dig through the files for the X rays showing the lodged plastic.

"Well, whatever the D.D.A. has in mind, we won't uncover it tonight," Bobby said. "We can but wait and see."

"I'm beat," Eddie said, standing up. "Think I'll head for home to remind my family what I look like."

"There're some things I got to take care of, too," Mercer said, following him out.

In the hall, Eddie stopped him. "I wouldn't want you to get the wrong idea, Mercer. They called me in. I didn't just . . . you know."

"Okay."

"I'm here to help," he said.

"Good," Mercer said softly. "Help is good."

A voice mail message from Detective Mingus was waiting at his desk. The return number was answered by a woman. "Just a minute," she told him. "I'll go get Lionel. He's lying down."

Lying down? Mercer checked his watch. It was a little early to be pounding the pillow. A very long couple of minutes later, Mingus picked up on his end. "Got something for you," he said, "but I'm not sure what."

"You okay? You sound kinda croaky."

"I'm lucky I'm not sitting down to a barbecue dinner with Darion."

"What happened?"

Mingus filled the lawyer in on the shard being a part of a sacrificial cup, how that led him to the discovery of Bay Bay's corpse and, more recently, to his brush with secondhand corrosive poisoning. "I'm pretty much back to normal now. But Bay Bay'll never be the same."

Mercer scanned the notes he'd just scribbled. "So Bay Bay had a cup like the one that got busted at Darion's. You think he might've been at the crime scene? Maybe he killed Darion? Or, maybe he saw his brother kill Darion?"

"Any of that, I guess."

"Then who killed Bay Bay?" Mercer asked. "And why?"

"Bay was so sick he wanted to die. But there are a lot kinder ways to do it than a Drano martini. Whoever served that up didn't much care for the man. That would rule out Ken Loc, who doesn't strike me as stone killer material to begin with."

"Well, it's all interesting." Mercer looked up to see something else that was interesting: Vanessa entering his office and taking a seat in the client chair.

"Anyway, counselor," Mingus was saying, "Bay Bay getting murdered has to be connected somehow. I figured you'd want to know."

"You're a good man," Mingus said.

"Remember that if I get up on the stand tomorrow. Remember I'm a sick man, too."

Mercer replaced the receiver and looked at Vanessa expectantly.

"We haven't been connecting very much lately," she said.

"I noticed." They'd had lunch a few weeks—no, he thought, it was closer to a month ago. She'd said something to the effect that since the preparation for the trial was taking up so much of his time, it seemed the perfect opportunity for them to "reevaluate their relationship." It sounded like seven kinds of bullshit to him, that the only reevaluating she'd be doing would be figuring what to wear when she went out with Barry. But there wasn't much he could do about it. Particularly not with the trial approaching.

She looked pretty good sitting across from him.

"Well, Daddy made a suggestion," she was saying, "and I swear I didn't say a word to him about this . . . he suggested . . . only if you were all right with it . . . that, maybe, it might be a good idea if I could apprentice you and Eddie during the trial?"

"Apprentice," he repeated. "How do you see that working exactly?"

"I guess I sort of hang out with you and do the running and the fetching and stay out of everybody's way and try to pick up on some practical criminal law experience."

"I didn't think your daddy was very fond of criminal law."

She smiled. "He's been known to change his mind. He wasn't very fond of you, either. Anyway, as you told me in no uncertain terms, I am lacking in experience. I guess one of the reasons I got so mad that night was because I knew you were right."

"Okay," he said.

"I can understand if you feel it might— You just say okay?"

He nodded.

"Thank you, Mercer." Damn, he loved that smile. He had to fight himself not to make too much of it.

"We'll start in the morning," he said. "Meet us here no later than a quarter to nine and we'll drive downtown together."

"I'll be here." She indicated the notepad filled with his scribbles from his conversation with Mingus. "Looks like you're going to be working tonight."

"Fact is I'm pretty well set for tomorrow," he said.

"We could have dinner," she said. "You could fill me in on what to expect in court. It'd be nice. Like old times."

"Persuasive argument, counselor. Sold."

They left his office and she ducked into her own. She returned with a sports bag and a tennis racket.

"I didn't know you played," he said.

"Just took up the game," she said.

In the elevator he suggested they go to a restaurant from their courting days. She wondered if it wouldn't be simpler to just pick up a pizza and a bottle of Chianti on the way to his place.

He let her choose the topping and the wine.

38

"**O**kay, Mr. Gomez, you're on," Judge Land said at precisely 9:31 A.M. the next morning.

Watching the D.D.A. stand, thank the judge and walk jauntily toward his witness, Dennis Farley, Mercer felt pretty much out of it. Vanessa, sitting at the defense table on the other side of Eddie, raised a hand to stifle a yawn. It had been a very nice but very late night with her leaving his apartment a little after two o'clock. He had to try to stay alert.

"Let me begin by clarifying a point," Gomez said. "Detective, did you bungle the crime scene investigation?"

"No, sir. A crime scene isn't a sterile environment like an operating room. Things get misplaced. Accidents happen. It's a little more difficult to locate evidence in an alley than in the lab."

"Speaking of the lab, Mr. Early asked you quite a lot of questions yesterday about a plastic shard that was removed from the victim's throat by the assistant coroner. Could you tell us in your own words what happened at the lab? Did you misplace the piece of plastic?"

"Well," Farley said, ducking his head in mock embarrassment, "I admit I may have misjudged its significance. But I didn't *misplace* it. I mean, it wasn't *misplaced*."

"What happened to that piece of plastic?" Gomez asked, so brightly that Mercer sat up straight in his chair. He heard Eddie mumble, "Oh, shit, here it comes."

"What's going on?" Vanessa whispered.

Burris swung around in his chair and stared into the visitor section. Mercer glanced back too, just in time to see Redd giving his client a little two-finger kiss.

When he swung back, Farley was grinning at him from the witness chair. He said, "It was kept with the victim's possessions, bagged and labeled, just like it was supposed to be."

"You're sure of that?" Gomez asked.

"Absolutely. I found it last evening and turned it over to you."

Gomez backtracked to the prosecution table and picked up a plastic bag. Mercer noticed two other evidence bags resting in front of Gloria Olivette. He tried to maintain a calm appearance but his body was reacting with alarm.

"I'd like this placed into evidence, Your Honor," Gomez said, handing the judge the baggie.

"Objection, Your Honor," Mercer said. "We weren't notified of any new evidence."

"Would opposing counsels approach the bench, please?"

When they were standing before her, Judge Land said, "Please explain, Mr. Gomez."

"It could hardly be called new evidence, Your Honor. Mr. Early introduced the subject of the plastic chip himself. As Detective Farley just testified, Mr. Early's questions prompted him to seek out the object, which he did in a swift, professional manner. He turned it over to me last evening and I summarily sent a fax covering the discovery to Mr. Early's office."

"I didn't get any fax."

"My obligation is merely to notify," Gomez said. "Not reorganize the method by which Mr. Early's firm handles incoming information."

"Enough," Judge Land said. "Objection overruled. The contents of the bag go into evidence. Proceed, Mr. Gomez."

Eddie was shaking his head as Mercer returned to the table. Perfect. That's exactly what he needed: criticism. He said, "Take a walk, Eddie. Call Melissa. If there's a fax from Gomez, have her read it to you. Make notes. Find out when it was sent."

"Isn't this something Vanessa could handle?" Eddie asked.

"She could, but I want you to do it."

Vanessa gave him a puzzled look, but he didn't have time to reassure her he was slapping Eddie's wrist, not indicating a lack of faith in her.

Gomez seemed to be shifting into high gear. "Detective, when the assistant coroner removed the plastic shard from the victim's mouth and you expressed your initial belief that it lacked evidentiary value, did anyone at the autopsy disagree with you?"

"Yes, sir. That would be Detective Lionel Mingus, the officer of the law who the suspect shot in the head."

It was such an astounding thing for Farley to say that Mercer was slow to respond. Time seemed to stand still. The deadly silence was broken by Vanessa's hissed command, "Object."

Mercer got to his feet and did just that. He could hear the spectators murmuring, the crack of Judge Land's gavel. He closed his eyes and commanded himself to throw off his stupor.

"Mr. Early?" the judge prompted.

"Yes," he said, heading back on track. "I don't recall any trial, much less a decision, regarding who may or may not have shot at Detective Mingus."

"C'mon," Farley yelled from the stand, "a beat cop saw Burris fire point-blank at Mingus."

The judge nearly cracked her gavel calling for order. She was just a step away from apoplexy, glaring at Farley. "The jury shall disregard everything that just emanated from Detective Farley's overactive mouth.

"You understand where you went wrong, Detective? Maybe not. Let me elucidate. One, there was no question pending and until there is one, you keep your mouth shut. Two, it is not your job to assist the district attorney in arguing objections. Three, and this is most important of all, the next time you pull a stunt like that in my courtroom it'll cost you a grand and ten days in the county."

Farley sat there pretending to look contrite. "Sorry, Your Honor," he said.

Judge Land banged her gavel again and ordered Gomez to proceed.

Which he did, much too confidently, Mercer thought.

"Sir, you were telling us that Detective Lionel Mingus said he believed the plastic shard might be of some significance in determining the murderer of Darion Mayfield?"

Farley turned to face the jury. "Yeah. That's what he said."

"Do you know why Detective Mingus was present for the autopsy?"

Mercer was confused. Gomez seemed to be getting his witness to admit that he was under investigation by Internal Affairs. And Farley seemed eager to answer. "He was investigating Burris for . . ."

Mercer was on his feet, objecting loudly, attempting to talk over the fat detective who raised his voice, too. "He was checking out Detective Burris for Internal Affairs."

Judge Land lost it. "Sidebar, now. No, make that my chambers. The witness and the jury will remain right where they are."

Mercer followed Gomez from the courtroom.

When they were inside Judge Land's chambers, she slammed the door. Mercer was surprised the woman had the strength to move the slab of thick oak that easily. "Mr. Gomez, what the hell are you trying to do here? Provoke a mistrial?"

Gomez slunk back into the judge's oxblood leather sofa. "I'm not sure what you mean, Your Honor."

Judge Land was now beet red. "You've introduced information that is not admissible, that, for all I know, is blatantly incorrect."

"I really haven't—"

"Don't play me, Mr. Gomez," the judge said sternly. "I'm talking about your question that prompted your witness to reply that the accused was under investigation by Internal Affairs."

"Oh," Gomez said. "I'm sorry, Your Honor. I was just asking about the piece of plastic. I'm not sure how Internal Affairs came up."

Mercer sat quietly. He'd objected to Farley's comment, but, in fact, he wasn't too upset by it. He knew whom Mingus was really investigating. The problem was figuring how to get it into the records without putting the IAG detective on the spot by forcing him to provide that information.

The judge stopped scowling at Gomez to look his way. "Since Mr. Early seems to have nothing more to say in this matter, allow me. There will be no further mention of Internal Affairs without first advising the court. Is that clear enough, Mr. Gomez?"

Gomez waited for a few ticks of the clock before nodding and saying that it was.

Back in the courtroom, Judge Land admonished the jurors to make no assumptions about what may or may not have transpired in the chambers conference. She then ordered Gomez to proceed.

"Detective, has your initial opinion changed about the evidentiary value of that piece of plastic?"

"Yes, it has."

"Tell us how it has changed."

"Well, after Mr. Early made such a big deal about it, I began to wonder why. I mean, he's a smart man. If he thinks this hunk of plastic is worth taking up the court's time—"

"Answer the question, Detective," Judge Land said.

"Yes, ma'am. Anyway, last evening I returned to the victim's apartment with an evidence technician. He brought along a vacuum cleaner that he used on the victim's rug near the window that the victim flew out of."

"Did the vacuuming turn up anything?"

"Yes, sir. A few more pieces of plastic."

Gomez returned to his table and picked up one of the remaining two baggies. Mercer stared at the final bag and wondered what the hell was keeping Eddie with the information from Gomez's fax.

"Are these the pieces you found?"

"Yes, sir. Them's my initials on the tape there."

Gomez handed the baggie to the judge. "For entering into evidence, Your Honor."

She nodded.

"Tell us briefly what happened after you found the pieces, Detective," Gomez said.

"We took 'em to the lab and checked 'em against the piece taken from the vic's throat."

"What did the comparison indicate?" Gomez asked.

"The pieces matched."

"And what did that tell you?"

"That the cup, or whatever, was broke in the vic's apartment. And, since he had the piece in his throat, it was probably broke right before he went through the window."

"Why right before?"

"Something like that gets caught in your throat, you dig it out unless you got some bigger problem on your mind, like flying through space."

Farley paused, anticipating the mumbles from the spectators.

"Why don't you give us your professional opinion of the events leading up to the victim's death?"

Mercer leaned forward.

"My educated guess is that the killer," he turned to Burris, "attacked the victim when he was drinking from a plastic cup. Maybe punched him. Swung something at him, shattering the cup and driving part of it into his throat. Then the attacker shoved the victim through the window."

"That brings us back to the matching pieces of a broken cup," Gomez said. "What was your next move?"

"Well, with all those little pieces of plastic on the rug, I asked myself if maybe we might be lucky enough for the killer to have stepped on one."

Mercer wasn't aware of Eddie's return, until he heard him whisper, "Check this."

It was a sheet of notepaper on which Eddie had scrawled the contents of Gomez's fax. It was not good news.

He showed the paper to Burris, pointing to a description of the contents of the third evidence bag. "Pieces of matching broken plastic recovered from shoes in suspect's closet."

Burris read the words, then looked up, smiled, and shrugged.

Damn the man, Mercer thought.

"I took the news about the broken plastic to Judge Runyon, just down the hall, and got a search warrant for Burris's place."

Mercer's mind was racing. He saw that the judge was frowning and guessed she wasn't happy about Farley seeking a warrant from Old Reliable Runyon instead of from her.

"You went to the suspect's home?"

"Yeah."

"What were you looking for, Detective?"

Another minute and it would be too late. *Come on, think, dammit*, Mercer commanded himself.

"We were looking for the suspect's shoes. To see if we could find any pieces of plastic matching the ones we found on the carpet."

"Did you?"

"Your Honor," Mercer said, rising, "I object to this whole line of questioning."

Judge Land looked surprised. "On what grounds, counselor?"

"On the grounds that the prosecutor has failed to inform the defense in a timely matter of the objects he has attempted to place into evidence today."

The judge sighed. "Come hither, gentlemen."

When they had gathered, Judge Land said, "Mr. Early, are you challenging Mr. Gomez's statement that he faxed you information about the new evidence?"

"He faxed it, Your Honor, at 11:43 P.M. I'd like to know what time the search warrant was issued."

The judge looked at Gomez. "I'm not sure I know . . ."

"Mr. Gomez," the judge said, heatedly.

"In the neighborhood of six o'clock."

"And it took the detective four hours to enter a closet and retrieve the suspect's shoes?"

"Detective Farley was hungry after his day on the stand and the events of the evening," Gomez said. "The detective informed me of the outcome of his search well after ten o'clock. I informed Mr. Early's firm as soon thereafter as possible. Mr. Early knows this sort of thing happens. It wasn't that long ago when the shoe was on the other foot and he was lecturing me on the subject."

Judge Land stared at the prosecutor, then nodded. "Sorry, Mr. Early. If I had a walker handy, I'd give it to you, because you haven't got a leg to stand on."

Mercer nodded ruefully.

Back at the defense table, a wide-eyed Vanessa looked at him with curiosity. Eddie said, "Well, you tried."

Mercer ignored them both to focus on Gomez and his witness.

"I ask you again, Detective, were there any matching pieces of plastic embedded in the suspect's shoes?"

"Oh, yeah. In a pair of Air Jordans, size eleven and a half, in his closet."

As Gomez waltzed back to his table, his cocounsel raised a black carrying case from the floor. She opened it and withdrew two white-and-black gym shoes in an evidence bag. Gomez carried them and the bits of plastic to the bench.

"More evidence, Your Honor." He faced Farley. "What does the discovery of the plastic particles embedded in the suspect's shoes tell you, Detective?"

"That Claude Burris over there had been in the dead man's apartment at the time of the murder."

It was all the jury needed to hear. Mercer saw their minds closing shut.

"Thank you, Detective." Turning from the jury, Gomez shot Mercer a quick wink and took his chair.

Mercer approached Farley as if he had something heavy on his mind. "Detective, given that I haven't had but about ten minutes to analyze the evidence myself, or even consider it for that matter, maybe you can help me with a few things. Do you mind?"

"Always glad to help."

"The lab failed to turn up any pieces of plastic in Darion Mayfield's apartment during the initial investigation, right?"

"There was a lot of . . . stuff up there. Drug residue, broken glass, spilled wine, dirt in general. The man wasn't the neatest housekeeper—"

"Answer yes or no, please. Did they find any pieces of plastic?"

"Not to my knowledge."

"But you found it yesterday evening, long after the fact, using your handy dandy vacuum cleaner?"

"It's truth, like you're sayin' it. Of course, I had the advantage of knowing what I was lookin' for."

"I don't suppose, in the intervening weeks, somebody might have put those pieces of plastic there for you to find?"

"Gee, I don't think so, counselor."

"Suppose we were to look at your shoes right now, Detective? Think we might find one of those plastic shards?"

Farley stared down at his expensive, highly polished oxblood loafers. "Maybe." He grinned. "Considerin' I was exposed to the little pieces last night."

"And the night of the murder, too, I imagine. You did visit the apartment that night?"

"Yeah. Sure. I could have picked some pieces up that night, if I was wearing these bluchers."

"Do you know where Detective Burris was arrested?" Mercer asked.

Farley frowned and said nothing.

"Your Honor," Mercer said, "would you inform the—"

"Yeah, okay," Farley said. "He was arrested at the Mayfield apartment."

"So couldn't he have picked up the plastic shards then?"

Farley thought for a beat, then grinned. "No. The shoes he was wearing when he was arrested would be at the lockup."

"But between the murder and my client's arrest, couldn't he have visited the crime scene?"

"Not for any legitimate reason," Farley said. "The apartment was secured."

"As a vice cop he would have no reason to visit an apartment where drugs may have been sold?"

"Wait a minute," Farley said. "You're tryin' to confuse me. He wouldn't have any reason to be there after the apartment's owner was dead and gone."

"Unless he suspected drugs were somehow involved," Mercer said.

"Objection, Your Honor," Gomez complained, "Mr. Early is asking Detective Farley questions about his own client's state of mind."

"Objection sustained." The judge told the jury to disregard the question.

"So, Detective Farley," Mercer said, "can you state unequivocally that Detective Burris could not have picked up those plastic shards on a visit to Darion Mayfield's apartment at a time after the murder?"

"Well, no, I can't. But—"

"Officer Farley, in the early stages of your investigation of the murder, were there other suspects on your list?"

"What do ya mean?"

"I mean, did you, as a professional of many years' standing, find an assortment of people who may have had reason for wanting Darion Mayfield, a man engaged in a nefarious activity, to die? Maybe addicted clients who thought he'd cheated them?"

"I guess maybe there were a few people didn't care for the man."

"How many?" Mercer asked. "Five? Ten?"

"I'm not sure."

"What does it say in your murder book?"

"Seven, eight names."

"And what happened to them?"

"We closed out our investigations of them when an eyewitness identified the suspect as the man seen fleeing the crime scene."

"On the strength of just one witness, you focused your entire investigation on my client?"

"We're lucky when we get one good witness," Farley said.

"What happens if your good witness is a liar, or maybe he's touched in the head or just makes a mistake?" Mercer asked.

"I said *good* witness. We check out statements that important very thoroughly."

"You personally checked out your witness?"

"Yes, sir."

"And you were thorough?"

"Yes, sir."

"Thorough like you were when you misplaced the victim's head and then ignored the pieces of plastic that the deputy district attorney now seems to feel are vital to his case?"

"I object, Your Honor. Mr. Early is badgering the witness."

"Move on, Mr. Early," Judge Land said. "We've already heard the shaggy-dog-ate-my-evidence story."

"All right, Your Honor. Detective, I'd like to clear up one other matter. A while ago, you mentioned something about Detective Mingus being shot by my client."

Farley blinked in surprise. He turned to look at the judge. "Do I answer that, Your Honor?"

"Hearing no complaint from the prosecution, I imagine you do."

"Okay, then. Yeah. Your client shot Detective Mingus."

"Mr. Farley, you have almost thirty years in service. Have you ever heard the term, 'accidental discharge'?"

Farley cocked his head to one side, winked, and said, "You mean in a sexual connotation?"

Again Farley got the courtroom audience to laugh.

"No, Detective, you're thinking about premature ejaculation. But we're not here to talk about your sex problems." Even the judge laughed at that one. Mercer continued, "Have you ever accidentally fired your handgun?"

The laughter stopped.

Gomez objected, of course.

"I'm just trying to make a point, Your Honor," Mercer said.

"Do it quickly. Answer the question, Detective Farley."

"I don't understand what that has to do with anything, Mercer."

The lawyer was surprised that Farley addressed him by his first name. But he didn't let it distract him. "Think back to 1997, Detective."

"Your Honor?" Gomez whined.

Mercer ignored him. "Let me help you remember. You had a suspect proned out on the ground. With your gun drawn, you tried to cuff him one-handed. According to your report, he flinched and you flinched, too, firing a shot into his back."

Farley was pushing against the chair, as if trying to put distance between himself and Mercer's words.

"That'll do, Mr. Early," Judge Land said. "I felt you

deserved a little leeway to counter Detective Farley's earlier gaffe. But that'll do."

"Just a couple more questions, if it please the court?"

"Two," she said.

"Thank you, Your Honor. Detective, when you shot that man, paralyzing him from the waist down, was it an accidental discharge or was it attempted murder?"

Farley said quietly, "It was an accident."

"Accidents do happen, Detective," Mercer said. "By the way, who cleared you of that shooting? Could it have been . . . Mr. Gomez?"

The D.D.A. had turned a strange red-brown color.

Farley said nothing.

"I suppose we can take your silence as a yes," Mercer said, walking to his chair at the counsel table and using it. "Small world, huh?"

"Since it seems Mr. Early is done," Judge Land said, "we'll take our lunch break. Trial will commence at one-thirty P.M."

In the lockup, Burris was as jubilant as Mercer had ever seen him. "Damn if you didn't carve up that fat boy," Burris said. "You're gonna have to watch your back for a long time, but, damn, that was a good show."

"It ain't the final act, Claude. The jury still thinks Mingus was investigating you for IAG. They think you're dirty and that means you probably wasted Darion."

"Convince 'em I didn't."

"It might help if you told me how those pieces of plastic got stuck in your sneakers."

"Make up whatever you want. I went to the crime scene and tromped around."

"It doesn't work that way," Mercer said.

"Then screw the shoes."

"They'll lend weight to Ken Loc's testimony. Maybe enough weight to send you to the death room."

"Then I guess I die," Burris said.

"How'd you get the plastic shards on your shoes?"

"How do you think?" Burris said.

"You told me you were there that night. Did you break the plastic cup when you hit Darion?"

"Naw. I didn't see any plastic cup. What I saw was an asshole snorting coke."

"You want to die, Claude?" Mercer asked.

"No."

"Then give me a shot at saving you. Tell me how those pieces of cup got stuck to your shoes."

Burris stared at him for a few seconds. He lowered his voice to a whisper. "I was there when it went down," he said.

"You were there?"

"Not in the goddamn room. I was in the parking lot when Darion went out the window."

"You must've seen who did it."

"Maybe. Maybe she did it."

"She?"

"There was a white broad . . . lemme just lay out the whole deal. I pull up and hear this crash. I get just a glimpse of glass raining down and a body hitting the Dumpster. It's gotta be Darion. Who else?"

"What the hell were you doing there?" Mercer asked.

"I had some dumb idea of staking out the place until a serious buy went down. Maybe some showbiz jagoff that'd catch a lot of press. Then nobody, not even you, could stop me from putting the smart-ass little prick away for a few years. My timing was as good as always. I'd just parked and cut the engine when it happened."

"So all that stuff about Redd being your alibi was pure bullshit?"

"Pretty much." He grinned, scratched his cheek. "I been fucking with you, Mercer. I knew about 'tells' when you were still in kindergarten."

The young lawyer was nearly beyond exasperation. "Okay, let's keep to the point. You were there in the parking lot. Ken Loc Ansol was supposed to be down there, too. You see him?"

"There were a lot of cars. He could have been in one of 'em. I didn't see him."

"Tell me about the woman."

"It took me a few seconds to realize what the fuck had gone down. When that kicked in, I headed up to his apartment."

"Why?"

"Why'd I go up?" Burris shrugged. "Natural instinct? Making sure it was him took the dive? I don't know. But I did. When I step out of the elevator, I see this broad in the hallway. She's stoned, staggering around, carrying a fucking laptop computer under one arm. Got a plastic bag full of white powder in the other hand. She's heading for the stairwell."

"It was probably a woman named Alice Adams," Mercer said. "Did you try to stop her?"

"Why? To shake her hand? Fact is, I didn't think she killed Darion. She was too stoned. Darion was probably flying so high, he thought he was getting on the elevator."

"If she didn't do it, she saw what happened. You'd have saved yourself a lot of grief if you'd grabbed her."

"Yeah, maybe."

"But you went into the murder scene instead," Mercer said. "And I got a nasty idea why."

"What would that be?" Burris stared at him with more than a hint of defiance.

"You saw that bag of powder in her hand and figured there was more where that came from."

Burris actually laughed. "Some opinion you got of me. But you're right. I knew where the fucker kept his stash. I grabbed it and got the hell out of there before Darion's neighbors let their curiosity give their courage a boost."

"You stole his goddamn drugs."

"How the fuck do you think I was able to pay you?"

"Aw, hell."

"Money doesn't know where it comes from," Burris said. "If it makes you feel better, think of it as antidrug money. It's loot taken out of the drug trade."

Mercer closed his eyes and tried to clear his head

from the bullshit Burris had just put there. "Okay," he said. "Let's shove all this to the side and think about what's going to happen this afternoon. Gomez is going to be putting either Mingus or Ken Loc Ansol on the stand. I was prepped for either one, but now I've got a problem with Ansol."

"Why? If he's playing straight, he'll be my fucking alibi. He musta seen me going into the building after Darion landed."

"From what I can gather, his statement is that he saw you leaving the building just after the fall."

"That's bullshit, unless he had his eyes closed when I went in."

"You're sure."

"You think I did it."

"I think you're capable of just about anything, but that's got nothing to do with the way I pursue your defense. I don't go into a courtroom to lose."

"That's good," Burris said. "For both our sakes."

39

That morning, just before the trial started up again, Mingus entered the attorney conference room to find Farley on his cellular. "If the arrogant black bastard don't come through, I say fuck him and the prick who runs him."

He expressed a bit of alarm when he saw Mingus, lowered his voice and ended his conversation. "You're some creepin' Jesus, Lionel. Anybody ever tell you that?"

"You're the first."

"Sit down, why don'tcha, take a load of shit off your feet."

Mingus sat. With a grunt, Farley bent down to retrieve his morning cup of Fong's Palace coffee.

"Got any idea when Gomez is going to put Ken Loc on the stand?" Mingus asked.

"Maybe today. I'm bringing him in after lunch."

"Why were you hiding him from me?"

"From you?" Farley said. "Jesus, man, but you've got an ego big as the Ritz. We just been trying to keep the weasel alive and kicking until he's had his say in court."

"You think Burris put a hit out on him?"

"Somebody did. He got shot the night him and you went for your ride," Farley said.

"No shit?"

"Gervey and me were parked, waiting for him. Saw you drop him off. He was heading for the Kittyhawk when it happened. Drive-by. Big fucking Mercedes. I figured the hell with the shooter, it was more important to get Loc to a medic. Turns out he was just winged. Tore the flesh off the inner part of his left arm.

"So we get him fixed and I pack him away all nice and tidy. But the asshole sneaks out and we find him staying with some dame in Inglewood. We grab him again and put him back in the safe house where he won't be found."

"In Chinatown," Mingus said.

Farley stopped. "How the fuck . . . ? That's a guess, right?"

"Fong's Palace," Mingus said, pointing to the coffee cup.

"Gee, Lionel, maybe you are a detective under that thick black hide. Yeah, we got him in a little place near Fong's."

"There was a Fong's carton at Bay Bay's, too."

Farley nodded. "Ken Loc thought his bro' was headin' for the homeland and wanted to say good-bye. We took him some moo shu and chitlins. Not that the bastard could do much eating."

"When was that?" Mingus asked.

"Three, no, four nights ago. We stuck around for maybe an hour, then split. Bay Bay went out hard, I understand. Anyway, Loc'll be testifying today or tomorrow and he'll be off my hands. Then, I won't give a damn if Burris or any of the other fucks shoot him or serve him on toast."

"Which other fucks would that be?"

A bailiff came to the door and nodded to Farley. He stood up, rolled his eyes. "You don't have any idea what's goin' on, do you, Lionel? You're as clueless as that little brown wetback, thinks he's the one winnin' his case next door. You bozos don't have any fucking idea."

Mingus sighed. "You got that right, fat man," he told the closing door.

It was nearly noon when Gloria Olivette informed him that he was free to go to lunch. But she cautioned him to be back before the afternoon session began at one-thirty. "David's putting you on the stand next."

His plan was to drive to a nearby restaurant for a quick sandwich and a beer. But when he left the elevator on the parking level, he spied Farley standing beside the driver's window of a parked black sedan, a new Mercedes 600S. The fat man was waving his arms in an agitated manner. Walking in that direction, Mingus began to pick up some of Farley's words.

". . . I'm tellin' you, we're on your side . . . it's the fuckers runnin' you who're out to get him . . . they're screwin' with you, you dumb cunt." Suddenly, the fat man reached both arms inside the window, apparently attacking the car's occupant.

There was a flash and an oddly hollow bang as the gunshot reverberated against the low ceiling.

Farley flew back away from the Mercedes, bouncing against the front fender of a parked Explorer with a thud and sliding to the cement floor.

Mingus broke into a run, hand going for his 9mm.

Another bang and flash and Farley's fat body twitched on the ground. Then the Mercedes's engine roared. The sedan zoomed back, the driver's tinted window sliding up.

Mingus was between the car and the exit. The Mercedes, facing him, seemed to be vibrating, a steel bull getting ready to charge.

"Stop," Mingus shouted, assuming the stance, pistol steadied on left open palm. "LAPD."

The sedan bore down on him, horn blaring. His finger began to contract against the trigger, but the car was upon him in a flash and he leaped backward, the 9mm sending its round into the ceiling of the garage.

He had a sense of déjà vu at that last second. It was

the same car that had nearly left him for rubble on the way to Alice Adams's home on Impala Terrace.

He'd landed sprawled over the trunk of a Chrysler. Turning his head, he saw the 600S taking the rise into the street and away. He holstered his weapon and eased off of the rear of the car, being careful to consider every painful joint and bone. He was bruised but not broken.

Farley wasn't so lucky. One bullet, the first probably, had done some damage to his upper chest. The stomach wound seemed to be the more serious. Blood gurgled from it like water rising from an underground well. Mingus knelt beside the dying man and pressed the heel of his hand against the wound to stanch the flow.

"The stupid bitch," Farley was saying. "Believed them over me . . ." He stared at Mingus. "Jesus, Lionel, bullets hurt."

"Lie still." Mingus heard footsteps. He shouted, "Man's been shot. Get a medic."

"She's goin' after my partner and Ken Loc."

"Where?"

Farley opened his mouth, but no sound came out. Only a pink froth. Then, "Seventeen . . . Dragon Lane . . . Fa . . ." He coughed up blood. "You see the cunt who—?"

He coughed again. A shudder went through the fat man's body. And he was gone.

Mingus removed his hand from the man's damaged stomach. He noticed something that had been snagged by Farley's coat sleeve. He plucked it free—a press-on fingernail decorated with the number from a two-dollar bill.

"I didn't have to see her, Fats," he said. He closed the dead man's eyes and stood.

He used a handkerchief to mop Farley's blood from his hand and cuff, then stuck the red-stained rag into his pocket with the broken fingernail.

Two middle-aged women—one white, one black— stood frozen, staring down at the body. "Go get a cop, ladies," he said, then added, perhaps unkindly, "Make yourselves useful."

He moved quickly to his car and headed for Chinatown.

Redd, Redd, Redd. She was all Mingus could think of as he rolled down Broadway. Damn, if she hadn't played him like a fool. Right from the jump, that night at Buckie's, she'd sent him out to find Ken Loc and Alice Adams, the only two witnesses she knew of who could put her boyfriend away. She'd been following him the night he found Ken Loc at the Kittyhawk, had taken her shot and missed.

But she'd got to Alice Adams before him. How ... shit, the static on his telephone. The bitch had bugged him. She'd heard Ida Bevan give him the address. She'd even phoned him right after, to get an idea how long she'd have to kill the Adams woman before he showed up.

Now, she was ahead of him. He didn't know how she'd discovered where Farley had stashed the ex-con. Maybe the fat man had slipped up and told her.

There was no time to try to find an empty section of curb in Chinatown. He pulled into a lot. Ten bucks, for an hour or all day. The last time he'd used his badge instead of cash, he'd returned to find his radio and hubcaps missing. He slapped a ten spot in the Asian attendant's hand and headed for Dragon Lane, a half block away.

The narrow streets were busy with foot traffic, mainly Asians and tourists, strolling past or into chock-a-block two-story commercial buildings with curved, neon-outlined roofs. Some people found the area colorful and picturesque. Mingus thought it looked crowded and desperate. He wasn't much for fake pagodas and gold-painted plaster of Paris elephants. And he wasn't crazy about the soundtrack—relentless rickey-tick music mixing with the best of Britney Spears.

Fong's Palace was at the corner of Ord and Dragon Lane. Glancing through its window, he spotted Al Gervey waiting at the counter with a bag full of food. He entered the establishment.

Gervey was not pleased to see him. "Mingus?" he said, nervously improvising. "You eat here, too? I was just picking up some grub for Dennis and me."

"No time for bullshit, Gervey." Mingus was searching the restaurant. "Ken Loc here with you?"

"I don't know what you're talking a—"

"I don't have time to ease into this. A woman just shot and killed your partner. She's a few minutes ahead of me, aiming to give Loc the same treatment."

"You're crazy, Mingus. Dennis can't be dead."

"Then he sure had me fooled."

"Oh, Jesus. I told him it wouldn't work. You don't screw with those guys."

"What are you talking about?"

"Oh, hell, what do I do now? I can't handle this by myself."

The guy sounded like he was going off his nut. "Where's Loc? Is he at number seventeen?"

"What do I do?"

"You got two choices, as I see it. Stay here or back me up. I'm getting Loc to the Courts Building."

He ran from the restaurant and headed down Dragon Lane. It was barely a street, two blocks long, with garbage cans and bins making the already narrow passage barely passable for pedestrians, much less cars. Number seventeen was a puke-yellow two-story with bright red trim around the open front door. A badly painted golden dragon guarded the entrance to what looked like six apartments. Two in the basement, accessible via littered cement steps; two on sidewalk level; two on the floor above.

Farley had died before giving him the apartment number.

Mingus looked in the direction of Ord and saw Gervey huffing and puffing toward him down the lane, gun drawn, twisting his head every which way, as if he expected 360 degrees of trouble. Mingus waved to get his attention, then pointed to a window on the top floor. Gervey paused and shook his head. "The other one," he yelled.

The 9mm firmly in his fist, Mingus entered the building. It smelled of smoke and cabbage and fresh paint. The stairwell was a new pea green. It creaked under his feet, so he gave up any hope of surprise and rushed up.

The door to the apartment Gervey had picked out was closed and locked. It looked like it was made out of parchment. He took a few steps back and used his moving weight and shoulder to open it.

There was only one room. Not terribly clean, but comfortable enough if you didn't mind the heat. Or the smell. On an ancient TV resting on a Goodwill table, a talk show was playing out with four ethnically diverse women ragging on some poor son of a bitch who looked like he'd stepped into the wrong bar room. Ken Loc was in a corner trying to hide behind a soiled purple sofa. When he saw the detective, he blinked and then started to rise, smiling sheepishly. "Mingus," he said, making a sniffing noise. "Jesus, I thought you was the reaper man."

"It's a reaper woman and be glad I'm not her. C'mon, gotta get you out of here."

He heard Gervey in the hall.

"Where's Farley?" Loc asked. He sniffed again.

"Stone-cold dead."

"Oh, man. I tole him it was a dumb idea. All we had to do was stick to the plan. But, no-o-o. He's gotta show 'em who's boss." Ken Loc was starting to throw objects into an open canvas bag. "Showed 'em all right."

"Leave that shit, Loc. There's no time."

"True enough," Redd said. "It done run out."

She was using Gervey as a shield, her gun pressed against his neck. Well, fuck, she'd done it to him again, Mingus realized. She hadn't known the whereabouts of the safe house. She'd left the garage and then pulled over and waited for him to lead her right to their door.

Mingus studied her weapon. He thought it was a Beretta Centurion, which meant it might be a ten-shot or a fifteen-shot, depending on the load. In either case, too many rounds to hope for any miracles.

"Drop your gun, Detective."

"Think I'll hang on to it. You're gonna shoot us anyway, aren't you, Redd?"

"Maybe. Maybe not. Ken Loc, you see Claude Burris the night Darion took his fall?"

Loc was nearly jumping out of his skin, sniffling with every breath. Mingus wondered if it was the result of the nose injury he'd caused. More likely, it was the after-effect of the white powder that the excellent lawmen had been feeding him. "Which way you want me to tell it?" the ex-con asked.

"Try the truth for a change."

"I seen him." Loc sniffled. "He went into the building just after Darion landed."

"Hear that, Lionel? Man just gave me a reason to let you live."

"Me, too, right?" Loc asked. "I'm with the truth now. I got more I can say."

"The difference between you and Lionel," Redd told him, "is I kinda trust him. Which means I'm through with you."

The bullet exploded Ken Loc's face and slammed him against a wall already mottled with his blood and brain.

"You wanna put your gun down *now*, Lionel? And hold your arms out, like you're gonna start flappin' your wings. I really don't want to have to shoot you."

Mingus dropped his gun and did as she instructed.

She stepped away from her human shield. Gervey looked confused and fearful. "I don't get it," he said. "Loc was goin' into court to name the real killer, let Burris clean off the hook. Why you doin' this?"

"Don't gimme your bullshit, white bread. You think I don't know what's the hap? Your fat partner hated Claude so much he was gonna use a couple crackheads to put him away. I'm just playing Lady Justice, forcing the truth to come out."

"You think this whole thing was Dennis's idea? You got it all wrong. We were getting fucked, too. That's why we decided to help Burris, to make sure Loc told it like it was."

"Let's see. Do I believe that? Hmmmmmm."

She shot him twice.

"Guess not."

She used the pointed toe of an oxblood pump to turn the cop over. One bullet had caught him directly between his blue eyes. The other didn't matter.

"Jesus, Redd. You didn't play this so smart, sister. Never mind Loc, you take out two members of the LAPD, even sorry specimens like this dude and Farley, they gonna hunt you down."

"Don't worry about me, Lionel. Just make sure you remember what Ken Loc said. It's what they call a dying declaration."

Mingus didn't think so. As sincere as Loc had sounded, he surely didn't know he was about to die. But it was not in the detective's self-interest to argue the point.

Redd moved to the door. "So long, Lionel."

"Suppose I pick up my gun now, Redd. You gonna kill the last chance for Loc's confession to come out?"

She smiled. "I won't kill you, honey. I'll just lame you real bad. Leave that gun where it be. Stick around here till I'm long gone. Live yourself a nice long life. And be good to your big-ass grandma girlfren', hear?"

He watched her strut out the door in her tailored gray pants suit, gun in hand, like she was headed back to the office after a light lunch. He picked up his gun from the ratty carpet and slipped it back into its holster. Since there didn't seem to be a phone in the room, he got out his cellular and sat down on the couch. The room was filled with the coppery smell of blood mixed with gun smoke. Keeping his eyes up, cutting off his view of whatever happened to be lying on the floor, he dialed Robbery-Homicide direct. There were some crime scenes an officer of the law simply couldn't duck out on. He hoped David Gomez would understand why he was not going to make it back to court that afternoon.

40

"Gentlemen, you're starting to repeat yourselves," Mercer said. "Since my client has been answering your questions truthfully, his answers aren't going to change. I think it's a wrap."

The interrogation of Claude Burris had gone on for over an hour in the small interview room at twin towers. Extra chairs had been brought in to accommodate the two RHD detectives assigned to the Mildred "Redd" Doremus trackdown: a sleepy-looking Caucasian named Carmody and Virgil Sykes, Mercer's friend and sometime bungle ball teammate—and David Gomez. The deputy D.A. was present merely to observe. The detectives did the questioning.

At the start, Burris had read a declarative statement, hastily prepared by the firm, that he had absolutely no knowledge, not even a suspicion, that Ms. Doremus had been committing any crime, murder or anything else, involving him or his current position as a defendant in a murder trial. Accepting that, they moved on to whatever they could pry out of him that would facilitate their hunt for the missing murder suspect.

He wasn't sure where she lived, thought she may have had a place in the Valley and another in Hollywood. He had no clue if she worked or at what or where her money came from, though possibly from illegal funds acquired by her imprisoned pimp husband. She had an arrest record for prostitution. That should tell them something. He gave them two phone numbers: her cellular and one other; he'd assumed it was a home number but he wasn't really sure. He couldn't come up with the name of any relative or friend or anybody she might turn to. He doubted it would be her husband. Maybe women she'd worked with in the life, but he didn't know any of their names either.

Sykes said they'd be talking to Sweets Doremus later in the day. He asked about vehicles at the suspected murderess's disposal. Burris dutifully described the cars he'd seen her drive: a new Mercedes, a Cadillac SUV, and a Land Rover, all of them black, but he had no idea of the plate numbers or if they'd been purchased or leased.

"The woman's going 'round on a killing spree for you," Sykes finally said, "and you don't even know where she lives. You did have a relationship with Mildred Doremus?"

"Yeah."

"Suppose you give us an idea of the nature of that relationship."

During their short session prior to the interrogation, Mercer had reminded Burris that this was the most potentially dangerous question he'd be tossed. The answer could snip away his last threads of credibility as an officer of the law, damaging his chances in the murder trial and setting him up for serious new criminal charges. "Ms. Doremus's husband was abusive," Burris said. "He damn near killed her. I took him off the streets and she was grateful. That was the basis for our relationship, as you call it."

Carmody wanted to know the extent of her gratitude and Mercer asked him to be more specific.

"Were you sleeping with her?"

"My client doesn't have to answer that. It won't help

you find her. He's told you he doesn't have any idea where Ms. Doremus is or how to reach her, other than by phone. Can we close this down now?"

Sykes was smart. Talk was he'd be moving into Farley's slot in the RHD chain of command. He asked, almost casually, "Detective Burris, you wouldn't be holding back on us because you're in love with the woman?"

Before Mercer could caution Burris, his client said, "I'm not holding anything back. The time I spent with Ms. Doremus was special. We didn't waste it by talking about day-to-day bullshit or past histories or weeping about things that weren't working out. Our relationship, to use your word, had nothing to do with how I lived my life away from her or how she lived hers. That was what made it special."

That closed Sykes down. When Carmody tried to get back to what Redd might have confided during their "special times," Mercer ended the session.

"What do you think?" Burris asked, when they were alone.

"You sounded sincere."

"I don't know where the fuck she is," he said. "I mean, part of the whole deal is she's this goddamn sexy mystery woman who loves my ass. I don't know anything about her past, how she got hooked up with Sweets. Once I got her on her feet after the damage he did, she disappeared for a while. One night she called and came over to my place. That's the way it's been going ever since. She calls the tune."

He leaned back in the chair and stared at the ceiling. "Last I heard from her, everything was cool. You saw her in court. She look like somebody who was getting ready to cut down three guys?"

Mercer had to admit that she hadn't. He said, "Those detectives don't seem to know much about her. But they'll be loading up on information damn quick. And they will find her. If there's anything they can get out of her that could put you on the spot, tell me now."

Burris slumped forward and stared at Mercer. "She'll never do anything to hurt me. But, Jesus Christ . . . three guys. The things we don't know about the people we sleep with."

At a little before seven that evening, Mercer was in LaLa's, nursing a Grey Goose and tonic at a table for two as far away from the bar and the bandstand as he could get. He'd been there nearly twenty minutes and he had that goldfish-in-a-bowl feeling. Redd's murder spree, aside from shaking up the trial, had sent the media into a feeding frenzy that made it slightly dangerous for him to stay in any one public place for too long.

He relaxed a little when he saw Lionel Mingus's large presence at the door.

The detective paused to give a waitress his order, then slid in opposite him. "Too-Good tell you about Ken Loc's final statement?" he asked Mercer.

"He waited until five. I guess it might've taken that long for him and the D.A. to decide it was exculpatory evidence that had to be shared."

"He was on the horn with her about it when I started my sessions with the Robbery-Homicide dicks. Jesus, it's been a day. I swear to God, Mercer, never mind dead people. If I just see somebody with their eyes closed, I'm running the other way. That goddamned Farley went out in my arms. I can still smell that ugly stink of blood."

"Maybe you oughta go get some sleep."

"Sleep? Hell, I don't want sleep. I have enough nightmares when I'm awake. I want booze. I'm dry. Been jawing all afternoon. Telling the same story over and over."

"You saw a lot of death today. It's going to take its toll."

"Yeah, yeah, yeah. I already made the appointment with the shrink. I know the routine. I've seen dead guys before and I'll probably see more of 'em before I join their club."

"How'd it go with Too-Good?" Mercer asked.

"He wasn't so happy to hear his ace witness had provided an alibi for your client."

"I can't figure out why he isn't giving up," Mercer said. "All he's got left in his backpack are an arguable motive and those plastic shards in Burris's sneakers. Slim pickings."

"He had some sleazy-looking dude in the office, a felon from the way he was being pushed around. I heard them mention Burris once or twice."

"Catch the guy's name?" Mercer asked.

Mingus shook his head. "I was too busy telling the pea brains in the office the same damn story about Redd and her crimes I'd already told RHD with Gomez present."

The waitress set a serious-looking cocktail in front of him. The detective winked at her, said, "Thank you, sister, and thank you, Lord," and sipped his drink. He smacked his lips, made an mm-mm-good sound. "Now that's therapy."

"What kind of questions did they ask?"

"Basically, all they wanted to know was why Redd was killing people. I told them what she told me: they were trying to railroad Burris."

"What should they have asked you?"

Mingus took another slug of his drink. "Why they were railroading him."

"Farley had a heavy hate against the man."

"It's not that simple," Mingus said. "According to both Farley and Gervey, the frame came from higher up. Their part of it was to deliver Ken Loc primed to put the finger on your client. But here's where it gets tricky. Something happened to seriously piss off Farley. Gervey swore to Redd that the fat man had turned the plan around and Ken Loc was going to get your client off the hook. 'Course, he was talking into Redd's gun at the time. She didn't believe him, obviously. He sure sounded sincere to me."

"Farley wasn't acting like a friend of Burris's in court," Mercer said.

"He sure was bitchin' about something this morning before the trial started. I don't think it was you or Burris."

Mercer considered that. "Suppose circumstances turned us into the lesser of two evils for him. He might still want to put us through as much shit as he could, knowing that whatever dirt he threw on Burris, Ken Loc's testimony would eventually exonerate him." He polished off the Grey Goose. "Be a help if we knew who ordered the frame."

"You sure Burris don't know?"

"Hard to tell, because the man lies like a rug. But my guess is if he knew that, he'd use it to try and get out of jail. He's not happy there."

"Maybe I'll get Redd to tell me if I see her again."

"You think she knows?" Mercer asked.

"Both Farley and Gervey thought so. They tried to tell her she was being conned by somebody into getting rid of the people who were trying to help Burris."

"Darion was going to testify against Burris in the perjury trial. Could Redd have killed him?"

Mingus thought about it. "No. She'd have to have known Darion's murder would put Burris on the spot."

"So who did kill him?" Mercer asked. "If we knew that, we could probably figure out everything else."

"I keep thinking about the broken cup and seeing a similar cup at Bay Bay's. Maybe he killed Darion."

"Why?"

"Hell, I don't know. Maybe he got his AIDS from one of Darion's needles."

"You said Bay Bay was drinking some thick red wine out of his cup, right?" Mercer said.

Mingus nodded. "Blood red."

"But according to your man at the lab, the residue on the broken cup was white wine."

"Right."

"That would suggest a communion ceremony a little more ordinary than Bay Bay's. More like the one at Darion's daddy's house of worship. I saw for myself that the Rev had trouble with his anger around Darion."

Mingus grinned. "When I told Loc's psychic friend Eula that he was doing some driving for Darion, she said that I'd got it screwed up. He was driving for the church. Could be he was driving for the Reverend. Hell, that's why Loc was parked at Darion's, waiting for the Rev who was upstairs, beatin' on his boy."

"I like it," Mercer said. "But we've got to nail it down."

41

The Church of the Redeemer was on Arlington and 47th in South Central L.A., a large clapboard building wearing a fresh coat of white paint. From the outside, it was not unlike Bay Bay's house of worship, except for a blue neon cross on the roof that stood out against the orange sunset sky. A light box in front read BIBLE STUDIES TONIGHT AND TOMORROW.

Mingus parked in a small busy lot just off the side door. He and Mercer sat in the car, watching members of the congregation arrive for their studies. "Guess you can put your lock pick away," Mercer said. "The place is jumpin' and you definitely look like a man in need of bible study."

"You better slump down out of the light," Mingus said. "The Reverend's followers find Burris's lawyer out here, they might decide to send you down for a game of hot-coal baseball with Bay Bay."

Both men got out of the car. Mercer merely exchanged his front seat for the more shadowy rear. Mingus headed warily toward the church. He was not familiar with the layout of this particular house of worship but he figured it wouldn't be much different from those he'd attended in the long ago. There would be a kitchen where, if luck was with him, the plastic communion cups would still be resting in the sink, cleansed of their pale dregs after the previous Sunday's services.

He followed a short man with a semi-Afro, thick glasses, and a leather-bound bible tucked under his arm. They went through the door and into a foyer that led to a stairwell that went up, probably to the church proper, and down, probably to the kitchen. The man with the bible went down. So did Mingus.

There were ten or more members of the Reverend Mayfield's flock down there, filling up on coffee from a pair of identical chrome machines. Mingus made a survey of the room, nodding to those whose eyes he met. The sink was spotless. And empty.

Annoyed, he focused on a cupboard with closed doors. He was wondering if anyone would stop him if he started poking around in it when an obese woman in a flower print dress tapped him on the shoulder and asked, "Would you be so kind to get me a cup, brother?"

Because the communion cups were on his mind, it took him a few seconds to realize she was talking about the coffee variety. "Sure," he said. "They in here?"

He threw open the cupboard doors to an assortment of glasses, plates, bowls, coffee cups . . . and communion cups. He reached out, plucked a coffee cup from the group, and handed it to the woman.

"You were on TV today, right?" she asked. "On the news about those murders?"

He thought he had avoided the media completely, but in getting from the murder scene on Dragon Lane to the Criminal Courts Building, maybe a camera or two had caught a glimpse of him.

"Not me," he said. "I got nothing to do with murders. I sell men's shoes."

"I could've sworn it was you." She was staring at him. "Musta been some other handsome black man. Won't you have a cup of coffee with me?"

"Sorry, sister. I have renounced the Devil's brew," he said piously.

The woman shrugged and moved on. After her departure, he quickly grabbed a communion cup and closed the cupboard doors. If he'd been on TV . . .

He was heading up the stairs when the Reverend appeared, a big, rawboned man who almost filled the doorway. Mingus closed his right hand around the cup and moved it behind his back. He had no intention of confronting the Reverend, even though he suspected that this so-called man of God had taken the life of his own son. First, they would make sure that the cup matched the shard. Then he and Mercer would decide if a visit with the Reverend was in order.

The Reverend Mayfield stepped back to allow him to pass. "Not going before the studies, are you, brother?"

"Just heading out for a little fresh air, Dr. Mayfield."

The man was staring at him. "Do I know you?"

"I don't think we've met," Mingus said. He shifted the cup to his left hand and extended his right. "Lionel Morgan."

"A sincere pleasure meeting you, Lionel," Reverend Doctor Mayfield said. He was a two-handed shaker, sandwiching Mingus's in what was nearly an embrace.

The detective's glance fell on a ring on the Reverend's left hand. A thick, buttery gold with a crucifix in relief at its center. "That's a handsome piece of jewelry, Reverend," he said.

"My parents gave me that when I graduated from the ministry. A long time ago."

"Well, I'd better go catch a little air while I can," Mingus said, even more anxious to make his getaway.

"Lionel, you don't have to obfuscate with me. I know what you're doing."

Mingus felt his heart flop over. "Beg pardon?" he said.

"You don't have to hide your weaknesses here. If you need to go smoke a cigarette, you can say so."

"Right," Mingus said. "I'll just go light up where I won't be bothering anybody."

"Good man. But don't take too long. We'll be starting the studies in just a minute."

Mingus nodded and backed out of there.

The two conspirators sat in temporary obscurity at a table at the Inglewood Fatburger, ignoring and in turn being ignored by a group of preteen boys hopping and bopping in their drag-ass baggy finery. Mercer was working on a large, soggy stacked bun sandwich. Mingus was sipping an after-dinner soda. On the table in front of them were the piece of plastic he'd found in Darion's apartment and the cup he'd just confiscated.

"No question, they're the same plastic," he said. "On the broken piece, you got the letters 'ist.' On the solid cup it says, 'Cruor Christi.' Christ's blood. It's used for communion."

Mercer put down his sandwich, wiped his fingers, and picked up the cup. "I'm on board for this. But what we got doesn't mean a hell of a lot. Even if the cup was exclusive to the Reverend's little place of worship, he could have given it to Darion any time."

"There's gotta be some way to prove Ken Loc drove for the Rev. A canceled check; somebody saw 'em in the car together. Something."

"We'd still have no way of proving Loc was waiting for him on that night." Mercer took a bite of his disappearing burger and grinned suddenly. "But we really don't have to prove a damn thing."

"What are you talking about?"

"I've been working on a backup plan in case everything else failed. I got another suspect picked out, a scary-looking junkie customer of Darion's who was cooping near the crime scene. The guy's in bad shape, and I don't like making his life any tougher. I'd feel much better throwing Reverend Mayfield to the jury even if he wasn't guilty."

"Suppose he comes up with an alibi?"

"How could he?" Mercer said. "We know where he

was: at the apartment in a rage, tossing his son out the window."

"I've got more," Mingus said. "At the autopsy, I noticed this indent on Darion's cheek. Like two lines intersecting. Mayfield wears a big honkin' gold ring with a raised cross on it. I'd bet you a hundred bucks that's what branded Darion's face. If I'm right, I don't care how many times the Rev's washed his hands, gold is soft. There'll be some DNA on that ring."

Mercer grinned. "My cocounsel asked me if I thought I was the black Perry Mason. He may have had something there. I'm gonna put that old boy in the witness box and Perry Mason the hell out of him."

42

Mercer spent most of the premidnight hours in his office, reading everything he'd been able to download from the *L.A. Times*'s archives on the Reverend Doctor Harlan Mayfield. There'd been a lot, starting in August of 1965 when, in his early twenties, he'd walked the riot-torn neighborhoods of Watts, preaching a street-level gospel that was generally considered to be a major force in establishing peace in the city. He'd personally saved the life of a young white police officer whom an angry mob was about to tear limb from limb. Mayfield had emerged as one of the acknowledged leaders of the African American community, while the cop, George Heathrow, used his sudden ten minutes of fame to begin a promising political career.

Both men were called to civic duty again in 1992 during what were labeled the Rodney King riots. Heathrow, then a state senator, began casting an eye on the mayor's office; and Mayfield, already firmly established, extended his popularity well beyond the borders of South Central. In 1993, a city magazine selected him among "The Favored Fifty: The Top Movers and Shakers of Our Town." By 2001 he'd risen to the nineteenth position in the chart, just below basketball's Shaquille O'Neal and above architect Frank Geary.

Mercer was concentrating on a 1998 interview with the Reverend in which he was complaining about the quality of black films and television shows when a voice cooed, "Burning that midnight oil?"

He nearly jumped off the office couch.

Vanessa was standing less than a foot away, wearing a shimmering white dress she hadn't had on earlier that day. "Sorry, honey, didn't mean to scare you."

"Surprise might be a better word." He swung around so that she could sit beside him. "What brings you down here this time of night?"

"I . . . needed to pick up some notes. Daddy may be letting me stick with you on the trial, but he's still got me working on civil cases, too." She picked up the downloaded pages he'd been reading. "What's this all about?"

"Prep."

"These are articles about Reverend Mayfield."

"I think he's gonna help me free up Claude Burris."

"How?"

"It's what an old law professor of mine called the Last Defense. When nothing else works, you shake the jury's belief in your client's guilt by throwing them a surprise suspect who looks just as guilty."

"You're going to suggest to the jury that the Reverend murdered his own son? Who'd believe it?"

"I do. So does a smart cop."

"Lionel Mingus?"

He frowned. "Where'd you get that name?"

"Well, it's surely been in the news today. And he's on the prosecution witness list. Last night, when I walked in on you, you were on the phone, making notes. I saw his name."

"You read upside down?"

"One of the first things I was taught in law school. You and Mingus friends?"

He had to think about it. "Yeah. I guess we are."

"Well, before you subpoena the Reverend, don't you think you should run it past Bobby first?"

"Why?"

"Because they're friends."

"Maybe you're right," he said. "You up for a drink?"

She shook her head. "I've got to go." She stood. "See you in the morning."

He stayed with his research on the Reverend for another half hour, but his thoughts kept hopping to Vanessa. He wondered where she'd been in her nice white dress. Had Barry Fox been waiting downstairs for her?

Yawning, he gathered the downloaded material into a folder, turned out his light and trudged to the elevator.

He heard someone call his name. It was his former klepto client, Eugenia Coulter, emerging from Joe Wexstead's darkened office as naked as a jaybird.

"Hey, Mercer," she said lazily, "come join the fun."

Wexstead appeared in the doorway behind her, clutching black-and-red-striped boxers to his privates with one hand and trying to grab her wrist and pull her back with the other.

"I think I'll pass, Eugenia," Mercer said. "Three's a crowd." He stepped into the elevator. "Lookin' good, Joe."

As he traveled down, his amusement at catching Wexstead and Eugenia at play turned to self-pity. Even a creepy little weasel like Joe had a woman.

43

The next morning there was a note on Mercer's desk from Bobby Carter. "My office. Immediately."

The partner looked uncharacteristically frazzled. He greeted Mercer with, "Are you out of your mind?"

"I'm the last person who'd know," Mercer said, trying to lighten the mood.

"You seem hell-bent on self-destruction. I care too much about you to sit back and let that happen."

"I appreciate your caring, Bobby, but I don't know what you're talking about."

"Dragging Reverend Mayfield into your courtroom?"

Mercer felt a flash of anger, but he did his best to control it. "She couldn't wait to go running to you with the news," he said.

"She?"

"Who told you I was going to subpoena the Reverend?"

"How I found out isn't the subject of this discussion. My God, Mercer, haven't you done enough to the poor man, defending his son's killer?"

"I'm not defending Darion's killer. Reverend Mayfield killed his son."

"You can't believe that."

"I'm not operating on a whim here, Bobby. Just hear me out."

Mercer told him about the cup, the ring, Ken Loc, everything he knew, even the Redd connection. When he'd finished, Bobby said, "It's nothing. It's all speculation."

"Not if the ring matches the mark on the victim's face or has traces of his DNA."

"For every expert who calls it a match, there's two to say it isn't."

"But the DNA—"

"First you have to get the ring, then have it tested and then, if by some miracle there's evidence of Darion's DNA on it, that is when you subpoena a man like Harlan. You don't do it on the come."

"By then the trial will be over."

"For that to concern me I'd have to have even the tiniest faith in your theory. Mercer, the idea that Harlan could not only murder his son but also send a . . . a *hitwoman* to murder others to cover up the crime, is ludicrous."

"Reverend Mayfield killed his son in an unpremeditated rage. Darion was the kind of boy who could piss off Gandhi. I don't know if he sent the Doremus woman off on her kill spree or if that's coming from somewhere else. That's not my concern, really."

Bobby emitted a derisive snort. "You're off the rails, son. I tell you this: you are not going to force that fine old man to take the stand."

Mercer stood up and headed for the door. "Watch me, Bobby. You just watch me."

He left the office shaking. Part of it was anger with Vanessa for betraying his confidence once again. Part of it was fear that Bobby could be right.

He went to Eddie's office. "I want you to issue a subpoena for the Reverend Harlan Mayfield."

"You're kidding?"

"I look like I'm in a happy mood?"

"Yeah, well, this ain't gonna make you any happier. I

just picked it up a minute ago." He held out a sheet of paper. It was a fax from the district attorney's office, adding one Gerald Callebrio to the list of prosecution witnesses. "Any idea who this guy is?" Eddie asked.

"No, but I bet our client does." Mercer looked at his watch. "We've only got about ten minutes before we have to leave for court. Try to get that subpoena in the works."

"There's a G. Callebrio has a pet shop in Santa Monica," Eddie said on the drive downtown. "Couldn't find anything else even close in the listings. If the guy takes care of animals, I don't see what use Gomez is going to make of him. Witness maybe."

For the first time, Mercer welcomed his cocounsel's chatter. It required no response. He himself was not in a communicative mood. Nor, apparently, was Vanessa. He wondered if she felt even the slightest bit guilty for running to Bobby. Not that Bobby wouldn't have found out about the subpoena eventually. It's just that Mercer would have preferred to avoid the confrontation until after the Reverend had been served. That way he wouldn't have had to defy a direct order from a partner of the firm.

"Whoa, look at this," Eddie said, drawing his attention to the crowd surrounding the CCB. Thanks to the murders, it had doubled since the previous day. "They sure love their blood, don't they?"

The atmosphere inside the courtroom seemed more highly charged, too. Mercer scanned the faces, half expecting to see Redd grinning back at him.

Gomez and Gloria Olivette were seated at their table, the little man beaming with a confidence that gave Mercer a seismic shake.

As soon as Burris was delivered, he asked, "Who's Gerald Callebrio?"

"Why?"

"Why do you think? He's a new witness for the prosecution. You know him?"

"He's got a pet shop."

"I don't think Gomez is going to be asking him about the price of puppies."

"He, ah, has another line, too."

"You guys should turn down the volume," Eddie cautioned.

"What line?" Mercer whispered.

"He middle-mans drug sales."

"Shit."

"I'd heard he got busted," Burris said. "I probably should have mentioned it to you."

"You think?"

"He's got a rep as a standup. I thought maybe I'd luck out."

"Yeah. You're real lucky, Burris."

"So I got more grief down the road. He can't damage me here, right? Mingus heard Ken Loc alibi me."

"Gomez will correctly identify Ken Loc as a hype. And, him being no longer of this world, the statement is not direct testimony. Still, it might've worked for us if a witness hadn't shown up to let the jury know who made off with Darion's stash the night of the murder."

Burris looked suitably shaken, but that accomplishment didn't improve Mercer's mood.

Judge Land began the morning session on time, as usual. She instructed the jury to ignore anything they may have heard or read about the case or anything the media may have suggested was related to the case. They were to stay focused on only the information provided them in the course of the trial itself.

She then nodded to Gomez. It would have been lovely if he'd called Mingus to the stand, but Mercer wasn't expecting that kind of favor. As soon as the words "Gerald Callebrio" escaped the prosecutor's lips, he was on his feet with an objection that the defense had not been provided timely notification of this new witness.

Annoyed, the judge bid the two opposing attorneys approach. "Once again, Your Honor, the information was faxed to Mr. Early's office."

"At eight o'clock this morning." Mercer handed the fax to the judge.

"It was supposed to go out last night," Gomez said, frowning. Some poor clerk would soon be suffering a chewed ass.

"Well, 'supposed' doesn't quite cut it, Mr. Gomez," the judge said. "An hour's notice does seem inadequate. What are your needs, Mr. Early?"

"I'd like to consult with my client. And I'd like to find out just a little about Mr. Callebrio other than his name."

"How much time?"

"I could use a day," Mercer said, knowing he was pushing his luck.

She shook her head. "We've already lost an afternoon because of yesterday's . . . extraordinary circumstances. I'm loath to prolong this agony further. Why don't you postpone the appearance of your mystery guest, Mr. Gomez, and make do with another witness. That'll give Mr. Early time during the lunch break to chew the fat with his client and send his minions to gather information about the mysterious Mr. Callebrio."

"Mr. Callebrio is the prosecution's final witness, Your Honor," Gomez said.

"What about Detective Mingus?" Mercer asked.

"We've decided not to call the detective."

"He has information crucial to this trial," Mercer complained.

"Then call him as a witness for the defense," Gomez said. "But I warn you. He's not terribly reliable. Got a little problem." He raised an imaginary glass to his lips.

Mercer glared at the prosecutor. If he put Mingus on the stand, Gomez would do his best to make him look like a prime candidate for a drunk tank. The "alcoholic" brand wouldn't just invalidate the detective's testimony, it could lead to forced early retirement.

"Well, Mr. Gomez, as much as I loathe delay, you leave me no choice but to give Mr. Early the morning to take the edge off of your surprise.

"Please use the time well, Mr. Early. And should you decide you want to add Detective Mingus to your list, for God's sake give the prosecution due notice. I shall expect both of you gentlemen to be ready to roll at one o'clock sharp."

44

Mingus arrived at the CCB that morning to discover his presence was no longer required in the case of *People* v. *Burris*. Angry at the abrupt dismissal after the hours of preparation and general bullshit Gomez had put him through, he headed for his office at Parker Center. Ordinarily, it was an easy hop, but to avoid the gamut of video cameras and pushy pretty people with microphones he had to leave via an underground passage, circle the block, and then walk well past Parker Center, doubling back to enter through a less-busy rear door.

At his section of the Internal Affairs Group, he nodded to the few detectives present, poured himself a cup of bitter coffee, and checked the assignment board. His name had not been put back in the hopper.

He wasn't all that anxious to get back to the grind. But he wanted to keep busy at something. His previous night's dreams had been haunted by images of blood and death, and he'd awakened in the early dawn with a yell, scaring Bettye and, in truth, scaring himself. He was beginning to think all that talk about post-traumatic stress might be a little more than just psychobabble.

Restless, he wandered down a few floors to Robbery-Homicide where he was greeted by a mixture of moods, from hostility to what he interpreted as guarded acceptance. They'd all heard that Dennis Farley had died in his arms and that he'd done his best to stop Al Gervey from a similar fate. It was just as well that they didn't know that his stupidity had led Redd to Gervey in the first place.

"How come you walked away from that room, Mingus?" Paul Hibbler asked. He'd been on the receiving end of Mingus's elbow during the fight that had broken out there. "The bitch just shoot white cops?"

"You can ask her when she gets picked up," Mingus said. "What's the chance of that happening, by the way?"

"Found her car," a dick named Duke Wasson said.

"Where?"

"A couple patrol cops spotted it parked on a street in San Marino."

"San Marino, huh." Mingus smiled. It was a lily-white upscale suburb twenty minutes away from downtown L.A. that had served for many years as the national headquarters of the John Birch Society. Ditching her car there was Redd's idea of a joke.

"Car give up any secrets?"

"Sykes and Carmody are over at the lab now checking that out."

He located the two Homicide detectives looking over an attractive Asian tech's shoulder as her latexed fingers worked the keys of a laptop computer.

Carmody was the first to notice him. He tapped his partner and Sykes turned, nodded, and went back to his vigil. Carmody continued to eye him warily. That was the curse of being in IAG.

"I had some off-duty time," Mingus explained, hoping to relax the man. "Thought I'd see what you got."

"A Gateway laptop belonging to Alice Adams, or as she preferred to be known online, scriptchick99," Sykes said. "I'd say it definitely puts her on Mildred Doremus's scorecard."

"Anything else in the car?"

"Just the manual in the glove box," Carmody drawled. "Nothing in any of the crannies or on the carpet. No gas receipts, pink slip, any of that kind of crap. Just a spare and the jack and the usual shit you find in a trunk. Woman's either very neat or very, very careful."

"But she left the laptop," Mingus said.

"It was jammed under the front seat," Sykes said. "Like maybe it had been resting on the floor in back and slid up in there when she hit the brakes."

Mingus nodded, but he couldn't help but think Redd may have wanted them to find the machine for some reason. "Anything of interest on the hard drive?" he asked.

"Some correspondence," the tech said. "A calendar. Quicken. Notes. I haven't started to log it all."

"Any kind of diary?" Mingus asked.

"Not so far. There are some movie scripts. That's what the owner did for a living."

What was it Ida said the Adams woman had written? *The Price of Sisterhood.* A ghetto coming-of-age story. It gave him an idea. "How many movie scripts are on there?"

The tech hit a key and the monitor changed colors. A half dozen old-time movie camera icons popped into place. Mingus scanned their captions. *Why We Puff Lye, The Soul Sisters, Dime Honeys.*

"I thought this Alice Adams was supposed to be white?" Mingus asked.

Sykes chuckled. "She did seem fascinated by our cultcha," he said.

A title struck Mingus full force. *Bumpy, O.G.*

"You see something, Mingus?" Sykes asked. "We're open to all ideas."

"The killer must've shagged the computer for a reason. Something on it must be important."

"Maybe she just wanted to boost a computer," Carmody said. "Pricey things."

"There's that," Mingus said. "But you're gonna be going over the files, right?"

"That's the plan," Sykes said. "Financial records might give up something. The calendar."

"I got some time on my hands," Mingus said. "You want to print out those scripts, I'll give 'em a read for you."

Sykes cocked his head and gave Mingus a look. "You working on something?"

"You're gonna be printing the files out anyway. Cut me a copy. It's not like I'd be taking anything away. It's just putting another pair of eyes on your evidence. Maybe I'll see something somebody else'll miss."

"I get the feeling you have a personal involvement in this," Sykes said. "You and this killer lady got any kind of history you neglected to tell us?"

Mingus had decided not to muddy the water by mentioning that Redd had been his snitch. When he thought about it later and realized that it would probably come out once she was apprehended, he regretted the omission. He could straighten it out now, but he probably wouldn't get the *Bumpy, O.G.* script if he did.

"My personal involvement," he said, "is that I saw her kill two of my brother officers. So, like I say, I'd like to help out."

Sykes turned to the tech. "It disturb anything inside or outside the machine to print some files for the detective?"

Every computer whiz Mingus had ever dealt with regarded the rest of humanity with disdain. This one answered Sykes in the negative, the expression on her face suggesting only an idiot would have to ask.

45

The afternoon session did not go well for Mercer.

The firm's investigators had discovered that Gerald Callebrio was quite an entrepreneur. His pet store, though a front, turned a comfortable profit. It was a drop in the bucket, however, when compared to the fortune he'd amassed acting as middleman in a series of major illegal drug sales. He was a man with a bankable reputation, trusted by lords of the Cali cartel and Russian mafia princes alike.

For reasons not quite clear even to the vice cops who'd been involved, Callebrio had been picked up a week before. There'd been no need to disturb most of the animals with a thorough search of his store. A tip had suggested that a record of his most recent subrosa sales could be found by lifting a panel from the bottom of the tarantula cage.

It had been impossible to discover the details of the deal he'd made with the district attorney's office for giving up Claude Burris.

Too-Good Gomez easily led his witness through a story so simple even the woman at the far right of the jury box, the one Mercer suspected of operating at diminished capacity, absorbed every word.

The day after Darion Mayfield's death, Claude Burris

had come to him with the request that he broker the
sale of a variety of drugs that Callebrio knew to have a
wholesale value of approximately three hundred thousand dollars. Not one of his larger deals.

How did he know the value?

Well, he had brokered their original sale to the deceased Darion Mayfield the previous evening. "Just
hours before his unfortunate death."

He was certain it was the same "merchandise," less a
pound or two, because he recognized the packaging.

Since Burris was a motivated seller, the buyer received the merchandise at the bargain rate of one hundred eighty thousand, plus an extra eighteen thousand
for Callebrio's broker fee.

Was the transaction in cash?

"Always. I prefer pictures of President Cleveland.
Some clients prefer bills that are more commonplace,
but the thousand-dollar bill simplifies the count."

Thousand-dollar bills were used in the sale of the
drugs provided by Detective Burris.

Gomez asked Callebrio if it would surprise him to
learn that five one-thousand-dollar bills were found in
Detective Burris's apartment. Mercer had objected, but
not before Callebrio had answered that it wouldn't surprise him a bit.

"Mr. Callebrio," Gomez said, "you are now under in-
dictment for participating in the sale of illegal drugs,
correct?"

"Correct."

"And no one in the district attorney's office has made
any promises to you of any kind of inducement for your
testimony in this trial?"

"I have received no promises whatsoever from your
office."

"Then why did you agree to come here today, to say
things that could actually damage your case when it
comes to trial?"

"I have a reputation for cutting a straight deal. When
it became clear to me how Detective Burris came into

possession of the merchandise I brokered for him, I realized I had to come forward."

"I'm not sure I understand what you're saying," Gomez said.

Mercer objected. "I understand what he's saying, Your Honor. And it's unsubstantiated and irrelevant."

"Quite correct. Objection sustained."

"Your witness, Mr. Early."

Mercer had no clear plan of attack. But he made the effort.

He called Callebrio a drug peddler, pushed him for an approximation of the quantity of heroin he had been brokering annually. Asked him if he'd figured out how many children under fifteen that much heroin might have killed. Gomez objected repeatedly, but Mercer argued that the questions went to the witness's character and Judge Land overruled most of the objections.

Finally, Mercer got to the heart of Callebrio's testimony. "Did you see Detective Burris push Darion Mayfield through that window?"

"No."

"Do you know for certain that Darion Mayfield did not make a present of the drugs to Detective Burris?"

"It seems rather unlikely. But no, I don't know that didn't happen."

Mercer should have ended his cross at that point, but he was feeling a surge of confidence. "Mr. Callebrio," he asked, "you mentioned to Mr. Gomez that you were the middleman in the original sale of the drugs to Darion Mayfield. Who was on the other end of that deal?"

Callebrio turned to Gomez, who was already on the rise. "Relevance, Your Honor?"

"If the victim had just participated in a drug deal a few hours before his death, Your Honor, it seems that the identity of the other participant in that deal might have some relevancy."

"Overruled."

Callebrio frowned. "I don't know the gentleman's name. He was a new client. A visitor, not from this country."

"But it is possible that he may have sought out Darion Mayfield later that evening?"

"There would be no reason for them to meet. They had nothing in common."

"That's not so. He and Mayfield were both drug dealers, possibly drug users. How can you be so certain they didn't meet, have a little cocaine, get in some kind of argument that led to a fight that ended with Mayfield's death?"

"I am certain because the gentleman spent the evening with me. He is not a drug user. He is an Afghani freedom fighter who, as a key supporter of the Northern Alliance, was allowed to return to his pre-Taliban occupation of exporting heroin and cocaine. He is a hero in his country, unlike your client who is a corrupt policeman who evidently did see Darion Mayfield that evening and killed him and stole his property."

"Nonresponsive, Your Honor," Mercer found himself shouting. "Move to strike all reference to my client."

Judge Land ordered the reference struck from the court record, but it had done its damage to Mercer's case and to him.

He had no more questions for Gerald Callebrio.

At the defense table, Vanessa and Eddie stared at him with what may have been sympathy but he took to be pity. Burris was furious. "You just lost my fucking case," he said as the bailiffs arrived to take him back to twin towers.

"Right," Mercer said. "And all you did was steal a dead man's drugs and use a snitch to sell them."

Burris leaned close and hissed, "Remember, Early. I go in, you go in with me."

As the bailiffs led him away, Vanessa asked, "What was that about you going in with him?"

"Guess the man loves me so much he wants me for a roommate."

46

"That son of a bitch. That *son* of a *bitch*."

Mingus threw down the Alice Adams script for *Bumpy, O.G.* and leaped to his feet.

Bettye came into her living room from the kitchen. "What's that all about?"

"I gotta call somebody."

"Okay. Just try to keep that kind of language down a little. I respect my neighbors and they respect me."

"I apologize, honey," he said, his hand reaching out to the phone sitting on an end table.

It was seven-thirty. He and Bettye had eaten early, but Mercer was probably just sitting down to dinner, or getting ready to. He dialed the apartment and got the answering machine.

The lawyer wasn't at his office, either. But he answered his cellular phone.

"Where are you?" Mingus asked.

"Driving around, trying to figure out a place to get drunk where they don't know me."

"You don't sound so good."

"Got pushed into cross-examining a dope dealer without any kind of prep and let the slimeball beat the hell out of me. Then when I returned to the office, I

ound out Bobby Carter stopped Reverend Mayfield's
ubpoena from being served."

"He can do that?"

"It's his law firm," Mercer said. "Or half of it is."

"Well, put that aside. I got something'll make you
mile. Come on up." He gave Mercer the address.

"Your place?"

"My lady friend's." He replaced the phone and
valked into the kitchen to tell Bettye his homeboy Mer-
er was paying a visit.

"Lionel, the place is a mess."

He looked around the spotless kitchen. Then he
valked back into the living room. The only thing messy
a there was the cushion on the couch his butt had
ented and the movie scripts scattered on the coffee
able. He'd gone through them all, surprised that he
ked the way they read. Alice Adams might've been a
vhite cluckhead but she knew how to come correct. He
icked out *Bumpy, O.G.* and stacked the rest.

The lawyer arrived ten minutes later. Mingus kept the
ntroductions brief. Bettye made sure they had coffee
nd sugar cookies and then left them alone to what she
alled "their business."

"Nice woman," Mercer said. "Attractive and under-
tanding."

"Man, that's not the half of it. She makes me feel so
ood I don't even know I'm me. Anyway . . ." He went
n to tell Mercer about the computer that had been re-
overed from Redd's car. Then he held up the script.

"Alice Adams wasn't hanging with Darion just for
rugs and the occasional boot knock. She was pumping
im for story ideas. And this is one hell of a story."

"About Darion's predecessor, Bumpy Lewis?" Mer-
er asked.

"Oh yeah. It's kinda told from Darion's viewpoint,
vhich makes it even more interesting."

"You want me to read it, or you gonna give me the
ist?"

In the interest of time, Mingus opted for the latter.

When he'd finished, Mercer said, "Darion wouldn'
have just made up something like that?"

"It explains a hell of a lot, including how a jackass like
him wound up running that candy store. What I hear
the boy wasn't smart enough to make up that kind o
shit. If Reverend Mayfield read the script, we got a
whole new thing happening here."

"Well, screw the subpoena," Mercer said. "Let's go
double-team the old boy and see what happens."

At the Church of the Redeemer, a new bible studies
group was considering Pontius Pilate's big decision, ac
cording to what Mingus could hear through the open
window.

"The Reverend there?" Mercer asked when the de
tective returned to the car.

"Large and in charge. He thinks Pilate maybe got a
bum rap. Old Pontius did his best to push the crowd into
letting Jesus go. When they voted to crucify him, i
wasn't Pilate's fault."

"That's the modern interpretation: nobody's respon
sible for their actions," Mercer said. He opened the car
door and got out. "It's not my fault. Boo hoo."

"Where you going?"

"He'll be in there making up excuses for Pilate for a
while. Let's go see what we can find in his office."

Mingus checked to make sure he was carrying. The
Reverend might be a bit long in the tooth, but he was
still a powerful-looking man.

His office suggested an occupant of slighter stature. I
was a small but comfortable room on the upper level a
the very rear of the building, smelling of furniture pol
ish and incense, with a hint of some sweet pipe tobacco
Nearly every spare inch of flat surface was covered by
books, folders, magazines, or newspapers. More books
lined two walls, adding to the room's closed-in feeling
The areas surrounding the windows on the remaining
walls were covered by framed diplomas, certificates, and
letters to the Reverend from celebrities and politica

gures, including several presidents of the United tates.

Mingus was checking out a warm message of friend- nip from one of the presidents, just to see if it sounded s stiff and inarticulate as the man used to, when Mer- er called his name. The lawyer had opened a leather riefcase and was pointing to the object on top: a copy f the *Bumpy, O.G.* script.

"Damn if that don't nail it down," Mingus said.

He was distracted by the sounds of car doors slam- ing and engines starting down below. He looked arough a window. "Bible party's breaking up."

"Good timing."

They heard heavy footsteps approaching down the all and then Reverend Mayfield was filling the door- ay. Mingus, still at the window, was directly in his line f sight. The Reverend's face tightened in a mixture of nnoyance and perplexity. Entering the room, he said, What are you doing in my off—?"

He stopped when he saw Mercer, script in hand. "Mr. arly? What's going on here?"

"We'd like to talk with you, Reverend," Mercer said. About where you were the night Darion was killed."

Mayfield looked almost relieved. "I've heard about our idiotic theory. Should you be foolish enough to ring it to public attention, I'll pick you clean. Every- ning you own, today and for the rest of your life, will be aine. And I may even have you thrown in jail as an af- erthought. Now, get out of here, the both of you."

"Who was it told you about my idiotic theory?"

"That's of no consequence. Clear out now, before—"

"Where'd you get this, Reverend?" Mercer asked, olding up the script.

Mayfield blinked and lost some of his steam. "I . . . a nember of my flock asked me to look at it. Put it down nd get out."

"Any good?"

"I'm no judge."

"What's it about?"

The big clergyman looked exasperated. "It's about man who turns to God when all else fails."

Mingus chuckled. "That's quick thinking. We know it's really about Bumpy Lewis, an Original Gangste who sold drugs out of Inglewood. When all else failed he didn't turn to God. He turned to his cousin."

"That would be you, Reverend," Mercer said. "Bump Lewis's cousin. Who'd'a believed it."

"Cousin and silent partner," Mingus said. "According to that script, you put up church money to seed his operation."

"That script is . . . a delusional fantasy," Mayfield said "The young woman who wrote it was mentally unbalanced. A demented drug addict and pervert."

"Nice way to talk about one of your flock," Mercer said. "You got a lot of white junkies attending services Reverend?"

"If you don't leave here immediately . . ." He seemed unable to summon up an adequate threat.

"Thing is," Mingus said, "birth records can be checked to make sure who's related and who's not."

That seemed to restore some of the Reverend's confidence. "You can't find what doesn't exist."

"You mean what no longer exists," Mingus said.

"Detective Mingus, I'll bet your group commander Eldon Kyle, doesn't know you're here hassling me, doe he?"

"I'm flattered you know who I am, Reverend. But m guess is Commander Kyle and a whole lot of other folk in this city won't be thinking too much about me when they find out what you've been up to."

"That's it, gentlemen. Hit the road, before I get really angry."

"We know what that's like," Mercer said. "Better ge away from that window, Detective."

The Reverend was not amused. He grabbed the phone. "You two are making a very big mistake."

"If you know who I am, Reverend," Mingus said "you know I was there when Ken Loc Ansol was sho down. Just before he died, he said he was driving you the night your son died and that you were up in the apartment when it happened."

"You're lying through your teeth, Detective. Ken Loc said nothing about me." The phone receiver began to squeal. He looked at it as if he couldn't remember how it got in his fist. When he placed it on its cradle, the silence did little to ease the tension in the room.

"That's some information network you got going, Rev. You know what Mercer's thinking. You know who I am. And now, best trick of all, you know what Ken Loc said just before he died. There's a real short list of people who could tell you that."

Mayfield gawked at him, momentarily frozen by the mistake he'd just made. Then he thawed. "I'm just assuming . . . I have no way of knowing, of course, what the man said. I suppose he could have lied. My point is, I was nowhere near where my son . . . I was at a dinner for the mayor. People saw me there."

"I saw you there," Mercer said. "But by then Darion had been dead an hour or more. You were talking up a storm with the mayor, looking wild, like you'd been through a real rough time."

"You were there? At the dinner?"

Mercer shifted his approach. "Nobody's saying you went to see your boy with the idea of doing him in. What happened? Were you on your way to the dinner, and he called you? Got you to tell Ken Loc to drive you there instead?"

"This is all—"

"Darion was flying high, I bet. Him and the white girl both. Your own son, flesh of your flesh, telling this ofay chickenhead serious family secrets that she was going to put in a movie for the whole world to see. Anybody'd lose it, Reverend. Were they laughing at you? Mocking you? Drinking wine out of your little communion cup?"

Mayfield shook his head, as if trying to loosen and throw off a memory. He turned to Mercer, in near fury. "Leave. Here. Now."

"Reverend, not that we don't appreciate your hospitality," Mercer said, "but we've got to be running along."

"Yep." Mingus headed for the door. "Got this meeting scheduled with a couple Homicide dicks who're trying to find the woman killed Ken Loc and the others."

"As your excellent sources probably told you, Alice Adams's laptop computer was recovered today," Mercer said, following the detective to the door. "We want to make sure the detectives check out all the details in that 'Bumpy' script of hers."

Reverend Mayfield's eyes followed them as they left the room. He was deep-breathing like a bull.

They made as much noise as they could leaving the building and slamming the car doors.

As Mercer steered his sedan off the church lot, he asked, "He checking us?"

"Got his face pressed against the window," Mingus said.

"Good. Maybe he won't keep us waiting." He drove to the corner, made a left turn, and eased against the curb under a tree whose full leaves surrounded them in shadow.

"You don't think we overdid it?" Mingus said. "He eats a gun, it won't help the cause any."

"He's too much in love with his life," Mercer said. "That's why he's gonna go running to get somebody to make sure we don't fuck it up for him."

"You called it," Mingus said. "There he goes."

47

The Reverend's Jaguar sped north. Its color was so white it seemed to be glowing in the night—a good thing, because, traffic being light on Arlington, Mercer was forced to give it a long lead.

Staying more than a block behind, he saw the Jag take a sharp left onto Olympic Boulevard. It then continued west straight as a bullet past darkened storefronts into the high-rent district.

When the Reverend turned right onto Highland Avenue and entered the Hancock Park area, Mingus said, "I bet I know where he's headed. I followed Farley to a house on this street not too long ago. He had a short and sour powwow with a guy he obviously didn't like. Not that I ever heard of a black man Fats liked and surely not one who was living in a better neighborhood than most whites can afford."

Mercer knew of a black man who was so damn proud of his "place in Hancock" he probably had a picture of it on a T-shirt. He kept his eye on the white car gliding north on Highland and hoped that was its destination. The thought of what they might find there both intrigued him and twisted his gut.

"That's the house," Mingus said as the Jag glided against the curb directly in front of an English Tudor separated from the sidewalk by a high wrought-iron fence. "The guy who lives there looked familiar. I just can't come up with the name."

"Barry Fox," Mercer said, guessing but also knowing it had to be. "Takes care of things for the mayor."

The Reverend was struggling with the handle of the gate as they drove by.

"You know Fox?" Mingus asked.

"We've got mutual friends." Mercer eased his car against the curb and parked. Half a block behind them, the Reverend finally got the gate open and rushed through it.

He'd disappeared inside the house by the time they went through the still-open iron gate.

At the heavy wooden front door, Mercer reached for the brass knocker. Was she inside? he wondered.

An elderly black man in livery opened the door. "Yes, gentlemen?" he asked. A fucking butler. Perfect, Mercer thought.

"We're with the Reverend," Mercer said.

"I'm not sure—" the butler began.

The two men pushed past him. "Don't worry, Uncle Ben, we can find him," Mingus said.

They entered a large living room, richly carpeted, the furniture a mix of antique warmth and sleek, contemporary sterility. A large slab of modern art splatter was hanging over a cold fireplace big as a cave.

"Out back," Mingus said, as the butler hurried past them and pushed through French doors leading to the rear of the property.

A lighted pool dominated the space. To their left was a darkened square structure attached to the house. Maybe an office or a gym. Beyond the pool near the rear wall was a coach house or garage. Separating the glowing rectangle from the main building was a long wooden deck. The butler hobbled across it to a table where an intimate candlelit dinner had just been interrupted by the highly agitated Reverend. Barry Fox was trying to calm the big man down, while Vanessa looked on in confusion and surprise.

Her surprise intensified when the butler called their attention to the two new uninvited guests who were approaching.

"Mercer, what in the world . . . ?"

Barry's hand on her arm stopped her. "I think your ex-boyfriend may be here to see me," he said, standing and placing his napkin on the table. He was wearing a white silk shirt with slightly puffy sleeves and dark velvety slacks. He looked like a black buccaneer. "Am I right, Mercer?"

Mercer was conscious of Mingus giving him the fish eye over the ex-boyfriend comment, but it was not the time to bring the detective up to speed on matters that he hoped were irrelevant. "We're here to have a chat with you and the Reverend."

"Judging by his condition, I think you've given Dr. Mayfield a difficult enough time tonight. Why don't we let him drive Vannie home?"

Mayfield gave him a grateful nod.

"Jody," Barry said to the butler, "I think you should head for home, too."

"Let me clear the table first, sir."

"I'm a big boy, Jody. Every now and then it's good for me to pick up after myself."

"As you wish, sir. Breakfast at seven-thirty as usual?"

Barry nodded, and the butler disappeared inside the house.

"What's this all about, Barry?" Vanessa asked. When he ignored the question, she turned to Mercer.

"*Vannie* should take a cab home," Mercer said to Barry. "We'd like the Reverend to stick around."

"What is going on?" Vanessa insisted, much to Barry's annoyance. He raised a hand to her in a silencing gesture, the sort of thing that, had Mercer done it, she'd have slapped his face. Now she took it and liked it.

Barry picked up a phone that rested beside his dessert plate and pushed one key.

Mercer assumed he was speed-dialing a taxi company. But a dim chirp sounded in the coach house. "Busy?" he asked and clicked off the phone.

He turned to Mayfield. "Doctor, it's time you and Vanessa were on your way."

Mingus took a step forward. "You're a cheeky fella," he said, smiling at Barry. "The Reverend's not gonna—"

A clicking sound echoed across the pool's glowing green surface, sending the waning charm of the soft lights and candle glow even further south. "What was that noise?" Vanessa asked. She turned to look at the coach house.

Mercer looked, too, but all he saw were shadows.

Mingus didn't bother looking. He'd heard enough clips being fed into enough weapons not to have to see the damn thing to know it was there. "So long, Rev," he said. "You know what the Good Book says: 'Evil men can't sleep 'less they've done some mischief.' I bet you're gonna snooze like a log tonight, huh?"

Mayfield frowned and walked away toward the French doors.

"There's something wrong going on here," Vanessa said.

"Nothing to worry about," Barry said. "We'll talk to-morrow. All will be made clear. Now run and catch up with the Reverend Doctor."

She seemed reluctant, but she took a few steps in that direction. "See you in the morning, Mercer?"

He stared at Barry, who said, "He'll be at work bright and early as always, right, Mercer?"

"Bright's probably not the best word," Mercer said.

She gave him a puzzled smile and went to find the Reverend.

What seemed like a second after she'd gone, Redd stepped from the shadows of the coach house. She was wearing tight black denim pants and a black "Shave-Ice Is Nice" T-shirt cut to expose a slice of taut and tan stomach. She'd exchanged her handgun for something bigger and deadlier, an automatic rifle with a shoulder brace and a curved magazine.

"You figuring on starting a war, Redd?" Mingus asked.

"Maybe a li'l skirmish," she said.

"Let's take this inside," Barry said, leading them to the attached building. It was a screening room. Framed movie posters on the wall. *Lady Sings the Blues, Titanic, Soul Food, The Candidate.* Soft sofas faced a flat video monitor of an almost obscene size.

"This where you and your pals kick back, huh?" Mercer said.

Barry gave him a lazy smile. "You carrying a weapon, Mercer?"

Mercer raised his arms. "Just so there's no mistake," he said, "I dress on the right."

His host gave him a perfunctory pat down.

"Now you," Barry said to Mingus.

Redd used the pointed barrel of her weapon to lift Mingus's jacket. Barry removed the 9mm from his shoulder holster.

"You missed the one he's got hanging off his belt," Redd said. She smiled at Mingus. "The one I bought for him."

Barry gave her a curious look but said nothing. He turned to the lawyer. "What is it you want, Mercer? Let's see if we can't do some business here."

There were a few overstuffed chairs on rollers. Mercer spun one around and sat down. "Since you asked, I'd like the Reverend to come down to court, take the stand and confess to his son's murder. Then my client Claude Burris can go free."

Redd's green, oddly serpentine eyes flicked to Barry. Hard to figure what she was thinking.

"The way you screwed things up in court today, he'll probably go right back in."

"Then I'll have to get him back out again. But let's take it one trial at a time, Barry. What's the deal? Why'd you frame him?"

To his credit, Barry didn't blink an eye. "I think you got me confused with a fat detective," he said. "I'm doing all I can to help you, Mercer, as Redd fully knows. But from what Vannie tells me, you're letting the team down. Instead of focusing on Claude's innocence, you're running around trying to build a case against the Reverend Doctor."

"Hey, Barry, did we just hitch in from Macon, Georgia, on a peach truck? Your boss's best pal did the crime. The only way he'll stay free and clear is if Burris takes the pill for him. Case closed."

Redd stayed silent, observing them, hand caressing her weapon as if it were alive.

"Jesus, isn't anybody paying attention to the way things work in this town?" Barry said in exasperation. "The trial is a one-shot. Once Burris is set free, that's the ball game. Nobody will go looking for another suspect. Trials like this are too expensive to repeat."

"What the hell you talking about?" Mingus said. "You can wiggle that snake tongue of yours any whicha way, you know damn well your plan is for Burris to take the fall."

The detective's words scraped away some of Barry's cool. Anger drove his voice up an octave. "Listen, you stupid fucking rummy cop, you don't talk to me in that tone. Get it? I made this lady a promise—a goddamn promise—that Claude Burris walks. And he will if his lawyer gets back on track."

"You ain't fooling anybody, Slick," Mingus said, moving forward, getting in Barry's face. "You promised. You know what a promise is to a politician? It's what a dog turd is to a dog, something you drop every so often that's got no practical use." His hand shot out and grabbed the front of Barry's silk shirt, jerking him forward. "And if you ever even dream of dissing me again like that, they gonna be picking up pieces of your skinny uptown ass all over South Central."

Mingus pushed the man away, sending him stumbling to the carpet. Barry got up, flushed and breathing hard. "Kill him," he said.

Redd raised her eyebrows. "Kill Lionel? Why'd I want to do that?"

"Let me count the reasons. I'm keeping you out of

il. I'm saving your boyfriend's life. And one more
ing." He crossed the room dramatically to the *Lady
ings the Blues* poster, swung it out on hinges, and ex-
osed a wall safe behind it. A few twists and turns and
e safe was open. He reached in and removed a huge
lastic bag filled with white powder so that he could get
something behind it—a thick packet of cash.

He replaced the cocaine in the safe and tossed the
ick money stack to Redd, who caught it with her left
and. She glanced at the figures on the wrapper.
Twenty grand." She lined up her weapon on the detec-
ve's chest. "Fun is fun, Lionel, but bidness is bidness."

"I can't argue about the twenty thousand," Mercer
aid. "Nice pay for the twitch of a finger. But the rest is
ullshit, Redd. You've got to know that weasel doesn't
ive a damn about you or Burris. He's got just one
genda, to keep Harlan Mayfield smiling and passing
e plate every Sunday. He wants Burris to be found
uilty. When that happens, you'd better make sure your
esigner duds are lined with Kevlar."

"Goddammit, Mercer, you've been a disappointment
ll around," Barry said. "I guess it's just as well we get
d of you, too. We'll find a good lawyer who'll do a bet-
r job."

"Why not Vannie?" Mercer said sarcastically.

Barry smiled. "As we both know, Vannie is an excel-
nt piece of ass, but what we need is someone who can
oo a jury, not go down on them."

The words tore into Mercer but instead of striking
ack at Barry, he turned to Redd. "Your friend here has
real up-to-date attitude about women."

"Redd knows I respect her ability."

Barry didn't catch the slight narrowing of her eyes.
le might have been good at seduction. But throw the
an something to take his mind off his dick and a whole
other Barry showed up, one who had such disregard
r the ladies, he stopped paying them much attention.
ven when they were packing heat.

Mercer wasn't about to make that mistake. "Ask you

something, Redd? Why'd you wait so long to take Farley out? Why not pop him even before the trial?"

She looked at Barry. "How'd you put it, honey? You said I should worry about the witnesses and you'd handle the cops."

"Farley was another disappointment," Barry said. "He took the money and then he fucked us."

"I believe that, Slick," Mingus said. "It's exactly what Farley and his partner told me. Only they said you've been paying 'em to sink Burris, not save him."

Barry turned to Redd. "These nuckers don't know you like I do, honey. They don't realize you're too strong to let them mess up your head with their lies. Let's get this done. Drop 'em and we'll dump 'em."

"Night's still young," Redd said. "What'll it hurt to hear a few more of their lies?"

"Think of the timing, Redd," Mercer said. "Farley's been hammering Claude from the jump. Why'd it take Barry so long to let you go after him?"

"You got an answer for that, Barry?" she asked.

"Fats wasn't doing any real damage. He was letting Mercer make him look like a fool. That was the plan. But he wanted more money. I guess I should have paid him, but I'd already given him a small fortune. To show he meant business, he had Callebrio picked up. He knew the felon would sell Burris down the river. That's when I saw Fats had to go and told you so."

"Fats didn't order the raid on Callebrio," Mercer said, as if he knew it for certain. "That came from the mayor's office."

"That's a lie."

"Barry, I'm getting the drift you the one with your pants on fire," Redd said.

"Then maybe you'd better let go of that lead sprayer." Barry had Mingus's old gun in his hand. It was no match for her automatic rifle. But the rifle was aimed at Mingus and his weapon was pointed at her bare belly button.

Redd wasn't happy. "You're too much of a pussy to—

Barry shot her. He'd seen something—a slight shift of stance, maybe—that allowed him to anticipate and cut short the swing of her rifle toward him.

The shot slammed her against a sofa. She looked surprised. Then perplexed. The rifle was getting too heavy for her. Before it slipped from her fingers, she tried once more to aim it at him. Barry shot her again. Then Mingus was on him, the impact tumbling them both to the carpet.

Mingus was on top as they struggled, one big hand wrapped around Barry's and the gun, squeezing. Barry tried to knee the detective and Mingus shoved his free forearm against his opponent's neck and bore down. Gurgling, Barry began to wiggle and writhe under him.

"Ease up," Mercer said, patting Mingus on the back.

"Why?"

"Because we want him to live. At least until we can get him into court."

With a disgusted grunt, Mingus removed his arm. Standing, he twisted his gun out of Barry's hand. Then he swung it flat-sided against the man's head.

Redd had fallen, the rifle landing on the carpet about six inches from her right hand. The movement of that hand caught Mercer's eye. "She's not dead."

Mingus was beside her in a flash, down on one knee. Her hand was still moving toward the weapon. He put his hand over hers. She looked up at him. "Am I crying, Lionel?"

"No, ma'am."

"Good. Never wanted him to see me cry." She winced in pain. Blood was pooling on the carpet from her wound.

"Barry can't see anything at the moment," Mingus said.

"Barry? Who the fuck cares what Barry sees?"

"Mercer, we got to get a paramedic in here."

The lawyer scanned the room for a phone.

Redd squeezed Mingus's hand and whispered, "Don't let him see me."

Mingus looked confused. "Who?"

"Daddy, o'course. He see me, he'll be rollin' on top o' me again. Gotta hide."

"Don't worry. He won't see you."

"Lionel? How'd you get here? I sure didn't know ..." The pain that had been in her face disappeared and she smiled. "Next time," she said. And died.

Lionel stood.

"There's a phone out on the table by the pool," Mercer said. "I'll go—"

"Don't bother. She's gone. Dumb little chickenhead." His eyes were wet. "Well, counselor, you the man. What now?"

"Call the cops, I guess."

"Yeah, that's smart," Barry said. He was lying on his back on the carpet. Glaring up at Mercer. "Call the cops. They're going to want to know why you busted in here with that murder mama and why the drunk cop shot her."

"You sayin' I shot her?"

"It's your gun."

Mingus grinned. "It was reported stolen six years ago. I think you stole it."

"Okay," Barry said, sitting up, rubbing his neck. "We got off on a bad start. Bringing the police in won't serve any purpose, because whatever you two tell 'em, I'll tell 'em something else. And I'm the guy they're gonna believe because, and I say this with the utmost respect, people in law enforcement hate you guys."

Mercer couldn't argue with that. "What's the deal?" he asked.

"Let me make one phone call and you can name your price. Hell, Mercer, if you want, you can take Bobby's place on the ticket. I can swing that. Mingus, how'd you like your old job back at RHD with an extra couple of grand in cash in your pocket every week?"

"What do we do about Redd?" Mingus asked.

"You let me handle that. Off the top of my head, I'd

say one of her cars will go off the road and down into a canyon where she and it will burn to a cinder."

"And Reverend Mayfield?" Mercer asked.

"That's out of my hands."

"Then what happens to my client?"

Barry's face hardened. "There's nothing anybody can do about Claude Burris. He's already dead. A dead man walking. Don't concern yourself over things that can't be changed, Mercer. One phone call and it's a happy ending for the rest of us."

Mercer turned to Mingus. "What do you think?"

"I love a happy ending," Mingus told him.

"Me, too," Mercer said and punched Barry in the face. It took another whack of Mingus's pistol to put the man out.

"I think we ought to call in Sykes and Carmody," Mingus said. "Let them take it from here."

"Not just yet. Barry was right. Heathrow will pull strings, evidence will vanish and we'll be lucky if we don't wind up serving time. I've got a better idea." He crossed the room and swung back the *Lady Sings the Blues* poster. Barry hadn't locked the safe.

Mercer took out the bag of drugs. "This looks suspiciously like it came from Darion's stash."

"What are you going to do with it?"

"Take a page out of Barry's book and set up the setup king." He dropped the drug bag at Barry's feet. He asked Mingus for his gun.

"I just got it back a month ago."

"Barry used it; he gets to keep it." Mercer fit it under the unconscious man's hand. He grabbed Redd's rifle and tossed it to Mingus. "Fair exchange?"

The detective checked the weapon. "Could come in handy, the state the world's in."

Mercer was studying the two bodies, one dead, one only sleeping. He picked up the bag of cocaine and sprinkled some of its contents on Barry Fox's face. The sleeping man breathed in and wrinkled his nose.

Mingus moved toward him, holding his rifle like a club. But Fox didn't wake up.

Mercer replaced the drug bag beside him, gave the room the once-over and said, "I think this will play."

"We gotta leave the front door open," Mingus said. "Don't want to give Mr. Slick's lawyer anything like illegal entry to gnaw on."

"We'll dump some of the coke on the stoop," Mercer said, "then trail it through the house like bread crumbs leading here."

He looked at the unconscious man. "There are some things I have to check out before we split. You might have to hit him again."

"Take your time," Mingus said. "I'll be happy hitting him all night long."

The next day, there was only one news story that anybody cared about.

Barry Fox, an associate and close friend of Mayor George Heathrow, was arrested in the early morning hours at his Hancock Park home on suspicion of having shot and killed murder suspect Mildred Doremus. Clothes and other items suggest Doremus had been hiding from police on the premises. A large quantity of cocaine was present and it was thought that the shooting may have been prompted by a drug-induced rage.

Fox's relationship to the murdered woman is as yet unknown, as is his involvement in the assassinations for which she has been accused. At present, no known connection exists between Doremus and Mayor George Heathrow. The mayor has been unavailable for comment, but it is thought that the scandal might close down His Honor's campaign for governor even before it started.

When Mercer stepped from the elevator into the C&H reception area, Bobby Carter was on his way out. "Mercer, good. I wanted to talk with you before I . . . Let's go to your office."

There, Bobby declined Melissa's offer of coffee and

got right down to it. "Harlan Mayfield called me this morning in a frantic state, begging me to come there to talk to him about a matter he said he couldn't get into on the phone. I'm sure it must involve Barry's arrest. I was hoping you might know something about it."

"Why me?"

"Vanessa told C.W. you and a detective were at Barry's home last night. Harlan was there, too. Everybody was behaving oddly. What've you been up to?"

"Let's stick to your question about the Reverend," Mercer said. "My guess is he's probably down on his knees right now, praying to the Lord that Barry's not planning on trading him in on a reduced sentence."

"You're not going to start in on that theory of yours?"

"Theory? It's gone beyond theory. Last night, Detective Lionel Mingus and I had a talk with the Reverend about a lot of things. Like his family ties to the late drug dealer Bumpy Lewis. Mayfield, the guy you wouldn't let me subpoena, then went running to Barry expecting the Fox to get Mildred Doremus to add Mingus and myself to her hit list.

"Barry was definitely up for that idea. It just didn't work out the way he'd planned."

Bobby looked shaken. "My God. What the hell was Barry thinking? Consorting with an assassin. Plotting murders. And if you tell me Harlan was part of that, after everything that's happened, I suppose I have to believe you. What do I say to him?"

" 'Good-bye'?"

"He's our client," Bobby said.

"So is Claude Burris, who is still on the hook for a murder Mayfield committed."

"How do we balance the books?" Bobby asked.

"You have to get your client to confess. Tell him the accidental murder of his son is a crime he can probably plead out. No premeditation. No intent. Darion was stoned, pissed him off. He slapped the punk, who tripped and went through the window. The tough part will be explaining why he didn't come forward earlier. But the D.A. is going to be looking for reasons to go light on him.

"If, on the other hand, Mayfield refuses to step up, I'll owe it to my client to open the lid on the whole ugly mess. Right now, only a very select few know that Barry had Mildred Doremus kill all those people to save the Reverend's ass. If proof of that surfaces, Mayfield will be tied to four very premeditated assassinations—two of the victims cops. Nobody will be going easy on him then. And, if that isn't incentive enough for him to confess to a much lesser crime, remind him that he'll be dragging the mayor into the soup with him. And the mayor won't like that."

Bobby stared at the young lawyer.

"Barry Fox had no reason to go out on a limb like that for the Reverend. He wasn't the guy Mayfield saved from an angry mob in the long ago."

Bobby was silent for a while. Then he said, "You mentioned proof?"

"Oh yeah. I, ah, came into possession of a pretty impressive file on the Reverend that Barry was keeping under lock and key at his place. Lots of very nasty stuff in it, including a videotape of the Reverend thanking Barry for 'taking care' of a young woman who'd written a film script that would have caused him grief."

"Where'd you find this?"

"In a file cabinet in Barry's bedroom closet. Like that wouldn't be the first place anybody'd look. I figured him for the kind of rat who'd hang on to things he could use if he ever got caught in a trap. There was a nice thick file on your running mate, too."

Bobby took a deep breath. "Ex-running mate," he said. "I spoke to him an hour ago. He said he was too old and too weary to have to go through the ordeal of running with a scandal like this so close to his doorstep."

"I know," Mercer said. "We had a little chat around three this morning. I just wanted to let him know he was in safe hands. I had his file and Barry didn't. He agreed to get a message to Barry. It's why you won't be hearing my name or Mingus's mentioned by Barry ever again."

"What the hell happened last night, Mercer?"

"Nothing you want to know about."

The senior partner stood. A bit shakily, Mercer thought. "I'll relay your advice to Harlan. I imagine he'll take it to heart. I would. But I can't help but wonder why you're giving him the option. If all you want is to free your man Burris, why not just turn over the videotape and whatever else you've got?"

"There'd be a domino effect," Mercer said. "No sense hurting a lot of people if you don't have to."

Bobby nodded. "Was I in Barry's files, son?"

"Not that I saw," Mercer lied.

48

George Heathrow not only dropped out of the gubernatorial campaign, he also stepped down as mayor "for reasons of health." One of his last acts in office was to pressure the district attorney not to seek the death penalty in its case against Barry Fox. It was a little short of the help Fox had been expecting, but, considering the charges against him and considering what steps could be taken to make his lengthy sentence even more of a living hell than it was, he went along with Heathrow's demands.

By following the advice of his lawyer and confessing to the murder of his son, Darion Mayfield, the Reverend Harland Mayfield was sentenced to a five-year term at the facility at Lompoc, California, a deal hammered out behind closed doors in the D.A.'s office. The murder charge against Claude Burris was dismissed but, because his woman was dead, his freedom was bittersweet. And brief. Within days, he was arrested again for dealing in drugs. But before he could be brought to trial, he fell victim to a particularly virulent form of hepatitis B that quickly took his life. The disease was common in prisons, but Mercer, recalling Barry Fox's description of Burris as a dead man walking, pushed for an investigation. It was discovered that one of Burris's fellow pris-

oners, assigned to the hospital, had several vials of
germs and viruses among his possessions. It's possible
that Fox hadn't had to pay him to infect Burris. His
name was Sweets Doremus.

It was shortly after Burris's death that C.W. and
Bobby summoned Mercer to the conference room to
tell him that, unlike the other young lawyers whose ap-
prenticeships were coming to an end, he was being offered a junior partnership.

"Full partner in four years?" he asked.

The partners laughed. "That may be pushing it," C.W.
said.

"There'll be a bit more money, some perks. I'm sure
we'll be able to work things out to your satisfaction,"
Bobby said. "You'll need an office in this wing. Possibly
the one I used when my daddy was still active. You can
fix it up however you want."

"Within a certain budget, of course," C.W. added as
he led Mercer to the door. "We're losing Vanessa, by the
way. She's decided to join Park, Woodrow in San Francisco."

Mercer hadn't kept up. He hadn't spoken with her in
months, other than to mutter the polite things one says
in the course of a workday. But the news that she was
leaving saddened him. When love ends, it never goes
away entirely.

"It's a good firm," C.W. said. "Park, Woodrow."

"But not the best," Mercer said.

"No," C.W. said, smiling. "Not the best."

Melissa was waiting with an expectant look. "Well?"
she said.

"We'll be moving down to the other end of the floor,
the partner end."

"No shit?" she exclaimed.

"No shit," he said.

She gave him a hug and went off, presumably to
spread the news.

He picked up the phone and punched out a number.

"IAG. Mingus," said the voice on the other end.

"They made me a junior partner, Lionel."

"Of course they did," Mingus said. "Listen, I was gonna call you. I think we should have dinner tonight. At LaLa's."

Mercer said that sounded fine.

They met at eight.

After they ordered drinks and chatted for a while, Mingus passed a manilla envelope across the table.

"What's this?" Mercer asked.

"Something for your files."

The envelope contained three photocopied pages, all from the *Huntsville Alabama Times*. The first featured a grainy but recognizable class photo of an eighteen-year-old named John Parker who, according to the headline, was "UAH Student Wanted in Coed's Death."

Mercer looked up to find Mingus staring at him without expression.

The second page was from an earlier edition, a photo of the paramedics wheeling Gisela Redmond from Mercer's old apartment building, with an insert of her school photo. That headline read, "Drug Overdose Leads to UAH Coed's Death."

"Where'd you get these?" Mercer asked.

"A buddy let me go through Burris's stuff before it got carted up. I guess I was looking for something of Redd's, but there wasn't anything. Soon as I got a look at—what's the name?—John Parker's photo, I pulled those sheets for you. What was Burris doing with them?"

"Forcing me to defend him."

Mingus frowned. "How'd that work? I mean, I guess it musta been a little tense for you back then, before the girl's brother came forward, but—"

"Before what?" Mercer asked.

"It's all in there."

Mercer looked at the third sheet. It was headlined, "UAH Student Describes Sister's Death." There was a picture of Gisela's brother Hank, or as the caption had it, "Henry 'Hank' Redmond." The article described a despondent Henry breaking down at the inquest and informing the judge that he and his sister, Gisela, had illegally entered the apartment of a fellow student who was away at the time. Gisela had been experimenting with heroin and injected herself with a fatal amount. Unable to rouse her, Henry called 911 and, because he himself was under the influence of an illegal drug, fled the scene. The article ended with the information that, "as a result of Henry Redmond's statement, the Huntsville PD has rescinded an arrest warrant for John Parker, the student who had resided at the apartment where the fatal mishap took place. The police remain concerned for Parker's safety, however, since he has been missing since the Redmond girl's death."

Mercer didn't know whether to laugh or cry. "All these years looking over my shoulder," he said. "I could have gone back any time."

"You didn't know you'd been cleared? Never mind. I see the answer on your face. So Redd and Burris traced your history."

"Used my fingerprints."

"When they realized you'd never gone back home, that you were still using a different name, they musta figured you didn't know about the brother. And they stuck it to you."

"This is a big thing you've done for me, Lionel. It's giving me a new life."

"Yeah, well, you still have yourself a serious problem: that law degree you got isn't exactly legit."

Mercer's elation disappeared. "You going to report me?" he asked sarcastically.

"Not in this life." Mingus looked at his friend's pained face and felt like a big-mouth fool. "I'm sorry, Mercer. I sure didn't mean to rain on your parade like that. It just came out."

"Rain on my parade?" Mercer said, his face breaking out in a broad grin. "Hell, brother, you brought the parade. Before I sat down here, I thought I was wanted for murder back in 'Bama. You took that all away. You are the bomb."

The two men high-fived.

"You not so bad yourself," Mingus said. "Damn, Mercer, we did good this time, you know it? We beat city hall, dumped a mayor, took a couple of bad guys off the boulevard. Can't ask for more than that."

"Guess not," Mercer said.

The bustling room suddenly quieted. Mercer turned to see that George Rose was on stage, microphone in hand. He broke into a rousing rendition of Teddy Pendergrass's "Life Is a Song Worth Singing."

Mercer looked at his friend who seemed mesmerized by the performer, tapping his big hand against the table, lost in the song. He was surprised to realize the music was getting to him, too.

He leaned back in his chair, nodding to the beat. Life was a song worth singing. He was young. The future looked big and bright. There were trials to win. Women to woo. Sooner or later his past would catch up with him, but he'd worry about that some other day.

Turn the page for a special preview
of Christopher Darden & Dick Lochte's
explosive and provocative new legal thriller

Lawless

Available in hardcover from
New American Library

"**W**hat made you decide to study the law?" Mercer Early asked the intense young man seated at his table. Kennard Haines, Jr., blinked behind his rimless glasses. Sidone Evans, the other member of their party of three, seemed amused by Haines's hesitation.

They were on the final, cup-of-coffee phase of their lunch at The Pantry, a crowded downtown L.A. restaurant owned by an ex-mayor of the city—Mercer, a junior partner in Carter and Hansborough, the most powerful black law firm on the West Coast, and Evans and Haines, C & H's two newest associates.

"I suppose my father was a big influence," the young man finally said in what some might have assumed to be an affected British accent. Mercer knew it to be the real deal, the result of the boy spending the first seventeen of his twenty-two years in England where his father had served as chief counsel for Altadine Industries. Ken Haines, Sr., was now an advisor to the White House, adding considerable caché to Junior's apprenticeship at the firm.

Sidone's family credentials—father a beat cop, mother in family planning in Detroit—were not quite as impressive, but her top-of-the-class performance at the University of Michigan Law School had opened the firm's doors to her.

In the several weeks that both associates had been kicking around the office, Mercer purposely had tried to build up some immunity to Sidone's beauty, which was a match for her academic standing. It wasn't that she was too young—maybe six years separated their ages—or that either of them was otherwise hooked up. He'd learned a hard lesson in the importance of keeping his personal life out of the office. And, of course, there was always the possibility of a potential sexual harassment suit, which was definitely to be avoided. So he was forcing himself to look past those ripe lips and alert bright eyes when he asked, "What about you, Ms. Sidone? What made you go for the law?"

"You first," she said.

He smiled. "Now that's a lawyer's answer. No sense giving anything away unless you have to. Points."

Kennard Haines frowned. "I didn't realize this was a test."

"Testing isn't my game, Kennard. The test comes when you step into the courtroom and anything you say or do, any blink of an eye or stutter or deep sigh may turn off a jury. You get a failing grade and your client gets screwed."

The boy looked sullen, but that was okay. Sullen faded quickly. Arrogance, stubbornness—those were things that could become a problem.

"Well?" Sidone asked. "I'm still waiting for your answer."

"Why'd I study the law?" he said. "I could say it was the money. Or the power. But the fact is: if you're a black *man* in this country, it doesn't much matter if you're a brother sleeping in the park or you're Denzel Washington, odds are the day will come when some cracker cop will be on your butt about something. When that happens you damn well better know more about the law than anybody else in the room."

"Sometimes it's smarter not to let them know how smart you are," Kennard Haines said.

"Example?" Mercer asked.

"On a visit to Manhattan, I just happened to be walking near a liquor store minutes after it had been robbed. So I got picked up, along with every other black man in the vicinity. There were quite a few of us. But I guess I was the only one using phrases like 'racial profiling,' so the police shoved me around a little more than the others. It might have gotten a lot worse if my dad hadn't had a friend in D.C. Metro make a call on my behalf. I could have saved myself some bruises by just keeping mum."

"Well, yeah. I didn't mean to suggest you should fly in the face of adversity," Mercer said. "Sometimes *keeping mum* is the smart play."

Noting Sidone's smile, Kennard said, "I'm sorry. I'm not big on slang. What should I have said? 'Keeping zipped'?"

The young woman shrugged. "I don't know. 'Chilling,' 'going baltic,' 'marinating.' Don't worry, Ken. I think you're at that point where uncool turns cool."

He grinned like he'd been paid a high compliment.

Mercer was starting to like the boy. When they were headed out of the restaurant, he decided another compliment wouldn't hurt. "If I *had* been testing you at lunch, Kennard, know what would have earned you the most points?"

The boy shook his head.

"You may be the only graduate of the Yale Law School I've ever met who didn't feel it necessary to mention that fact every couple minutes."

Kennard Haines, Jr., grinned. "I figured everybody knew," he said.

On the drive to the Criminal Courts Building, Sidone said, "Mercer, it would've been lame for me to ask you about the trial in a public dining room, but is now okay?"

"Sure."

"The client, Julio Lopez, was a fugitive from justice, right?"

The statement was correct, if a bit lacking in detail. Lopez had been convicted of murdering his stepfather,

Arne Vargas, the owner of a popular Olvera Street bodega, who had been the young man's caretaker and molester for nearly ten of his nineteen years.

Deputy U. S. Marshals Tom Kinderman and Jim Hubble were transporting Lopez to Wayside Park, a facility about sixty miles north of the city, when their prisoner complained of stomach pain and asked if he could relieve himself at the next opportunity. Hubble had laughed at the notion. The more simpatico Kinderman had pulled into the nearest service station.

When Lopez somehow managed to fit through a small window at the rear of the lavatory and disappear into the wind, it was Kinderman who took the heat and Kinderman who eventually tracked down Lopez to the San Pedro warehouse where he'd been lifting and hauling in the guise of an illegal named Luis Gordo.

It was Kinderman who confronted Lopez in a dark alley near the warehouse.

And it was Kinderman whose skull Lopez crushed with a lead pipe.

"Our client was a fugitive, sure enough," Mercer agreed as he maneuvered his Benz through the thick, slow midday traffic. "That's because I wasn't his attorney then. To my knowledge, I have never lost a trial where the client was truly innocent."

That innocence had come to light several months after the verdict, when another of Arne Vargas's young victims, a busboy in his establishment, left a suicide note in which he confessed to the crime. By itself, the note would probably not have been enough to get the guilty verdict overturned. However, a search of the dead boy's room disclosed the missing murder weapon, a knife smeared with Vargas's blood and skin particles, and a jar containing a noticeably absent body part of Vargas's afloat in alcohol.

Unfortunately, neither Lopez nor the lawman pursuing him seemed to have received the news in time.

"Even if he was innocent of his stepfather's murder," Sidone said, "there is no question that he offed a Deputy U.S. Marshal."

"And, according to *Tennessee* vs. *Garner,* a person must submit to even an unlawful arrest if the peace officer is acting under an existing fugitive warrant," Kennard added.

"You two have been talking about this, eh? That's good. And you disagree with the plea?"

"Not exactly," Kennard said. "It's just that the deputy marshal was performing his duty. The client admits killing him. We can't see a jury eagerly accepting this as an act of self-defense, no matter what the exigencies."

"Well, let's check out those exigencies. Suppose you're on the run from a crime you know you didn't commit and Deputy Marshal Kinderman draws down on you in an alley. What would you do?"

"I doubt I'd grab a pipe and hit him with it. I'd try to run, maybe. If that were not possible, I'd probably put up my hands."

"Even if putting up your hands meant spending a life behind bars? Suffering the same kind of sexual molestation that had turned your childhood into a nightmare? All for something you didn't do?"

"We're not arguing about Julio Lopez's motive," Sidone said, coming to Kennard's defense. "Sister Justice definitely had something in her eye during his trial. But that didn't give him the right to off a deputy marshal who was acting under the rule of law."

"The opposite of what Julio Lopez was doing," Kennard said.

Mercer had forgotten what it was like to be so fresh and so trusting in the rule of law.

"Okay," he said. "Putting aside man's natural instinct for self-preservation, what you both seem to be hung up on is the fact that the deputy marshal was just doin' his duty. Correct?"

They nodded.

"So you see where my defense is going?"

Sidone smiled. After a few seconds, so did Kennard. Points for them both.

Now in Hardcover

#1 *NEW YORK TIMES* BESTSELLING AUTHOR

CHRISTOPHER DARDEN

& DICK LOCHTE

LAWLESS

"[A] literary dream team."
—*Entertainment Weekly*

New American Library

L.A. JUSTICE

CHRISTOPHER DARDEN

& DICK LOCHTE

"EXCITING." —*Chicago Tribune*

"A STORY THAT TWISTS AND TURNS."
—Laura Lippman, *Baltimore Sun*

"GRIPPING." —*Sunday Oregonian*

World-famous prosecutor Christopher Darden and award-winning novelist Dick Lochte return with Deputy DA Nikki Hill and a high-profile murder case that takes hold of her life—and won't let go.

"[A] FRENZIED PAGE-TURNER...Darden's legal smarts and Lochte's sure prose touch work well in tandem."
—*Publishers Weekly*

0-451-20541-3

To order call: 1-800-788-6262

New York Times **bestselling author**

Sheldon Siegel

Criminal Intent

Lawyers Mike Daley and Rosie Fernandez
have put aside their differences as former
husband and wife to become San Francisco's
top criminal defense team. But a new case
could bring it all crashing down, changing
everyone's perspecitve on truth and
justice—and life and death.

0-451-20953-2

"FULL OF TWISTS AND TURNS."
—HOUSTON CHRONICLE